RONALD FRAME

The author was born in 1953 in Glasgow and was educated there and at Oxford. He has written five other books, including the prize-winning novel WINTER JOURNEY, a collection of short stories, WATCHING MRS GORDON, and A LONG WEEKEND WITH MARCEL PROUST, which comprises seven stories and a short novel. He has recently received the Samuel Beckett Prize for his first television play, *Paris*, and he has also won PYE's 'Most Promising Writer New to Television' award. His latest published collection, a novel and fifteen stories, is called A WOMAN OF JUDAH.

Ronald Frame

SANDMOUTH PEOPLE

For Imogen Parker

The poem 'Christine', part iv of 'Novelettes' by Louis MacNeice from his *Collected Poems*, is reproduced by kind permission of Faber & Faber Limited

A few memories of ephemera were jogged by a programme in the second BBC Radio series *When Housewives had the Choice*

Copyright © 1987 by Ronald Frame

First published in Great Britain in 1987 by The Bodley Head

Sceptre edition 1988

Sceptre is an imprint of Hodder and Stoughton Paperbacks, a division of Hodder and Stoughton Limited.

British Library C.I.P.

Frame, Ronald
  Sandmouth people.
  I. Title
  823.914[F]   PR6056.R262

  ISBN 0-340-42320-X

Printed and bound in Great Britain for Hodder and Stoughton Paperbacks, a division of Hodder and Stoughton Limited, Mill Road, Dunton Green, Sevenoaks, Kent TN13 2YA (Editorial Office: 47 Bedford Square, London WC1B 3DP) by Richard Clay Limited, Bungay, Suffolk.

'THE terrible thing about this world is that everybody has his reasons.'

From JEAN RENOIR's 'La Règle du Jeu'

PROLOGUE

Late one April evening, in the middle-1950s

The body of the man was lying face-down in the glistening dew. Leadbetter saw by the headlights of the police car parked on the verge.

It was a cold evening. The body would be as stiff as a board by the time they managed to transport it to a mortuary.

Leadbetter shivered.

The man's identity seemed to be known from what he had been carrying in his pockets. The two policemen stood shaking their heads. A voice spoke behind them, from the scatter of spectators. 'This is a rum do, and no mistaking.'

Selby Parva was the last place where Leadbetter would have expected to be brought up against a murder. His sister called it 'the quietest village in Somerset', and he had supposed that she had invited him here for two reasons, because a visit must become an event in such a spot and because she knew that peace and fresh country air would do him some good. Now, taking a walk on his first evening, he had chanced to come across the scene of a murder.

As he stood in the chill air, drawing heavily on his briar pipe, he remembered the book of local history he had found on the shelf beside his bed and which he had casually perused before dinner. There had only been time to glance at the chapter dealing with the earliest inhabitants of the neighbourhood. He had read that there was evidence to 'place' a number of ancient sites of worship and sacrifice in the vicinity of Selby Magna and Selby Parva: mostly they had been dedicated to the spirits of fertility, giving rise to speculation that the two Selby's, greater and lesser, had been a designated centre of magic ritual for a wider area.

Leadbetter looked again at the body lying on the grass. He suddenly noticed that the positioning of the limbs wasn't quite natural. The arms stuck straight out at approximate right angles to the torso, and the legs were both splayed in different directions, like a frog's in water.

He realised he had only presumed that this must be the spot where the crime had been committed. Perhaps that had been an automatic deduction to make in the circumstances, but he saw now that it was not properly a deduction at all, because he hadn't applied his full reason to the matter.

As he stood beside the body's place of rest he wondered why his reading of a few hours ago should have come into his mind at the particular moment it had! Why had he made an unconscious association between the two!

It happened that he now found himself looking towards a point several feet to the left of the watching policemen—and whom should he see standing there, shivering like himself, but. . .

At which juncture a buzzing sounded on the switchboard, and the reader laid the novel, open pages down, on her lap.

'This is the Sandmouth Exchange. Which number do you require, please?'

Alma Stockton's is the voice of Sandmouth.

As the week's rota specifies, she sits in the telephone exchange of an evening and operates the plugs and cables by which the residents of here and beyond make contact. At all times she speaks calmly, and sometimes—whenever she receives a panting, slobbering call that is a professional hazard—quite firmly.

She knows that not everyone cares for the sound of her voice. She delivers in a neutral tone and accent she has taught herself from listening to the announcers on the wireless. Some people seem to hear its falseness. Others tell her she comes across as cheerful, or efficient: these are compliments. Still, it bothers her whenever a caller becomes irritable, or takes pains to make himself or herself sound superior. It's at such moments that Mrs Stockton is required to be all the calmer and more careful in pronouncing her vowels. Once or twice in the course of an evening a woman like Mrs Harkness will snap at her impatiently or a Miss Roach-type will put a lofty ring into her voice. Others speak to her with great reverence, almost as if she were a fount of rare knowledge. A man once told her she was 'the voice of Pythia', and when she asked who 'Pythia' was when she was at home he told her her home was at Delphi: she was the oracle, and whenever she chose to speak it was always 'in a divine ecstasy'. (A madman, she'd told herself in those younger days of impetuous innocence, and briskly transferred his call.)

Alma Stockton—she has never confessed it to anyone except her husband—is not above temptation. In the pool of light from the lampshade, in the silence of these three evenings a week, she is conscious of communicating the links and severances between people as she plugs them in. Maybe she hesitates for a second or two after she makes the connection, then she is distracted by a word or a tone of voice so that she forgets to disconnect herself.

She brings her knitting or darning with her, or a library book (she likes Howard Spring, and Beverley Nichols, but whodunits fill the time most easily), and she knows that whoever takes over from her—Olive Welch or Mrs Dodds—has a certain picture of her, as a very domesticated sort of woman. She lets her voice slip a little when she's speaking to them but she also knows they think of her as dedicated and vigilant when she's on the job, that is another part of the picture of her they receive. She has trained her features to show only cheerful tiredness at the end of her evening shift; she closes her book or winds up her ball of wool and lances it with her steel needles, then she looks up at the skylight and comments on something that's happened in the town; or the state of the weather, or the number of stars. They mention their day, and ask her a question about her family. Packing up to go she remembers the name 'Pythia' and the man she did not encourage in his

7

classical ramblings about her 'Delphic tongue', and she ponders on something she may have overheard in the course of her five-hour shift.

At night she walks home by herself, along Charlbury Drive and Clivedon Grove. They're on the heights, where the better class of residential avenues are. After that it's a downhill journey for her, and as she walks she sees more clearly the town spread out beneath her. Bedroom lights are being switched off. By half-past eleven the bats and the other unseen flying things are all airborne. They pass overhead and all she hears is a soft whirring of wings on flight sonar. Somehow they always avoid the tangle of telephone wires which she knows complexly thread the darkness.

Tonight, as ever, she walks smartly past the vicarage garden with its gloomy yew and cypress trees. In her mind's eye she sees the rough draft of next Sunday's sermon reposing in a drawer; she pictures the upstairs rooms where the good (as the Reverend Aldred is so fond of saying) lie safe in their beds, blessed with the deep sleep of the just. (Personally she has her doubts about the equation of virtue and sleep.)

Tilly Moscombe, whom Mrs Stockton entertains in her kitchen, also seems to detect something untoward in the atmosphere of the vicarage, but she won't tell her what. Tilly is silent on the matter, as she is silent concerning the domestic intimacies of other households in the town where she is shown hospitality.

Mrs Stockton is of the opinion that the girl picks up by sight and sound considerably more than people imagine, and interprets that knowledge by some system of logic uniquely her own. It may even be that, perversely, Tilly tries to *become* these people, sitting in their kitchens, watching how they go about the dull, ordinary business of their lives. Tilly Moscombe at sixteen years old *gives* herself, but not as the vicar talks of 'giving' and wanting nothing back in return. Tilly is stealing all the time; Mrs Stockton sees it in her eyes whenever she asks her a question and the girl clams up, she's stealing the intimate details of their lives and hoarding them away—and, later, putting whatever construction on them her mind allows her to.

When Mrs Stockton overhears on the telephone at work, she believes it's curiosity to blame, there's the simple thrill of being somewhere you shouldn't be. But Tilly makes no bones about it, she doesn't have to contend with her conscience: in turn the people she visits understand *their* dependence on *her*, and they know she humiliates them. She humiliates them because she offers back a perfect emptiness: she doesn't make faces, she isn't rude, she isn't anything at all—except silent and thoughtful and sometimes with a smile playing under the skin on her face.

Tilly's odd life is jumbled up with memories of her own daughter who only lived weeks. She remembers the difficult birth, in a period of the War with regular, nightly black-outs. The delivery was by candlelight: a long, madly fraught business. She lay on the bed remembering her great-grandmother, a Sandmouth worthy who read the patterns in china cups and told the weather to come by sticking out her tongue and tasting the wind, and she worried at the time that it wasn't a good omen.

It's stupid to think there are omens of good or bad: least of all passing under the lacework of telephone wires on a moonlit night when the town on its wooded hill looks so small set against the sweeping spectacle of the sea. Of course not. But the echoing silence on her walks home disturbs Alma Stockton.

Fearful people—as the War made plain, as Alma Stockton hears occasionally in the tone of voice on a telephone line—they can also be the most desperate, to save what it seems they must lose.

Tilly Moscombe didn't know it, she couldn't know it, but she was walking on the perimeter edge of childhood, towards the far side of the tried and familiar, into the uncharted, the country of wild lions . . .

> '**I**T'S all got something to do with the new Britain and apparently it's an absolutely splendid idea.'
>
> TERENCE RATTIGAN, '*Harlequinade*'

The next morning,
Saint George's Day

Nicknames were positively encouraged at Minster Court Preparatory School. Probably fashionable precepts on pre-adolescent psychology were less to account for such a state of affairs than a belief favoured in the Headmaster's study that the use of nicknames among the boys was thoroughly 'traditional' and British. (No one could be sure if an extremely conventional or extremely liberal principle was being established: which was one of the reasons why unorthodox parents were starting to show an interest in the establishment, as well as the dyed-in-the-wool variety who are a respectable school's bread-and-butter custom.) Re the nicknames, the Headmaster's wife thought they were 'good for building character'. The moral of her pep talk to the boys on the subject was twofold: either you fought and disposed of the nickname once and for all, or you hardened yourself to a point where you accepted it manfully as a part of your identity.

At eleven years old Simon Jope believed it was unsound thinking. Although he was a day boy with perfectly ordinary sleeping habits at home (if it was anyone's business), he'd had the experience of being called 'Bedpan' for the whole of his second year. If his father had been a doctor like Nigel Dick's, it might have made sense. But he wasn't medical, he was a hotelier, and young Jope hadn't been able to fathom the connection at first: only gradually had he realised that the name was really a comment on his social standing.

It wasn't till this last year that he'd overcome the stigma of having the background he did. A few boys in his class had parents in trade, but not many: one father was a wholesale fishmonger in Poole (the son became—not very originally—'Stinky'), another father owned and managed a self-made plumbing business (the boy became 'Ballcock' to the school). Jope couldn't play down his own father's trade: it was accessible to anyone who walked up the flight of white steps and into the front hall of the Clarence Hotel on the promenade. His family life was public property as no other boy's at Minster Court was.

There were some parents staying in the hotel for the Saint George's Day activities. Young Jope saw them looking at him in his school uniform and he knew they presumed, as the parents they had for guests always did, that he must be visiting the premises. Usually those who stayed gave the names of Home Counties farms or solid London squares when they signed the visitors' register, and they could only have imagined he was one of their kind. Already at eleven years old Simon Jope was conducting himself in such a manner that he would appear no different from anyone else at Minster Court. But inside himself, and half-aware of the transformation taking place, he was turning into a wry, wary observer of life.

A few sets of parents were colonialists home on leave, with tanned hides and elasticated drawls and (Jope's father told him) always an eagle eye on the prices. The parents appreciated the chintz lounge and the separate writing-room and the cocktail lounge at the back. (Mr Jope was thinking of converting the writing-room into a television lounge, a democratic touch—Gilbert Harding for some, 'The Grove Family' for those who kept up with that—but he delayed, knowing it wouldn't go down well with the school trade.) They brought Harrods' library books with them to read—Compton Mackenzie and J. B. Priestley were favourites—and they wore carpet slippers in the bedrooms, and were in bed no later than eleven o'clock. They didn't tip well, but the staff had orders always to be on their best behaviour with those bluff, well-connected fathers and their sharp-featured wives who sat as J.P.s and organised charity bazaars and lifted plates and cups to the light to inspect their cleanliness.

Mr Jope recognised that 'diplomacy' was the first pre-requisite of a hotelier, and he'd tried to inculcate the virtue in his son. Sure enough, Simon had started to view the random hotel life through his father's eyes, as classifying itself according to specific types and situations. Sometimes guests arrived in a delicate physical state: they were run down, or they were recuperating, or they were experiencing the unaccustomed cold of England. They had to be handled with proverbial kid gloves. Often they wanted a willing ear to speak into, and you had to compose yourself and appear sympathetic. Some of them were out-and-out liars and others—sadder cases, the boy's father said—could no longer distinguish the truth from their inventions.

Once they'd unwittingly sheltered a man who'd absconded on bail, and the police had tracked him down to the hotel. A chamber-maid had discovered that a guest's suitcase was filled to overflowing with used pound notes but he left hurriedly before a decision could be taken what to do. (The pound notes that spilled down the staircase in his haste to be gone more than covered the total of the bill he hadn't paid.) A middle-aged couple with a bland surname and an uncanny resemblance to each other had shared a room with a double-bed for most of one week. A very attractive woman wearing dark glasses and a wide picture hat like the Gainsborough Lady and stylish white trousers had asked for the best room and lain low for a few days, and it was only when she'd gone away that Mrs Jope realised who it must have been: Kay Kendall.

The weekend trade was more dubious than the weekdays'. A separate morality existed for it, one the boy—like his father—had accustomed himself to. Guests arrived in pairs, the men for the most part hearty, the women with them silent, inclined to look over their shoulders. Sometimes they each carried a suitcase and took the keys to single rooms; more often they were sharing and only gave themselves away when they became confused as to who wanted tea and which newspaper delivered in the morning and did they prefer to read Godfrey Winn or William Hickey first thing. The names signed in the register were either unexceptional—'Smith', 'Jones', 'Brown'—or they were flights of erotic fancy brought on by elation at a safe arrival and escaping undetected: 'Lovejoy',

'Prickett', 'Allcock', 'Stiff'. The boy's father smiled to them as he smiled to all the other guests, as if there was nothing to mark these ones as any different. The men would take possession of the key as if they were officially sharing, and the women would seem to relax a little, only giving a searching backwards glance as they stepped up on to the first treads of the staircase. In the dining-room in the morning the boy would notice the pair's drugged satisfaction at everything or, occasionally, the very opposite; they would be edgy, irritable, the man would assert himself with the waitress, the woman would sit with her elbows on the table-top and her chin in her hand, eating nothing and staring out the window at the frothy sea in the bay.

Simon Jope's wry, wary eye saw it all. At eleven years old he was also beginning to see through the deceits people lived by.

Like the man with the balding head and the sandy moustache who had arrived the night before and signed his name into the register as 'Arthur Brown' from 'London', whistling 'The Happy Wanderer'. The boy had noticed him trying to catch his attention, timing his departure from the table so their paths would exactly coincide. He was dressed in a checked tweed suit, the kind the Duke of Windsor wore in newspaper photographs, only his had lost its shape and looked—as his mother would have said—'past its best'. The man kept twitching his shoulders, as if the jacket was uncomfortable. The boy had the feeling that the garb was intended to make the man blend with the other guests, whom he sat at his table observing with such persistent attention over the top of his newspaper.

'Off to school, are we?'

Jope jumped.

'I—I beg your pardon?'

The man had been standing behind one of the columns in the hall.

'You're off to school now?'

'Yes. Yes, I am.'

'Oh well. Mustn't keep you.'

He spoke in flat city vowels, which the hotel's guests would usually try their best to cover up. Sometimes the 'Mrs Browns'

14

who came at bank holiday weekends spoke in the same way, but they never said much, only 'yes' or 'no' to the waitress at the breakfast table and the rest kept for whispers.

'Yes,' the boy said, and nodded.

'Nice hotel, this,' the man told him, turning his head to take note of the two pairs of parents' legs disappearing up the staircase.

'I'm glad you like it.' Simon Jope thought a 'sir' unnecessary in the circumstances.

'Oh yes, I do like it. Very much,' the man said, not even bothering to sound enthusiastic. 'Your dad's, is it?'

'Are you—are you on holiday?' young Jope asked, ducking the question.

'Sort of,' the man said.

'I hope you enjoy . . .'

'I've been thinking,' the man interrupted, 'I don't know what to look out for. In Sandmouth. Maybe you could show me? Later? Could you?'

'We've got maps . . .'

'No, I don't mean that.'

The man smiled tensely; the skin pulled tight on his thin face.

'A chat, *that's* what I mean,' he said. 'We could have a chat. You and me.'

'I don't come back till . . .'

'*That* doesn't matter.' The man spoke quickly. 'Not at all. So long as I know you're coming.'

'My father . . .' the boy suggested, seeing no alternative to mentioning him, 'my father would be very willing to . . .'

'*You* know all the right things to say, don't you?' the man said, letting his tetchiness show.

'Do—do I?'

'Must be a very *proper* school you go to, is it?'

' "Proper"? I don't know.'

'No, I bet you don't.'

'I'm sorry?'

'I'm interested how you see everything, sonny. What *you* could tell me would be very different from what your dad would tell me. Do you get me—what I mean?'

The boy nodded his head, although he didn't fully understand. He would have to consider this on the walk up Hill Street.

'So, I'll be waiting,' the man said. 'When you get back. By the way, I'm Mr Brown . . .'

'I'm sorry, I have to go now,' the boy said, noticing the time on the wall clock behind the reception counter and seeing in the corner of his eye that the man was holding out his hand.

He was relieved to get away. His parents had told him to let them know at once if any of the men guests tried to involve him in a conversation. They meant the men who sometimes came to the hotel by themselves: their eyes gave them away— either the weak, watery, shifty sort or the dull, lifeless, staring variety that bored straight into you—and for some reason they always had great difficulty knowing what to do with their hands, their fingers fluttered or the wrists hung loose and they never seemed able to forget about them as other people did. But this wasn't like the other times it had happened: the man was too open, and he'd caught the traces of impatience in his voice. He guessed the man didn't care for him, or care for what the masters at school were always reminding them of, his 'chances' in life as a Minster Court boy.

He ran down the flight of front steps on to the promenade. It sometimes happened that you heard that tone in people's voices, which let you know that while you both chatted amiably enough there was another feeling in play, only neither of you admitted that it was there: the other person's contempt of you. The boy didn't know what grounds they could have for disliking you when they knew so little about you: all they knew was how you *appeared* to them, how you dressed and spoke and had your hair cut and who your parents were and if you were at a prep school. He was often asked, 'And which school do you go to?' 'Minster Court' sounded grander and more pompous than it really was, but people couldn't know that. (And, he'd begun to wonder, maybe that was the point: that the school *should* sound grand and pompous to people who didn't know any better?)

The white Lagonda passed him as it passed him every morning. He rounded the corner of Britannia Terrace into George Street. In the distance he saw the man from the bank.

16

'Looks as if he's sat on a poker,' one of the other day boys at school was always saying about him. 'Pokerbum.' Simon Jope's eyes concentrated on the man. Pokerbum used to walk on the same side of the street as he did and would come close enough to let him see his glassy brown eyes which were the famous giveaway. Knight at school followed him as he came out of his garden in the morning; he said there was a *Mrs* Pokerbum. That discovery had prompted Simon Jope to puzzle, precociously, just how many wives there were in the town you never saw, who married and lost their old self when they became Mrs Somebodyelse and their life just became their husband's. Knight had changed the words of the song: 'Bumbo, Bumbo, Does your mummy know, You're going down the road to see a little laddie-o . . .'

At school he noticed how boys all spoke in the same way about 'females', as the term was; they mentioned their mothers, and sometimes their sisters, but they didn't talk about girls or women except the bits under their frocks you never saw. Last year a boy had brought an American magazine back from London in his trunk: there was a colour photograph of a naked woman sitting up a tree with her legs wide apart. Some of the others had turned pale when they saw that scarlet tulip under the trim triangle of hair, looking like an enflamed eye. When they'd stopped blanching they talked about ramming a length of gaspipe into her. Someone else, Norris, suggested a broken bottle . . .

The young woman from the department store appeared ahead of him. She was called Mavis Clark. Her big breasts bobbed up and down on her chest. They were real tits. She would look so haughty whenever boys smiled to her, but she was actually quite common. Under her wide turquoise skirt *she* had a sleeping eye too: a tight red tulip, closed now but only waiting for an opportunity to be opened wide. A woman's fanny was supposed to be wet and hot, and if you put a finger near it it was sucked inside. Sometimes when you passed near Mavis Clark there was a slightly fishy odour. Today she crossed George Street in front of him, tits jumping on her chest. Was she pursuing Mr Pokerbum from the bank? If she was, she was wasting her time.

The boy hurried on another few yards, jumping over every

17

third paving stone, then—as he came to the corner of George Street—he turned and looked back.

Mavis Clark from the store was speeding towards the bank. Mr Pokerbum was sorting through his keys, or pretending to: at that same moment Simon Jope saw him lift his head and stand searching along the street.

Who was he looking at? Mavis Clark?—or at himself, because he suspected he used the nickname 'Pokerbum'?

He almost collided with a man on the corner. 'Look out, Roger Bannister!' It was one of his father's businessmen friends, the bank manager Mr Braddock in his fitted overcoat and hat and carrying a rolled umbrella.

'It's an important day for you boys, isn't it?' he said in his most cheerful voice.

'Yes. Yes, sir. It is.'

'Major Fitt. A very fine man.'

'Yes, sir.' Young Jope nodded his head. 'He's giving us a speech, sir.'

'I envy you. I'd love to pop along myself. Do you think I could come?'

'I'm sure you could, sir.'

'It's men like that who've kept this Britain of ours "Great",' Mr Braddock said, passing on.

'Yes, sir,' the boy called after him.

Above Arbuckle's the grocers on Hill Street, the flag of Saint George was quietly unfurling itself. Mr Arbuckle and his daughter with the withered arm stood looking up at it.

They both turned and beamed at the boy as he walked past. Like Mr Braddock, they realised the treat that was in store for him. Heroes (even if it was from another war, not the one just past) didn't walk among ordinary mortals except on an unforgettable, blue diamond day like today.

★

Under a scrubbed and optimistic April sky of high breezy clouds, Howard Trevis walks smartly downhill into the town. In starched white collar and cuffs. He walks with his back held straight and his arms marking time with his legs.

He looks directly in front of him, incurious to see into gardens and houses and the domestic arrangements of other

18

people's lives. Away from home he seldom thinks of his wife. She occupies a particular compartment of his life. His business life is quite separate and distinct from that. The walk into the town is the passage between the two.

He's more likely to think of his mother than his wife. That seems only natural to him. He has known his wife for two-and-a-half years; he has known his mother for thirty-one. After his father died she'd had to be two parents to him. Sometimes he thinks of his grandmother, and his Great Aunt Mildred and Great Aunt Lilian, and their cousin Miss Sedilia Ellis: they all of them occupy his memories more than his father.

Sometimes he thinks of school and certainly more often than he does of his wife. That also seems natural, because between the ages of five and eighteen half of his life was spent in classrooms and dormitories and on playing fields. He remembers faces and names. It irks him to remember some of them. They weren't the happiest days of his life, but he would be hard put to decide what were. Maybe his happiest days are still ahead of him?

It irks him most of all to remember Cox and Dovey, who were his tormentors. Yet they are a more consequential element in his life's history than he can allow his wife to be. For years after he'd left school they filled his dreams. Occasionally he's thought he's seen them, when he's been driven in someone else's car or as he's come walking out of the bank. His boarding school was in the next county, so it's unlikely but not impossible that their paths might re-cross. He doesn't know what he would say to Cox or Dovey if they should walk through the door of his office, with its neatly lettered sign 'Senior Cashier'.

He hated Cox and Dovey. They still terrorise him. For all he knows, he might kill to save himself from Cox and Dovey. They used to tell him they knew everything—'*Everything*!'—about him. He would turn hot and cold with sheer uncontrollable panic whenever they approached him. Sometimes he checks through the list of new names on his registers of customers, and the two he looks up first every time are 'Cox' and 'Dovey'.

Keeping up a steady pace as he walks helps to keep the phantoms of the past at bay. His heart takes even beats, his blood circulates freely. He holds his head and back straight for the sake of his posture.

He has markers, and he checks his watch against them. His walk takes him sixteen minutes. He knows he is his own best time-keeper and not the same people he passes every morning, who might be a minute or more behind or forward.

After the Town Hall clock, his last marker—but an unreliable one—is the Jopes' son from the Clarence Hotel as every day he doesn't turn his head but allows his eyes to search him out. The boy has noticed of late, he feels sure, and for the eighth or ninth morning in succession he keeps to the opposite pavement.

He is a good-looking lad, eleven or twelve years old. He likes to think there is a resemblance between them: the boy, and how *he* looked at that age. Maybe the boy is better-developed. He has broad shoulders and strong legs, visible between his grey flannel shorts and fawn-and-navy top stockings. He ought to do well on the rugger field. A few times Mr Trevis has just chanced to take a walk out past Minster Court's grounds and he's tried to spot him among the foraging limbs in the scrum or marshalled with the others for line-out practice. In six or seven years' time it may be he'll open an account with the bank. He might be the under-manager by then. Or they might be in Bournemouth, or Salisbury, he and Maureen. Things would have picked up by that time on the money front: they'd have a detached house of their own, with a high hedge and privacy, and a car.

At the door of the bank he permits himself to look back along George Street, at the boy springing along the pavement. If he could be that age again, he thinks, how might he determine that he grew up differently from how he had?

Envy pricks him, for the boy's chances. His parents will pay to send him to a better school than *he* went to. With those strong legs he won't let a Cox or a Dovey back him into a corner. He'll cycle into the nearest town on Saturdays and smile at pairs of girls in convent capes and berets. He has a father, he doesn't have a Great Aunt Mildred or an Honorary Great Aunt Sedilia. He still has to choose whichever life he wants for himself.

The girl Clark from Crockers' store passes the boy and teeters across the street on her absurd heels. She sometimes comes into the bank, on personal business; she leans forward so that her breasts lie on the counter and he hears the clerks sniggering.

Mr Trevis sees the boy looking over his shoulder as the heels squawk. He bows his head and fumbles with the bunch of keys to open the double pair of front doors. Who has the boy been looking at?—the girl, or past her at him?

He feels he's been unduly indiscreet, incautious. It isn't typical of him at all.

He realises he has started the day badly. He concentrates as he rams the key into the lock of the outer door and gives his wrist a half-twist.

He remembers his wife now, in the house in Walnut Avenue. At such moments he doesn't conjure up her features: she exists for him as an idea, as an abstract—she represents a certain way of life he has committed himself to. He is uncomfortably aware that she is becoming his conscience.

He hears the girl passing behind him. He pauses on the top step and then he does what he knows any other red-blooded young male would be expected to do: he gives her a sideways look as her heels carry her off.

'Not attending!'

He swings round.

'Mr Braddock! Good morning, sir!'

The branch manager with his rolled umbrella and fitted coat smiles benevolently from under his Anthony Eden hat.

'Security risk there, my boy. Must be careful!'

Mr Braddock smiles broadly.

'Won't say a word to Mrs Trevis!'

Trevis smiles, pretending to be grateful. He unlocks the inner door and holds it open for the manager, who indulges in a forgiving wink.

He locks the inner door behind them. The manager removes his hat and slips his arms out of his coat. Today he's wearing a buttonhole, a red rose. He notices his subordinate's surprise.

'You're very forgetful, aren't you, you young men?'

'I'm sorry?'

Mr Braddock is still smiling; he cocks his head.

'Saint George's Day, Mr Trevis. Although we'll trust there are no dragons left to slay in Sandmouth.'

The smile stays fixed on the chief cashier's face. For no reason he can think of he is continuing to see the Jopes' sturdy son, his muscular legs in the grey flannel shorts taking those seven-league boot strides across every third paving stone, kicking a hard leather ball out of the darkness of a straining, sweating rugby scrum.

★

Nothing touches us in our lives, Mrs Dick thought as her husband went through the motions of scrutinising the newspaper headlines. Or hardly anything does: a war overseas, a budget, threats to supplies so that we might be living on rations all over again. But only *self*-interest causes that interest. Otherwise . . .

It wasn't only the experience of their lives here in Sandmouth, which sometimes felt like being smothered by a weight of soft pillows (the feathers harmless enough, until concentrated into that killing bulk). Beyond Sandmouth it was the malaise of hundreds of other small towns, and larger towns, and the great cities. People were smothered by an unthinking faith in unquantifiable things: Britain's continuing greatness, the future, possibilities, an era dawning—like light being beamed into darkness at a son et lumière in some cosy, calendar-pretty village. Go inland from Sandmouth and there was the dreamy English idyll that still sustained the country: but in that rolling landscape of grassy ramparts and combes you were prevented from seeing whatever lay beyond the next range of hills and what lay beyond that: there was no height, and no sense of perspective.

The young, of course, would demand their opportunities. Their elders wouldn't be sure what they were, they might resent their offspring their chances, what they called their 'rights'. Jack would consider he must be as good as his master, almost: he would half-believe it.

Sometimes Mrs Dick was privy to very treacherous thoughts which seemed to strike at the root base of those assumptions everyone lived by. Even the War: that had never been explained, she felt, then or after. It hadn't been like the first

22

conflagration, which her father and uncles had served in. Glory
hadn't been possible—even the glory of a thatched village on
the lid of a tin box of biscuits—because it can't be possible in a
war that's planned on radar or in bunkers and where the killers
only make contact with their victims according to paper
instructions. Here in Sandmouth they'd only *heard* the planes,
distantly, above the clouds, and they'd hoped they weren't
going to receive any falling message from the skies. (Newspaper photographs showed the shells of bombed churches, so
hoping had seemed more sensible than praying.)

She didn't ask her husband, who had served his time at sea:
she was determined she wouldn't. But the questions didn't
become any less important to her, and considering them so
often had made them no more easy to solve. She felt she didn't
even have *clues*. A 'right' or 'wrong' conclusion is possible only
where the puzzle has a solution, a kernel of truth, be it trivial
or profound.

No clues, no solutions and maybe none possible. Like
husbands, and wives, and having children. Right or wrong?
And like building houses for homes—nests—as the birds do,
and living to survive, to eat, and never knowing who the real
predators were. Perhaps the wooden horse brought to Troy was
divine code, the shorthand of disregarded gods: and maybe the
world still blindly, miraculously, thrived on the cuckoo
principle?

★

The town of Sandmouth is built on a sheltered escarpment
between two lines of chalky cliffs, directly above a bay. The
sweep of hillside is steep, particularly in its wooded upper
section, and the appropriately named Hill Street presents the
driver with some awkward zig-zags before it considerably
straightens out for a gentler descent into the town proper.

The oldest-surviving buildings are a clutch of late
seventeenth-century cottages dating from the town's fishing
days: not particularly distinguished relics of the past, any of
them, and badly in need of repair. They now lie empty,
although there is some talk of a local builder converting them
into holiday homes: but the expense of the operation would be
considerable and the moment isn't deemed to be quite right

yet. The town's architecture is mainly late Georgian and early Victorian: the spot's commendable qualities as a health-giving resort began to be advertised in the 1790s, largely on the prompting of the major landowner who found himself firstly 'embarrassed' in the financial sense and, before his programme of persuasion could have its full impact in society's higher circles, insolvent.

The 'prestige' development was a row of a dozen substantial dwellings called Britannia Terrace, now painted white and housing the Clarence Hotel as well as assorted offices and three private residences. Behind Britannia Terrace and parallel to it is the principal thoroughfare, George Street, which intersects Hill Street at a right angle: together, George Street and Hill Street contain most of the town's shops and hostelries as well as numerous other commercial premises and professional business offices.

West of Britannia Terrace are the War Memorial public gardens, the golf course and various outlying houses. In the other direction live the bulk of Sandmouth's residents. As a simple rule of thumb—in direct contravention of the proprieties in many larger resorts—the closer to the sea front and sea level the less a property's social desirability and hence commercial value is judged to be. Property value increases the higher a house is sited on the hillside; population and density of building simultaneously thin in a corresponding ratio to height above sea level.

Obscured by trees, sunk in tranquil gardens, the most expensive houses are on Greenaway Avenue and Rossholme Drive and Clivedon Grove: the houses themselves wouldn't disgrace Branksome or Virginia Water or even Weybridge. Also among a profusion of trees, Charlbury Drive and Claremont Avenue exist on a slightly lesser, but still elevated, plane. Among more modest greenery Hawthorn Avenue and Walnut Avenue are situated lower down, but they too look down on the rest of the town. Social aspiration is always upward, in the direction of the Avenues. Rather than allow a property to suffer a physical decline, Avenue-dwellers may let the bottom portion of a house and move upstairs, claiming that it's selfish to *use* a house so little: or, if even that will not remedy their plight, they might consider removing themselves altogether.

But that desperate solution has been employed only two or three times in the years since the War, and a distinct feeling was left in the air after the former owners had gone that they lacked courage, that in the best of all possible worlds still to come a solution would have been possible, if they'd just had the strength to wait and hang on a while longer.

*

At 'The Laurels', the Prentices' creeper-fringed Edwardian house at the top of the town (with egress on to both Greenaway Avenue *and* Hill Street), breakfast begins with the post.

The couple—not father and daughter, but husband and wife—sit at a George III mahogany dining-table. Everything in the room shines: the furniture, the silver place-settings, the silver pheasants on the side-board, the glaze on the oil paintings purchased from expensive London dealers, the parquet on which it's sometimes difficult to keep one's balance.

The mail rests on a small silver salver until Mrs Prentice appears with the tea. Mrs Prentice thinks a maid unnecessary to feed two people, but her husband insists on the salver, at least. He imagines it's how people in a house like 'The Laurels' were in the way of conducting themselves before the War. She allows Cedric his fiction, although she knows better, that 'The Laurels' was occupied by the Starkeys, the stingiest couple in the town. Mrs Prentice knows perfectly well why it was that her husband chose to marry her, or someone in her mould— because she was to be a talisman, his introduction to a higher way of life—and she is fully aware that they have never been able to discuss any of the differences that exist between them. She feels they are *both* of them aware that such is the state of circumstances, and to her ear it makes an odd silence at the start of every new day.

Mrs Prentice has three letters to open this morning. One is from a schoolfriend who occasionally writes: she lives in Petersfield and is the mother of three children and she passes on her chit-chat about her comfortable, unexciting life, about a pony called Primula in a paddock and toadstools on the lawn and problems with the maid, and did she remember that girl who was in their form at Malvern, Virginia Something from Wales, she was sure she'd spotted her emerging from the Savoy

Grill, flirting with a white-haired man who had his arm round her waist. 'What's the world coming to, for heaven's sake?'

The second letter was from her sister. Rosalind, she realised, did not care overmuch for Cedric. Rosalind and her husband farmed in Herefordshire and they both prided themselves on being practical, down-to-earth types. That wasn't wholly the case, but she knew they purported to disapprove of materialists like themselves, be they professional or not. Cedric's being in law wasn't allowed to cut much ice with Rosalind. What made her doubly disapproving was that she seemed to imagine the family was 'above' the fusty dealings of lawyers with commercial clients and a secretary operating the telephone: even a father like theirs had been better, because he'd been a surgeon before he hit the bottle. More seriously there was Cedric's background, or lack of it: Rosalind, farmer and crypto-snob, was quite clearly of the opinion that she'd somehow betrayed them all.

It was an unfair judgment on her, Penelope Prentice was convinced. Ros on her rolling acres in Herefordshire must have forgotten the anxieties of life at home: *she* hadn't. Now she was close enough to be able to visit her mother every day if she chose to, which was more than Ros was (literally) in a position to do; Cedric would remind her of arrangements he'd made to have this or that seen to and repaired—could her mother be there when the workmen arrived?—and she would feel this marriage had worked practical good not just to herself. Also, she had much less to occupy her than Ros, and the memory of what she'd escaped—of what they'd both escaped—couldn't be worked out of her system, even if she'd wanted it to be.

'Penwythy' had had a sad history. Every year the house had seemed to lose more of its grace: the glass panes cracked in the casements and replacements were too expensive to afford, a bird smashed through a stained glass skylight in the roof and the hole had to be boarded up, tiles kept slithering off the roof and underneath one particularly affected spot a puddle would form on one of the bedroom floors. Their own history, hers and Rosalind's, couldn't be distinguished from 'Penwythy' 's. The worst interlude had been their troubled later adolescence, when the two of them had panicked that they weren't going to

26

find a husband who would rescue them from the shared responsibility for it. Every dance on the local circuit they'd gone to had been an agony of suspense: not knowing if they would be left standing partner-less on the side-lines of over-dressed spectators. It became easier for Rosalind, because she began to blossom and her duckling stage was suddenly behind her; until the same metamorphosis happened to her, her younger sister had had to take her chance with the rest of the field. The older brothers of the district—stiff-backed and invariably jug-eared—favoured her with their attention while Ros started to be received into the ranks of the great and untouchables. Once a grey-haired widower flattered her with a prepared speech about her 'vernal virtues', and all she wanted for herself was to look like the ripely maturing Rosalind. A beanpole boy at Oxford reading for the cloth had taken a shine to her for two or three months and pestered her with sickly poems that didn't rhyme properly and which attributed her goodness of heart to God's smiling benison on his chosen ones. (Damn God's benison, she wanted to tell him: when do I start to look like my sister?) Another boy called Edward Harrap had once danced with her and, drawing her close to him, had whispered in her ear that he was wearing no underpants. ('How dreadful to be so forgetful,' she'd told him, and swanned off, for the first time actually imagining—as she still reeled from the shock of the confession—that her body was changing, distinctly for the better at last.) Such had been her early initiation into what articles in magazines referred to as 'affairs of the heart'.

She put her sister's letter down. So long ago but unforgotten. Was the reason Rosalind couldn't forgive her now because she'd eventually found her own prettiness?

'Anything interesting?'

Cedric was watching her.

'It's just from Ros.'

'How are they?' he asked, as if he was really concerned and didn't merely enquire for duty's sake. He was kinder to them than the pair deserved; he was a kinder man than *any* of them deserved.

'Oh . . . Fine, I think.'

He nodded, then meticulously sliced the top off his boiled egg.

27

Sometimes she'd caught him looking at Rosalind—rather oddly for a brother-in-law, in a wondering but also familiar way, not so very different from how he looked at *her*. Ironically country life—lots of fresh air and (apparently) hard work and no cosmetics—had only served to point up Ros's good looks, her fine features, and managed to lend her, somehow, a sensual appearance on top of everything else. She was conscious that no amount of Cedric's money she spent on herself could bring her close to that state of voluptuous, earthy ripeness Herefordshire seemed to bring out. Perhaps she'd worried the potential of real glamour out of herself in the years just after the War, when there was no brother still alive to take over the house and her mother seemed to lose the will to interest herself in its upkeep.

Just occasionally she wondered perversely if, for Cedric, Rosalind and she might not have been interchangeable at the start, sharing all that past as they had done? He'd fallen romantically in love with, not herself, but with the atmosphere of 'Penwythy'—mistaking the dampness and economies of their life for a kind of polite English decadence?

'We should go and see them,' she heard him say.

She didn't reply as she folded the letter.

'We could do with a change of air, Penelope, no? It's nice country.'

She returned the letter to its envelope.

'It wouldn't take us long.'

She nodded slowly.

'Yes, we *could*,' she said.

'We can think about it?'

'Yes,' she said. 'Yes, we can think about it.'

She picked up the third letter. It was inside a blue air-mail envelope with an American stamp and frank. Kate, of course. At this moment she didn't think she was in a mood for being regaled with the wonders of domestic life on the other side of the ocean.

'In the meantime . . .'

Mr Prentice got to his feet.

'Time waits for no man. Saint George's Day or not.'

His wife looked over at the carriage-clock.

'Oh, is it? I'd forgotten.'

28

She didn't know what difference its being a saint's day made to anything. Maybe tradition had it that it was a day for miracles?

Mr Prentice kissed her on the cheek. She always felt that *he* must think he was being very romantic. He would lean towards her so carefully and respectfully, as if she were some fragile artefact of great value. Which, in social terms, was exactly what she had been to him from the word 'go': an untouchable woman who had suddenly become a bargain for the taking.

'I've got Pargiter coming in early.'

She raised her eyes quickly.

'What for?'

'Hasn't really said. Something to do with the house.'

'Doesn't he have his own men?'

'I'm sorry?'

'Money men. People like him usually do, don't they?'

'You sound rather disapproving. Is he as bad as some people make out?'

'You *have* been hearing things about him?'

'A mixture—grudging envy, let's say, and admiration—the usual. Wealth normally wins people's respect in the end, though.'

'What do they say about him?'

'Oh . . . "Where does it all come from?" "There must be some hanky-panky somewhere" . . .'

'Maybe there is.'

'They could find that out, if they wanted to. If they didn't enjoy putting him down so much. He's sharp, Pargiter, he's not going to leave himself open.'

'I suppose what they mean is "how?" '

' "How?" ' Mr Prentice repeated.

'How does he do what he does? His methods. Are they fair?'

'He's a businessman, Penelope.'

'Well, you're a lawyer, Cedric. So remember'—she tried to smile—'you have the honour of your profession to uphold.'

'All this concern for my profession, my dear?'

'For *you*, Cedric.'

The smile spread: a beguiling smile which her husband appeared to find confusing.

'He's coming for legal advice, Penelope. Which is precisely what he will receive. No less and no more.'

'Make sure you charge him the full amount then. More if you can. Then we don't need to go to Herefordshire, we can have a spree in Paris on the proceeds!'

'I can see Herefordshire doesn't greatly appeal,' Mr Prentice said, smiling.

'No, not greatly.' His wife touched his arm. 'Gang warily with Mr Pargiter.'

'Is it worrying you?'

'Well, he's not the best sort to do business with, is he? You don't *need* his business.'

'He's coming in person. Quite an honour, wouldn't you say?' Mrs Prentice shook her head.

'And what are you going to do with yourself today, dear?'

'Read Kate's letter before anything else, I expect.'

He always asked her and she always eluded the question, fenced him off. She stood at the window watching him set off down the drive, wearing that silly bowler hat he *would* insist on putting on his head and, ever prepared, carrying his rolled-up umbrella. At the curve in the driveway he turned and waved, and she waved back. After six years of marriage she never failed to find the moment touching, even when he was least on her mind.

He walked off again, behind the banks of rhododendrons and laurels. She looked at the address on Kate's envelope, 'Mrs Cedric Prentice'. Kate had been much kinder about the marriage than Ros: it was only the fact of Cedric's additional nineteen years which, at the beginning when she discovered, had diminished her enthusiasm a little, not his vague South-ampton background. Sensible Kate (sensible *then*, how she'd been at school) had appreciated it was the only practical, decent, *dignified* solution.

She wasn't so sure that Kate retained her full complement of sound common sense after three years in America. Finding there fewer of the barriers and distinctions she'd been used to living by in England, she seemed less able to discriminate and judge, and some of her enthusiasms now struck her correspondent as almost absurd. Or maybe she just envied Kate her new *joie de vivre*, puzzled that it should still be possible after the age of thirty.

Mrs Prentice didn't think she could cope with the letter at this juncture, not at this moment. She had to have her bath and she wanted to put some clear varnish on her nails and wax her legs.

She saw the day ahead. At quarter-to-one Mrs Lenny would appear: she would take her coat and hat off, roll up her sleeves, and slip her apron over her head: the window sashes would be pushed up, and then they were off—the real business of the day at 'The Laurels' could begin.

Before that, in a corner of the morning sometime, before Mrs Lenny arrived and as she was making her decision about what to wear in the afternoon for her little indiscretion—while she had quiet, and she was still her own mistress—she would unseal the envelope then, she would brave herself for the full gamut of Kate's crazy effusiveness, the glorification of America the Beautiful.

★

Alma Stockton surfaces momentarily from sleep. Tilly Moscombe is on her mind and she imagines she sees her face in the crumples and folds of the bedroom curtains.

The house is empty, everyone has gone, she realises: it *sounds* empty, abandoned.

Except for Tilly Moscombe. But when Mrs Stockton looks again at the curtains the face is nowhere to be seen: the ridges of the curtains belong to peacocks and urns—strutting, turquoise peacocks and solidly handsome urns ungreened by lichen. Tilly Moscombe by comparison is almost nothing at all, less than the running shadow of a thought.

★

'Prince Charles is keeping tadpoles.'
'Is he?'
Silence.
Betty Messiter glanced over the top of her '*Daily Graphic*'.
'Are you remembering I'm getting my hair done this afternoon?'

Her husband smiled wanly as he continued his search of the breakfast table.

'What *are* you looking for, Brian?'

'Just the marmalade, dear.'

'It's there in front of you. For heaven's sake, Brian, are you going blind?'

'Sorry, dear.'

'And it's not *just* "marmalade". It's Frank Cooper's. I might as well get the stuff at the W.I. market, for all the difference it makes to you.'

'I—I did know really.'

The *Graphic* was raised.

'In future I'll keep it for guests.'

'Yes. Well, whatever you like, dear.'

Silence.

The pages of the newspaper rustled.

'I thought Greta might have written by now to say she was coming.'

'I'm sure she will.'

The newspaper was lowered again. Mr Messiter instinctively feared the worst.

'I see. She *will*, will she?'

'I . . .'

'I'm glad you know my old schoolfriends better than *I* do, Brian.'

'Of course I . . .'

'Where Greta's concerned, nothing's "of course". She's the least "of course" person in the world. I should have thought you might have known *that* by now.'

'I'm sorry. I only meant . . .'

'She's probably forgotten I asked her. You could get too much of that scattiness.'

The newspaper was raised aloft.

Betty Messiter hated the late starts, but she hated too long a day even more. They could still be sitting at breakfast at ten o'clock, which broke with the habits of a lifetime. The retired life wasn't much to her liking: Brian had sold out to the Cypriot who'd been so desperate for his cardboard box business and they'd got good terms for the sale, but she would have preferred to live by the rituals they'd had until the year before

32

last. She now recognised the disadvantages of premature retirement: she was only fifty-seven and Brian sixty-one, an age when many men still had much vigour. Brian had seemed to have less and less vigour ever since his abdication from business responsibilities. She had deliberately let him choose his future for himself: now *she* couldn't be in a position to be upbraided about anything.

'I'll need a lift to the hairdressers.'

'Yes, dear.'

'The car could do with a wash before you take it out.'

'I'll do it at lunchtime.'

'I thought—'

The newspaper was lowered, the voice softened a little.

'I thought we could get a few holes in this morning.'

The voice had softened because only Brian Messiter was a bona fide member of the Sandmouth Golf Club. As a special weekday morning privilege, wives were permitted on the greens if their husbands were in attendance. (For most of them with working husbands, she'd wryly realised, that was an impossibility. Trust the Golf Club Committee to be so crafty about it.)

'Yes. Yes, I didn't know what you were planning . . .'

'Don't you want to go?' She asked the question with little gentleness.

'Yes. Of course, Betty.'

The newspaper rattled.

'*This* morning?' her husband checked.

'That's what I said. I'm not going to go *after* I get my hair done, am I?'

'No. No, of course not.'

'I hope I don't get that stupid Brenda girl washing it today. She doesn't do a good job at all. Someone should say something. She's not getting a tip from me at Christmas-time.'

Mr Messiter didn't offer a reply.

'She's got some very common habits. She scratches a lot. It's very unhygienic.'

'Yes. I suppose . . .'

'She's too simple to make conversation with.'

'Oh.'

'Marmalade, Brian.'

'I'm sorry?'

'Haven't you forgotten to do something?'

The marmalade pot was duly replaced on the saucer Mrs Messiter insisted should always go underneath. The lady of the house sighed. She liked to make sure the little points were attended to: she had no intention whatsoever of letting her standards slip now that they were in a town with different neighbours and where they could have taken advantage of other people's ignorance of them both. Plates had doilies; there was always a tea-cloth on the tray; the picquot tea-pot had a padded chintz cover; the 'serviettes' (as Mrs Messiter stipulated they should be called) were rolled up and pushed into a couple of cracked ivory rings, bought from the oddments cupboard in 'Arbuthnot Antiques'.

'So, it's the golf course,' Mrs Messiter said, in a very positive, final-sounding tone of voice which would brook no questions.

'Yes. Certainly, dear.' Mr Messiter resolved to be positive too.

After a few seconds' thought, Mrs Messiter lowered the newspaper and asked with more concern, 'Is the car clean enough for the golf course?'

'I don't . . .'

'You could clean it *before* we go . . .'

Mr Messiter nodded, consenting.

'Anyway, I've my blouse to iron. I'd better do your collar and cuffs. Which shirt are you wearing?'

'For golf?' Mr Messiter asked helplessly.

'For golf,' Mrs Messiter said slowly. She drew breath ominously. 'What else, for goodness' sake?'

The newspaper was raised again. Dior has lifted his skirts yesterday, and every woman in the land should be taking note . . .

'The Viyella one, maybe?' her husband suggested.

The collar was starting to fray, Mrs Messiter knew, but the shirt looked the part, from a distance: equipping Brian with new clothes as well as herself with all those *she* needed was another of retirement's headaches which put her on edge. (Sandmouth noticed what you wore, and remembered.) First the awful imprisonment of the menopause—lasting years longer than she'd read that it was supposed to—and now these irritations of their long, long days.

'All right, then. Leave it out for me and I'll give it a going-over,' she said, reducing the height of the newspaper by a couple of inches. 'When I've done my blouse.'

'Thank you, dear.'

As much as anything else, it was Brian's habitual surrender on every point which had disorientated her since their move to Sandmouth. He used to be much more assertive, a man with opinions. Now he bent to her like a reed, and made her feel as if she was always a contrary wind.

For a few seconds she smiled over the top of the newspaper, with a measure of tenderness even. Then for the first time she noticed the spots of tea spilt on the tray-cloth.

'Oh *really*, Brian.' Shhe stared at the vandalism. 'Can't you be more careful?'

'What, dear?'

Her voice and face became shrewish whenever she was flustered, she knew that. But it was a clean tray-cloth, for heaven's sake. And one day soon she would have to remind Brian to mend his bathroom habits.

She sighed.

'Lid, Brian.'

'I'm sorry?'

'The Cooper's. The *lid*, Brian.'

She was so frightened of lapsed standards. The rituals were for his good too, didn't he see that? She closed her eyes, and shook her head; she made a suffering mouth and knew it was only wasting lipstick, but there was more at stake than Yardley lipstick from the reduced oddments basket in Crockers' to save a few pennies.

She opened her eyes and caught sight of herself in the carefully positioned gilt mirror behind Brian's head. The house had several carefully positioned gilt mirrors on its walls. Mrs Messiter was quite sure it wasn't her vanity which had instructed that they should be placed where they were. When they'd moved to Sandmouth she'd realised just how much depends on a first impression. She'd soon discovered a breed of woman here—'lady', rather—much rarer on the ground in Essex, where they'd previously lived: they wore woollen stockings, and thick ample tweeds, and scuffed, slightly down-at-heels shoes, and they spoke in good, county voices.

It was difficult to get the look exactly right. Mrs Messiter appreciated that her clothes had too much newness. They also didn't have quite the cut, but the clothes you bought nowadays didn't. She was below average height, and she valued heels for their ability to bring her up-in-the-world: but she tried to pick a dateless style of shoe. Woollen stockings made her legs look less thin. Her only real vanity was her hair, which received much more regular attention than any of the ladies she studied on Hill Street allowed. She had tried to ease the sly Essex vowels out of her voice: her accent had undergone a very definite readjustment since their move to Sandmouth. She now pitched her voice a little higher, which sometimes gave it rather a shrill, brittle strain to her own ear: but she found the vowels looked after themselves better that way. She was out on Hill Street and George Street with her basket most mornings, and had discovered the haunts of the favoured of Sandmouth: either 'The Wishing Well' (Tuesdays and Fridays), or the lounge of the Clarence Hotel (Mondays and Thursdays), or the W.I. market (Wednesdays).

'I think I'll tell them Brenda can't do me,' she said aloud, looking into the mirror and picking back strands of her hair.

'What's that, Betty?'

Mrs Messiter frowned and her forehead crinkled. She hated the diminutive: *that* diminutive.

'She hardly wets it,' she said, quite fiercely. 'She's a half-wit. Hair needs a good dunking.'

'Oh.'

'And she's common with it. She's got some *very* common ways.'

Mrs Messiter said no more. Mr Messiter looked away at the breakfast things. His wife used to tell him that the Cypriot gentleman Mr Kyriakides who bought the business was the commonest man she'd ever had the misfortune to meet. Just as well she hadn't heard his lunchtime conversation, and learned what it was he'd once laid out on a plate on top of the kitchen table in front of his Greek wife. The world was a lot commoner than Betty imagined it was at its worst.

'Maybe I'll say something?' Mrs Messiter couldn't resist adding as an afterthought. 'Do you think she should get the sharp edge of my tongue?'

She was beginning to pride herself on the 'tone' she could

36

bring into her voice when dealing with shop menials. Her husband considered it a not altogether happy new development. He was sure one could be purposeful but also tactful. Betty seemed to imagine talking down was a constituent of breeding and proper social behaviour. He hesitated about putting her right. She didn't like to be corrected on social matters.

'Well,' she asked, 'haven't you anything to say about it?'

Mr Messiter focused on the words 'Oxford Cut' on the marmalade pot label.

'Maybe—maybe things'll sort themselves out?' he offered.

He didn't look at his wife for a reaction. He heard a sigh, then the newspaper rattled noisily. He waited till the head was hidden behind it before he looked up to study the morning's headlines.

Two murders and a suicide among the rest, he read with his good long sight. 'H'-Bomb tests. Death threat to Lady Boyle. Thank God for Sandmouth, he thought: whatever he knew the town's failings of hospitality to be, and whatever the private little vicissitudes of every new day behind the frosted glass front door and pebbledash walls of 'Fairways' in its cul-de-sac of modern bungalows. By comparison with what you read in the newspapers—so he imagined it to himself, in a grandiloquent metaphor—it was like getting out of the rough and on to one of the sheltered, gentle greens he liked to play best, with or without Betty in her headscarf and razor-creased casuals: the twelfth hole, or maybe the fifteenth, possibly the thirteenth.

'It says here, Betty, they think they've found the Yeti's footprints.'

★

'Did you see the bunting at Minster Court?' Miss Spink asked Mavis Clark.

'Yes. They've got that old buffer coming.'

Miss Spink closed her eyes and counted to five. 'The gentleman's name,' she replied loftily to the junior, 'is Major Fitt.'

'How come he's so special?'

'He lost a leg. In the field.'

'What field?'

One-two-three-four-five.

'He was making a better world for us all. And the Germans caught him.'

'Don't tell me, "it was just one of those days"!' Mavis Clark laughed. 'Doesn't sound much fun to me.'

'War,' Miss Spink announced acidly, appalled by the girl's disrespect, 'isn't *supposed* to be fun.'

'It can't be *all* bad. I mean, you've got to laugh sometimes. Haven't you?'

'Well, losing your leg in the trenches isn't a laughing matter.'

'I saw his picture in the paper. He's laughing there all right.'

'Well . . .' Miss Spink hesitated. 'He's known for his spirit. His redoubtable spirit. That—that is the myth. The myth of the man.'

'Oh, I see.' Mavis Clark looked unconvinced. Then she brightened as a thought struck her. 'Don't see how a myth can be a man, do you?' She laughed again.

Miss Spink willed herself to keep her temper. Please.

'It was for *you* he lost it, Mavis Clark.'

'What? Lost his leg?'

'So *you* would be born a free woman.'

' "Born a *woman*"? That'd be a miracle, that's what!'

One-two-three-four-five.

'Born a baby, I meant.'

'I'd have been here just the same. Only we'd be serving a lot of krauts, that's all.'

Six-seven-eight-nine-ten.

'I don't think you understand.'

'It's ages ago, anyway.'

'Just a generation. And a bit.'

'Well, that *is* ages. It is to me.'

'It doesn't mean you should be disrespectful.'

'I can't go around thinking of Richard the Lionheart every blinking second.'

'Please moderate your language.'

'Or old Nelson. Or the blooming Duke of Wellington. Can I?'

'*They* are dead, Miss Clark.'

'So's this old fossil, I expect.'

'He's alive and he's here in our town,' a shocked Miss Spink retorted. '*That's* the difference.'

'Well, good luck to him,' Mavis Clark said. 'I've nothing against him, I'm sure.'

'I should think not.'

'He's got *his* life and I've got mine.'

'You might not have had yours—if it hadn't been for great men like him.'

Miss Spink could hear her voice betraying her—her emotional fever-pitch, her origins in the far mists of time, at the lesser end of South Norwood.

'Well, I've got it, Miss Spink, and I can't use it all up thinking about him. Can I?'

The older woman turned her back. Every fresh day was a trial to her. Mavis Clark would have to go. They were temperamentally unsuited for work in the same department. If it came to the bit she would just have to tell Mr Cheevy on the second floor, it was either her or Mavis Clark.

'That display could do with another scarf, Miss Clark.'

Mavis Clark made a face at Miss Spink's back. The 'Miss Clark' days were a penance for her having been so free, and they had to be suffered. It was worth it, though, just to be able to say what she really felt. What was the point of saying only what you thought other people would find agreeable? That was stupid.

'A scarf, if you please, Miss Clark.'

'What colour, Miss Spink?'

'A dark green. I think that would do nicely.'

'*How* dark?'

One-two-three-four-five. Miss Spink knew Mavis Clark went for the gaudiest colours she could find.

'*Medium* dark.'

'Medium dark green, Miss Spink?'

By chance there was just such a shade of scarf and the girl held it up.

'Thank you, Miss Clark,' said Miss Spink, receiving the chiffon square.

The younger woman watched the solemn ritual of dressing the stand. Miss Spink treated it as if it were a God-given rôle. Mavis Clark didn't believe in God, so she didn't believe He doled out rôles like this to dull, middle-aged women like Miss Spink.

She stood back and considered her surroundings. It was a boring-looking department all right, with boring-looking stuff for sale. If she'd had her own way it would have been lively and bright. People wanted cheering-up. They would have come if they'd thought that's what they were going to find. Miss Spink did the buying for it on the principle that all women must be like her: grey-haired, wearing those sober colours, with no man to dress herself up for. She never even looked inside a fashion magazine. The War might as well still be going on; maybe it was, inside her head? She didn't seem to appreciate the things *she* did: about hemlines for instance, that every quarter inch up or down your calf *mattered*, very much, and you were as dead as a dodo if you didn't heed.

'Yes,' Miss Spink complimented herself. 'Yes, I think that will do very nicely. A most fetching green.'

Mavis Clark considered how it was that they could see things so differently: they lived in the same town, they shared their daylight hours in each other's company, in the same square yards of space, and yet their opinions and tastes were so much at odds. Nothing seemed to have rubbed off, from one to the other.

Maybe if Miss Spink had been aware of such thoughts occupying the young woman's mind for these seconds, she would have been surprised: she could have received them as proof that Mavis Clark's nature was not entirely undiscerning, not wholly contrary. But the insight we have is blurred and partial. *She* knew that, as an instinct rather than as a precept, and Mavis Clark was sensitive enough to know it too in her own modern way, but one of the keenest misfortunes of our lives is not to know how to open and disclose to each other in the same instant of time.

*

Something slithers through the brass flap in the front door as Mrs Judd is crossing the hall and she knows what and from whom before she picks it up.

The postmark reads 'Cape Town'. She admires the perspective of Table Mountain on the maroon-tinted stamp.

She prolongs the waiting and makes herself a cup of tea. She sits down with the cup and saucer and the letter at the table in the dining-room. She feels her full attention is required.

Carefully she prises open the seals on the back of the envelope. The paper inside is thin and crinkly. She unfolds the pages and smooths them out on the table-top. Two pages, four sides, a respectable length of letter for a husband to write to his wife. The sheets are monogrammed with the name and address of a hotel. 'My Dear Frances' it begins.

Mostly it's about business and the people he's met. He mentions Cape Town, and the apricot-coloured countryside, and the white beaches, but the social life sounds much like England: Mrs Judd has to remind herself that South Africa is only the tip of a continent, that the rest of Africa lies behind it—like a crouching lion. He tells her the chaps are easy to deal with, they like seeing the Brits come out. It's a good life out here, he repeats, great weather, nice houses and cheaper than England to live, you don't have to lift a finger, no one's got a bad word for the life-style. He describes dinner at one colleague's home, and a picnic on a beach on False Bay with another man's family from Simonstown.

Of course, Mrs Judd knows, what her husband tells her is only as much as he *wants* to tell her. It is the seemly front he puts on his life, just as the existence they live in Sandmouth is a display for public consumption. But she can read between the lines. The wife who prepared the meal is called Avril, she reads again, and is very fond of swimming (as Charles is). The party on the beach included the three teenage daughters of the family and another couple.

She realises whenever she entertains Charles's colleagues and their wives to dinner in the house that they are watching her, they're preparing the words to exchange on their drives home in their cars. 'What does she know?', 'Hasn't she guessed?', 'How can she just sit there and smile?' In her turn, *she* is careful not to watch *him*, although she is aware that *he* is aware that she has a sixth sense on these occasions. In the past she has interrupted him on the phone and let him tell her it was 'nobody' and she has smiled back her most dazzling and brilliant smile; twice she has accidentally mentioned to a colleague's wife that Charles had to stay overnight for a company meeting recently and the wife has looked puzzled and told her, she's sure there hasn't been a meeting for the last three months. 'Maybe I'm getting confused,' she has twice replied. 'I get the months all muddled up.'

She believes he truly means it when he falls in love with the women he does. She has educated herself to believe that he can't help it. He doesn't neglect her as a consequence; quite the contrary, an absence makes him more tender and thoughtful on his return. He has always bought her presents, and she feels he doesn't do it merely as an appeasement, a salve to his conscience; the gift is always very carefully chosen, and he gives it to her because he knows it's exactly what she wants, whatever it is. None of the women has stayed the course, she's certain, but that is the way of mature love. She even pities the women, for the brevity of the affairs; she sympathises with them, knowing they must discover that their joy at being loved is only finite after all. She has total recall from her own experience of years ago to know how completely that feeling takes hold of you while it lasts, as if it must never end.

She has never forgotten the summer of 1947, nor any of the details and particulars. He swept her off her feet: the hoariest romantic truism of the lot, but quite *true*. He turned her head with love and she felt she was slowly, deliciously experiencing every hackneyed, clichéd condition in rotation. At the affair's zenith she could believe she was at the centre of all things, every sensation met in her and—enraptured by happiness— she was living in everything she saw: a flower blooming on a stalk, a wave rippling across a pond, she could even illuminate the existence of a sober brick set in a wall. No comparison was impossible to her imagination, she was so transported, so elated with the bliss of it all.

For each of those other women over the years the experience must have been an echo of her own: not as strong or intense, because hasn't it always been to *her*—to the memory of 1947's summer—that he's returned from his conquests? He has never confessed his guilt to her: she is merely relieved that none of his other affairs has approached the intensity of theirs. Occasionally she wonders to herself if our lives don't reach some peak—experience building to white heat—and all else afterwards is lived in the illuminating glow of that. Existence doesn't become 'less': the memory persists and cannot be lost. What happens subsequently is a kind of transfiguration.

Mrs Judd hasn't forgotten anything—becoming the flower, the rippling wave, the brick in the wall—and, weakness or not, it allows her to forgive. She doesn't deceive herself that the events of that period of her life can ever be repeated. But she chooses to think that experience isn't what's always being left behind: it endures, clear and fresh, in memory, and the memory becomes an unconscious part of daily routine. She knows that, several layers deeper down, the memory survives in Charles too: perhaps it's even in the way of an inspiration to him? She knows that *he* guesses her suspicions, and she notices an evasiveness in his eyes some mornings across the breakfast table. They never refer to their dinner parties of the evening before, they aren't the sort of host and hostess to perform an autopsy, even if the circumstances have been quite innocent. She can be confident that he would never be so indecorous as actually to lay his hand on a pretty woman's arm in her presence even if his attention were to fasten wholly on to her: she would merely stop looking towards that end of the table, she doesn't think she could bear seeing that look of devotion turned on to someone else, as it was once turned on her.

Mrs Judd refolds the flimsy sheets of paper and returns them to the envelope. South Africa is allowing Charles different opportunities. All that heat, the lush gardens, places called 'Darling' and 'Flesh Point', the drowning din of cicadas. But didn't he say it reminded him of England, lived under flawlessly blue skies and a boiling sun?

He's written her a letter that covers four sides of paper. He's conscience-stricken perhaps? Guilty because of what he has in mind to do, or has already done?—or guilty because he is encouraging the doubts that he knows must be in *her* mind?

He will be back next weekend, no time for her to write to him. She will wear something nice and listen to his stories, and dinner will be a menu quite out of the ordinary—dressed crab perhaps, followed by sweetbreads possibly—and the business of pretending she sees and suspects nothing will keep her buoyant, afloat, all will be up on the surface, daylight-bright as his own nature is, as is the good life he's enjoying on the Cape: and not a thought for anything else, for what hasn't been seen, for what—who knows?—may be seething and simmering in the darkness, waiting at day's end.

★

The Misses Vetch, purveyors of dairy products, will shut the shop in the middle of the afternoon. They have closed early every Saint George's Day for the last forty years, as their father did before them. Miss Madge, the younger, will climb up into the window and draw down the yellow sheeting on the wares by which the sisters make a living: bottles of cows' milk, goats' milk, ewes' milk, hens' and ducks' eggs, curds, thin and thick and whipping creams, soft cream cheeses, slabs of milk-fat cheeses, all displayed on the shelves.

The two sisters, dressed in their shop uniform of brown overalls and a felt hat apiece (Miss Bridget's is grey, Miss Madge's is a slightly darker shade of brown than her overall) watch the comings and goings on Hill Street. The temptation for chance shoppers is to judge from externals and to underestimate their intelligence: locals know better, that the two brains under the felt hats function as finely tuned barometers in all matters pertaining to social rank and distinction. It would pay to be a fly on the wall when the doorbell rings behind the day's last customer.

Miss Bridget and Miss Madge know the history of everyone who claims to belong to the town. They carry the family biographies of generations in their heads. They chart the sudden falls and, more suspiciously, the sudden ascents of particular members of those same families. No one can assume for themselves, however lightly and (it might seem) inconsequentially, the vowels and gestures of a social order to which they were not born without the Misses Vetch noticing immediately. With approaching strangers, even if they can't hear their accents through the window glass, they can recognise the qualities of a proper lady or gentleman from what they observe. It's the ones who try too hard and too quickly to become an 'almost' lady or an 'almost' gentleman who, in their considered opinion, are the most dangerous elements in a community, most likely to disrupt its natural harmony for their own selfish, and usually mischievous, ends.

Standing on the shop's earth floor, everyone has a common humanity: but the sisters weigh and apportion just as they apply weights and fractions in measuring out the comestibles. Naturally they vary their tone and manner, although there is only slightly less do-as-you-would-be-done-by politeness shown to the servants of the big houses than to the owners. It's the Almost Ladies and Almost Gentlemen, risen above themselves in less than a generation, who encounter the determined silences and the subliminally-exchanged eye-glances across the shop and the terrible, deadly accuracy of the shiny copper weights hitting the plate on the scales.

★

In summer the visitors come. There is no sailing worth mentioning, so the trade is less profitable than it might otherwise be. Sandmouth's visitors don't have sailing people's money but they are almost always respectable, maybe quieter than the sailing fraternity would be. They come from the area west of London, and from Bristol way, and from the South Midlands. Sandmouth has a modest gentility and its visitors also have a modest gentility. There is no caravan park and no amusement gallery; none of the shops sells pink sugar sticks of holiday rock and there are no deck-chairs for hire. The Alhambra Theatre provides the only 'entertainment', in the conventional sense: sometimes a touring variety show performs for as long as a week in Sandmouth's 'high season', more often a repertory company stages one or two plays on two or three or four successive evenings, and on the remaining evenings a film is shown. There are no plans afoot to greatly alter the current state of things as they determine Sandmouth's commercial 'image'.

Only one development has taken place of late. In the year of the Festival in London the new owner of the Clarence Hotel organised an event at the height of high summer, one without any parallel in Sandmouth's modest and genteel recent history. The event's novelty and (it was agreed) oddness ensured a repetition the following year.

The preparations were undertaken with assistance from Copplestone's timber yard. A dais was constructed on the lawn at the side of the hotel and six chairs and two long trestle tables with white cloths placed on them. In front of the platform fifty assorted chairs from the hotel's public rooms were set out in rows.

The six chairs on the stage were provided for the local celebrities invited to judge the competition: businessman and managing director of Copplestone's, Mr Norman Pargiter, from the Old Rectory; Miss Meredith Vane (published novelist and

45

local resident); Doctor Quentin Dick, G.P.; Mr Cyril Braddock from the bank; Mr Leonard Cheevy (assistant manager of Crockers' departmental store); and the then Mayor, Major Richard Wailes (now deceased) of 'Greywalls'. It was suggested after both events that another, younger woman should have been included in the judging panel, since the purpose of the competition was to select a 'Miss Modern Personality' and a woman of fewer years than Miss Vane's might have been presumed to know exactly what was being looked for. (The wife of the hotel's owner had had the opportunity offered to her twice, but had declined it, preferring to share in the glory of the day by spectating.)

All the contestants completed each single stage of the test in turn, then they all went on to the next. They were asked to appear in smart day-wear, which might include a hat or not. Firstly each young woman was required to walk the length of three duck-boards set down on the lawn and back again, then mount the steps to the dais. On the dais various tests of social aptitude and deportment awaited them. Standing at the second trestle table, with its pristine white linen cloth, they had to pour tea from a teapot into six cups and present one cup and saucer to each of the judges. The next labour of the afternoon— to be undertaken in full view of both audience and judges— was to prepare a cucumber sandwich from various assembled commodities (a loaf of brown bread, butter, cucumber, salt, parsley garnish) and again to offer the result for inspection to the judges. The third part of the examination was more demanding: the young lady had to station herself in her finery in front of an ironing-board and, in view of the judges and spectators, she had to wield a hot iron and press a gentleman's shirt that had already been starched; a wooden coathanger was handed to the competitor and she had to place it inside the ironed shirt and let the finished article be passed for consideration by the judges. For the fourth labour an armchair was rolled into the middle of the dais: each of the competitors was required to sit down on the soft cushion of the chair as gracefully as possible, cross her legs, sit fully back, then lean forward, uncross her legs, and stand up. (The judges individually accorded a mark out of ten on their report sheets.) The fifth labour was performed at the same covered table where the cucumber sandwich had been prepared: half a dozen varieties of flower with additional foliage had to be assembled into a decorative arrangement in either a vase or a crystal jug—a time-limit of two-and-a-half minutes was set, and the display passed to the judging committee. The sixth and final labour each of the seven or eight contestants had to tackle was the most difficult and the most nerve-wracking in some ways (once more a time-limit was set, three minutes): using a fork and side-knife as tools they had to prepare a selection of fresh fruit and arrange it on a plate—the process included coring *and skinning* (obligatory) an apple, unwrapping a banana decorously and to make it appear seemly on the plate (some of the contestants let their embarrassment show, they diced the naked fruit furiously with the knife and lost points) and (a dash against the clock) unpeeling and parting into segments a blood-orange using the stipulated implements.

At the end of the practical stage of the competition the seven or eight young women were reintroduced: one behind the other they paraded along the duck-boards laid down on the lawn and then they re-mounted the three steps (sometimes a slip occurred) on to the dais. One of the judges—on both occasions it had been young Mr Cheevy from Crockers' departmental store—was standing waiting and he proceeded with the aid of a sputtering microphone to ask each of the contestants six questions, to help the judges assess the intellectual calibre of each potential 'Miss Modern Personality'. (It was a matter of intense debate if this was a fair method of discrimination.) The questions were drawn from the following, in any combination:

'Which one tip would you offer to help ensure a perfect roasted joint for a Sunday family luncheon?'

'Is the Welfare State a good or bad thing in your opinion?'

'Which three qualities of Sandmouth life do you appreciate most?'

'Does charity begin at home?'

'If Barbara Goalen asked to swap places with you, (a) which piece of advice would you give her concerning either housework or your job and (b) what would be (one) the main asset and (two) the main disadvantage of finding yourself in Miss Goalen's position?'

'If you found lumps forming in your gravy, what would you do?'

And finally (one or other was compulsory), either:

'In half a minute or so, give your verdict on the achievements of Anthony Eden' or 'How would you advise our judges to keep shampoo out of their eyes when washing their hair?'

At that point for all but one of the contestants the event was effectively over. The judges conferred over their notes for a few minutes and then when a verdict had been arrived at, an announcement was made by local businessman and entrepreneur Norman Pargiter Esquire. An envelope containing seven guineas was then presented to the winning competitor (in both cases it was a lucky choice that the successful young woman was local and not one of the rather smug and self-satisfied holidaymakers); in addition the winner received two pairs of stockings and the very same iron already used in the competition, presented to the event free courtesy of Crockers' store and allowed to cool so that it could be packed into a box. Plus of course (the audience appreciated) the prestige of being Sandmouth's 'Miss Modern Personality' for an entire twelve months, in these exciting modern times in which everyone played their part.

*

Beneath the wet clay lie the origins of Sandmouth.

The pit is marked off with ropes and interested or bemused faces peer over the edge. Parties of schoolchildren are brought to gaze respectfully at the slough of mud and reddish clay.

After cleaning, the finds are exhibited beneath glass in the cases of the tiny museum. Mostly they are Roman, relics of devotional life: sections of a broken altar stone, fragments of a frieze, copper and pottery vessels.

The experts admit that these items are insignificant compared with what is yet to be uncovered. Their greatest ambition is to find the fabled gold head of Diana, goddess of war and love, celebrated among the Romans and their spoilers alike. They believe that beneath the temple may lie relics of an earlier pagan religious site: the evidence of a more barbarous philosophy of life and death than the later Roman one. Perhaps, eight or ten feet down, skeletons await discovery:

shackled, severed at the neck, conceivably bled to death.

It has been established that far underground, beneath the hill on which Sandmouth is built, run fast arterial channels of water: very probably one of these, now blocked, emerged at the surface as a well-head and in the mists of ancient time the cult of water-worship was developed here. The water bubbled up from hot caverns between warring layers of rock and spurted into the air, frothing and foaming like a geyser. The well was the point of communication between humankind and the vast, almighty forces of the underworld: the sulphurous water was drunk for its beneficial, restoring properties, the sick came here to be cured, gifts were offered to the gods and lesser gods in return for the boon of bodily health. In some dark periods of history it even happened that individuals were offered as live sacrifices, necessary victims to guarantee the safety of the community: the miserable brevity of human existence was traded for the assurance of eternal spiritual life.

So, who can be certain what trophies of past and future time lie sunk beneath the hole in the ground? The archaeologists have their theories and hopes. The golden head waits for modern adoration, its eyes caked with clay; a young girl picking buds and an old man in a long beard—spring and winter—revel daintily on a strip of frieze; the skeleton of a man or a woman lies face down, with stick hands crossed and bound.

Far beneath those, the waters churn, rushing beneath the hill. In local farmyards today there is often a well with a constant supply of fresh, sparkling water, cooled and chilled by its long, roundabout journey to the surface: a straightforward, diluted version of the magical element that inspired such pious worship in the early settlers of these parts.

The hot water directly beneath the site spits and seethes, as it has during the fifteen hundred years since the seam was filled and stoppered with clay and stones in a frenzy of hatred for the Romans. It's an improbable fancy that if the stones and clay are dislodged by a too earnest, too scrupulous archaeologist, the force of the jet might turn him into a flying man, propelling him high across the rooftops of unsuspecting Sandmouth.

But who can be so certain that those omnipotent forces of

the underworld are *not* waiting for their moment? In the annals of divine time, fifteen hundred years is only the fluttering of a god's eyelid in sleep. The fissure in the seal and the explosion of boiling waters could happen any day: a national saint's day when the flag flies is of no significance to the great earth and water gods—this particular day would be just as good (or bad) for the purpose as another.

★

The crocodile file of archaeologists is wending its way downhill.

Mr Selwyn watches the eight or nine persons it includes from the window of 'Arbuthnot Antiques'. Seen 'en masse' they look like itinerant prospectors, with their spades and sieves and trowels. Apparently Sandmouth is founded on richer substrata than even the most optimistic had ever dared to hope.

The telephone rings.

'Good morning. This is "Arbuthnot Antiques".'

A woman speaks, enquiring whether or not the shop offers valuations.

'For a small charge, madam.'

'Yes, of course. I have too much, you see. Too many things.'

Mr Selwyn hears the quavering tones of age and recognises the familiar fear of penury in the voice.

'We'll certainly give them a looking-over, madam. Discreetly, it goes without saying.'

'Oh yes. Please.'

'I then submit figures to Miss Arbuthnot. And she makes a final decision.'

He takes a note of the name and address.

'Miss Arbuthnot' is a fiction, his own invention: a commercially justifiable ploy, he feels. 'She' has never appeared in the shop nor spoken to any customers on the telephone, but 'she' engenders respect by virtue of her surname and her aloofness. Reference is made in very small print on the shop's receipts to a 'Miss M. Arbuthnot' ('M' for 'Matilda'?), but it is the flourish of Mr Selwyn's signature that attaches itself to any financial transaction. There have been awkwardnesses: particularly insistent customers, a man called Arbuthnot probing every

50

twiglet on his family tree, a government officer inspecting the records of antiques businesses in the area (a tip-off from Customs concerning skulduggery by a cartel of Dutch dealers).

To Eric Selwyn, antiques seem a very favourable commodity to be trading in at present, and he believes the business was quite a shrewd move on his part—without or (preferably) *with* the tacit cooperation of 'Miss Arbuthnot', a sleeping partner if ever there was one. He takes full account of the new people coming into the town—he is a 'new man' himself—and he realises from their custom how necessary is the service he provides, offering them these specimens of a waxed and polished past (without—by choice—woodworm holes and any major signs of renovation): they buy from him for a reason he cottoned on to long ago, because they want to own an ambience, one which creates for others an image of inherited substance and position, substrata of time and family. Mr Selwyn doesn't condone or condemn: it befits the traditionalist spirit of these times, with all its strident, confusing, smokescreen talk of egalitarianism. (People's social aspirations will always be upward, won't they?) The past, Mr Selwyn appreciates, is the inspiration of this new Elizabethan age: sylvan villagers in doublet and hose gambolling under a maypole, villagers of a later era lighting bonfires to warn of the enemy at sea and spreading the news from clifftop to clifftop and shire to shire. An oak coffer is just the job in a modern hallway and holds masses, linen or blankets or toys; a mahogany dining-table shows its patina best by candlelight, and seems able to raise the general tone of conversation more effectively than the best food and wine can; burnished copper pans make attractive pot plant holders, and it isn't difficult to drill a hole into the underside of a blue and white Chinese vase and wire it up as a lamp-base. The old should be adaptable, Mr Selwyn believes, and he is constantly on the look-out for what might be given a serviceable second life in these functional 1950s. He strips what he guesses to be worthless paintings out of interesting frames, then regilds the wood and inserts sheets of mirror glass (bevelled or plain-edged); he recycles salt boxes to hang on walls as letter racks, and—more innocently—he commends the usefulness of embroidered firescreens to hide the fronts of television sets.

Chance callers to 'Arbuthnot Antiques' come into the shop for casual interest's sake, or because they've recognised an object like one they own and they're keen to discover what it's worth, or because it's raining outside and the shop doesn't look unwelcoming. Selwyn can sum them up at a glance, but it's the occasional miscalculations he makes that allow him to be charitable. The incomers who have settled in Sandmouth constitute his principal contact with the public, they have become his regular customers. More and more, though, Selwyn's business is with others of his kind. He buys from smaller shops where he can, and in turn shops in larger towns buy from him, and perhaps he may sell them something which will end up in a London showroom eventually. The profits increase from stage to stage but the risks grow greater too. Sometimes Selwyn has a hunch to hold back on a sale and here 'Miss Arbuthnot' comes into her own. The suggestion is made that the lady sees each item as it comes into the shop, that it is her lameness which prevents direct dealings with customers; when her leg is causing particular pain she inevitably delays— and that's when Selwyn slow-pedals on a deal. Miss Arbuthnot, he also explains, is sometimes 'sentimental', and now and then she will not approve a sale which *he* has already pledged himself to. Sentimental or not, Miss Arbuthnot—to judge from what her junior partner recounts of his conversations with her—is fixed and dogmatic in most of her decisions; her opinions can be made to sound like firm and eternal pronouncements from on high, and as a rule no one is much inclined to argue or pursue the issue further if she refuses or fails to commit herself.

Whether his invisible mentor Miss M. Arbuthnot would survive a removal to Salisbury or even Cheltenham isn't clear to Selwyn. Really he needs to ask *her* opinion on that, but of course—irony of ironies—he cannot. It would be betrayal of a kind, he can't help feeling, after the luck she's brought him: but he wonders if dealers aren't sharper-witted in larger towns and able to see through a ruse like 'Miss Arbuthnot'. Mr Selwyn does know that, in a certain sense, he would miss her and he would be only half the man that he currently is without her. Miss Arbuthnot, he's begun to realise, is now not to be so easily got rid of.

She is a minor myth in the town. No one knows where she lives: 'some miles outside' is all the curious are ever told, so 'some miles outside' it is. Interest in her has fallen off a little after three-and-a-half years. Some people think that the passage of so much time means that she *must* make an appearance before too long: others, that it only confirms the fact of her reclusiveness. The Misses Vetch in their dairy don't recognise the name, so assume her to be an incomer and don't take up the matter of her health with Mr Selwyn. One or two worldly minds have hazarded a guess that she isn't a maiden aunt, fire-breathing type of matriarch at all, and have confected a further fiction according to which the woman is young and mysterious and attractive and—dare it be said—Mr Selwyn's mistress: she is also assumed to be his patroness, and more than likely is neither 'Miss' nor 'Arbuthnot' but a rich man's restless and weary young wife.

Mr Selwyn has super-keen antennae which enable him to pick up on these secondary flights of fancy, and he doesn't deny them or give them credence. They add to the complexity of the situation, and in the meantime he is content that it should have as many embroidered strands, as many heaped strata, as is possible.

However, Mr Selwyn is resolved not to be intimidated, neither by the rumours nor by his own image-making that has prompted them. Miss Arbuthnot, safely distanced from Sandmouth and to most ears sounding formidable and gaunt and distinctly of the older generation, will not be the final guarantor of this young man's prosperity, of that he is convinced: but her demise and its date require careful consideration.

His spirits stay high. At thirty-two years old he has alertness and stamina in plenty, and quite enough cool objectivity concerning his own abilities to know that Sandmouth is only a very temporary stopping-place on the journey to somewhere else entirely.

*

Diana lies another eight feet down beneath the deep topsoil within the cordoned rectangle of interest. Her head is gilded and severed from the rest of her body, which will never be located.

The head lies at such an angle that her finders will be able to joke (with relief, with the thrill of discovery) that she must have lain there listening for sounds carried down from the real world of buildings and roads and people. The eyes in the gold head are plugged with clay, which may only have intensified her concentration. (Another slightly laboured, archaeologist's witticism.)

Humour is invariably a defence of sorts. Who among us can afford to be absolutely certain about the lady's capacities? From her dark safeness, perhaps she has been in contact with surface life in a way that exceeds our powers of understanding. She has her own shrewd knowledge of our doings.

. . . a Latin goddess.

Diana was supposed to promote the union of communities. There appear to have been Greek elements in her primitive cult, and she was identified with the Greek Artemis at an early date. She was especially worshipped by women. She was perhaps originally a spirit of the woods and of wild nature, brought into friendly relation with the Italian farmer and his family.

From her association with Artemis, Diana took over the character of a moon-goddess; and, since Hecate was sometimes identified with Artemis, of an earth-goddess. She had the cult-title 'Trivia' from being worshipped, like Hecate, at the crossways. (*Oxford Companion to Classical Literature*)

★

Black GIs were once seen in the town, driving through in a jeep on a day's leave from the air base at Ringwell. One of them went into the chemist's and asked Mrs Stratton for a packet of extra-large condoms. She didn't bat an eyelid and told him that that article had been in very short supply and they only had regular size. What's regular? the GI asked, and Mrs Stratton, disregarding, said no one else had any complaints.

'But you see, ma'am, it's like this. What *I* need . . .'

It was as far as he got. Mr Stratton came through from the back of the shop and asked the man for his rank and number and base. The negro told him, or made something up to tell him. Mr Stratton asked him to kindly vacate the premises. The man opened his mouth to object and Mr Stratton reached out his hand to the telephone.

Mrs Stratton had a crisis of conscience immediately after-

54

wards, that they might be endangering the collective virtue of the town's young women. Her husband shifted uncomfortably. He'd been embarrassed for *her* sake, he explained, hearing a woman spoken to like that.

'I'm a woman of the world,' she said.

'*Our* world,' he told her. '*Our* world. That's what we were fighting the Gers for. For our standards. God was on our side.'

And on the Americans' side, they both thought without saying. Blasphemously Mrs Stratton tried imagining God with an American accent, like Spencer Tracy's, and she smiled at her husband, who nodded, misunderstanding, thinking she cast the seconding vote.

★

Enter Tilly Moscombe, in ankle socks and Start-rite sandals.

Sandmouth is the extent of Tilly's experience of people and places, more or less. She has never been anywhere else since she was four years old. Sandmouth is the sum of Tilly's knowledge of the world.

And she perhaps knows more about the town than the town is willing to think that a girl like Tilly Moscombe *could* know.

A stranger would realise there's something wrong with the girl from a couple of dozen yards away. Most obviously she doesn't seem able to walk as other people do, in a straight line. She is lop-sided and seems to meander and career erratically, side-on, with the clinging gait of a crab. One foot plods to the right, the other to the left, but even limping and lumbering Tilly Moscombe with her dished man-in-the-moon face is capable of speedy progress through the streets of the town.

To Sandmouth in general it's debatable if she ever *knows* where she wants to go, if she even has the power of simple volition. An animal instinct—no more than that—leads her home. Certainly her limbs appear to have a life of their own. At some point there is a crucial failure of communication between the brain and her nerve-ends, and that is as much as most people have been able to decide about Tilly Moscombe.

Others have persevered and discovered that conversation of a kind is possible with her. She is entertained in certain of the town's households because, as Alma Stockton has recognised,

55

she functions excellently as a listener, having such a limited command of reply. Opinions differ on the girl's capacity to understand what is being said to her. Perhaps those who are easiest with her expect the least: those who are not so comfortable in her company suspect that she is able to assimilate and retain information, but selects it by methods peculiar to herself. 'Eyes in lubricating oil, that girl has,' one of the Reverend Aldred's Ladies' Circle is fond of remarking behind the good man's back, as if she is proud to have originated the metaphor. What the expression confirms is a discomfort that the more charitably disposed of the population are conscious of in her presence: they admit her to their kitchens and serve her what's left in the teapot and any soft biscuits or stale gingerbread that require eating, but something disturbs them in the way her eyes ceaselessly move quite independently of that lolling body, seeing into all the corners, sweeping over addresses on envelopes and (unless one is careful) lines of private correspondence. Compared with other people's, her eyes are expressionless, like the rest of her scooped face, and therein lies the difficulty: how is one to gauge her thoughts and shape one's own responses accordingly? Every common exchange between persons surely requires that play between the eyes and mouth to start the business of human interchange: the gaze is often complicated by deceit and guile, but in Tilly Moscombe's case it's possible that she has no conception of deceit or guile or else the opposite, that she can't recognise any of the polite, positive virtues and her nature is shifty and untrustworthy to the core.

Of the little that *is* known about her: she is either sixteen or seventeen, and lives in her own room in the staff wing of 'Hallam House', Lady de Castellet's home. She came to Lady de Castellet when she was four years old, in the early days of the War, and it seems appropriate that her history belongs to that confused, unreal epoch, which—notwithstanding its brief elations—still seems to most people like a sinister crack running through the neat, reputable fabric of their lives. Since then the consensus of opinion has been that Tilly Moscombe is related in some dark way to Lady de Castellet. It is out of the question that the child is the spinster's own, a love-child: the fact of pregnancy could not have been concealed from Sandmouth. Just as Tilly Moscombe's history belongs to the time of the War, so also it belongs to the kind of family the burghers of Sandmouth read novels about, where Money exercises sovereign power and sway behind the scenes, shifting wealth and influence among competing heirs and siblings and bastards by means of secret wills with codicils and elaborate and misleading legal gobbledygook. To the truly percipient, Tilly Moscombe is part of a grander design, a minor figure woven into the panorama on a tapestry—like the tapestries of medieval chases hanging in nearby 'Melfort Hall', claimed to be unsung masterpieces of English art—where by long and accepted tradition every single element serves some symbolistic purpose in the whole.

*

Miss Spink too had cause to remember the posse of negro servicemen. She was standing in for Miss Mansell in the days when 'Accoutrements' was a separate department and haberdashery was banished to the other side of the staircase. Two of them had come swaggering in in their uniforms with caps doffed, politely enough, and swinging their arms like golliwogs, Miss Spink thought.

They asked if she would kindly direct them to—they discussed the matter between them—'medical aids' or, possibly, 'surgical appliances'.

'I'm afraid we haven't anything like that,' replied Miss Spink, far from green where customers were concerned. 'We have domestic *household* appliances.'

'This would be rubber, ma'am.'

'I see.'

'We've tried the drugstore.'

'The chemist?'

'That's right, ma'am.'

'Medical or surgical, did you say?'

'Of a personal nature, ma'am.'

Miss Spink's eyebrows drew together.

'But the drugstore had none left, you see.'

'Is it—are you very...?'

'...desperate? Yes, kinda.'

'I see.'

Miss Spink swallowed.

'But the chemist couldn't oblige you, sir?'

'Nor his wife.'

'I see.'

'I guess that's it.'

'Maybe you should see a doctor,' Miss Spink suggested quickly; then she suddenly felt a little unsteady on her feet and had a horrible intuition—muddling around in the pit of her stomach—of what this conversation might conceivably mean.

'Maybe he should,' the other man said, 'see a doctor. Who'd you recommend him to, lady?'

'There's a surgery across the road.'

'Who do I ask to see, ma'am?'

'Ask for Doctor Dick.'

'Begging your pardon, ma'am?'

'Doctor Dick. He's *my* doctor.'

'You mean that's his name? It's not what he does?'

'Oh yes, he *is* a doctor.'

'But he's "Doctor Dick"—like that? Not a dick doctor?'

'I'm sorry, I don't think I quite understand you . . .'

'He's a doctor, sure, I see. I thought maybe he must be a specialist.'

'Not that I know of. He treats everyone. And everything.'

'I've a kinda big complaint, you see, ma'am.'

'Oh.'

'Very big. I don't know if I should explain to you or not.'

Miss Spink was saved an explanation by the fortuitous arrival of Miss Mansell, last of the handful of departmental heads personally appointed to their posts by the original Mr Crocker in the 1920s. She advanced to the counter in queenly fashion, her wrists tucked inside Tudor cuffs, her lorgnette resting by a gilt chain on her black bombazine chest. No mere male ever entered her department without her seeking out the explanation: a black man, nay two of them, was quite unheard of.

'Perhaps I can be of some assistance, Miss Spink?' she said, noting the woman's expression of concern.

' "Spink"?' one of the fellows said, and smiled.

'That is my principal assistant's name, sir. "Miss Spink".'

'It's an unusual name, lady.'

'I wasn't aware so, sir.'

'Where we come from, it gets a real *weird* pronunciation.'

Miss Mansell blinked slowly. The voices made her think of Scarlett O'Hara, plantation coons, white verandahs, rustling crinolines and lacy parasols . . .

'Comes out kinda like "Spunk".'

Miss Mansell nodded. No explanation was coming readily to her, but she too had an instinct—an unpleasant, sinking sensation—that these two negroes were really talking smutty, very smutty indeed, and that there was a distinct danger that the situation was about to escape her command.

'Just comes out . . .' The other man repeated him and laughed with his thick lips pulled back.

Miss Mansell had never cared for Americans anyway, so she felt it no great disloyalty to request Miss Spink, in her best Cicely Courtneidge voice, to please go and summon the gentlemen on the second floor. She believed their services were required. And would she please take the lift and be quick about it.

Of course the servicemen had gone by the time the second Mr Crocker arrived in the open lift, wrestling with the bars of the gate before Miss Spink could stretch out an arm from inside the cage to release the handle. Miss Mansell pointedly did not look at Miss Spink during her conversation with Mr Crocker, to save them both the embarrassment of acknowledging that each had comprehended the unsavoury quality of the servicemen's talk. One wasn't required to recognise specifics—words and meanings: but even so, Miss Mansell considered, it was quite out of the question that a woman should permit her natural dignity to be in any manner compromised, given that the two genders were as they were today—quite distinct and (thank the good Lord) apart.

★

In Sandmouth's midsummer pageant, Ruth Aldred, the Reverend Aldred's daughter, is due to appear as a lady-in-waiting of Good Queen Bess, a particularly demure Lady Hamilton, a guest at a *fin-de-siècle* country-weekend, and a city girl waiting for her beau to return from the First War. They are all of them brief, secondary roles.

Performing in the pageant is an obligation. Sometimes it seems to Ruth Aldred that all her life is a matter of obligation. Sometimes it seems to her that the only reason she is tolerated in this life is because she is the daughter of the vicar of the church of St Andrew and St John. She includes herself in the company of all her father's 'good women': small good in a small town is as much as she believes she is capable of doing or considered capable by him of doing, although she knows that—regarding her—her father cannot read the whole story.

Her mother died when she was born. Two children should have been born, but the second proved too much for her frail mother and both she and the child died together, locked in a frantic, agonising struggle for life.

It was the worst beginning she could have had, of course. It imposed the primary and fundamental obligation on her: she'd grown up as her father's daughter but also as the sole woman of the house, a surrogate for her mother. She accepted the rôle as her necessary right. It wasn't herself but her mother she reserved her sorrow for, and her dead sister. All her sentient life she'd felt she was only atoning for the guilt of surviving.

On the surface it had been a lonely life thus far. She noticed people pitying her, even when she was being at her most sociable at church functions. They didn't see *all* of her, she consoled herself: only the quiet, prim, very slightly masculine exterior. They didn't see *inside* her: they couldn't understand that she too, Ruth Aldred, had her own reserves of strength.

Certainly no one in Sandmouth could have had cause to suspect the sea-change their vicar's daughter worked on the real world which they shared with her. In its essence, it had nothing to do with them, since it concerned Constance; she'd christened her dead sister with her mother's name, none other seemed appropriate since they were buried together for all time and could have no need of names between them. Constance, still unnamed, had come into her bedroom on the evening of the day her father had seen fit to tell her about the tragedy: or, rather, she had walked into her own bedroom and found Constance already there, in a corner of it, as if the room was Constance's and *she*, Ruth, were the interloper. A christian name had helped to define her, and with it seemed to attend certain facial features. Constance's face was prettier and more

60

feminine than her own, but she didn't envy her rediscovered sister on that account. After their shared schooldays at the school in Merioneth, Constance started to dress differently too: she wore more modish clothes than Ruth, better cut, flattering, not at all like the decorous, no-nonsense body-coverings which their father's 'good women' contented themselves with. Constance heard what went on in London, and twice she'd taken her up on the train for a day away from Sandmouth.

It wasn't all a case of Constance leading and Ruth following. They confided in each other a good deal, and then Ruth did much of the talking; Constance listened, quite intently, and registered approval or disapproval with a nod or shake of the head. Sometimes *she* suggested what should be done and Ruth in her turn listened most attentively.

The two sisters had become inseparable. Even at mealtimes Ruth smiled across the table to where she knew Constance sat listening. They slept side by side in the darkness of the bedroom with the cedar tree outside which had always been 'Ruth's Room': the double-bed had been her parents' and the room had been theirs too for the short time that they were able to share it. To Ruth it seemed fitting that another Constance should be using it in her mother's stead.

Sometimes she wondered if they would have grown up so happily together if the situation had been otherwise and her mother had lived. She felt they shared an experience whole and entire because they both came from the same bloody, lightless place in their mother's interior, which they were the only two ever to have known. That made them as close as conspirators. What freak chance had decided that Constance should hold back while Ruth was allowed to make her exit first?

It puzzled her to think, could I have *done* anything? If it had happened the other way about, would Constance have reached back to help *me* in some way? Did I abandon her?

She recognised that it was the merest chance that had made her 'Ruth' and not 'Constance'. She *might* have been Constance. She persuaded herself, maybe she *was* Constance. Constance had had as much right to the privilege of 'life' as she did.

Thus Ruth Aldred was able to see the situation for herself, in the round, from inside *and* outside. Thus Ruth Aldred was deeper and more complicated than the folk of Sandmouth—good or not—suspected. She knew what they thought, but it stayed in the dim nether-reaches of her mind where such matters belonged, not in the forefront where Constance thrived: her smarter, prettier, sweet-smiling, never-to-be-forsaken sister.

★

Occasionally the Bendall boy comes into the bank.

Normally two hatches are in operation at the one time; from behind the wooden screen, at the back of the room, Howard Trevis can see the customers as they enter. When the Bendall boy appears and stands in one or other of the queues to be served, he asks whoever is attending at that hatch to see to some other piece of business behind the screen.

The boy's turn comes and Trevis finds himself looking into his face and holding out his hand to receive the order from his uncle.

He can hardly focus to read what it says. His eyes steal across the counter to where the boy's hands lie on top of each other. He has long straight fingers; not like the stubby, grubby fingers of Sandmouth commerce which he has to serve on Friday mornings when an extra hatch is opened. He has shiny nails with clear cuticles; tiny gold hairs sweep up from his wrist on to the back of his hand. Trevis tries to imagine him in rolled short sleeves, and with his tie off and the front stud of his collar undone.

Trevis delays the business for as long as he can. The boy always thanks him politely when he's done and has handed back the order book. He watches him leave—the co-ordination of legs and buttocks inside the flannel trousers—and then he summons the cashier back to his place.

Inevitably he has to retire to the cloakroom. Washing his hands afterwards, he looks at himself in the mirror above the basin. There's something wolfish about the image at such moments: seeing it used to alarm him, but he has now—almost—accustomed himself to it. The eyes still confuse him, with that fixed jellied stare. His skull is elongated, he has two lines at either side of his mouth; the map of his beard casts half his face in shadow. He's not the man who looks out of the wedding studies at home. He can't believe that the cricketer's fresh face in the school team photographs is the father of this one. He doesn't know if Maureen notices: maybe the wedding photograph on top of the bureau is more like an icon to her, its 'reality' becomes less as the months recede and they pass into years. That's how *he* feels, confronting it from his armchair in the evenings as he fills his pipe with tobacco: he views it through plumes of smoke and remembers certain moments out of his life—his mother telling him that his father smoked a briar pipe, escorting Maureen to a dance and woodenly partnering her and feeling like the one male dummy in Crockers' window in George Street, Maureen's mother serving them Sunday afternoon tea on a tray laid with a lace cloth and lace doilies.

The clock ticks in their back living-room—it was a wedding present—and he wishes that it didn't. The ticking seems to make the rooms—all the rooms in the house it reaches to—feel smaller.

At the end of every evening, when the wireless has been switched off and the newspaper neatly folded, he steps outside for some fresh air while Maureen attends to her ablutions in the bathroom. From the garden he watches the lit window upstairs and sees Maureen's shadow on the frosted glass.

His 'breathers' have lengthened over the months. Sometimes the fancy comes into his head that he could open the latch gate and walk out on to the road and go anywhere in the town he wants to.

Maureen would lie in bed patiently waiting and imagine he was only getting up his courage to allow them both their conjugal rights. She would wait all night if he made her. Every time she pats his shoulder after he has withdrawn and rolled over on to his back, the breath heaving in his chest: as if he's a well-behaved schoolboy who deserves favour. For all he knows she does it just for simple relief's sake, because they've got the ordeal over and done with till the next time.

In that respect—their grateful relief—they come closer together than at any other point in this life they're meant to be sharing, his wife of seventeen months and himself.

★

Betty Messiter had decided they would take the long way round to the golf course. She wanted to make some purchases in the Misses Vetch's dairy; also she imagined herself rather dashing in her golfing-tweeds, and had no objection at all to being seen in them. So it was that the Hillman drew up a few feet from the shop. In a weary-sounding voice Mrs Messiter asked to be taken to a point in line with the front door, thank you very much. Mr Messiter freewheeled the little distance downhill and made the mistake of not securing the handbrake so that when his wife was stretching out her legs and cork-screwing round to get out of the car it continued rolling forward. She made a very undistinguished exit and landed on the pavement in a semi-crouching position, hands grabbing at air. Somehow she didn't go down. As she recovered her balance she turned round and glared at her husband. Mr Messiter tried to look suitably concerned; he pulled on the handbrake and realised it was going to be one of their difficult days.

Mrs Messiter's thin face became thinner still as she walked into the shop. She ran her tongue over her teeth, convinced she'd smeared them with lipstick as she landed so unceremoniously on the pavement. She couldn't taste any, though.

There were no customers inside the shop. 'Good morning,' Mrs Messiter announced in her Phyllis Calvert voice. Neither sister replied or even looked up. In truth she had always thought the two of them quite off-hand and wondered how it was that the other customers could put up with it. Clearly some of them didn't have to—the sisters treated them very courteously; perhaps incomers had to serve their apprenticeship first.

Mrs Messiter pulled the knot of her headscarf tighter under her bony cusp of chin. Even for the golf course she wore toilet water and she realised the funny little women were probably envious of her panache. She still felt she had lipstick on her teeth and now she was afraid to open her mouth. When the younger sister came to attend to her she pointed at the eggs she wanted and mumbled how many through her lips.

'No, the small ones. If you please.'

The woman virtually tossed the eggs into a box. Then she stood and just stared at her as the doorbell rang and more customers entered the shop.

'Anything else?'

Not even a 'madam', nor a 'Mrs Messiter', although she'd left her name on orders in the past and they must know perfectly well who she was. What a sinister pair they were.

'I really don't think so,' she said, reaching into her willow pannier for her purse. She preferred to pay cash rather than have an account: it was an old habit Brian had encouraged in her, pay for something on the nail and make sure it's yours. She felt it was more genteel to live on account, but habits of a lifetime are ingrained.

The doorbell rang again. Miss Madge handed her the eggs as she stood counting out the money and she became confused with her hands reaching everywhere and she dropped the purse. She snatched at the box of eggs as the purse flung loose change and notes on to the earth floor.

No one offered to help her to pick up the money. Stooping down she became embarrassed that people would be adding the money up and thinking it didn't amount to very much.

The fine earth on the floor was soiling her white gloves. She was aware her face was firing. She fingered the knot of scarf under her chin, then realised she was streaking herself with the filth half of Sandmouth had trodden on.

She pulled herself upright. She counted the money out wrongly and had to start again. The woman stood waiting, with her hand held out, while the doorbell rang and, behind her, another customer entered the shop. When she'd paid correctly, Mrs Messiter shut her purse and replaced it in her basket.

As Mrs Messiter said a chilly 'thank you' and wished the woman 'good day' in her grandest voice, she heard the most recent arrival in the shop start talking, in a quietly-subdued and pukka Home Counties voice. She gave the woman a tight smile as she turned round. The other customer responded with a very faint smile and a puzzled frown: should I recognise you? it seemed to be asking, have we ever met? Is it likely that we would have met anywhere before?

The doorbell sounded particularly dismissive as Mrs Messiter stepped outside in her pick-me-up heels. As she stood waiting for pedestrians to pass, she wished the Hillman wasn't a Hillman. She deserved a Humber at least.

She angled herself carefully into the front seat, paying attention that she didn't dislodge the headscarf in the process. She pulled the door shut and stared frostily ahead of her. Her husband asked her something as he lifted off the handbrake—remembering not to say 'Betty', although it was the habit of a lifetime—but she affected not to hear.

He understood instantly, another habit of a lifetime. Inwardly he sighed; outwardly he attempted to look just cheerful enough, but not *too* cheerful, in case she thought there was a conspiracy afoot and Sandmouth was wanting her to suffer for being Brian Messiter's wife.

★

The Tierneys are famous in Sandmouth for their quarrels. The habit is generally put down to the mother's fiery Celtic blood, which she has passed on to her son. But the quarrelling is perhaps less of a 'habit' than a way of life.

The couple own and run the garden shop. 'Florists' was always too weak and watery a word for Mrs Tierney to stomach, and she preferred to call the business 'Tierney and Son, Floricultural Specialists'. (The adjective was discovered skulking in a dictionary.) Since then the signboard has been altered, to 'Mrs Bella and Mr William Tierney, Floricultural Specialists'. Mr William doesn't care for the word 'Floricultural' but it was as much as they could agree on to have his name included, so 'Floricultural' it remains.

It strikes some customers as more than a little ironic that the fiercesome Scotch couple, forever barking at each other and stomping about the shop, should be dealers in such sensitive organisms as flowers. It's as if the Tierneys, mother and son, had seen through the exercise of flower-giving many years ago. In humble mood recalcitrant husbands purchase a bunch or two, intending to placate a wife at home, while Mrs Tierney shakes water from the stalks as if the blooms had done her some personal injury; relatives or friends cautiously choose the correct, tactful, peaceable colour and fragrance for an invalid, and sullen and silent Mr William, never a man with patience to spare, gives the impression that *he* understands it's done only as a kind of peace-offering and as a sop to their consciences, as a minding before the patient's condition worsens and the final decline begins; the wreaths in which the Tierneys specialise also seem to constitute a futile and petty gesture of self-interest according to their wholly unsentimental appraisal of human behaviour, an 'I'm sorry, please think the best of me' once the worst has happened and the end has come and, too late, regrets crowd in thick and fast. On the other hand Mr William is less ferocious with the children who come to buy spring posies for Easter and Mothering Sunday; he even lays a hand on the locks of the prettiest little girls and is willing to risk taking a penny or two off the price if he feels it might tease out a smile. Mrs Tierney sees, but appears reluctant to offer any criticism on this one point: probably she realises the darkness of her son would know no bounds if she did.

Otherwise there are no holds barred between them. Mrs Tierney's manner is put down to the one verifiable item of personal history that is public history, namely the absconding of Mr Tierney (Senior). Mr William has inherited his mother's firecracker disposition. Some days tempers have exploded soon after the shop has been opened and watered and they have fallen out with each other by nine o'clock. The rest of the day's business may be conducted without a single word being exchanged between them: money is grabbed out of customers' hands, wet change dropped into their palms, the door is kicked shut behind them if they fail to close it themselves, anyone handling goods is told off in no uncertain fashion, any males are scowled at by Mrs Tierney while her son treats the women brusquely and monosyllabically, staring past them at move-ments in the street and only looking at them when the wind has blown their coiffure out of shape or cold sores are budding at the corners of their mouths or when they have the mark of the curse on them.

Some people find their behaviour amusing, others are upset by it. There have always been rumours that the couple are worst at the time of a full moon: that they have been spotted on Windmill Hill on the morning of the midsummer solstice clad in white sheets, that they bathe in the cold sea by starlight, that no cat ever escapes from their back garden with any of its nine lives. Floristry and floriculture (they also grow flowers on allotments) are presumed to be a peculiarly deman-ding business: more of a calling, a vocation, and the Tierneys must be blessed in some way that others, uninitiated, aren't equipped to understand. Their oddness and their unhappiness with each other is how they've paid for their talent.

Occasionally of an evening their voices can be heard with especial clarity if an upstairs window has been left open. The tone of the voices is unmistakable even if the matter of the conversation remains obscure and difficult to fathom. 'Hammer and tongs' is how their neighbours describe these interludes: 'all hell let loose'. No one knows if the arguments are about anything in particular: or if the details have been lost sight of and the atmosphere of hostility is just a habit, like a war. Maybe in the future something will have to be done about it, although it will need a brave man or woman to take the first step.

As it is, the Tierneys are a famous (or infamous) feature of Sandmouth life. The town has a way of including everything and everyone, even such rebels by temperament. It isn't a matter of resisting: Sandmouth decides. Its slightly insipid resort appearance deceives in certain respects. Sandmouth stands at the outermost edge of Thomas Hardy country: a sly, suspicious, unpardoning land, home to an inbred race reared apart, who've forgotten other lands and races that might exist beyond the last rampart of grassy combes and hills. Here in Sandmouth the vista of sea to the south doesn't necessarily guarantee wider mental horizons.

Personal eccentricities are permissible, only if they don't interfere with the prevailing modes of self-interest: when the Tierneys become an embarrassment to the general decorum others regulate their lives by, a request will be made to the authorities. In a democracy such as Sandmouth, the will of the majority is paramount.

★

'Very interesting, I'm sure.'

Miss Perry had been describing the religious rites of Bali and Miss Watkin was rather in the dark as to its relevance in the circumstances.

'Of course,' Miss Perry said, 'I'm not quite sure if it *could* be done up into a speech, or—or even if I'm capable of delivering it myself!'

A pause followed. Miss Watkin felt obliged to speak, and not only because she was a guest in the house.

'Oh yes, Miss Perry,' she said. 'I'm *quite* certain that you could.'

'Are you?' Miss Perry nodded her head thoughtfully. 'Yes. May-be.'

She'd visited Bali once when she was out in Singapore staying with her brother. A very pleasant time she'd been having of it in Tanglin with Hugh's Orchard Road friends, but she'd found herself with itchy feet.

'Good and bad are precisely balanced, they think,' she repeated. 'They're always battling with each other. The spirits, I mean. Some people here think good has to triumph, because it's Britain—'—she brought her eyebrows together (not very patriotically, Miss Watkin thought)—'and then you get your weary-willies and moaning-minnies who think we're all going to the dogs, nothing's how it used to be.'

Miss Watkin nodded, understanding that much at least.

'But my Bali friends,' Miss Perry said, 'for them it's a struggle every day of their lives. They're in the thick of it, you see. The devil speaks in one ear, and a good god in the other. They both get to work on him. Or her. Neither, you see, has the "right" to win. No moral expectation. Morality is all flux. Do you understand, Miss Watkin?'

Miss Watkin suddenly felt from the sharp, schoolmarmish tone of voice that she was being reproached in some way. She pulled herself up in her chair.

'Yes. Yes of course, Miss Perry.'

'Now, Miss Watkin, the first question is, do you think Sandmouth would be interested?'

Miss Watkin guessed the proper answer.

'I suppose it's not for me to . . .'

'Of course not. But you must have an opinion.'

Miss Watkin decided to risk an untruth.

'Oh, then I should think so, Miss Perry. I should think *so*.'

She heard her voice sounding rather weak. She didn't know if the vicarage would be quite the place for such a talk: devils and good gods prancing about, woolly dragons one minute and invisible the next, and dusky natives banging gongs and cymbals. What a muddle. It all sounded rather dubious. And only half-remembered. But for social appearances' sake she felt she must approve: be polite.

'I'm sure we should all . . .'

'Yes, Miss Watkin?'

'Find it—well, of great benefit. I'm sure so.'

'To know how our brothers and sisters live *their* lives?'

'Yes. Yes, indeed.'

Miss Watkin managed a smile. A wary, tepid smile.

'Yes, indeed,' she repeated.

It was 'brothers' and 'sisters' now, was it? Whatever next? Under the skin perhaps, people's internal organs *might* be much the same. But it was the skin that mattered, wasn't it, and its colour. As for the space inside people's heads, that was another matter entirely, and even in the genteel sitting-room of 'Walberswick', discreetly scented with pot-pourri, Miss Watkin felt that the strip of sun-faded blue floor-runner between her and her hostess might as well have been a raging, roaring jungle torrent at full spate.

*

A boy at school called Hislop once told Trevis that during the black-outs in London, the first thing men of a certain persuasion did was to rush to one of a select number of public lavatories in the metropolis. Inside each of these famous 'cottages' a crowd would assemble, a heaving mass of bodies and limbs collected together in the darkness. The lavatories had become so packed that if you'd genuinely needed to relieve yourself, you wouldn't have been able to force your way inside.

Hislop hadn't specified what actually took place in the fetid, dank, airless darkness, only feet away from the innocents passing by on the King's thoroughfares. He'd merely raised his eyebrows and whistled through his teeth and dug his hands deeper into his pockets.

The picture stayed in Trevis's head, almost like a memory. For him the War was taking on a halcyon quality, although he hadn't properly experienced it from the fastness of the school in Somerset. In a black-out men could be united in their simple desires, there and then: there wasn't the rest of your life to spend obliging people's propriety by concealing your feelings, in the moment when death might have come striking down out of the skies you allowed them to well up out of you. In the darkness of a public place faces were unseen, identities were anonymous: all the terrible thing was reduced to was touch, relief, congress with a stranger—he could be a negro or a yellow Chinaman, a spiritual man of the cloth or a policeman in civvies.

In his pipe-dreams at his desk he was in a lavatory in somewhere low like Clerkenwell, and by a flicker from someone's match he was able to see that the shape packed next to him in the murk was the Bendall boy's.

It was the boy's hands which laid themselves on *his* body first. All he could do was reciprocate, encircle his waist with his arms, explore with his fingers for the buttons on his trouser waistband.

The rest of the encounter only came to him in his dreams at night, lying beside Maureen. For the most part the office in the bank with its brown panelling and ticking clock on the mantelpiece was a curb on his imagination, and even with the door closed it refused to rise to the bait.

He would dream of the boy while Maureen lay awake and dutifully said nothing about what they both knew was his failure to do the manly thing in the circumstances. Once a week, he'd read, was generally regarded as often enough: but even that was proving an impossible dictum to comply with. Perhaps once every ten or eleven days he tried and managed something: he would feel a dribble of his seed spurting into its legally approved sump and he would tell himself that he was only suffering from nerves.

The rest of his seed—in plentiful supply, he was relieved to discover—was reserved for the porcelain toilet bowl in the bank's Gents. Immediately he would flush it away and take care to remove any evidence that might have spilt on to the floor or the rim of the bowl.

The wolfish face would look out from the mirror as he washed his hands, a custom instilled into him by his mother and two great-aunts and which he performed like an automaton. He was thinking instead of the wedding photograph at home in pride of place on top of the bureau—himself, with Maureen's arm linked through his—and he found himself feeling unaccountably cheated.

There must be something in the air to make Mr Blinney think it is a Sunday.

Every sabbath he dresses in his suit and white shirt and collar and walks up Hill Street to stand outside the Reverend Aldred's church. He waits till the doors have been opened and the first of the congregation emerge before he launches into his accustomed diatribe against the profane leaders of the alien hordes. To the departing worshippers the names 'Hitler' and 'Mussolini' are as much part of Sunday morning's ritual as the handshake with the Reverend Aldred and the prospect of one o'clock lunch to come. From the little knoll ringed by gravestones Mr Blinney proclaims that when the War is finally over, the victory will belong to the righteous of this island, this sceptred isle—God's chosen people.

There must be something in the air this Saint George's Day to persuade him that the world would benefit from his message. He dresses in his frayed suit and unstarched white shirt and collar and walks up Hill Street. He fails to notice that there are more cars and pedestrians about than usual, and takes up his position outside the Reverend Aldred's church. He stands on the knoll waiting, ringed by gravestones. He waits, but the doors don't open.

Mr Harold Blinney, a bachelor in his late middle-years, is a man of custom. So, being in his wonted spot, he begins at last. Der Führer and Il Duce and their alien hordes will suffer the humiliation deserving of the infidel, Mr Churchill bears the nation's pride as his tryst, the dragon-slayer will lance the blasphemous, infidel beast through its evil heart.

The words rise into the cloudless blue, the wind on the heights catches them, they scatter far and wide, smithereens of sense borne aloft over rooftops and swept, southwards and ever higher, out to open sea.

★

On the intersection where Hill Street and George Street crossed, Mrs Judd stopped and looked across at Tilly Moscombe stamping along the opposite pavement.

She felt sorry for the girl, such a rambling life she led. And how was it that she perceived her life—as only in the present tense? Was she able to remember anything?—steering herself between the past and what was yet to happen, as most other people in their right minds did.

Mrs Judd wondered what time it was in South Africa. How often in the day—or night—did she occur in Charles's thoughts?

She knew *she* couldn't have lived without the past. The future was a menace, and every time she came down into the town she was thinking of the next time, and would people's expressions be different when they looked at her, because at last they positively *knew*?

The past was safer ground. Of course she had cause to reproach herself for not having seen through Charles earlier. Yet it wasn't that simple, her terms weren't appropriate. There wasn't anything to 'see through' in the usual sense. Her husband's feelings for her had been quite genuine. In all probability no one had meant more to him than *she* had.

The truth about the past was two-fold, she realised. It included the best part of her life: it also included much else, strictly on the periphery of her own experience, and she was reminded dozens of times a day that this was a marriage that 'worked' only under the severest limitations—tolerance was all and mattered rather less than understanding.

If she'd had a job, maybe she would have thought about these things less. But Charles was insistent that she didn't go out: it was pride on his part—and perhaps indifference for her needs—and she felt that if she were to do it against his wishes it could give him an excuse to make his business trips more frequent, their masks would slip.

Maybe this marriage of theirs was really only an extreme version of other marriages?—and every married couple lived among minefields, and kept to a straight and narrow track of polite, social behaviour with themselves and with the company they were required to keep?

It comforted Mrs Judd to think she might not be alone in that respect. And at least she had the material security and compensations Charles's other women friends didn't have. Their 'freedom' didn't count for much if they could let their emotions get the better of them during these brief interludes and rule their lives for them.

Which at least was a predicament Tilly would never know, for good or bad. Eyes screwed up, Mrs Judd looked after her, pitying her. Maybe she should do what certain other women did and invite her into her house. She suspected they did it for very loneliness, which was a hard thing to concede. She wanted Tilly to *know* that she pitied her. Maybe that was a wrong impulse, though. But the alternative was to offer nothing at all. The moral lesson of her own life was surely that to experience a measure of true feeling, of however short duration, was better than to have known none. The girl might see that she did it to have an object for her pity: in that case she needn't come to the house a second time—or else she just might be able to recognise the simple instinct to do a little good that had prompted it, and in her turn pity *her*.

★

Every Wednesday was spring-cleaning in the bungalow called 'Avalon'.

The Bassetts were famously lithe and nimble for their age, somewhere in the late sixties. It was Mr Bassett (retired from the office of a printing-works in Salisbury) who attended to the windows. He scrambled across the sills in stocking-soles, as surely as a mountain-goat, applying a sponge first, then a chamois to the panes and metal frames. He opened the hinged panes and swung a leg and arm out like a trapeze artist, flailing with his sponge and chamois. Somehow he contrived to whistle at the same time, often a melody from 'Showboat' or 'Carousel'.

Mrs Bassett meanwhile took up all the rugs and carried them out into the garden; she hung them over the washing-line and batted like a demon. When she'd finished, she set to sweeping all the floors with a broom. Dusting was Mr Bassett's province and he flicked into every last corner and refuge with devastating accuracy. He joined his wife in the bedroom and together they stripped the bed bare and beat the mattress. Mrs Bassett took the sheets into the kitchen and filled the sink while Mr Bassett began the precise business of disinfecting the bathroom. The lavatory bowl was scrupulously brushed and repeatedly flushed.

While Mrs Bassett was in the kitchen steeping the sheets she wrung out the sponge and chamois a second time, washed the window-pail and started cleaning down the fronts of the cabinets. (Interiors were emptied and cleaned every third week.) Mr Bassett reappeared and immediately got to work on the cooker with another sponge and a nail brush, whistling as he scrubbed it of a week's spills and splashes. Mrs Bassett disinfected the pail, then disinfected the sponge and chamois before tackling the sheets. Every other day barring Sunday is a clothes-washing day in 'Avalon' so Wednesday is by way of a respite in that respect.

With his tasks in the house now successfully accomplished, Mr Bassett (whistling the same melody with which he began) can now turn his attention to his principal duties of the day, in 'Avalon's' well-tilled, fully utilised, one third of an acre.

★

Miss Meredith Vane was up with the lark and by quarter-past-eleven she has had enough. She leaves the bureau which is also her writing-desk, and walks over to the mirror behind the console table.

She looks from the jaded specimen of middle-age in the mirror to the image shown on the jacket of her last novel, *Memory is a Lonely Place*. There she is photographed in sophisticated pose: she wears a borrowed black velvet dress cut low at the shoulders, her hair is swept up into a bun, her neck strains to lift her jaw clear of her chins. The camera is set at an angle and she looks upwards and beyond, a quiet and knowing smile on her face. Otherwise the closest resemblance people see in her is to Nancy Spain.

Miss Vane makes a point of describing her characters' exteriors: for that, is it not, is how we first perceive a person, and on which we must base a first impression? As for herself, she has a full, squarish face, and hair (black, dyed) normally pulled up into a ring and held in place by combs; she is stocky, has graceful hands, and most frequently wears a shaggy, fisherman's jumper with a pair of red or navy canvas sailing trousers bought on account from the chandler's. On public occasions she dresses up: she looks as elegant as, say, Ginette Spanier, with her ballerina bun and wearing a waisted frock and long gloves. Her very best outfit is a tailored cotton piqué

75

suit from Lachasse, navy-blue with white beading on the lapels: it's seldom given an airing in Sandmouth but it's believed that it is what she wears to her luncheons with her publishers when she makes her occasional overnight visits to London. Caught sight of standing on the platform waiting for the 7.17, she appears ten years younger than her usual Sandmouth self, and in that situation she admits her femininity in a way she normally doesn't. To those who have never had the privilege of seeing her in her fitted costume at a town function, she is rather lumpish and ungainly, and certainly distracted: much more given to her Art than to the artifice of self-presentation. It's assumed that all authoresses are like her. Some, who haven't read her books, believe she is a kind of seer, above the full and routine concerns of every day, a dweller on a plane apart. Her behaviour is attractively eccentric. Walking along George Street she will stop in her tracks and click her fingers because she has remembered something, she will pick a fallen leaf off the pavement if its colour attracts her, she befriends the waifs of the cat world, she may spend twenty minutes or half-an-hour perusing another novelist's book in Stanley's the Stationers, then mark the place with a match till next time, or she will select a complete stranger (most often a woman) and go up to her, introduce herself, ask her do you like lilies, is blue preferable to green, come and have tea with me in 'The Wishing Well' and tell me your life-story.

Miss Meredith Vane is one of Sandmouth's 'characters' and it would be a staider place without her: also a less cerebral one, because it is recognised that, along with two or three others, Miss Meredith Vane—whatever the truth of her age, whether she chooses to wear her hair in a ring or a bun—represents the higher influences of 'Mind'. What she may lack in physical height she more than makes up for in the loftiness of her intelligence; she writes books, which is an exalted calling in life, and her welcome eccentricity is just a facet of that, a brain and sensibility overflowing with curiosity and wonderment at the world. Or something of that sort.

Now it is general knowledge that she has embarked on another novel—referred to variously as a 'story book', a 'novelette', a 'play'—and Sandmouth looks forward to all sorts of absent-minded, unrestrained behaviour in the months to come. A rumour is currently circulating that this time Miss Vane is turning her attention to the town that has been her home for the last twenty-three years. Miss Vane has heard the rumour and knows that people will forever flatter themselves that they must make interesting 'copy'. Even so she realises that writers (of a certain standing, naturally) may reach a watershed in their professional life when they imagine they need stray less far from their 'base': that the local should be enough to provide them with the matter from which axioms on conduct and character are extracted.

Not drily, however. Miss Vane believes that the mental eye has to be satisfied. It requires colour, a little spectacle, some dash. Her readers want 'escape', within limits, they want taking out of themselves: living one life and reading about another, that is the nub of it.

So, for the next few months, it's the fisherman's jumper, the sailing breeks, and combs rammed into her hair. (She must continue to dye her hair, though, because Miss Vane takes a more careful and critical view of herself than Sandmouth might imagine. Put bluntly, greying hair would lose her her mystique and include her in the pedestrian ranks of the ageing.) She knows that clothes and the externals most certainly maketh the woman in the public estimation. Repeated behaviour enforces an image; she seeks to control the image and reputation and not vice versa. Mercifully Sandmouth isn't capable of making acute literary judgements, or perhaps she wouldn't have survived this long; she will concentrate on what she knows modern Sandmouth does supremely well, seeing and making its moral deductions on character from the impression that is offered to it.

*

The major concession to seaside commerce in Sandmouth is the Lavezzolis' Seafood Restaurant and Ice-Cream Bar. Both have a reputation that extends beyond this particular reach of the South English coastline and the industrious and enterprising Lavezzolis have grown sleek and prosperous and wholly respectable on the profits of the business.

Only the sister Caterina was known in the locale before the War. She had come to London with little money and set up as a dressmaker; she'd moved to Bournemouth in an attempt to find a kinder climate, more like that she was used to, and then when the War started she was advised that it might save her 'possible embarrassment' if she were to conduct her business at a discreet distance from the resort, from somewhere like Sandmouth. (The Jewish custom in particular was very unforgiving about Italian participation in the War.)

In Sandmouth she was like a sore thumb at first: she had hoped to lead a quiet and unexceptional life for however long the War lasted, but she might as well have walked through the streets brandishing the Fascist flag. Suspicions were allayed after only a few months when the good women of Sandmouth discovered the wonders Signorina Lavezzoli could achieve with the minimum of materials and at minimal expense. By the second year she was being greeted quite cheerfully on Hill Street and George Street and on the promenade by wives and their husbands, who would wish her 'good day!' and no harm at all. The policeman who served in the town then was obliged to call on her twice a day. He would wait for a break in the whirring of the sewing machine and would knock on the front door politely.

'Are you in, Miss Lavezzoli?' he would ask.

'*Si, si. Ah' meen.*'

If the man was fortunate, she would add in her mangled English, 'I go make coffee now. You will like—?'

Her brother Stefano and his wife Marta left Italy in 1948, less discontented with affairs in their homeland than fired by what Caterina wrote in her letters. The couple couldn't speak half-a-dozen words of English between them when they arrived, although their children had picked up a good many more from Americans: they couldn't fritter time chatting anyway, except with Caterina and each other, and they got their heads down to the task of establishing a livelihood. In Sandmouth they quickly became a byword for hard work, and the sums owing on the restaurant were paid off inside three years. The ice-cream parlour was the next inspiration, opened in the Festival Year. Even Bournemouth didn't have anything quite like it: wicker tables and chairs, three picture windows commanding a view of the promenade, striped awnings flapping above the little terrace outside, terracotta pots of geraniums

78

and peonies. The elder Lavezzolis knew enough English by now to take orders and discuss in simple fashion the relative virtues of different flavours and to be able to enquire after the customer's own business or health; Angela and her younger brother Carlo were striking-looking in a way no one else in Sandmouth except the Bendall boy was, and people—for untold and disparate reasons—liked to be served by them, to have Angela's pretty face smiling down at them and to watch swarthy Carlo's manly strength and tight Latin buttocks as he cleared the table, muscles straining under his starched white shirt. Their being Roman Catholic (with Jewish complications) was neither here nor there.

It was only in very recent times that Sandmouth had seemed to cool somewhat towards the ice-cream family. Perhaps the slow distancing chiefly had to do with their gathering success. Doing decently well in business is admirable, especially if the hours involved are long and hard, but a point is reached when industry becomes disturbing if it seems to be obsessive and when the reward of prosperity loses its moral stamp and is seen to be vulgar, ill-bred, and not a quality of the angels any more.

The Lavezzoli clan all lived in 'Elmhurst', up on Rossholme Drive at the top of the town: they'd picked the house up for less than it was worth because they offered to pay the owner— a retired Navy man—cash. The purists and traditionalists were offended by the green roof tiles that replaced the worn and cracked red ones, and by the crazy paving paths that were laid, and the plaster model donkey pulling a barrow beside the front steps, and by the florid script which appeared on the gate-posts, announcing that the property had been re-christened (in memory of a deceased sister) 'Casa Fulvia'. Those good folk of Sandmouth still struggling to make a go of things in the new decade were nonplussed, even offended, by the sight of the Jaguar with whitewall tyres supplied by a dealer in Bournemouth, and by the extravagance of Mrs Lavez-zoli's clothes. (It was observed that while she was ring-less in the restaurant, the outline of rings and stones made bulges under her gloves as she attended to her shopping in town.) A grandmother showed up, then a great-aunt, morose white-haired women in black habits who seldom ventured into Sandmouth but who could occasionally be caught sight of taking the air on the Avenues. Carlo drove his own car, a racy little red MG which spluttered up Hill Street on his late nights home from Bournemouth. And, worst of all, Angela Lavezzoli had turned out to be some kind of genius and astounded Sandmouth and her family by winning herself a place at Oxford.

The Jaguar was parked in the station yard. Portly Mr Lavezzoli in a lightweight navy blue suit that billowed about him stood on the platform as the first train of the day from London pulled in. The door of a first class compartment opened and he saw his daughter lifting her luggage down from the rack. The porter was summoned with a loud whistle and Mr Lavezzoli advanced with his bulk to her assistance.

He shouted his welcome.

'Angelina! Angelina!'

As the porter took charge of the suitcase and vanity-case, the pater familias gave his daughter a bear-hug, or tried to.

'Ti trovo bene. Sei contento di ritornare a casa? Tutti voglioni vederti.'

Angela extricated herself from his hold.

'Hello, Fa,' she replied briskly in English, and in a clipped accent her father didn't recognise, no more than he recognised the contraction. 'Gosh, what a journey. Am I late? Dreadful dash across London, you can't imagine.'

She used to return from visits to London with her mother loaded with band-boxes and parcels tied with shop ribbon. Now she was carrying some books under one arm. *Sweet's Anglo-Saxon Reader* her father deciphered with some difficulty as he slipped his hand through the other arm.

'Cosa ci racconti di Oxford?'

'Oh fine, thanks. I really like LMH now.'

'Ti sei divertito con gli amici?'

'Oh, lovely.'

'Dove abitano?'

'Beaconsfield. They've a super house. A bit Spoils of Poynton-ish.'

'Come?'

'Henry James.'

'He is your friend's father?'

'I'll explain another time.'

'Angelina, da un bacio alla nonna quando la vedi. È tanto che ti aspetta.'

'Rightey-ho, Fa. Povera nonna, è ancora raffreddata?'

'Sta un po'meglio.'

'E Zia Guiliana?'

'Better. She wants to hear how you like Oxford.'

'Oh. Moltissimo. I think I've cracked it.'

' "Cracked it"?'

'E gli vomini—they're so nice, the men. I'm sorry I'm only going to be home a week.'

'Carlo, he can't be here to meet you. He's gone for winklies.'

Angela's sigh was inaudible to her father.

'*Winkles*, Dad—'

The luggage was fitted into the boot, the porter was lavishly over-tipped, and Mr Lavezzoli and his famously clever daughter climbed into the Jaguar. The engine thrummed to life, the whitewall tyres crunched on the red gravel, and the porter was left counting the coins in his hand, breathing in the perfume the young woman attired in caramel and cream had left behind her.

*

The announcer before 'Housewives' Choice' said it would be 'a good drying day', so Howard Trevis's wife has taken his advice.

She doesn't like to disturb the Prestons next door with the wireless, so she only listens to it in the living-room. When she's in the kitchen therefore, she turns it off. Sometimes she thinks she would like to hear what the voices are saying—or not even that perhaps, what she really wants (but is unaware of wanting) is to hear the wash of human sounds. But there is always work to be done, and the wireless set is too cumbersome to think of moving it.

She begins running things through the wringer when they've been Rinso-ed and (those that require it) starched. She squeezes them out first, feeds them between the rollers, turns the squeaky handle several times—pushing and pulling hard because for some reason the handle has become stiffer recently—and watches the tablecloth and pillow-cases as they fold over on themselves in a pile in the sink.

Her hands and arms, the bottom halves up to her elbows, turn red. The sense of touch disappears from the tops of her fingers. But there is no helping it, so she doesn't dwell on the discomfort; it doesn't occur to her that she should.

★

At Minster Court Preparatory School the bunting's up. Food has been laid on the trestle-tables in the marquee and flies have discovered its whereabouts. Masters have their instructions. The paint is dry in the requisitioned kitchen-staff lavatory, now the Ladies' Cloakroom. The first Daimlers and Humbers have rolled up the driveway and on to the makeshift car-park on the top lawn. Parents are stepping out, mothers dressed like galleons in the glory of full sail, fathers in tweeds or dark suits with or without buttonholes. Labradors and setters are put on leashes and choke-chains and taken for some brief, busy exercise.

Mrs Symington-Berry watches from the french windows of the Headmaster's study in the private wing. Her husband is re-acquainting himself with a list of pupils' christian-names.

'Some of them have probably no more idea than you do,' Mrs Symington-Berry pronounces.

'What's that, dear?'

She doesn't answer but steps back to where she can see herself in the mirror.

'Where's Fitt?' she asks.

'The Major, dear?'

'Whatever he is.'

'Maybe the train's late.'

'Today of *all* days.'

'It'll only take three or four minutes. Harry's picking him up.'

' "Blake",' his wife corrects him. 'Not "Harry". How many times—'

'I always think of him as—'

'Who said?' —the lady lowers her voice—'who said we have to get everything "just right"? *Your* words.' Mrs Symington-Berry glares at her husband in the mirror. 'So he's "Blake": not "Harry".'

Her husband nods at her, then inclines his head to the page of names.

'If things aren't right today, Philip, we can just forget it.'

'I'm sorry?'

'Blake *has* gone to the station?'

'In the car. He'll bring him back. It's only a few minutes—'

'It'll be time to begin in a few minutes. All this is presuming he's on the right train, of course.'

'I'm sure he will be.'

'Well, I wish *I* was. What makes you think he can get himself on a train? You saw his letter. He wouldn't pass Common Entrance.'

'Well—' Mr Symington-Berry smiles charitably. 'Well, it's excusable.'

'*Why*'s it excusable?' his wife asks, turning from the mirror and fixing him.

'You're—' The Headmaster, inspired by the day's importance, finds a sudden, momentary surge of confidence in himself. 'You're very discriminating about academic standards suddenly, Lavinia.'

Anger sparks in Mrs Symington-Berry's eyes for a second or two. She might be tempted to reply in kind if the day's momentous nature weren't acting as an oppressor on *her* spirit.

'I repeat,' she says. 'Why is it excusable?'

'Well, he's done his bit, I suppose.'

' "Done his bit"? Is that one of your teaching expressions?'

The Headmaster's teaching abilities are a subject of mutual dispute between the pair in the confines of their private rooms.

'He's one of our heroes,' the Headmaster replies simply.

'Maybe he's a hero, but can he get on the right train?'

'Oh, I expect so.'

'Well, we'll see.'

'I . . .'

'Yes?'

'I thought . . .'

'Thought what?'

'You seem . . .'

'I seem *what*, Philip?'

'If you don't mind my saying so—a bit, well, nervy.'

'I am not "nervy"!' Mrs Symington-Berry replies indignantly.

'You *are*, I think.'

'Oh, just memorise your names, Philip. For heaven's sake—'

Through the french windows a procession of cars can be seen approaching up the driveway. The drivers turn and negotiate the front wheels up on to the front lawn.

'No sign of Blake.'

'What's that, dear?'

'They're not here yet.'

The cars bounce along the top lawn. Mrs Symington-Berry eyes the extravagant hats and realises that this Saint George's Day is being treated as another Speech Day.

'We shouldn't have done it,' she says.

'Well, it was *your* suggestion.'

'Saint George's Day was. Not Fitt.'

'You didn't say "no".'

'That's right, blame *me*.'

The Headmaster clears his throat. 'I'm not *blaming* you, Lavinia—'

It's an ancient, enduring argument. The private wing often rings to it. Mrs Symington-Berry favours the philosophy that life should approximate to a garden party as often as that state of affairs can be arranged. It may well be occasioned by feelings of guilt about the general standard of education provided on the premises. Certainly the standard is no lower than that of many similar institutions: but to her way of thinking there does seem to be a discrepancy between what is promised (or at least held out as a possibility) in the shiny brochure and what is most frequently attained—or, more to the point, not attained. Her husband has acted on the commendable principle of employing young men fresh out of the older universities and with respectable degrees to their names: but somehow, however respectable and persuasive the degree appears on paper and in the brochure, the man has all too often failed to match up in the 'character' stakes.

That blanket judgement glosses a multitude of probable sins, but a headmaster and his spouse can only be privy to so much information of a personal kind. Nonetheless they believe it necessary that they should both work together, energies harnessed, to ensure that the school continues to have a good name. Copies of their brochure are posted as far afield as London, Sussex, Hertfordshire, Gloucestershire and Devon; in that they insist that such attention will be given as to provide

84

pupils with a 'fully grounded education in academic compe-
tence and the social niceties'. On the latter count Mrs
Symington-Berry (her own education was Quaker and directed
at the conscience) considers that parents—on the current scale
of fees—should be allowed to appreciate the school as a
properly functioning social organisation. One method of their
appreciating it has proved to be the rite of the garden party . . .

Mrs Symington-Berry is conscious she looks her best in
festive summer wear. Hats suit her, unlike most women: with
her height she acquires a grandeur and a dash her own Quaker
teachers would have disapproved of, but life is ordinarily so
dull and has been ever since the War, so why shouldn't people's
harmless whims be indulged, didn't they deserve it, and wasn't
she only providing others with a free (if 'free' was the appropriate term) show anyway?

She rallies when she sees the roof of the Jowett pass through
the archway and turn towards the house.

'They're here! At last!'

Her husband closes his register. 'I'll never remember . . .'

'If you say surnames, they think it's a custom, it's what
they're paying for.'

The Headmaster watches his wife half with wonder and half
with alarm. It's true that she has helped to make the school
what it is—fashionable—but he thinks he sometimes detects
a detached, almost mercenary quality to her. It may be that she
merely states things aloud that already exist at the back of his
mind—by some quirky wifely telepathy—but the business of
hearing them spoken is no less disconcerting to him.

He walks towards her, meaning to wrap both his arms round
her waist, when she darts forward for her handbag. 'Battle
stations!' she says, undoing the clasp and looking inside. 'God
help us . . .'

The Headmaster is relieved that no one is privileged to see
behind the green baize-backed door. He couldn't conceive of
this life without his wife's presence, but she occasionally
shows a bluntness and directness he would prefer others
shouldn't know about—even, he's been driven to telling her,
himself.

'Very apt, I'm sure,' he says, with the brave attempt at a
smile.

She's looking through the french windows and perhaps catches his reflection.

'What did he do?' she asks.

'Who?'

'What's-his-name.'

'Oh. Distinguished himself somewhere. Lots of medals.'

'In the War?'

'The First one.'

'Good God—'

'Flew out of a trench. Lost a leg. Jerries captured him.'

'And you think that'll go down well, do you?'

To the Headmaster it sounds as if his wife is making an accusation.

'He wrote a book,' he says. 'Read it once. Queer title. *A Leg to Stand On.*'

'Does he drink?'

'No idea.'

'Why did you invite *him*?'

'You wanted to make it special. Suggest someone, you said. You didn't say "no" when I told—'

'Just pray to God we get to lunch,' she interrupts him.

The french doors are thrown open and out they stride, on to the paved terrace. Mr Symington-Berry follows his wife, a pace or two behind. He is content to walk in her shadow. He wouldn't have the nerve to stage-manage such an ambitious spectacle by his own devices. He lacks the social confidence for that. His wife told him it would add 'kudos': that was reason enough for him to agree. It has also added expense, but on the whole (it's a crude fact of the headmaster-ing life) such activities tend to keep the parents on *their* side—and with one new prep school seeming to open for business every week along the South Coast, they can't afford to fall behind the times, fall out of step and so out of the race.

★

At the annual church bazaar Miss Meredith Vane makes a sideshow of herself and her talent. It began as a humorous remark exchanged between herself and the Reverend Aldred, a piece of whimsy which, very oddly, she couldn't clear her mind of.

86

The upshot was the first of Miss Vane's appearances at a rickety card-table—placed at an unfortunately noisy spot midway between the jam, marmalade and chutney stall and the skittle run—where, as far as it was possible in the circumstances, she sat creating. People necessarily had expectations, and these had to be accommodated. So she made a point of sucking the end of her fountain pen every so often—actually inserting the blunt, rounded end between her teeth and nibbling on it for several seconds—and drumming her fingers on the shaky table-top and looking absently into the distance.

Miss Vane's appearances at the annual bazaar were considered rather successful by her, a little less so by the vicar (her personality was perhaps a mite intrusive?). In fact people were variously intrigued, amused, humbled, or turned into sceptics by what they saw and heard. The scribblings were laid out on the table-top after each page was completed and offered for public criticism, both helpful and unhelpful. In the way of amateur verdicts the best so far elicited has been 'the workings of a genius mind' by the wife of the proprietor of 'The Wishing Well', who suddenly found herself the sole spectator at the table; the very worst Miss Vane has had to endure she only partially overheard, when one vulgarly-spoken, freckle-faced teenage lad from the wrong end of the town sniggered and whispered to his chum, all it was good for was bog paper, and his pal opined that it had already been used for that purpose. (They departed in gales of laughter, to upset next the staid demeanours of the ladies at the 'Odd-Balls' counter of knitting wool.)

'Bringing the Muse down to the level of Sandmouth' was how the Reverend Aldred originally described the event, more tellingly than he might have intended. Frankly, he had been afraid to be seen as pouring cold water on the suggestion when Miss Vane proposed more of the same a second year, and he had weakly capitulated. Thereafter it was difficult to recommend any alterations in the event, already half-way to being established as a Sandmouth institution.

★

Mr and Mrs Berry lost their way immediately after the War.

Philip Berry had been looking for a job in civvie street. He hadn't liked the cap-doffing to men who'd been sitting on their back-sides all through the War. Like all the others, he'd expected better, but it seemed to be all the way back to square one. Then, out of the blue, a ship-mate invited him to join him in running an estate agency he was starting up in Guildford.

'But I don't know anything about that kind of work, Pinky.'

'It's easy. I'll teach you, old chap.'

Berry (as he was called in those days) discovered that his character wasn't very well suited to either the persuasive harangue or the famous soft touch Pinky tried to instruct him in. Berry's wife let it be known after several months that she wasn't overkeen on the 'trade' aspects, and that she believed Pinky Taylor's methods (and 'motives', she added darkly) required constant attention and scrutiny.

It was by the most fortuitous timing that an obscure great-aunt of Mrs Berry happened to decease—her main recommendation in her niece's eyes was that her brother had once farmed rubber in Malaya—and, like two waifs in a Victorian novel, they found themselves in receipt of more money than they had dared to imagine might come to them. The Will had two stipulations: one was that a proportion of the estate was to be held in trust and the interest was to be paid as income; the other was that the beneficiaries should agree to the inclusion of 'Symington' in their surname (a hyphen or not was left as an optional matter).

Symington-Berry, the former Petty Officer, had heated words with his supposed partner in the office one day in front of a customer and the two of them agreed—there and then, in front of the client—to part company. Thereupon Mr and Mrs Symington-Berry considered the possibilities of buying a size-able residence for themselves and running part of it as a private hotel. At the same time it chanced that an educational establishment housed in a Pevsner-listed building—a manageable Edwardian version of Gothic—came on the market, in a part of the world neither of them knew very well and which had no previous knowledge of *them*.

It wasn't easy at first. Every rogue in that line seemed to get wind of them: masters who couldn't teach, cooks who couldn't cook, matrons who couldn't put on a bandage and fainted at the sight of blood, a gardener who couldn't tell a bedding-out plant from a weed. Eventually, though, they learned the knack of homing in on the imposters (or most of them): and they hoped that they themselves presented what would seem to be an artlessly authentic front to the world. Occasional misfortunes occurred: an inspector committed the text-book gaff of leaving his hat behind and returned to find the most unorthodox of the young masters playing sardines in the stationery cupboard with the new intake (the young man published an experimental novel the next year, much praised in London, and he left them to take up the literary life; Mrs Symington-Berry lived in perpetual dread of something more commercial, a novel which would be a take-off of life at a preparatory school, appearing in print); the cook chanced to serve prunes for breakfast on the morning the whole school set out to visit the Festival of Britain exposition in London; it was discovered that a young matron was charging threepence a time to the senior boys for each lingering 'good night, sweet dreams' kiss; and most improbably, Mr Smith taught the rudiments of mathematics for a whole term before his husband phoned the school from another similar establishment, and it was discovered 'he' was a 'she' meaning to make a new life for herself/himself.

Those were the high-tide—or low-tide—marks on the way to establishing Minster Court as a healthy going and growing concern, in what was a very shady corner of the educational garden. Mr Braddock at the bank considered it one of Sandmouth's financial success stories; there was now a waiting-list of prospective parents and pupils; Gabbitas Thring were keen to hear of impending vacancies on the staff. The Symington-Berrys had achieved much in only a handful of years, and if they had been slightly more relaxed individuals they might have had due cause to think they could rest on their laurels for a while—to 'stand easy', as Pinky Taylor might have said—and take time to catch their breath.

★

London, of course, was where you went to live if you thought you were of Trevis's persuasion.

There he'd seen men in crowds, singly and in pairs, and he'd *known*. At school his classmate Hislop's favourite saying used to be 'It takes one to know one'. From his own observations they fell into different types: the single men might look ordinary enough but were betrayed by a predatory sharpness in their eyes—or else they were the docile variety with bland, featureless faces, from which all the character seemed to have been drained. The men who walked together often had facial and bodily characteristics in common, and he wondered from seeing that if the search didn't take two forms, both equally destructive: either you quest for your ideal, who may be heterosexual but who ceases to be ideal once he has been seduced, and who, if he's the same way as yourself, loses some of that mystique of the ideal by submitting himself to you—or alternatively you search for someone you might try to resemble as closely as possible, and the two of you only approach oneness and completeness by manufacturing a 'look', a narcissistic mirror-image. Trevis would think, maybe men like him—hating how they were—they wanted to find some way of loving, not another person, but themselves, and they did it by turning themselves into their partner. In a curious way he felt he wanted to *be* the Bendall boy: Bendall looked how *he* had always wanted to look, Bendall was a straightforward girl-fancying male such as he had never had the choice of being. There was nostalgia in his craving for Matthew Bendall: a wistfulness for the person he'd never been allowed to grow up as.

He craved the joy of undressing Bendall, of fondling him: but the boy would have been contaminated and made worldly by the contact. The pleasure Trevis felt at the moment lay in not knowing how much Bendall was capable of understanding. It gave him, Trevis, a power of corruption which he could feel stirring in his groin.

Sometimes, though, it wasn't the wish for mastery that was uppermost in him. A good-looking man who gave grounds for doubt would walk into the bank and the need to assert was taken away from you, the compulsion to be mastered took over; the desire to accept the nature of your ways and not to feel there was any further option possible to you, either confessing to them or concealing them. The other man *knew* and you couldn't deny or resist.

Between the two of them he suspected he was a lost soul. He diligently performed his duties in the bank, he performed—less well—his duties at home. He saw the way stretching ahead till he was of pensionable age and he left the bank and a daughter came to visit them both and Maureen in her stout later years dispensed acts of goodness about the town, as the Trevis women had all done. He would make the effort to keep himself lithe and narrow-waisted at least: he would attend to his appearance and maintain standards—shoes polished, tie tightly knotted, collar and cuffs stiff with starch. And, with any degree of luck, after another forty years he would look in the mirror and the image of the wolf floating beneath his features would have completely faded and gone.

★

'Mrs Symington-Berry?'

'Yes, that's correct.'

'I'm Mrs Huntley.'

'I'm pleased to meet you, Mrs Huntley.'

The two women shook hands.

'I'm so looking forward to hearing Major Fitt.'

'He's resting for a few minutes first.'

'Of course.'

Mrs Symington-Berry felt uneasy, prey to a dim premonition.

'I've been wondering, Mrs Symington-Berry . . .'

'I'm sorry, Mrs Huntley?'

'You're not one of the *Hove* Symingtons, by any chance?'

The Headmaster's wife smiled hesitantly.

'Indirectly,' she said.

'I beg your pardon?'

'I have never lived in Hove myself. But certainly relations of mine have.'

'The rubber Symingtons?'

Mrs Symington-Berry felt her mouth straining to keep the smile in place.

'My Great-Uncle Symington,' she said.

'Percival Symington? Gertrude's brother?'

'Yes. Yes, that's right.'

'I *thought* so.'

Mrs Symington-Berry tilted her head warily.

'We were in rubber too, you see,' the mother announced.

The Headmaster's wife made a circle of her mouth. 'Oh?'

'Your great-uncle was a neighbour of ours. In fact he was, Uncle Percival to us as well!'

The woman laughed.

'What a strange coincidence,' she said. 'I come half-way round the world and who do I meet but Percival Symington's great-niece!'

The woman laughed again.

Mrs Symington-Berry deigned to give a perfunctory nod of the head.

'Yes. It *is* a small world, isn't it?' she said, quite drily.

'And now we're paying you to bring up Christopher!'

Mrs Symington-Berry's eyes narrowed at the woman. It was one thing having to be cornered on a personal matter, having to pretend an intimacy with a branch of the family that had always given itself superior airs to her own . . .

'I trust our policy of education here, "drawing out the child",' she said, echoing the words she'd put together with Philip for the brochure, 'will not be construed as a mercantile arrangement.'

The words came out sounding rather more caustic than she'd intended them to. For a moment the mother looked quite startled. Mrs Symington-Berry stretched her mouth wide to a speech-day smile. The woman tried to mirror it on her own face.

'I'm sure you *don't* think like that, Mrs Huntley.'

The name was intended to distance, to establish a proper equilibrium between them.

'No,' the woman replied, a little nervously to Mrs Symington-Berry's ear. 'No, of course not.'

'I thought not.'

'I'm sure Christopher is—very happy.'

The time-switch smile left no trace. 'I am sure, Mrs Huntley, we are attending to his potential as a growing person.'

Mrs Symington-Berry frowned to hear the words she was speaking. She was aware she only quoted the brochure when she was put on the proverbial defensive: what she and Philip referred to in the privacy of the house wing as 'a Landseer', the stag-at-bay routine.

'Yes.' It was the mother's turn to start nodding. She was too inexpert to know how to lose her smile. 'I'm quite sure you are.'

A mystique must be seen to attach to the business, Mrs Symington-Berry had realised in her saner moments of reflection. There was nothing more likely to kill the uncomfortable confusion with the commercial which some parents made to their faces than a general rarefaction and abstraction of the methods involved.

'But now,' the Headmaster's wife said, 'you must excuse me, Mrs Huntley.' (The 'Mrs' received a particular emphasis.) 'I believe I can see Lady Herbison. I simply *must* have a word.'

The most effective recourse was to find a title and shelter yourself behind it as best you could: as Lady Herbison herself had done, who had left school title-less and had married a most distinguished man in his seventies, now too fragile to be exhibited in public.

'*Will* you excuse me, Mrs Huntley?' Mrs Symington-Berry repeated. (Unambiguous stress on the woman's marital and social status.) 'I *must* waylay her Ladyship.'

She knew she was being watched as she beat her retreat, so she had no option but to raise her gloved hand to Lady Herbison, whom she had met only once before. Her son was a curious child with an old man's head set on a pixie's body, and whose christian-name she couldn't think of for the life of her. But any social embarrassment with Lady Herbison—not exactly a candidate for the 'Brains' Trust', although clever enough to bag Sir Montagu—would be preferable to more of the grilling she'd just undergone. In future on such public occasions she was going to have to plan her manoeuvres in advance, with shrewd caution and cunning.

*

Mr Ferris stood in 'The Gyft Shoppe' and his thoughts were not of Sandmouth and the here and now but of the War and the potential for virtue that it had allowed unassuming people. Small men became great in their comrades' eyes; unsung old ladies smelling of lavender kept their eyes trained to spot a German spy in a country lane or in the High Street and each in her way had the 'Odette' spirit and became a heroine of her country. If there had been a clearer distinction between the two conditions, war and peace, then he might not have dwelt on that time as he did. But the years following 1945 had made this new age seem like a continuation, with so much want still left over.

Maybe it was odd that he should have felt so much for the spirit of those War times when history had played a kind of trick on him by making him too young to serve in the First and not fit enough to have an active role in the Second. During the last he'd offered his services at least, and landed himself a job in the Navy accounting office in Southampton. No job would have been wholly tedious so long as it was part of the War effort, and he often used to remind himself of the greater end they were all working for, King and Country and the freedom of its people.

He was always hoping someone he would recognise would walk in, by accident. Instead he mainly saw the visitors to the town, and there weren't too many of those. Now he closed the shop from mid-November till the end of February, because it was cheaper not to heat and light it. The time went by more quickly than he dreaded it was going to. He would remember the War, and the one before; he would remember his wife, and each year he found himself drier-eyed, less agitated. He became rather lazy in his habits during his hibernation months, and let dishes pile up in the sink and clothes go unwashed if he felt like it. He believed there had to be some compensation for growing older and just surviving the years. When he'd still had Doris around, there hadn't been an opportunity for reflection: not of that kind anyway.

Doris wouldn't have approved of either his slovenly winter habits or of 'The Gyft Shoppe'. She might have *seemed* to: everyone used to speak of her 'sweetness'. She had had a pretty face certainly, but he'd always known when the thoughts behind it weren't in sync. The sweeter she appeared, the more sceptical and hesitant *he* became. The years had made her seem to be sweeter, on the outside, and he'd never been sure why that should have been, what secret it concealed.

At her funeral, announced in the newspaper as 'private', an unidentified man had shown up and Ferris hadn't had the courage to ask, 'And who might *you* be, sir?' They'd shaken hands and looked into each other's eyes, but no words were exchanged. The stranger must have been about his own age, or perhaps a little younger. He'd made his way from the cemetery before Ferris had an opportunity to ask anyone else who he might be.

All the time since then he'd wondered. Conceivably he might have been a relation but he looked like none of those who had gathered for the service. Possibly he might have had to do with the munitions works where he'd encouraged Doris to put in some of her time after he'd offered his own services and Southampton had accepted him: possibly *there* lay an explanation—or possibly not. He always kept a weather eye open for the man in Sandmouth but he'd never spotted him.

He wasn't able to forget. He wished the matter of the man's identity could have been as tidily disposed of as Doris's things were by the woman who came calling from the church. Instead it rankled; it was now a perplexity to him. It stopped him becoming attuned to his condition of widower, and somehow it prevented Doris from becoming elevated in his thoughts as a deceased wife surely deserves. (He often puzzled: how many mysteries are there on the periphery of our life which we don't even perceive?) She wasn't cast in a quiet golden light, not yet at any rate. He couldn't think of her—just as he couldn't think of the War—without imagining her in his absence, when he'd been in Southampton and not at home to collect the images that must sustain him after her death. In Southampton he'd felt he was doing all that a trained book-keeper with a perforated lung could do to help a war to be won, and he'd hoped the same impulse was firing Doris to give of her best too. He was a patriot, he always had been and always would be: Doris hadn't objected when he'd told her about Southampton, she'd sounded almost relieved as if now his frustrations must be at an end—with his office work and his Home Guard duties he wrote about in his letters to her, he would be making as full a contribution to the War effort as he was capable of. She smiled as sweetly as ever when he was at home, and when he was back in Southampton she wrote replies to his letters that were brief but seemed to say sweet things. He heard someone in the office speaking about another man who offered his women friends whispered sweet nothings in their ear, and it struck him as a strange and prophetic harnessing of words. It further occurred to him in gloomier moments of introspection in Southampton that maybe the War wasn't everything in the world, that he'd been happy to make a loop of thoughts for himself—but now an unspecified danger threatened to break the circuit.

What it was he never did find out exactly, because to all appearances things stayed just as they had been before. When the War finished he hummed and hawed about another book-keeping job and only went into Crockers' fusty accounting-department at the top of the store because he was assured by the now-departed Mr Wilfred Crocker that it would take a man like himself to get the figures into any kind of order. It was flannel, but sounded agreeable, and made their move to out-on-a-limb Sandmouth seem a less wayward step to have taken.

The door of 'The Gyft Shoppe' opened. Mr Ferris had a glimpse of a responsible-looking couple with two children before he turned and looked away. He preferred that he should seem to be interrupting his business to confer attention on customers. You had to be careful, though: once last autumn a couple of the breed the newspapers were calling the 'teddy boys' had saun-tered in and he hadn't lost a second in putting on a stiff military bearing. They hadn't come back.

Mr Ferris took a cloth out of a drawer and dusted the glass top of the serving counter. Underneath was a display of varnished shells. The pink sea urchins were proving the most popular, even though they smelt a bit inside. There was a family of spiky purplish conch shells. A blue starfish was glassed inside the dome of a paperweight: he lifted the lid of the counter and pulled out the price label, four and threepence. Some ordinary seashore shells had been resined and threaded together to make bonny strings of beads. There were phials of coloured sand—strictly worthless—but decorative; most cus-tomers only thought of the souvenir value when folk purch-ased something from him, he liked to think he was selling them memories. (The pink and puce layers of sand came from coves thirty miles along the coast, but Mr Ferris didn't see that it was necessary to confuse people needlessly.) In years to come they would remember their younger selves—the men with heads of hair, the women keen to show themselves in their summer frocks, the children manageable and eager—and the souvenir would have ceased to be a *thing* but a kind of key instead, a sesame to other summers. Whenever Mr Ferris felt especially prone to self-doubt or he imagined the past was mischievously making tracks round him, he reminded himself that his vocation in life now was the happiness business.

A few words reached across to him from the family as they inspected the items on the shelves. Foreigners. He couldn't make the language out at first. He wondered if it could be Dutch, or Danish. Then he had a horrible suspicion what it must be.

'Sieh da, Johannes, ein Leuchtturm!'

Mr Ferris lifted his eyes. They were all blonde-haired, and had squarish, rather flat, not unattractive faces. The children had bright blue eyes and white teeth.

Mr Ferris tugged at his shirt collar. It had never happened before, not like this.

'Rumfasser. "Alles Gute aus Sandmouth".'

He didn't recognise the name at first, the sound of it had become so mutilated.

The father was looking at him. Mr Ferris coughed into the back of his hand and pretended to be studying one of the framed watercolours on the opposite wall. The man's blue eyes turned in the same direction. He tapped his wife's arm.

'Sieh mal, Hanna, meinst Du nicht auch das ist toll?'

'Ja, hervorragend. Die Farben sind auffallend.'

'My wife, sir,' the man said, 'is a painter.'

Mr Ferris delayed a few moments. Then he smiled, miserably. He'd only ever sold a couple of the paintings, to natives of the town, and neither of them the soundest sort. He didn't understand these modern pictures at all: he liked places to look as they really were, not streaky and twisted and out of perspective. He had bought them because the art student who'd come into the shop with them had seemed to have even fewer clues about prices for that sort of thing than he did.

'Brechung,' the wife said, looking intently through a pair of spectacles, 'auf beiden Seiten.'

'Refraction, my wife is saying. At both sides.'

Mr Ferris coughed again. He'd never heard such rot.

'May I congratulate you on your excellent taste, sir, in stocking these paintings in your shop.'

They were so bloody polite with it.

97

'I believe this is called "naive art",' the man said. 'Am I correct?'

Mr Ferris wished that he couldn't hear, that he wasn't in the same room as them. Now the children were being told to look too, at this artistic miracle.

'May I ask the price of this painting, sir?' the man asked.

He'd chalked it on the back. He couldn't remember how much. He thought quickly.

'Twenty-five quid,' he said, inventing wildly. 'Pounds—'

The man nodded his head.

'We would like to buy this painting, sir.'

Mr Ferris took his time walking out from behind the counter and crossing the shop. He smiled sourly and didn't look at any of them. Gingerly he lifted the picture off its hook and was careful that no one was able to see the back of it.

When he had it in the back room he peered at the board the canvas had been mounted on and tried to decipher some figures. It looked like three guineas. He smiled to himself, awed by his own daring.

When the painting was wrapped up in brown paper he felt he had cause to be more polite than he would otherwise have allowed himself to be. Certainly he had tied the string very tightly, so that the man had difficulty pushing his fingers through, but nothing seemed to ruffle this family—any more than losing a war could have done. He wondered what hideous knowledge of depraved doings they carried about in their consciences, seen or partaken in by them. They looked well-fed, which he couldn't understand, and their expressions seemed unburdened. They were enjoying their—the modern word—'leisure'. A place-name or two from him could have changed all that. But he felt it in himself to be charitably disposed this morning, to spare them the lash of time just past. That would never become just 'history', it was an interlude of human—inhuman—experience too terrible to fade.

At least he had that assurance as they offered him their pleasant, smiling 'guten tag's and 'auf wiedersehen's, which he let glance off him. He felt surer again of the past, and stood proudly and resolutely in present time because of it. Even the memory of Doris was an easier one as he watched the four of them depart into the blustery blue English day with the twenty-five pounds safely deposited in the till and without a single word of courtesy or good-bye passing his lips as they turned and gave him their stupefied grins of farewell.

★

'Mr Symington-Berry?'

'I'm sorry?'

'We haven't met. We're Anthony's parents.'

The Headmaster narrowed his eyes at the middle-distance.

'Anthony Beddoes,' the father said.

'Ah, yes.'

The eyes detached themselves. Handshakes all round.

The man's wife stared quite forthrightly at the Headmaster, with far more attention than he was used to eliciting from pupils or staff.

'We *have* met before, Mr Symington-Berry, have we not?'

'Have we?' he replied vacantly.

'Yes, I'm sure—'

'Not here?'

Often parents were disconcerted by the Headmaster's habit of staring at a point behind one or other of their shoulders— but not Mrs Beddoes, who managed to persist.

'Not here,' she said, 'no.'

'I don't—'

'You did live in Guildford at one time?'

'Guildford?'

'I'm sure you must have.'

'Briefly. In that—general area. Very briefly.'

'I met a Mr Berry at a land agent's.'

'Really?'

'You didn't try to sell me a house? You're not *that* Mr Berry?'

'No, I—don't think so.'

The Headmaster smiled an electric smile.

'Are you *quite* sure?' the woman repeated.

The smile on the Headmaster's face was broad enough to power a generator.

'You're confusing your Mr Berrys, Diana,' the husband said, also smiling.

'I don't *think* so. Remember that house out at Garston End?'

'Oh, *I* remember,' the husband said. 'The Victorian one?'

99

'No, it had beams. And a red roof.'

The Headmaster might have been trying to hypnotise the entire 'A' and 'B' rugger teams ranged for a line-out a hundred and fifty yards away, on the playing-field directly behind the couple's heads.

'Perhaps we met a relation?' the husband was suggesting vaguely.

'I—I have a cousin in those parts,' the Headmaster heard himself replying. 'I have the full name of *my* side of the family.'

'Yes, quite,' the husband said, nodding in agreement.

His wife wasn't convinced.

'He spoke like you. He tried very hard to sell us the house.'

'Not my way at all,' the Headmaster said. He laughed, concentrating on the middle post of an 'H'.

'Of course not,' the husband assured him.

'He said there were two other couples interested *and* a member of an aristocratic family.'

'Sounds like an—' The Headmaster wavered momentarily. '—an enterprising fellow.'

'I don't know who the two other couples and the aristocrat were. The house was on the market after that for a full year and a half. Our surveyor'—the woman hitched up her fur collar— 'our surveyor told us it was riddled with damp. Riddled with it. He said the house should have been at least six hundred less.'

'Well, well! What a business!' the Headmaster exclaimed with another throaty laugh, inching himself leftwards of the couple. 'Good try from Huntley there, did you see?'

The husband turned round. The Headmaster was fully aware that Mrs Beddoes was studying his profile.

'Is Andrew keen on rugger?' he asked genially.

'Anthony,' his mother cut in.

The Headmaster chose not to say anything; he must appear distracted, eccentric, above the petty details.

'At their Public Schools,' he said, 'we hope they will get the proper encouragement. That they do here.'

'Yes, yes,' the husband nodded in agreement.

'In the end, of course,' his wife announced grandly, in cut-glass syllables, 'they closed the agency down.'

It took all the powers of concentration and deceit the

Headmaster was capable of to carry his performance for the next fifteen or twenty seconds.

He narrowed his eyes even more, straining to see into the far distance.

'Almost a touch-down there!' he cried.

The husband nodded, and sympathised.

Damn Pinky Taylor's eyes, making a mess of things and getting the news of it plastered everywhere. When had it happened? He hadn't heard about it going bust. No surprise, of course. Pinky Taylor couldn't have run a tombola stand. Never mind selling sham-Tudor houses in Garston End that you could smell rotting the moment you stepped in the front door. Like those rookery nook houses in theatre farces: the whole enterprise was a damned botch, a fiasco. Lavinia had been right all along.

'Nice try this time!' the husband called out above the shouts from across the field.

A few seconds too late the Headmaster waxed enthusiastic too. Even the man's wife had turned to look at the event.

'Don't worry,' he assured them, trying to sound jocular and keen, 'even if you think Andrew isn't, we'll turn him into a rugger-player. A-team man—'

'Actually,' the woman said with a little sniff which the cold might have caused, 'Andrew's Anthony.'

Be aloof, distracted, eccentric, the former Petty Officer Berry instructed himself: it's a headmaster's privilege, you're above it all. In the next few seconds he was hoping to God that Pinky Taylor wouldn't get the news of Lavinia's windfall and take it into his thick head to show up on *their* doorstep. He would get no further than that, the 'private wing' on the other side of his study was exactly that: 'PRIVATE', underlined, positively no admission without prior invitation.

★

'The Old Rectory' sits in open fields behind the town. In the early nineteenth century Sandmouth's parish church used to stand quite close by, on the highest point of ground in the district, until a freak storm in the 1830s caught it a sideways blow and sent half the tower toppling through the roof of the nave into the aisle. In the next decade a new church was completed lower down the hill, in its lea, and the old one was abandoned to weather and grass. Incumbents found the distance between the Georgian parsonage and the new church inconvenient and vexing, and in the 1850s a grey-brick residence was constructed only a hundred yards away from the church. The new house was called 'The Vicarage' and the old gracious 'Rectory' was allowed to retain its name. The church estates sold off the 'Rectory' earlier than they had intended, to meet the final costs on its replacement, and the building passed into the ownership of various Sandmouth notables.

The most recent of these is Norman George Pargiter. He isn't strictly a Sandmouth man. His mother belongs to the area although she married and raised her son in the northern suburbs of London. Her talk about Sandmouth and the coastline inspired her son with an interest for a place which he'd never seen: he spoke about it with markedly more affection than *she* ever did, and his peers at school used to imagine there must be a softer side to 'Knuckles' Pargiter's nature after all. Muddling at various jobs after he was demobbed and after his father died, he discovered that his mother had a cousin with a not insubstantial construction company to his name, which was based in a town between Sandmouth and Bournemouth.

Why not give it a try? He'd soon had a bellyful of civvy street, and the brawling for every job going. The law gave you your old job back if you'd had one before call-up; if not, it was *your* bad luck, another smile and a grab at your balls. No one gave the steam off a monkey's turd about the War any more, everything went back to being how it had always been. Before he made his discovery, he'd seriously been thinking about jacking it in and joining up again.

Instead he borrowed a car, got hold of some petrol coupons, and drove down to introduce himself. He humoured the bland, rosy-cheeked bachelor (a fairy? probably not; maybe it was schoolgirls he gave the eye to?) and he seemed to impress him with his invented stories of experience in the building industry. He stressed the family connection and behaved in such a thoroughly gentlemanly and enthusiastic manner that Mr Arkwright was impelled to ask the lad if he thought he could bring some of his smart ways down to this neck of the woods? Of course, when he stood tall on the rug in front of the desk to reply, he lied through his teeth: for all he was worth.

When he started in the job—the work itself wasn't the problem, and the money was enough—Pargiter found he didn't have the loose rein he'd bargained for. After less than a year he chanced to be introduced to one of his adopted 'Uncle' 's competitors. Archibald Copplestone had a fly, worldly, wholly pragmatic view of the trade and its intrigues. He invited the young Pargiter to his mock-Tudor home and the guest took immediately to the tumbling wistaria and the beamed rooms and the Bentley convertible in which they made the journey there and back.

About that time a plot of prime building land happened to be put up for sale on the (supposedly) 'open' market. Pargiter's 'Uncle' Arkwright was very 'near' (an Arkwright word) with the auctioneers and confided in his 'nephew' that he had arranged a division of future profits in return for a reduced buying-price. Since that—considered in the abstract—seemed somewhat underhand in itself, Pargiter had no compunction in reporting the state of affairs to Copplestone. His uncle's rival outbid at the public sale and raised an objection when the auctioneer on the podium appeared to falter. The particular auctioneer officiating that day wasn't fully au fait with the understanding previously arrived at and Copplestone's offer was accepted as the concluding business of the morning.

Pargiter's uncle discovered how the accident had happened, but on the very morning he had resolved to dismiss him from his employ he received a letter from the man himself, containing the information that he had been offered a senior post at Copplestone's. In fact the position was less secure than that, but in little more than eighteen months Pargiter had made himself indispensable to the company and so invincible: the official recognition of senior status followed after that as a matter of course.

Pargiter soon acquired the reputation for himself of being as sharp as a knife; some knowing souls claimed he was no better than a crook. He became engaged to Copplestone's daughter, but two months before the wedding was due to take place Margaret was thrown from a horse and dragged along cobbles with her feet still hanging from the stirrups. During the weeks she lay in a coma, Pargiter debated whether or not he was obliged to marry a crippled bride. Eventually she took a turn for the worse and died and he was spared any more heart-searching—a less than pleasurable new activity, he decided.

The father and mother went off to Madeira to nurse their grief, and while they were there Copplestone had a coronary and slumped forward, dead, on to a pontoon table in Reid's Hotel. Pargiter arranged his second funeral in six weeks. In the interval of days after the burial, an undignified scramble took place among the directors to secure acting control of company affairs. Pargiter enlisted the help of Mrs Copplestone, now the major shareholder. He persuaded her to call a public meeting, at which he appeared to make perfectly respectable and above-board what he had already convinced Mrs Copplestone was the only sound and sensible course for the company: *he* should be allowed to serve as the company's managing director, with all its onerous responsibilities. Two of the directors promptly resigned, but that was no more than expected: by the little he said then and afterwards Pargiter implied their action was unspeakable betrayal. Mrs Copplestone made her gratitude very evident, and for a time Pargiter thought she had designs on *him*, his body and soul. The wistaria-clad house in its ten acres was very desirable, but he didn't believe it was worth acquiring at *any* cost. In the event he managed to convince the sad, unsurely balanced widow that 'Mallards' held too many memories for her and that she would be happier elsewhere: perhaps in a new house which the company could have designed and then build for her? He persuaded her that 'Mallards' should not be vulgarised by public sale, and instead he contrived an 'arrangement' with the same firm of auctioneers his 'Uncle' Arkwright had dealt with on the sale of land whereby his own bid for the house—on various bank promises of funding—came out on top.

Still only in his mid-thirties, Pargiter was now Sandmouth's premier success story. He regularly frequented the Clarence Hotel with clients and 'acquaintances', those he didn't particularly want to be seen doing business with in the much grander hotels of Bournemouth. He gave generous gifts of cash to the church, he subsidised the building of the new memorial to the fallen and paid for the landscaping of the 'Norman George Pargiter War Memorial Gardens', public lavatories were provided as a company (rather than personal) bequest to the community, and he had his eyes beadily trained on the possibilities which the shabby Alhambra Theatre might afford him to improve his stock even further.

To confirm his familial bond with Sandmouth, Pargiter bought 'The Old Rectory', ostensibly to house his mother. In effect it was as a home for himself: 'Mallards' had begun to oppress him with its *Rebecca*-ish atmosphere—or perhaps, he wondered vaguely, guilt is claiming me? The wistaria-dripping mansion remained in his ownership, but he seldom visited it now. He much preferred the humbler, whitewashed Georgian 'Rectory', surrounded not by lowering copses but by—in summer—bright waving cornfields. With the sash windows open you could catch a whiff of the sea. The rooms were low and the windows and doors broad. No ghosts lurked in the house.

An unplanned advantage was that his mother—unlike her son—considered the house 'far too good' for her, and was happy in her own perverse, grumbling way acting as his housekeeper, preparing his meals for him, seeing that the maid kept the place dustless, letting him know whenever anything needed a lick of paint or even a new screw or bolt put in—then he would summon one of the workmen and get the repairs done on company time and money. Through his contacts in other businesses he'd had the driveway re-designed and laid with white gravel chips and the lawns taken up and drained and re-turfed. The beds were stocked with different displays for every season. There was a garage for two cars and a rotating white summer-house and a dovecot with a pair of imported white doves (natives of Madeira, as fate would have it).

'The Old Rectory' was the most enviable property in Sandmouth. As a house for modern times it easily outdid 'Hallam House': that was a grander edifice but its garden of rhododendrons and hornbeam and hemlock trees was overgrown and the lofty public rooms were said to smell of must and damp. The 'Rectory' was in tip-top form and (Pargiter liked to make a polite little joke about it) kept in the condition which had always been intended for it.

Opinions on Pargiter himself were more qualified. Certainly he *looked* the part of the successful self-made man—in his cravat and his waisted chrome-buttoned blazer from Simpson's he might even have passed as a dashing specimen of the

Hurlingham set—but the rumours concerning his methods of business had reached even the most ordinary households, although most people were ignorant of what the terms meant. They could simultaneously feel respect for his wealth and also disapproval of it: he showed there were opportunities to be taken advantage of in this day and age, yet (the higher orders decided) trade was trade, it always had been and always would be. Wisely Pargiter didn't overstep himself in the social stakes locally, and so he didn't antagonise the old guard. He was seen to actively do good in the town, although the sceptical recognised the useful outlet for self-promotion it allowed. Perhaps the very best that could be said of Norman George Pargiter was that he caused no extremes of opinion about himself. No one voiced a wish that he should live elsewhere because the town would be better off without him. People saw him as a potential benefit in respect of his money rather than for the quality of his personal character, concerning which there was a good deal of mystery and guess-work. He would continue to be tolerated so long as he didn't offend 'sensibilities' and either imagine he could lord it over Sandmouth or engage in what were too blatantly questionable business practices.

That was the status quo established between Sandmouth and young Mr Pargiter of Copplestone's on the dawning of this particular April morning. Both appeared easy with it. Pargiter didn't seem inclined to take undue advantage of the town, as his outside detractors warned that he was bound to do some day: for the nonce Sandmouth was disposed in his case to a mildly charitable view rather than the censorious.

There might have seemed no just reason why things should not continue just so, to the mutual contentment and benefit of both parties.

★

The party leave the main house of Minster Court. Major Fitt is first to descend the steps, assisted by two house prefects. Mrs Symington-Berry follows, wearing white gloves and an ostrich-feather hat. Her husband follows a step or two behind her. 'Nimrod' is banged out on a piano. Mrs Symington-Berry's mouth contracts as she mutters something about Winifred Atwell.

At a master's prompting, a decorous cheer goes up from the boys assembled on the lawn. The Major smiles and waves in their direction. Mrs Symington-Berry bows towards the parents and the white feathers flutter on her hat. Her husband extracts his fob watch and appears to be making a calculation.

The party walk towards the marquee, between the two herds, one of parents, the other of boys. The cheer of schoolboy voices is not repeated, the pianist inexplicably stops, and the silence is felt by some to be rather embarrassing. The Major smiles bravely as he has in every adversity and limps along, holding on to the shoulders of his two fair-haired, prepubescent crutches. Mrs Symington-Berry continues to bow towards the parents and some are reminded of Princess Marina. Her husband follows in his best Chester Barrie city suit; he looks at the grass and rolls his tongue around inside his cheeks.

The party have to pass between two files of prefects and monitors, half a dozen on each side. The boys take a few steps backwards to allow the Major's crutches to pass through them. Fitt has a word for each of the lads. Most of them are struck with wonder and become tongue-tied, but the last boy happens to catch the eye of one of the crutches who is ready to groan under the weight and starts to laugh. He remembers the nickname the school has given him, 'Tinleg', which sets him off again. The Major's port-wine face is at a loss to understand. He is famous for having joked with his men in time of grave crisis, but the joke eludes him on this occasion. Behind him, Mrs Symington-Berry's smile freezes. The Headmaster stares into the back of his wife's neck.

Mrs Symington-Berry coughs loudly. The boy doesn't heed it as a warning, but finds the embarrassment he's caused helplessly funny. Mrs Symington-Berry reaches forward her gloved hand and taps one of the crutches, Simon Jope, on the shoulder-blade. He moves off before the Major is quite ready, and the famous man clutches at the other boy as he loses his balance and falls forward. The boy has sturdy legs and is able to withstand the sudden shock of the weight dropping on top of him. The boy holds on to his arm and recognises from his experience on visits home the sour afterbreath of spirits; the cracked veins on the man's cheeks are another indicator, and his moist eyes.

Major Fitt struggles again for his balance. Mrs Symington-Berry, keen to assist, is only making the situation worse: none of the boys dares to come closer and the Major is unable to get a steady grip. The party totters the last few yards towards the marquee while Mrs Symington-Berry spouts anxious, breathless pleasantries about how special this day is proving for them all.

In the general confusion no one notices the guy-ropes secured by pegs to the turf. When the boy who's acting as the crutch falls against one, it grazes him on the knee but he keeps upright. The day's guest-of-honour is less lucky and, when his false foot catches the rope, he goes tumbling headlong.

Mrs Symington-Berry is following too closely behind him to be able to save herself and she is also felled: she drops with her full weight and dignity on top of the Major.

To the more worldly boys who are powerless to do anything but watch, there's something indecent about the way the Headmaster's wife is straddling the old man. After a few stunned seconds, hands start to grapple with the struggling limbs. The prefects notice that Mrs Symington-Berry's coat and dress have ridden up and her underskirt is showing and they are afraid to approach her from behind. Her husband does the manly thing and tries to pull down her frock and coat but tugs so hard against the top layers of summer material that he rips the stitching.

Mrs Symington-Berry hauls herself off the Major with a grimace of disgust. Her white gloves and the front of her powder-blue coat are streaked with grass stains. Her face looks terribly bloodless, not brick-red as the boys are used to seeing it when there's a temper 'on her'. She crouches on her knees over the Major and as her husband searches for the damage of split seams, she covers her mouth with her gloved hand and tells him she thinks she's going to be sick.

The reason becomes clear as she is helped to her feet. The Major is writhing. With disbelief the boys—and the parents who have surrounded them—see that one of his legs appears to be about a foot longer than the other.

'Jesus Christ!' a boy says. 'His leg's fallen off!'

Visible between the turn-up of his right trouser-leg and his black right shoe and beige sock patterned with brown lozenges is a length of silvery tubing and a leather strap.

Everyone stands horrified. Major Fitt, so famous for his ability to 'crack jokes' in adversity, only moans; he twitches like a landed fish.

Mrs Symington-Berry sprints off, her face yellow, her hand gagging her mouth. Her husband doesn't know what he should do or where he's required to be, and he runs off after her.

For several seconds people just want to look at what they would normally never have a chance to see: the limb inside the flapping trouser-leg. The Major squirms on the grass and another few inches of metal slip into public view.

'We've got to *do* something,' a father says.

'It's humiliating him,' a mother adds.

'Poor old soul,' another mother opines.

The most capable debate what should be done. If they attempt to carry him, the leg will only come further adrift. One father suggests they should prise the limb out of the trouser-leg, but a mother wisely says that nobody knows what might be holding it up.

'Not very much by the look of it,' one of the men cuts in with.

At that point, when no one is able to decide what's the best thing to be done, the Major comes into his own and shows his mettle. Flat on his stomach on the turf, he starts to deliver his famous chuckle that has already made him a television favourite. A smile wreathes his port-wine face.

'I was going to tell you boys,' he says, 'that you should—you should learn—to stand on your own two feet!'

A few boys laugh nervously, the ones who are always the first to respond when Mr and Mrs Symington-Berry intend they should laugh.

'Now,' the Major adds and chuckles again, 'I haven't a leg to stand on!'

This is the spirit that has endeared him to the British public: domineering and enduring, laughing out of grim adversity. Up and down the country he opens fêtes, judges WI flower shows, picks the most beautiful baby, presents school prizes. Today vicissitude has laid him low again but he confronts it with a smile and a retort.

The only recourse, he says, is for him to fix the leg himself. He instructs how he should be turned over on to his side. 'The lads can do it,' he says, and he smiles again at their eagerness as heads of neatly combed fair hair bow over him. Then, while the boys and the more intrepid or foolhardy of the parents watch, he unbuttons his trousers and wrenches them down over his underpants. He's also wearing an elaborate-looking corset contraption. It's too much for the mothers, who turn away. He asks one of the boys—then two of them when the first boy blanches—to pull his dummy foot. They pull, and the Major nimbly contorts himself so that he can extract his white hairless surviving leg out of the trousers. The trousers fall away to reveal (thankfully) not the stump of the leg mislaid in Flanders but a complicated superstructure of straps and hinges.

It's now too much for some of the boys, who wander off to sit down on the grass and hang their heads between their bare knees.

The leg is re-hitched in a minute and a half. Instructions are shouted services-fashion and the trousers are hoisted over the shoes by the bravest, least-squeamish masters, two to each leg, then pulled all the way up to the crotch. There's some additional manoeuvring with the top—or bottom—of the right leg, then the fork of the trousers is eased over the Major's private parts. The boys and those still spectating can't help noticing that the trousers meet with some resistance at that juncture. No one wants to, but the Major exhorts the team to pull hard.

'Harder!'

Everything falls safely back into place. As the Major struggles to pick himself back up, one of the masters has to remind him that his flies require doing up: Fitt beams, and although he would perhaps prefer to have the buttoning-up done for him, he nods his head agreeably and does the deed himself.

The event has been a trial for everyone concerned and the day's activities have yet to begin properly. The Major seems drained as he is helped to his feet. Boys, mothers and fathers meet each other's eyes unsurely, looking white about the gills.

Meanwhile, in the private wing Mr Symington-Berry is consoling his wife, who is holding her head over the lavatory bowl. She is still wearing her hat of ostrich feathers and her green-stained gloves and her unwieldy white handbag.

In the marquee the flies buzz around the food, unaware of the traumas on the other side of the canvas. They scramble

110

across the slices of veal-and-ham pie and the slivers of roast beef, and it's a moonscape of limitless delight to them.

On the top lawn of Minster Court the flag of Saint George flutters lazily from a flagpole. Boys and parents stand awkwardly in the spring sunlight, on this sod of England's green and pleasant turf. The Major gradually recovers his breath, supported by his two stalwart crutches; apparently he has forgiven the misadventure with the guy-ropes and is seen cracking jokes. The music master takes a liberty with the running-order of events and sits down at the piano in the marquee and knocks out something cheerful: 'You forget the little ploughboy, who whistles o'er the lea'.

The doors open in the private wing and the Symington-Berrys reappear. Mrs Symington-Berry is wearing emerald gloves, a puce coat, and a blue hat. She stops when she realises she's forgotten her handbag and her husband hastens inside to retrieve it. When it's been found—the white handbag she began with hastily sponged down—the couple make their way out at a stately pace on to the grass. Mrs Symington-Berry smiles and inclines her head, as if nothing untoward has happened. Her husband removes his fob watch and consults it. To the accompaniment of 'Jerusalem' rendered on the piano, Mrs Symington-Berry motions that everyone should make their way into the marquee where—she has decided for herself—the speech will not take place, but where lunch *will* commence. Inadvertently or not she marches past the spot where Major Fitt is resting on a chair. Her husband touches her arm but she fails to notice.

The festivities of this day of Saint George, those which haven't been scuppered, are about to be joined.

★

The sound of cheering wafted over rooftops and over high beech hedges into the garden of 'Linden Lodge'.

This will make a memory for her too, Mrs Mason thought, watching her daughter chasing something—an insect?—across the lawn.

'What is it, darling, a dragonfly?'

Sometimes Mrs Mason felt that Susan invented those butterflies and ladybirds she cupped her hands around and told her

111

mother she'd caught. When she came after her to see what it was, the palms opened and Susan laughed because 'it' had got away.

Harmless inventions, Mrs Mason thought, thankful for them: grateful that the 'distortions' of the outside world didn't reach them here, in the old-fashioned, scented garden of roses and lilies and cedars and linden trees behind the high hedges.

This was all she'd ever wished for her daughter: that she shouldn't know the terrible restrictions which history had imposed on her mother's growing-up. When she'd thought she had survived them—the War starting as she'd always dreaded it must, her father being killed at sea—their house in Kensington was caught in one of the last raids on London and almost half of it was seared clean away. Two walls fell out, the staircase collapsed into the shell of the house, the roof cracked and showered down timbers and tiles through the rooms. To save herself she'd had to roll across the tilting floor of her bedroom and jump from her window. Luckily for her she'd landed on the saving earth of a flower-bed. Her mother wasn't so fortunate: certainly she'd been on the floor beneath and had less far to fall, but when she jumped she'd gone crashing through the conservatory roof.

Her mother had never recovered, bodily or in spirits. She took Susan to see her grandmother as seldom as possible. One of the reasons she had married was to find a means of escaping from London and the oppressive memory of the past. She went back very rarely, and solely to visit her mother. It was the only—and unavoidable—part of her past she gave her child access to. Her husband's history was happier, and she let Susan hear as much about that as she asked to hear.

Her dearest wish was that the past shouldn't *have* to matter to them now: they were as free of it here as it was possible to be, behind their high beech hedges, in this seven-eighths of an acre where the seasons were carefully cultivated to always have something to offer the eye and pleasant memories to make in Susan's mind.

When she grew up and she was her mother's age, there would be no blurring shadows in her images of the past: they wouldn't be cramped and crowded and threatening like hers, inside the house as well as outside all would be dazzle and space—and perfect happiness inhabiting rooms awash with white light.

★

The hairdresser's was called a 'Salon' and had netted curtains at the two windows. Mr Gutteridge and his wife had often discussed the merits of the business being called not 'The Salon' but 'Piccadilly Stylings': however neither of them was sure that Sandmouth was quite ready yet to receive such a modern idea. So the business remained 'The Salon' in the meantime while Mr Gutteridge continued to persuade his clients (but not staff) that they should feel free to call him 'Paul'. It established a confidence, he tried to convince his wife: a man was in a unique position of trust in such circumstances. Mrs Gutteridge had her doubts, but she also realised that their surname lacked a certain—she wasn't sure what— 'romance' perhaps, not to say 'tone'. It was an additional complication that the name her husband had been christened with wasn't 'Paul' but 'Kenneth': 'Kenneth Clifford Gutter- idge'. How confusing for their daughter that she heard her father addressed as 'Paul' when she was in the salon and 'Ken' when she was at home and 'Clifford' when they visited her grandmother in Gosport.

'Why "Paul", Ken?' she'd asked her husband.

'Why not?' he'd replied.

'Well, Clifford's all right.'

'It's all right, yes. But I think I want it to be better than all right. Don't you?'

'I just wondered where you'd got it from.'

'It sounds—well, a bit Italian.'

'No, the "Piccadilly" bit.'

'Well, when I was in London—'

'That was Regent Street.'

'Near enough. That *is* Piccadilly.'

This was a damned stupid conversation, Gutteridge realised: and so did his wife.

'Well, why not?' he'd concluded it.

'Why not?'

'Anything that makes people think of London—'

He saw how some of his clients read everything in the

113

magazines as if it was gospel truth. They coyly showed him photographs of Kay Walsh or Glynis Johns and asked him, how did their hairdressers achieve that effect? He kept his replies abstract and technical.

'That's the professional approach,' Gutteridge told his wife.

Also professional was diluting the hair lotions in the back room, a trick he'd learned in Regent Street and which he personally attended to: professional was always putting a client next to the windows, so anyone passing would think you were crowded out even if it was a quiet morning: professional was educating the girl on the desk to allow the telephone to ring for at least ten seconds—seven, eight, nine, ten—before picking it up to take the booking.

They were doing well on the strength of it, and on his wife's thriving side-line driving out to some of the houses and farmhouses further off and doing washes, sets and perms on the spot. (Stout, middle-aged, farmers' wives had no interest in Piccadilly or Kay Walsh or marcel waves, but they paid with notes uncurled from wads they stored in teapots or inside clock cases. Even the headmistress at the Convent had a healthily feminine interest in her appearance, and was colour-rinsed in her private sitting-room, beneath a crucifix hung with a sagging, nearly naked Christ.)

The Gutteridges' daughter was being educated— expensively, and in élite company—at the Convent, and Christina's mother tried to keep her weekly appearances at the private wing as discreet as possible. Some of the girls' mothers came to 'The Salon' if they weren't in the habit of frequenting establishments in larger towns, and Mr Gutteridge turned a conveniently blind eye to the coincidence. (At school functions he smiled distantly, as if a face prompted only the vaguest recognition.)

The Gutteridge parents were C of E, if they were anything, but they superstitiously imagined that the sisters on the teaching staff of Our Lady of the Sacred Heart would give a kind of divine sanction to the social ambitions they had for their daughter. They could afford—just—to educate her above their own original station in life, and they considered it the best use of their money: Christina was receiving a better education than she would otherwise have had, and she was among girls who had a stability in their lives—moral and financial—which many of Christina's generation didn't. The salon's likely elevation to 'Piccadilly Stylings' was intended to ease Christina's own progress to greater things socially. Perhaps in another couple of years' time, if the plans went smoothly, there might also be a second salon: the Gutteridges had their sights on an ailing concern in one of Bournemouth's quieter districts almost wholly populated by retired and/or non-Gentile types, and with a surfeit of widows and spinsters careful of their appearance. The current owner had no business sense, and was losing out to the salons in town and the hairdressing departments in the stores; the Gutteridges had different ideas.

Christina still liked to come about the salon. She didn't offer to sweep up with the broom any more but sat and read the magazines and sucked a twist of barley sugar. Her father noticed that she would ask one of the girls on the staff to pour her a glass of ginger beer rather than do it herself; but how could he tell her that it was 'wrong' behaviour which the nuns wouldn't approve of, when he couldn't have found the words and wasn't even quite sure himself that it *was* wrong? She'd begun to leave the burrs out of her speech—except when she was flustered or threatening to go into one of her moods—and her parents didn't comment on the development, even to each other. Mrs Gutteridge made an extra special effort sartorially to match the smartest of the other mothers whenever she went to a parents' evening at the Convent, and she saw Christina approving: her daughter didn't blush and look at the floor as some of the other girls did, confronted by the ridiculousness of their mothers. She was obviously much less at ease with her father in those circumstances, however. Once when he'd been talking to Sister Patricia about English history, Christina had nudged her elbow in his ribs and cut him off in mid-flow: Sister Patricia had looked rather shocked, but the next moment she was talking about something completely different in her top-drawer, Home Counties lockjaw, sounding not at all like a nun but more like a duchess at a garden party. Sister Patricia had placed her hand possessively on Christina's shoulder, and both her parents (they caught one another's eye for a split second) were secretly satisfied.

Susan had developed an odd habit of referring to an 'it'. Mrs Mason shook her head at her.

'What do you mean, darling? What's "it"? Where?'

'It's everywhere.'

'What is?'

'It.'

Mrs Mason tried to laugh, in an unconcerned way. Susan's persistence in the matter alarmed her.

'What is "it"?' she asked patiently. 'You never tell me.'

Susan shrugged.

'Is it good?'

'No.'

'It's *not* good?' Mrs Mason frowned.

'No,' Susan said.

'Well, then—' Mrs Mason smoothed her daughter's hair with her hand. 'Can you tell me what?'

'It's bad,' Susan said without hesitation.

Mrs Mason heard how forced her own laugh sounded.

'It *can't* be bad, darling!'

'But it *is*!'

Mrs Mason didn't like to correct her daughter for answering back but sometimes she felt a start would have to be made.

'I don't think you're right, darling.'

'It follows me.'

'*Follows* you?'

'Follows me about.'

Mrs Mason hesitated.

'About where?' she asked.

'Everywhere.'

'Is it an insect?'

'Oh *no*!' Susan suddenly whooped with laughter.

'What then?' Mrs Mason thought the laughter not quite normal. 'Tell me, I haven't seen it.'

'I don't know.'

Mrs Mason shook her head. She told Susan not to worry, Mummy and Daddy were here.

She watched her daughter run off across the garden, looking happy enough. She wondered if the silly notion had anything to do with that awful Moscombe girl, the cripple, sort of. She didn't quite like to ask Susan: it wasn't the sort of thing she wanted to talk about with her, in case it upset her.

She would ask Nanny Filbert to keep a sharp look-out in case there was any danger on that account. In the meantime it was important that Susan should be able to accept her mother as a confidante, someone to be trusted and to be told all her secrets. She had hoped her child would grow up without any secrets, that everything could be open and declared between them both. Perhaps they were just temporary shadows and Susan would outgrow them—then all would be how she'd always meant it should be, in their own private, sun-lit garden kingdom.

★

Behind the closed doors of the private wing Mrs Symington-Berry slipped out of her social manner as easily as she did the gloves which she was never seen without. After a glass of sherry she would become considerably less the benign Lady Bountiful the town was used to, bestowing her smiles and patronage on all and sundry.

'That was the worst morning of my life,' she informed her husband. 'Which, let me tell you, is saying something.'

'Yes, dear.'

'Never again.'

'I'm sorry, dear.'

'Yes, Philip, I think that's exactly what you *should* be. And now I just wish everyone would go.'

'They will.'

'It can't be soon enough.'

'I didn't think he—'

'He couldn't have given a speech anyway, no one would have listened.'

'He took it all right.'

'I couldn't care less *how* he took it. I wasn't having him making a speech and that was that.'

Mr Symington-Berry poured his wife a second drink, and for himself a third.

'What did those people—'

'Ye gods, I was landed with some dreadful woman who said she knew Great-Uncle Percival. Out in Borneo or wherever he was. It was quite ghastly.'

'That was a coincidence.'

117

'Then she tracked me down and went on and on about Aunt Gertrude in Hove.'

'How strange.'

'It's not what she meant, of course. She was getting at *me*.'

'Why should—'

'For not being what she expected.'

'You don't think—'

'I don't think *what*?'

The Headmaster stooped forward a little.

'Maybe—you're being a little sensitive on the matter?'

'I don't think it's being too sensitive not to like when people are trying to humiliate you. This is not what I was brought up to, might I remind you.'

For better or worse, the ship's chaplain had intoned at the splicing ceremony: rather more of the latter than the former would have been Mrs Symington-Berry's verdict after eight years.

Her husband paused to consider whether he should repeat the worse incident of *his* day—the mother who remembered him from Guildford days—and allow them to compare woes. No, he decided, better not—given her precarious state.

'I don't think you quite understand what I have to suffer, Philip.'

'Yes I do, dear. Everyone—everyone—'

'Yes?' his wife demanded impatiently. Her husband had discovered a loquacious seam in him since he had taken up headmastering for a living.

'Everyone has had to cut their cloth. To suit the times. These new times.'

'I think I've had to do enough cutting, thank you very much.'

Mr Symington-Berry winced.

'I think—' he began.

'Think *what*?'

'I think we've worked wonders really. In a very short time. In another sense—'

Mrs Symington-Berry tapped the arm of her chair with her empty glass.

'Yes?'

'In another sense today has been very successful. Boys and parents have both had an opportunity—'

Mrs Symington-Berry stopped listening. Even in Guildford Philip hadn't lost the sense of fun she'd originally found herself drawn to. To begin with, he'd had a touch of the hero about him too, or were all women after the War prepared to see the best in their beaux? There was always that dreadful panicky feeling in the air—a bygone from the First War—that there wouldn't be enough men to go around. In the event, the impression she'd had was that there was a glut of them. How many other women were unable to lose a dark nagging thought at the back of their minds that, getting married so hastily, they might have jumped the gun?

They'd been married in Portsmouth. There had still been bunting everywhere: the feeling of occasion hadn't yet faded from people's lives. In an obscure way she had believed she was making payment for having survived the War intact. She'd thought Philip nice-looking, he was considerate and he was only *just* the wrong side of thirty, like her: he cracked a lot of jokes, laughed in a hearty way which she'd found so infectious. Other women must have felt the same about him, but his eye had only wandered to them occasionally in those early days. A lot of things he hadn't understood and still didn't understand about domestic life: but he wasn't any different from many other men in that respect, and anyway she realised very well the limitations of the domestic routine herself. (She'd always envied her cousins, having cooks and maids and not knowing one end of a broom from the other.) People had assumed—and still did—that they were 'made for each other', Lavinia and Philip, that they naturally belonged together. They'd bought themselves a pedigree dalmatian on their first pay from Pinky, and—even before Great-Aunt Gertrude's bequest—people assumed a comfortable, definitely superior manner of life. Already in Guildford, where they'd moved to first, she'd felt they were beginning to live through, and for, other people's eyes.

There was another little matter that, every so often, wriggled like a tapeworm in Mrs Symington-Berry's brain. The incontrovertible fact that, in the euphoria of landing that whack of Great-Aunt Gertrude's money and then getting a school which no one else wanted at a knock-down price, she'd let Philip invent a degree for himself on the prospectus.

119

At least he hadn't chosen Oxford or Cambridge, but London: somehow a metropolitan degree made her think there must be some way of disguising yourself. She knew that when there was an opening for a new member of staff, he always sifted through the candidates' credentials to ensure that no embarrassment might arise. Sometimes parents asked questions, but only out of politeness, and polite questions (as she was thankfully aware) are the easiest to deflect.

They didn't discuss the degree between them. But it was there, she knew, in the thoughts of both of them about the life they led. He was quite right, the school was proving a success, for certain reasons which they'd very pragmatically engineered: the adopted double-barrelled surname inspired confidence, that and the degree, and the fire-breathing man who trained the boys at rugger and was obsessed about the shine on their boots, and the spiel in the expensive-looking brochure they'd had printed concerning the health-giving advantages of the coastal elevation, and the recent introduction of such subjects as biology and chemistry into the curriculum. They should have been pleased with their achievement, proud even. Other than the silly business of the degree, they'd committed no moral wrong. And yet—

And yet, she couldn't help feeling, there was something sham about the set-up. Why else did they require 'Private' writ so large on the doors of the wing of the building where they lived, if it wasn't to allow them to be 'themselves' rather than the persons they purported to be? She guessed that Philip was surer-minded than she often gave him credit for being: he responded to the tenor of their times in a way that was the match of hers. She'd come from the lesser side of an affluent family and believed she had a complex about it. Philip perceived that parents were keen, sometimes desperate, to secure for their male offspring a background and experience conjured out of what they envisaged being the old social virtues— double-barrelled names, alumni among the Governors, strawberry teas in the summer (through someone else, Philip had located a supplier who provided them wholesale), Gilbert and Sullivan once a term, cavorting dalmatians and pups on the lawn—augmented by a discreet infusion of the new and modish: biology rabbits in hutches, a peculiar Scotsman called

Mr McIlwham who'd lived with a tribe of Amazonian Indians and who wore shorts and taught his own idiosyncratic version of anthropology plus geography plus the rudiments of chemistry, the annual camping trip for the top class to a fell farm in Cumberland (which she'd recently told Philip, positively and finally and for the *very* last time, she wasn't going to be seen dead on).

She also believed that Philip believed they were a truly enlightened couple. He *is* the man I married, she habitually had to remind herself; as if that put paid to any suspicion she had that his gaze concentrated unduly on each term's new young matron during School Assembly, or that she somehow wasn't the person she'd been before they came to Sandmouth but a grumpier version, less at her ease socially: as if it discredited any of the vague fears and premonitions she had for the future of Minster Court Preparatory School and its Headmaster and his spouse.

★

From a window Mrs Mason watches Susan as she runs about the garden, in the shade of trees and walls.

A child had been her only ambition in life, after surviving the rigours of her own girlhood in war-blasted London. Marriage had been the means to that end. The sacrament and its consequent rites had mattered more than the man perhaps, but in common with the other young women she'd known of her own station in life, she'd become the wife of someone socially suitable: in her case, a barrister. Now Allan kept her and Susan in a manner to which she believed they were both entitled.

Mrs Mason liked her husband well enough, as much as she could have expected to. She was confident that she didn't 'love' him—she never had; and it was another of her beliefs that love must be something that trips you up as you're innocently going about your business, like an object lying in the road, and it sends you tumbling so that for a while you see stars and after that you remain merely pleasantly dazed. Her own feelings had been nothing like that, not at all. She wasn't the sort of person to fall over objects inopportunely dropped in the middle of roads.

What she did believe of herself was this: that in some

women—she being one—the maternal instinct counts for everything. It was strong enough to defy the conventions of a marriage if, say, a husband were to prove unwilling or unable to sire a child: it was an instinct so compulsive and dominant that even a common morality such as people were trained from birth to accept wouldn't stand in its way. Another man would be found to do what was required and beyond that simple and necessary fact of life there was nothing more to be explained or apologised for.

Fortunately Allan had been able and willing: Susan was his, in a sense. Not in the sense that he could understand her or feel for her as *she* could. Of course not. Anyway, his public person—his work—must always come between him and any essential relationship. Susan realised her father was the 'provider' and that was quite enough for a child to comprehend. Mrs Mason didn't care that he should return home at the end of a long day and that he and Susan should provide a distraction for one another, as they seemed inclined to do. She recognised the danger of that—that she and not the father would become the figure of authority, the disciplinarian, the scolder (she'd flicked through the child-psychology books in a shop in Bournemouth)—which was why she went out of her way to be as accommodating with Susan as she could. It prevented Allan from winning the man's easy victory in the affection stakes.

A man couldn't discover the bonds between a mother and the child who will grow up into her likeness. The 1970s and 1980s would provide Susan with different opportunities from those that had been granted to *her*, but the 'truth' of their two experiences would be identical, more or less. (Mrs Mason enjoyed absolute-sounding terms like 'truth'.) Susan would perceive then why her mother had wanted them to be so close: because they were fated to be mirror likenesses of each other. From her months growing in her belly, Susan alone knew the dark, bloody interior capacities of herself, what she'd undergone to give her life: she wasn't expecting gratitude back, only the recognition that the two of them were sisters of the one flesh.

*

'What would *you* do if you were in the money, Tilly?' Mrs Lenny asks.

122

The girl stares.

'I know for sure. I'd get me a fur coat. That's for starters. Then for Vic I'd get a car. Like Mr Miller's Sunbeam Talbot only a bit bigger. And a bungalow somewhere—that's for us both—maybe those ones up on Rossholme Drive. Or even 'The Wyldnesse' would do. With a fitted carpet and a lounge. I'd get a china-cabinet and collect animals: you know, little glass animals, like Bambi. And all the things to go into the house like a television, and a refrigerator. I'd have pretty paper on the walls. Then we'd have to have holidays—'

Tilly continues to stare, open-mouthed.

Denise walks in and sits down at the table. She's Tilly's age, but doesn't speak to her. She's heard all her mother's talk before, dozens of times. She realises Mum only likes Tilly to be there so she can talk to her: she knows her family aren't going to listen to her any more. Dad's been getting a bit ratty about it too. Maybe it's to do with the Change of Life: terrible things happen then, much, much worse than the curse.

She doesn't know how Tilly Moscombe first got coming here. She's as thick as two short ones. People see her up at the top of the town; she lives somewhere in 'Hallam House'. Denise suspects she's not as stupid as she makes out—she *couldn't* be—maybe she comes here to spy? Why'd anyone want to spy on *them*, though? They're the most ordinary people in Sandmouth, sometimes Denise wants to scream to get out of the house and just to make her mother shut up.

Sometimes too, her parents get at each other: it's always got to do with *things*. Dad's trodden something into the rug or burnt a hole in the tablecloth, and why can't they get this or that? Then it *really* gets her down, living here. At least Tilly Moscombe can clear off out of it. Sometimes she's only in for ten minutes, if she starts getting under their feet: she just scoffs their tea and eats a slice of bread and jam or a biscuit out of the tin with Anne Hathaway's cottage on the lid, and then she's off. If everyone gives her that, how come she's not as fat as a barrel? There's tons about Tilly Moscombe that she doesn't understand.

Denise gives Tilly Moscombe one of her hard looks. It's not a tea-room they're running. Doesn't she see she's being *used*, so she'll listen to her mother?

Denise would like to work in Crockers', instead of filleting haddock through the back in Beresford's, where she's a dogs-body five mornings and two afternoons a week. Then she would have all those nice things around her every day. You have to be polite to the people, but she'd be choosy about that. The posh customers would get the best service, the properly posh, not the fakes: if you weren't so posh, you wouldn't get such good service. That would be her rule, and it only stood to reason. Dead simple really.

★

Howard Trevis was walking uphill on his daily journey home for lunch. The people who recognised him and volunteered a greeting told him it was a fine day, and he nodded agreement with them.

It wasn't until he reached the turning into Walnut Avenue that he looked up and noticed the blue sky and the high white trails of cloud. From the opposite pavement he heard the flag of Saint George slapping on the pole in Mr Herbert's garden, and he realised the wind had got up. The houses on Walnut Avenue usually caught any wind that was going.

He walked on, past the hedges and latch-gates and the house-names which his eye always noticed and read uncon-sciously. They were a litany of normality: 'Ferndean', 'Wych-wood', 'Tree Tops', 'Holmfield', 'Sunny Nook', 'Finsthwaite'. When they'd moved into the house they'd inherited the name 'Lyndhurst'. Neither of them felt strongly enough about it to suggest an alternative. It had a safe, very English ring to it, and the mind's eye saw that tile-hung street on its hill and the creeper-clad gabled residences in their quiet, leafy gardens. To the postman they were 'Mr and Mrs H D Trevis, 'Lyndhurst', 14 Walnut Avenue,' and it connoted nothing untoward or out of the ordinary, which was exactly how Trevis wanted the two of them to be seen. They presented a picture of decent, self-contained, harmonious married life to their neighbours, no doubt, and prompted no suspicions. Everything must be as it appeared to be.

Only, of course, it wasn't: not quite.

Washing smacking on a clothes-rope caught Trevis's atten-tion as he passed a garden with a double-feu. He looked back through the thin privet hedge and saw bed sheets like white

124

sails and slack, drooping underpants and oversized vests and a vast, unhooked corset with its attachments hanging down, like an article of chain mail. He also noticed a pair of child's blue pyjamas, the jacket throwing up its arms gleefully and the trousers aiming high kicks at the length of rope.

He stopped for a few moments to look. The pyjamas appeared full of the joys of spring, quite wild and abandoned with happiness. How could that conceivably be?—unless the bliss was to be free briefly of the child who wore them, a boy with all his nocturnal phobias and deceits.

At school he'd always worn striped pyjamas: you wore what everyone else wore, and obeyed the tacit principle governing school life—namely, that every boy should be as alike as possible. But that was only what he'd wanted, to be as much like someone such as Markham or Rogerson as he could be, to have their prowess in games and work, to share their blonde good looks and to speak in the same mellow tenor voice and to have golden hairs on his arms and to have the manly poise that they had, dignifying such ordinary actions as crossing the school yard or walking down the broad central staircase in the House. Markham and Rogerson wore striped pyjamas, and already their cocks seemed to hang heavily behind the cotton: they were two years above him and he didn't have the opportunity to see them naked, but sometimes they left their dressing-gowns open when they switched lights off and he used to convince himself that he could see a bush of dark pubic hair through the slit of the fly, under the trailing ends of the white draw-cords. There was a story that Markham stood up like a lamp-post in the morning when he woke up, and Trevis used to lie in his bed imagining the sight to himself.

None of that explained what happened. He'd heard the legends passed round the school concerning Quinn, but they didn't make the House any less loyal to him or to (the second) Mrs Quinn. It was as if that side of him had belonged to another plane of thought in your mental workings, and if you were summoned to his study to see him about something you had to make a conscious jump between what was happening and the remotest possibility of what *might* happen to you, but the two planes didn't properly coincide. Sometimes it seemed as if the man had a haunted, hunted expression on his face which even a fourth-former was capable of recognising, and sometimes he used to believe that the man's eyes alighted on him with particular frequency in the course of a lesson or a House assembly. But Mrs Quinn smiled through all the memories of his schooldays, and he'd never been quite convinced until his Lower Sixth Year that theirs wasn't a perfectly straightforward, unexceptional marriage between two people who'd wanted to have a shared life and a brood of children together. Even after 'It' happened—the 'It' which seemed to have no reason or sense to it—he didn't totally believe that it had, even though he knew he couldn't have invented the details.

He hadn't known that adults stuck their tongues into each other's throats, so he couldn't have *imagined* that happening when Quinn came upon him from behind late one evening in a dimly lit corridor of the labyrinthine building, which had been built by a Victorian philanthropist in château style as a convalescent home but had never been used as such. For those moments he seemed to float as Quinn cradled his neck and the back of his head with his squat fingers and reached all the way down into his throat with his tongue. At the same time another hand was roving inside his pyjama trousers, fondling what the House nurse had carefully warned them were called their 'private parts' and exploring the gully between his legs. Quinn took his hand from the back of his head, clasped the boy's hand in his own and pressed it against the fork of his trousers. The hot hand with the hairy knuckles pressed down on his and he vaguely felt the outline of the erection he realised later he had caused.

Nothing else took place, no other sin beyond that initial exploration. His own tool wouldn't do what Quinn must have wanted it to as he massaged it with his fingers that were stained yellow at the tips with nicotine. It resolutely refused to stiffen, even though Quinn was whispering to him not to worry, just to relax, there were only themselves.

He didn't tell anyone. They wouldn't have believed him. And even if they *had* found a way to believe him, they would have presumed he'd engineered the incident. In Quinn's presence he tried as hard as he could to give the impression that he had no memory of the occasion. To begin with he smiled more

126

at Mrs Quinn, because he felt he ought to be showing her pity, then in the fullness of time he felt less generously disposed towards her and decided that she was a fool not to see why her husband had married her—to credit himself with the appearance of normality—and so how could she be deserving his sympathy?

The event wasn't repeated. Trevis was constantly on tenterhooks that it would, and miserably unsure of what his own feelings and reactions would be if it did. He knew there could only be one decent gentlemanly response, but he wasn't so confident now that he belonged to the ranks of gentlemen, to the decent and righteous. For one thing they had unsullied consciences—they were like the products of the school, boys who grew up into men in pin-stripes or tweeds with untroubled, frown-less faces—and now he knew something about Quinn which they didn't. (Quinn himself was almost a caricature of a moustached, window-pane check county gent, just beginning to carry a little too much weight for his middling frame.) Worse, though, he had grave doubts about himself, his own virtue and degree of involvement: how much had he tempted Quinn, albeit unconsciously, and *how much was he wanting the episode to be repeated*? Wasn't it *he* who had caused the bunched swelling of flesh to iron in his trousers: so shouldn't as much of the blame be apportioned to himself?

The pyjama trousers and jacket flapped gaily on the washing-line as another updraught of wind caught them, and Trevis turned back to the solid virtue of Walnut Avenue, to the straight and narrow. He looked down at the pavement under his feet.

Responsibility preserved them both, Maureen and himself, it kept them the right way up. Otherwise . . . Well, he chose not to think what the alternative might be. It was necessary that he obeyed the 'rules', every single one of them, just as he had been required to do at school and in the House. Even though he'd learned that the reality of Quinn's character was so different from what it *appeared* to be, he'd continued to obey the rules all his life since then: scrupulously so, as if he didn't want to put himself forward as anything other than the model average specimen. More than that, perhaps, he'd come to half-accept now that he truly was the person he purported to

127

be. It was a vital solace—or semi-solace—to him.

Maybe he should cut himself a buttonhole from whatever was blooming in the garden? On the national saint's day it was a permissible indulgence, to allow him to pass as one of the crowd.

Washing smacked in other gardens. Sleeves somersaulted over washing-lines and seemed to be waving to him. Drying sheets, pegged out tautly, rumbled like rolling thunder. A saint's day, Trevis thought, and also the most normal of mornings in Sandmouth: and the thought was like a bullet to his heart.

★

'Bunch of huns,' said Mr Ferris, standing at the bar of 'The Anchor'. 'In they walk, cool as you like.'

He lifted his mug and stared into the beer.

'If I'd known they were huns, then I'd have put up the sign on the door. I didn't have a chance, though.'

He realised he was starting to sound defensive.

'Of course I pretended I had lots of things to be getting on with. But I saw them looking at everything, brazen as you like. Bloody cheek, I wanted to tell them, bloody cheek *you*'ve got.'

'What *did* you say to them?'

'Well, I thought of things afterwards I *could* have said. All I needed to come out with was something like "Nuremberg". That would have turned them white. Or "Hitler". Or "Dachau". Walking about as if none of it had happened and I wanted their filthy money.'

'D'you get many foreigners?'

'I didn't used to. God knows who it'll be next. I should put a sign on the door, "NO WOGS", that'd tell them. Those run-for-their-lives Iti's, they'll be over next. Like the Lavezzoli's. And the bleeding nips with their little slit eyes and finger nails out to here. We know what *they're* like, they're not all suddenly just like us, are they?'

Mr Ferris looked round the company for agreeing nods.

'What's the point of fighting them if the next thing they're over here with cameras round their necks, opening their wallets. They like the calendars—you know the ones, bits of polished slate with a pottery seagull on top and "Sandmouth" written on them. That's what they go for, seven and nine or

128

eleven and six, money's no object to them. It's the British folk never spend more than five bob because they can't, and go away happy with whatever they've got. They like the jar of striped sand and never mind if they can't afford a ship in a bottle. That went to an Australian bloke. I told him they took six weeks to make, and he asked me "Is it an antique, mate?" I wanted to tell him "*You* wouldn't know an antique if it had coloured flashing lights put on it and it rang bells. Mate." '

The others sympathised vaguely with their daily lunchtime drinking companion.

'I'm getting in new stock. Porcelain pigs for putting flowers in, and cream jugs like cows, with their mouths open for pouring and tails up for a handle. I'm having "Sandmouth" painted on them,' Mr Ferris said, tucking one thumb into the pocket of his waistcoat as he swallowed from his glass.

Someone said an encouraging word.

Mr Ferris continued. 'Three and eleven the pigs'll be. Good quality, mind you, no rubbish. I mean, Sandmouth's not just like any other seaside place.'

The others agreed with mutterings and nods of their heads.

'I think it has to go for the quality image. There's the future to think of, isn't there?'

No one replied to that. Perhaps they were a little mystified by the logic.

'The glass animals, *they've* been popular. And the set of three lobster pots, in three different sizes: miniatures, I mean, but it's real wicker. I believe some old dame makes them, she's in a home, but I tell people it's a fisherman. Like I told that Australian it was an old salt made his ship in a bottle, even though it's a policeman and his wife in Slough, they do them in the kitchen, one makes the ships and the other attends to the plaster of paris for the sea and then the shoving-in. With long stick-contraptions. But I don't know who does which. Which job, I mean.'

There was no reply.

'You don't have to tell the whole truth,' Mr Ferris said. 'I don't think so anyway, not all the time. Really, it's what people *want* to hear, what they *expect* to hear.'

'Have you asked them?' someone had the gall to enquire. 'If that's what they want to hear?'

'No. Well, not actually *asked* them. It stands to reason,

though, doesn't it? It's kind of romantic. A fisherman, an old tar. It's like another world to them.'

Mr Ferris heard himself sounding defensive again. He took two swallows from his glass.

'I think it should be our duty,' he said, on the strength of the beer. 'That's our purpose in a place like this. I mean—what do they call it?—the "leisure trade". People think we're lucky living here.'

Someone at the counter groaned.

'Well, it *looks* quite pretty,' Mr Ferris said. 'Maybe *we* think other places are, and then you find that's what they're thinking about us!'

The proprietor of 'The Gyft Shoppe' took another draught of beer from his mug. He felt he was starting to speak in unfamiliar terms.

'Supply-and-demand. You've got to give people what they want. That's the future.'

'Bollocks,' someone said. 'All they want's the past.'

'Well—' Mr Ferris swallowed from his glass. 'There's that side to it too. Then you just serve it up to folk. Get "Sand-mouth" painted on it and put a decent price on it.'

'Tell us, Bob, is that what *you're* in it for?'

Mr Ferris didn't know whether to nod his head or shake it. He didn't care to admit that the idea for the business had seeded itself in his mind after someone in Southampton had asked him if he was interested in buying four dozen china ashtrays that had been meant for officers' messes.

'I'm as patriotic as the next chap,' he said. 'More so.'

'What're you sailing us down the river for, then?'

'No, I'm not.'

'That's what you said.'

'I didn't say *that*,' Mr Ferris replied, not at all sure what it was he *had* said.

'You're just tarting everything up.'

'Everyone needs romance,' Mr Ferris declared, preferring his rendering and feeling that his meaning sounded conveniently obscure, maybe even profound.

For some reason his departed wife came into his mind at that moment. She tended to do so when unbidden, when he'd drunk too much. He tried to live with a solid, contented image of her:

when people spoke of her, he tried to envisage her as neutrally as possible. Then, suddenly, the picture would be lost, and mysteries abounded.

All told, the past was an uncomfortably sly and shifty commodity; not to be trusted sometimes, not an inch.

At least Doris hadn't lived to see the shop, though. Mr Ferris didn't know what she would have made of the wares he lived by: the crudely painted porcelain thatched-cottages with the wobbly bases, the letter-knives with malachite handles some-one had found for him in Portugal, the prancing glass animals, the half-dozen or so of the remaining twenty-six ashtrays (with 'Sandmouth' lettered on them) which he regularly had out on display. 'Nothing stays quite the same,' he would have told her if he'd had the chance, but he knew that it must equally well apply to the past life too.

'No, God deliver us from the wogs,' Mr Ferris said, knowing it would save his equilibrium and the conversation, steering them all into safer channels. 'After the Japs, it'll be nigbo's. I definitely don't want *their* hands reaching out. Bunch of thieves.'

There was an outbreak of nodding among the company.

'Don't lift a hand to help us. Up coconut trees. Or too lazy, lying in their hammocks fanning themselves, picking each other's nits. *They'll* be over next, mark my word: off the banana boats, grabbing what they can.'

'Britain's a lumber-cupboard,' someone said.

'We should just have left them,' another voice remarked. 'The darkies.'

'Where would we have been without them?' a discordant voice chimed. 'In the past. That old lord or whatever he was, before the de Castellets got here, the gambler, the bankrupt—that was money from the slave-ships . . .'

No one heeded.

Mr Ferris was swilling the beer around in the bottom of his glass.

'I mean, *they* really *are* the limit.'

He drank. The prospect of his demon—a chocolate-coloured coon standing in his shop—always alarmed and unnerved him.

'You've got to have standards,' he said vaguely. 'Limits.'

Limits on what was possible and not possible: what might be

allowed and what not allowed. Out of the dim and distant past, Doris seemed to be about to open her mouth to say something to him.

'Another one, anyone?' Mr Ferris offered in his heartiest voice. 'I'll be late in opening. I'm not opening on time for huns or dagoes. *They* owe *us*, I think. Having the freedom to go anywhere they like. Just let them wait,' Mr Ferris announced royally, his confidence momentarily buoyed and high.

*

Susan Mason has a Wendy house, bought and transported from Hamleys; and, although she has started to outgrow it, she spends some time of every day inside it. She has a set of dolls' crockery and miniature cutlery and her mother encourages her to set them out as if she were serving luncheon or dinner. 'Like Mummy does,' she says.

Mrs Mason takes care that Susan should be by her side when her luncheon guests arrive. A number of them are friends from school, some are the wives of Allan's colleagues, others are ladies of the town. She is concerned that her daughter should learn how females conduct themselves in company.

From the Wendy house the child hears the chatter and the trilling laughter of her mother's friends and acquaintances as they discuss Sandmouth and its ways. Occasionally there are interludes of quiet when Susan knows the voices are being lowered, but she cannot appreciate why. That must remain one of the mysteries of adulthood to her.

Nanny Filbert is supposed to be on hand, but while Mrs Mason's guests are in the house she keeps a low profile. Susan catches sight of the top of her head just bobbing above the window sill, where the armchair is. That means Nanny Filbert is in one of her cross moods when she doesn't like to be interrupted. That must remain another of the mysteries of adulthood to the child, why Nanny Filbert looks and speaks so scathingly when her mother isn't there to see and hear.

Things are simpler in the Wendy house. Susan has only herself to please or frustrate. Sometimes she plays at having a husband, but she always loses interest in that game after a while. A husband has to be out at his work, and he has to wear a suit like other husbands, and for the most part his conversation is pretty dull. Even Susan at four-and-three-quarter years

132

old recognises dullness when she encounters it. Just as her mother can, she is unconsciously aware, because no one in the child's experience lets the tedium rise up from the depths to the surface and shows it on her face quite as her mother does.

★

'We've arrived, Adele.'

'And to prove it we're here. No, Guy, the fact is not lost on me.'

'Smile for your public.'

The actress in her toning beige suit and coat and beaver hat opened her mouth wide for the station porter.

'Of course,' she said, 'Mewes isn't getting away with this.'

'Beggars can't be choosers, Adele.'

'Don't you mean "buggers", dear?'

'Not Mewes, surely?'

'It wasn't him I was thinking of. I've no idea about Mewes and frankly I don't care, but *you* could tell at a glance, darling, I know. It's enough that he manages to bugger up everything that has to do with me, good and proper.'

'I get the feeling you're not overjoyed to be here, Adele.'

'Whatever gave you that idea, my dear Guy?'

'Oh . . .' Pennicote shrugged his shoulders. 'Maybe just because we appear to be walking this way down the platform while the others have gone in the other.'

'*Not* accidental, my dear. I think I've had enough of them for one morning.'

'Well, you *are* Adele Adaire!'

'Very droll.'

'Well, you *are*. Aren't you?'

'Not just a pretty face, Guy.'

'Is it the only reason?'

'The only reason what?'

'Why you haven't gone on with them. Because you've had enough of them?'

'I don't seem to be very popular, Guy, do I?'

'Aren't you?'

'Give over, darling. Come on, do tell . . .'

'All right. A couple of—what shall I call them?—less-than-vintage performances. So what?'

'Amazing what their tiny minds won't forget.'

133

'Well, *you* should forget it. What the hell does it matter?'

The actress flung the fold of her cape-coat over her shoulder.

'Where are you staying?' she asked.

'Somewhere called the "Journey's End" Guest House. God help me.'

'That's where *I* should be.'

'Tut-tut, you know what they think of single men and single women sharing premises in places like this.'

'Yes, I know, Guy. But it's *you* and *me*.'

'Even so—*far* too risky, Adele.'

'Just think, I could say I'm your mother.'

'I'm trying *not* to think it.'

'I'm at somewhere called the "Camelot" Guest House. Mewes' secretary thought it sounded "patriotic", silly bitch.'

'Surprised she even knows the word.'

'Oh, it's a very demanding job she's got. She has to know how to use a telephone: how to hold the receiver, dial numbers, that sort of thing.'

'She can dial numbers? Uses her finger a lot, does she?'

'All the time. And if "Camelot" 's no better than Salisbury, I'm going to tell her to pull it out, and be pretty damn quick about it.'

'That's the spirit, Adele! Won and lost an empire!'

They turned when they reached the end of the platform and started walking back the other way. They heard the doors of a car banging shut in the station yard.

'That's them gone,' Pennicote said.

The actress breathed out.

'Let's have dinner tonight, Guy. *À deux*. It's the only chance we've got. We'll go to an hotel. There must be one. Dinner, just us, and we'll slag, slag, slag.'

'Most sensible thing you've said all morning, my dear Adele.'

'I've said *lots* of interesting things this morning.'

'Maybe it's just that I've heard them all before, then.'

'Yes. Yes, Guy, you probably have.'

The actress arranged the fold of her cape. Guy was the best of the bunch, but he forced her to confess to things she didn't mean to confess to. She could have let him go on ahead with the others in the taxi, but she'd held on to him, the age difference notwithstanding. She wasn't afraid of what he might say behind her back, because she knew it couldn't be worse than what he said to her face. After so many years of justifying herself, hearing the blunt truth spoken to her was almost in the way of a liberation.

★

Domesticity was a common undoing, Mrs Dick decided as she stood waiting for the kettle to come to the boil: it was also the only defence possible sometimes, safety and concealment in unthinking routine, hiding feelings behind marmalade-pots and cream-jugs. But the life trapped certain people, it became a cage.

On the back of the kitchen door she had pinned up a Diary of Events for the children to fill in themselves. She felt it let them *see* the system in operation: that a week was filled up with as many activities as possible, pleasant (Nigel's birthday party, David's trip to the Mumbles with the Redmonds) and less pleasant (Laura's visit to the dentist, Nigel's 'thank you' letters). The house was always in a state of commotion: school-bags thrown down and spilling on to the floor, a violin and piano competing against each other, the bath running, vegetables steaming, cut-out paper men shedding their fellows, a ball bouncing against the garage wall, the telephone ringing with messages for Quentin or the children, socks and underwear discarded on the upstairs landing, alarm clocks going off when they weren't supposed to, an escaped rabbit loosè in the garden, raps on the front door, a soup-pot boiling over.

A mother's fulfilment or just a cage for a wife, it was hard to say which. Her suspicions tended towards the latter.

Mrs Dick filled a teapot with water and measured in some tea. She hadn't tasted decent tea for years.

She sat down at the kitchen table in her tweed suit and picture hat. Neither went with the other, she knew, but neither had received an airing at Minster Court before. The other mothers noticed things like that. Was the hat new, had they seen it before, how much had she spent on it? It irritated her that *that* should have decided why she'd worn what she had: sometimes she felt the common manner of life they lived with other people was sucking her in and she was allowing other people's expectations of her to determine her actions.

She picked a chipped cup to drink her tea from, for perversity's sake. It was the first time she'd gone to a school function alone, and she sat wondering what they'd been saying behind her back. At least a doctor had a reasonable excuse for not attending, so she'd realised when Quentin had told her he had a full load and would she mind, would anyone think it odd if he didn't come . . .? He'd made it seem such a very casual decision when she knew they both knew what its significance was— here was a major point of public etiquette they were breaching.

Of *course* it was the case that they let other people choose for them how they behaved: it was the premise of their lives after all. Hadn't appearances come to be of the very essence in Sandmouth? She would realise it in a particular circumstance—picking what to wear for the Saint George's Day formalities at the school, for instance—but that was the most trivial manifestation of the matter. How people saw Quentin and herself and the degree of 'trust' they inspired was very important to them, and not just for professional reasons: what was necessary to them both was to know that they passed as a quite normal married couple.

Mrs Dick reached out and turned the knob of the wireless set. After a few seconds fingers strayed up a keyboard: Chopin, she recognised.

The music conferred a stillness on the objects in the kitchen. Mrs Dick felt quietened. It had been a ridiculous morning, and made to seem more unreal by her having to cope by herself. She'd come away realising how much the deceit of togetherness had become a habit with her.

Not that she and Quentin warred to any extreme extent, and certainly not in front of the children. Perhaps what she had learned from her marriage was that she had no strong opinion on the issue: she could either have taken matrimony or left it well alone. There was no single reason for her to distrust her own marriage: Quentin hadn't been unfaithful to her, so far as she was aware. But she looked at the other mothers and fathers at the school functions and thought, we could be paired quite differently, and she wondered what difference it would really have made.

They hadn't at all been made for each other, she knew, no more than for anyone else of an approximately similar social standing. She hadn't liked anyone more, which was the most she could say for Quentin's 'right' to be married to her, and she supposed the same was true for him. He hadn't appeared out-of-place in her parents' chintzy home, even though his talk was of masculine activities, rugby and sporty holidays with his medical chums. *She* had felt not uncomfortable in *his* parents' chintzy home, although she'd realised her conversation must sound rather trite, a bit Jane Austen-ish, the most arduous of her interests being gardening. Now, in their own chintzy home, the strands of conversation were deftly interwoven: the Calcutta Cup, begonias, taking Nigel out in the skiff, odd pairs of socks left over at the end of the wash. It all went painlessly enough, but she didn't know if painlessness should have been their ambition, if they weren't expending too much effort in maintaining a numbness of feeling, a status quo of bland, unconcerned politeness.

Their problems added up to nothing more melodramatic than that, she knew as the music trilled through the speaker in the wireless case. Maybe it was normal enough. But she wasn't able to keep her own dissatisfaction out of her face and her voice any longer. It showed itself when she least wanted it to appear. She saw Quentin trying not to notice, pretending even harder with people that everything was as sound and proper as it should be.

Melancholia was reaching her through Chopin's music. She closed her eyes. Perhaps she was reaching a woman's bad years earlier than she ought?

She opened her eyes again and looked about her. Sometimes the objects in the kitchen all had a deafening purposefulness about them, they clamoured to her that they all served a function: that *she* was a function too, and what was she doing about it, just sitting there and starting and looking guilty whenever someone walked in through the door? So much in the house required attention, and required it every day; she had a timetable to live by and no excuses please.

Mrs Dick sighed. On her worst days the simplest objects had the ability to intimidate her. When she was in a defeatist frame of mind the ladles and spatulas hanging on the rack, the sieves and whisks, the rolling-pin, even the meekest pastry-brushes—they all *demanded to be used*. It seemed to be their

137

intention that she should have no rest and no opportunity to reflect on the thoughts she could feel crowding into her skull.

She pushed her chair back, got to her feet, and slopped the remaining contents of her cup into the sink. Quentin would ask her how the morning had gone and she would tell him honestly, more or less: that Witt had made a fool of himself, that the Symington-Berrys had done their best to handle the situation, that David looked spruce (for once) and Nigel very responsible in his prefect's colours, that the lunch was edible, people had spoken to her and she had spoken to them, in fact she hadn't had a dull moment.

Maybe he would look surprised, and realise he had been impetuous. Or maybe he would see right through her, and understand that she was only putting a brave show on it. She hardly cared which, now that they'd reached the point where he could allow it to happen.

Mrs Dick found she was standing in front of the door into the hall, running an eye down the Diary of Events. The sense of what she was reading wasn't registering. She shook her head absent-mindedly.

There were days when she managed to survive the waking hours by not seeming to think at all, or by concentrating on such trivial matters that they blocked out all else. Those were like lost days. *But perhaps all her days were lost*, to a greater or lesser degree — she couldn't help the thought.

She believed that in some people's lives a watershed is reached, an event of such intensity that all that comes after it is a tailing-off and a falling-away. She didn't think she'd ever *had* a high-point in her experience. Instead she just seemed more and more to chip away at the possibilities she used to imagine for herself, in that strange interlude of months before she'd met Quentin and before she'd convinced herself of the wisdom of becoming engaged. Every day that came now seemed to be inching her away from the possibility of ever behaving any differently: she was hardly making any progress at all now in living her life, she'd weighted herself down into a rut.

Quentin could see that knowledge just by looking into her eyes. Now they had no proper surprises left to hide from each other; only the extent of their concealments to disguise.

Mrs Dick pulled off her hat. It had been a disaster with the suit. Perhaps Quentin would hear as much from one of his patients.

The picture hat with its broad fedora brim had been an eccentric purchase in the first place. Not a doctor's wife's hat at all: it belonged to the wardrobe of a woman who dressed in any devil-may-care way she chose, who didn't have a husband to offend or children to embarrass. A woman who acted just as she decided for herself and not as she believed she was obliged to; who had the confidence to know that, because she wished it, her life was her own—it was *her* property, *hers* alone, and no one else was entitled to any say in how she managed or mismanaged it.

★

'Perhaps—something to get me back up on my feet, lad?'

Major Fitt sits on a chair in a corner of the marquee. He watches the company quite amiably. He has spotted a tray of bottles under a trestle-table, only partially concealed by the white table-cloth.

The boy is obliging. He stoops down on the grass behind the table and disappears beneath the cloth. He fills a wine-glass out of one bottle, and then when that bottle is empty, he opens another and tips whatever it contains into the glass.

The Major stares at the concoction: he sniffs it, then tastes. The content proves to his liking, and quickly goes down the hatch.

The boy is very obliging and offers to refill the glass.

'Another of your interesting selections, young man, eh?

Through a flap in the canvas wall the Major spies the cricket pavilion twenty or thirty yards away and replies, yes, that's a good idea, but what if I goes somewhere a little more private to enjoy it this time, eh?

The boy makes another interesting selection from the bottles under the table while the Major slips unnoticed through the flap and makes as exactly as he can for the cricket pavilion. The boy finds him sprawled in a folding canvas chair on the verandah.

The Major accepts the glass gratefully.

'Nigel, is it?'

'Yes, sir. Nigel Dick, sir.'

'Better call you "Nigel", then, hadn't I?'

After several swallows the Major launches into the story of a binge they'd once had *before* they went out: no one had been supposed to know about it—and maybe it was *still* a secret?

'Some of them were so pissed they couldn't get their caps on. It was so boring, most of it, just sitting around. Then when you got the chance, it was like—I don't know—being let loose in an orchard or something, you tried to bag everything you could see. Just couldn't wait that day, then we got the call. Bad timing, I suppose.'

The Major swilled the drink that was left in the bottom of the glass, round and round.

'Are you *still* thirsty, sir?' the boy asked.

'It's hard work, you know. Having a name to live up to. Hot work too. Under canvas. Very hot, canvas. Tents. Don't mind if I do indulge myself one more time. Never touched a drop before I signed up, you know. Temperance family. Their sons are always the worst. And daughters. Mustn't forget them. Do you like girls, sonny?'

The boy blushed.

'Too young, I expect. As a matter of fact—what age *are* you?'

'Twelve, sir.'

'Well, then, I expect you'll be interested in girls quite soon. When you're too old for all this flying saucer nonsense. Big girls or little girls, it's up to you. I wouldn't want to tell you. Advise you. Don't see any today, though.'

'There are just one or two, sir.'

'Eh?'

'Girls, sir. Here today, sir.'

'D'you think they saw? Suppose they must have. Why were they here anyway, shouldn't *they* be at school too? Spankies for them. I'd hate to be at school again, really. All that tosh. "Happiest Days Of Your Life". Supposed to knock the corners off me. Headmaster called me a "lout". Said I'd come to a sticky end. He wasn't as stupid as some people made out he was.'

'Wasn't he, sir?'

'I wonder if it's worth a leg, though?'

'I beg your pardon, sir.'

140

'Probably you're not supposed to mention it, are you? Any of you? My famous leg.'

The boy fired.

'You were told not to look at it, I'll bet.'

'I—, I—'

'I do this for a living, of course, kind of. But was it worth losing a leg for, that is the question.'

The boy stood awkwardly, staring.

'I suspect—*with* it, I'd be holding down a job somewhere, or trying to. Never had a job in my life, you see. But the nobly legless—shall we say?—have a . . . rogue glamour. A rogue glamour. Yes, that's it.'

The Major smacked his lips appreciatively at the remark.

'I was always being asked for my memoirs. Give my name to it anyway, what the publishers had cobbled together. You'll find it on a second-hand book barrow one day, my boy. "*I* remember," you'll say, "that bloke. I gave him a drink or two. He spoke to me, a load of twaddle".'

The Major farted loudly.

'Safety!'

The boy retreated a couple of feet, blushing pink.

' "What're they asking for it? A shilling? Might be worth that. Question is, do I want my son to be reading this kind of thing? What's it going to mean to him, for Jesus Christ's sake?" '

The boy cleared his throat.

'I could find you another drink, sir. If you'd like.'

'What's that?'

'Are you still thirsty, sir?'

The Major broke wind again.

'Gas masks!'

The boy touched the tip of one of his ears, as if he could feel it burning.

'You're not one of those bloody pacifists, are you?'

'Pardon, sir?'

'All pansies and lefties. Don't let your son be a pansy or a lefty, will you? Send him somewhere they'll knock the corners off him. Not a tarted-up strawberries-and-cream place for nancy boys, like this one.'

The boy looked at the floorboards, frowning as if he might

have been trying to memorise the words for passing on later.

'Still, I never got served such interesting drinks anywhere else I went to, I must say.'

The boy nodded.

'*One* more I think, laddie. Then I'll have to be getting away.'

'Yes, sir. Certainly, sir.'

'Get the feeling I've outstayed my welcome here.'

The boy ran down the steps and off across the turf. The Major watched him. Good lick he was going at. Maybe they really *would* be his Happiest Days. If he was that age again and he was somewhere like here, what difference would it have made?

The Major felt his tenses were becoming muddled. You're born at one time in history, and that is your lot. You have two lives—the one around you, the close immediate one, and some of that you can sort out for yourself, say what *you're* going to do—and you have the other, which is all people in one place at the one time, 'history', and in that you've no choice. Somehow you have to live with the two: or between the two. But it's a loser's game. Thinking you could have lived your life differently if you'd had the guts, if you'd chosen to, also knowing that too much is decided for you to have that freedom.

The boy would never get away from that. That meant everyone under the sun was the same; strawberry teas made it easier to bear, but your palate grows tired of what it has to taste too often.

*

Tilly Moscombe stands inside a rhododendron bush, watching. She has no true remembrance, and no hopes or expectations of what may be to come.

She only watches, with her eyes expressionless.

She might be rooted to the spot. Somewhere above her the birds have started trilling again; a caterpillar clings to her sock, and a ladybird climbs the cuff of her cardigan. The grounds of Minster Court might be in the Amazonian rain forest, for all that either means to her. She doesn't hear the jungle tattoo. She cannot know that a person not able to be understood causes fear, and fear isn't responsible for its actions. A rhododendron bush is a hide, but no last protection.

142

Ruth Aldred wasn't certain when it was that she knew she had lost her faith.

But one day stayed fixed in her mind. A hot July afternoon when she was eleven or twelve. She had gone into Bournemouth with her father; he had promised to visit a parishioner in a nursing-home, and he'd suggested that she might like to look in one or two of the bookshops while he went about his business, then he would come and collect her in the car.

The heat sizzled in the streets of Bournemouth, she remembered it: dancing above the rooftops and softening the tar on the roads. Every surface had felt hot to the touch. She'd caught sight of a child eating an ice-cream sundae in the window of a tea-room; as they drove past her father noticed and asked if she would like one too. She'd been in one of her self-denying moods, and told him 'No, thank you'. Constance, sitting in the back of the car, whispered to her that she shouldn't be so hasty in her decisions; her father had been prepared for her saying 'Yes, please,' he had volunteered the expense, so why shouldn't she have accepted?

At the prearranged point her father stopped the car and let her off. As soon as she started walking she could feel the heat of the pavements through her socks and the soles of her sandals. After two or three minutes she came to one of the bookshops her father had suggested and she pushed on the door and went in. While she was inside browsing, a woman with a shopping-basket keeled over on the pavement across the street. Ruth watched through the window as people rushed to her aid. When the ambulance had driven her away, Ruth heard one of the female customers telling another that the old dear had had a heart-attack and died. 'Out like a light. That's the way to go. Hope I have an easy death like that.'

Easy, maybe, invisible Constance was saying at her shoulder, but undignified. How frail we are in our bodies, Ruth considered, feeling the afternoon had turned very solemn: we should all pity people more, since we don't know when we shall die, any of us—and then it will be too late to say or do the things we want to. (Constance, still at her shoulder, agreed with the sentiment.)

But for some reason Ruth felt especially bad-tempered that

afternoon. She became impatient with an assistant in the second bookshop who kept following her round and taking out the book she'd just looked at and checking it for damage before replacing it on the shelf. For spite's sake Ruth took down one book and, when the assistant in her apron had fleetingly turned her back, she returned it to the wrong shelf. The assistant knew something was wrong when she started looking, and glared at the girl. Ruth grinned at her and walked smartly towards the door. The assistant came after her but before she could open her mouth Ruth had let go of the door and it swung back and tipped the woman off balance. She fell flat on the floor with a resounding thud.

Ruth ran into another street, where she knew there was a second-hand bookshop. She saw a barrow outside, piled with books in crates. Most probably it was then and there—in that street, on that scorchingly hot day with people dropping around her like flies—that she lost what was left of her faith in the divine.

She was standing under the barrow's frayed and tattered awning when her eyes alighted on a book's cover and she picked it out. The Germanic script on the dust-jacket must have drawn her attention, so she would tell herself in later years. The book was called *Into Belsen*; the words on the inside of the jacket had American spellings. Inside consisted mainly of photographs.

For ten minutes or a quarter-of-an-hour the vicar's daughter stood turning the pages, until the shop owner came outside and asked if he could be of any help to her. She looked up and saw how red he was, cooked by the heat: perspiration trickled down his temple.

He asked her if she was feeling all right. She blinked at him. 'You've gone white,' he said. She closed the book and leaned forward to return it among the others. The sudden movement made her feel queasy and she steadied herself by clinging to the sides of the wooden crate of books. 'Careful now, love,' the man told her. She tried to smile, and as she did so she chanced to look up through a hole in the barrow's canvas awning and saw the polished yellow sun winking down at her. She closed her eyes and saw white streamers trailing out of where the sky must be. She swayed on her feet, her head fell backwards on

144

her neck, her knees buckled and gave way and then the man must have put his arms around her waist.

Inside the dark shop like a cave she didn't know where she was: under the shade of the torn awning, or in the back street of some vanished European city, or in a kind of dream made up of dead stick-people in striped pyjamas. What she saw first when she opened her eyes were the shelves of books, and a slash of sunshine where the real street must have been, and then an old woman looking down at her into her face, and she thought it must be the same woman who'd dropped dead in the street because her heart had stopped beating: an easy death, but undignified. But that woman had been thrown into a grave after all her fillings had been ripped out and the flesh flayed off her, so now it was stretched across the tight drum of a lampshade in some quite unsuspecting person's house. 'Waste not, want not,' as her father was forever telling her. A dog barked, and suddenly it was dead too, shot by the troops who'd come to save her. They were escorting her over a sea of charred bones, rattling under her bare feet.

A clammy hand fell across her brow. Ruth opened her eyes and saw the old woman was wearing a gold ring: where had the gold come from, out of someone's mouth or out of the sky? She panicked for a few moments, terrified what her history might be. Then she seemed to see the sun winking down on everything and everybody, as if all this could only be a joke and nothing was so very serious after all.

Years later, it seemed—and years older—she heard a familiar voice among the others. It called her 'Ruth', it was like another christening to her. 'Constance', she repeated, but the voice said more definitely, 'Ruth'.

'*Can you hear me, Ruth?*'

A doctor appeared. She felt too heavy to move but she found that she *was* moving, one foot in front of another, and she discovered that her legs weren't bones but had a covering of flesh on them and there were normal people in the streets as her father drove the car carefully, taking care and patience on the bends, women with proper hair-dos and men in dark business suits, some of them with hooked noses but all of them looking well-fed and no more than a little hot.

She wasn't able to sleep after her experience, not for many

nights. Another doctor in Sandmouth prescribed tablets to make her sleep, but the result was like extinction and she became afraid of never waking up again and always staying over there on the other side where everything was black and forgotten.

She didn't want to be forgotten and she preferred to lie awake struggling to put certain pictures out of her mind, asking Constance to help her, trying to think of absolutely nothing at all—a different kind of oblivion, as white as winter snow.

Another day that summer her father had to go back into Bournemouth, and he asked her if she wanted to come, but she shook her head, from side to side to side to side, and he understood that she never wanted to go back to that place again. 'We're having prayers,' he told her, and she found herself giggling. 'For Mrs Kerrigan. In the nursing-home. She would like them—' It was very impolite, of course, but she just kept giggling, she couldn't help herself, the idea was so ridiculous: a dying woman and she was saying prayers *now*.

Her father backed away, and left her. For that part of her life, everyone backed away and left her. Except Constance, who came to be with her more and more, lying beside her in the bed that had been their parents'. They lay together, not sleeping, discussing their father and mother, thinking some very peculiar thoughts.

Two or three years later, when she did go back to Bournemouth one school holiday, mysteriously the shop and its barrow and its owner had gone. She was so surprised, she wondered stupidly if it had ever been there, or if she had only imagined it. But how could she have cabbalized out of her imagination the things she'd seen photographed in that book—how could anyone have conceived of it without the proof of the images? Her father picked her up in the car, and she felt she was repeating the motions of someone else. He smiled benignly to her as he always did, seeming inclined to think the best of her. He said the right words—not about how she looked or what she was wearing but about the weather, about how Mrs Goodchild in the nursing-home was faring—and she honestly thought she would scream, so that she wouldn't have to hear any more of it.

Maybe the scream showed in her eyes, because the flow of

146

words stopped eventually and there was silence in the car. Then it was *her* cue to smile, through the windscreen.

Sorrowing 'Ruth' is appropriate, she was thinking, but really he should have called me 'Eve' . . . 'of the tree of the knowledge of good and evil, thou shalt not eat of it: for in the day that thou eatest thereof thou shalt surely die.' Not gods after all, knowing good and evil.

That was all fine and dandy for God in His Heaven: but the capacity for good in ourselves can only be appreciated by us and properly worked for if we have a notion of our potential for evil too. So Ruth perceived the human predicament. Now and then she would also ask herself this: what happens beyond *that* point—when evil tips the scales so decisively that we know a proper balance of good against it will never be possible?

Sometimes Ruth caught her father looking at her: he would seem quite anxious—much more so than his usual self—as if, perhaps, he was afraid of what he might discover about her. Or . . . or might it be only a trick of the light in the heavily Victorian vicarage with its stained-glass infills at the tops of the windows?

She didn't purposely want to upset her father, and what she perceived might be his inability to comprehend made her concerned in turn for *him*. She'd asked Constance if perhaps God had intended this particular state of affairs too: if she wasn't meant to be the proverbial thorn, the softly sibilant serpent come to test her father's faith and that innocence he was a byword for.

★

Neither good nor bad was Miss Vane's verdict on her own books. So she decided when she was out of the public gaze and could be herself: or rather, another one of her selves.

The books inclined towards the gothic and highly coloured: but fiction always heightened experience, did it not? Miss Vane liked a plot, she must have a plot. Sometimes—in retrospect, after publication—she thought that her books had rather too much plot, too many links and coincidences. But life was frequently over-written too, was it not?—story-lines often existed where you didn't suspect that they did. However, penned by whom—by ourselves or by Another Being—she thought it was not her place to speculate upon in her thoroughly middle-brow, middle-of-the-road novels. (If you stand in the middle of the road too far lost in thought, there's a very good chance that something unpleasant and very possibly fatal is going to happen to you.)

The complicated plots and vividly drawn locations and the larger-than-life characters comprised the 'commercial' bias of Miss Vane's writing. (That is, inasmuch as her work could be said to have ever proved saleable or profitable.) She also chose to believe that another Meredith Vane—this time the Girton aspirant who had taken a cold on the train journey to her interview and had had the misfortune of being grilled on a low, sagging armchair with a standard lamp shining down on her face—had a responsibility to her more serious-minded readers. They required something rather more substantial: hence she supplied—spliced into the narrative—some of her own thoughts on character and morality and 'the times' in general. She didn't care to go into anything too deeply, of course, unless her hypothetical 'serious' reader—she imagined a Hampstead woman sitting reading in a book-lined first-floor room in a tall, narrow, sea-captain's house, like a ship marooned on dry land—was led too far from the incidents of the story. Her publisher, old Mr Cresswell, sometimes coughed apologetically and quietly sidled the word 'editor' into their gentle, genteel conversation in the dusty office in Bloomsbury, but unfailingly she would bestow on him her most radiant smile of incomprehension—being her London self, who looked at least ten years younger than the Sandmouth version—and he would retire like a proper gentleman into his shell, seeming too uncertain how to deal with her feminine wiles. He wasn't, thank God, like those modern bookmen who trawled their young editors fresh out of the universities. Conveniently for Miss Vane, Mr Cresswell was an old-fashioned type of publisher: he printed a book because he thought it deserved to be printed, maybe because he was too set in his ways and feared a 'scene' if he were to raise an objection with any of his regular authors, and somehow, in spite of everything, he managed to survive by very occasionally—accidentally rather than by design—publishing a book that curiosity took to the top of a reviewer's pile.

Somehow Miss Vane survived too, largely by virtue of certain shares and bonds sagaciously invested long ago. The high point of her existence occurred every four or five months when she travelled three sides of the leafy square in Bloomsbury to reach the fourth, where 'Cresswell and Bone' had their four floors of cramped, warren-like offices, smelling so deliciously of coffee-grounds and old leather upholstery and printers' ink. Circling the square she would imagine she was following in Virginia Woolf's footsteps, Virginia's possibly following Vita's: or she was Dorothy Richardson, up from the sticks of Cornwall for the day, her mind humming with brilliant, diamond-bright, only slightly overstretched images. In her London clothes she was smarter than any of them, of course. Her own literary worth still wasn't properly appreciated, she felt, but that is the lot of certain authors: *they* are 'chosen' too: their faith uplifts them and in the fullness of ripening time faith is rewarded. Sometimes unfortunately it takes till after death, which is somewhat inconvenient: but some of us, she told herself, we live *out* of our time, ahead of the flock, and it requires our passing for the rest to catch up and learn too late the value of what they find they've lost.

★

No one, thought Mrs Dick, absolutely no one could write about this place as it actually is.

The older she became the more she saw that the hoary old adages about humans and their modes of behaviour are true. People really do turn into caricatures of themselves, their own clichés: and clichés are recognisable because they represent the truth about so many, infinitely many people.

Sandmouth would hardly be believable, written down. Mrs Dick pitied Miss Vane for the colossal task she'd taken on, if it was true that her literary sights were now turned on the town. She would find herself having to out-invent the worst excesses that the denizens of Sandmouth were capable of.

★

Nanny Filbert has a view of the garden from her room at the back of the house. It's a pleasant room, just as Mrs Mason has wished it to be.

The walls are papered with a pattern of fleur-de-lis. There's a bed with brass rails, and an armchair with chintz covers, and a table, and an upright mahogany chair with a balloon back.

Nanny Filbert sits there quietly of an afternoon, during the interlude of peace when her charge is asleep. *She* dozes too, but very lightly; at some point she always twitches awake, then she extracts a stub of cigarette from her deepest pocket, leans forward and lights the end from the gas fire. One of Nanny's little pick-me-ups. Mrs Mason doesn't know about her little afternoon luxury, but she wouldn't presume it possible, so where might the harm be?

Mrs Mason didn't know a lot of things. Maybe she thought she did, but Nanny Filbert wasn't one to make an issue of anything. She appreciated the quiet life. She had her meals at set times, she had her few creature comforts. Mrs Mason was bearable for the most part—except when she smiled in such a high-and-mighty way at the china dolls along the window sill. There was only another couple of bona fide uniformed nannies in Sandmouth, up at houses on Greenaway Avenue and Rossholme Drive, and Nanny Filbert was the eldest, so that made her doyenne of her kind in the town. Really everything was the best it could be. Only there were times in the day—when she wasn't quite ready for it—her mind would start reaching back, trying to recover moments like fast glittery fish darting beneath cold water . . .

She'd been sitting on the lawn of another house when the car had come swinging up the driveway. The doors had opened, and out had stepped—first, Mr Sangster, still tanned and lean as a whippet after his years abroad during which she'd taken the responsibility for Jonathan and for running the house; and then, behind him, had appeared a woman in a Susan Small suit and Breton straw hat and the 'doe eyes' everyone had that year. 'Miss Seymour' he'd introduced her as, and right away Nanny Filbert had seen what was brewing between the two of them. Later, another day, he'd gone so far as trying to explain to her: that Jonathan needed a proper mother, the 'right atmosphere' to grow up in.

'I thought that's what I *was* providing for him, sir,' she'd made so bold as to declare.

'Of course, of course,' he'd replied, like the man of reasoned diplomacy that he was when he was up in London or in any of his hot foreign lands. 'But, you see, a *mother* . . .'

She'd braved him with her steeliest look. Yes, the look was asking him, what exactly *can* a step-mother give your child that *I* can't . . .?

Thereupon the telephone rang and the conversation was hurriedly concluded. She heard it was a woman's voice speaking; she knew from Mr Sangster's gentle, wondering tone it was *that* woman again. How long are you going to be able to keep *this* up? she stood asking him in her head: it's not always going to be so honey sweet, God help you both.

Nanny Filbert hadn't clapped eyes on her own husband since one evening in 1943 when he'd gone out to buy some tobacco at the corner shop. He might as well have dropped off the edge of the world. Maybe it had come of marrying a younger man, she couldn't be sure. Anyway, Rob might as well never have been. And this precious woman will change too, she told herself every time the telephone rang; just watch what happens once you've carried your darling Miss Seymour-that-was over the threshold and she starts to think she owns the place and knows every single thing about what's what.

Nanny Filbert became a different person during the weeks of the wooing, and although she could still remember quite distinctly that afternoon sitting out on the top lawn and the car creaking up the driveway—all the colours dazzling, the sun spinning off the car's black roof—what happened after that, between the telephone calls which were like terrible rents and tears in those still, Surrey mornings and afternoons, it was greyness to her: like rolling a cloud over and over in her hand, or feeling for an object in the cold darkness beneath water . . .

The boathouse she remembered, and the long, narrow punt on its rope slithering in and out on the river tide, and an obscene thought which would come into her mind, which was the sort of thing Rob would have said to her as a joke. Long before the thing happened, she knew the boardwalk planks were soft and worn, and that Mr Sangster had warned her about letting Jonathan go too close: but being able to rescue Jonathan from the peril and showing his father that no one could love him as she did, no one could make the 'right atmosphere' except Nanny Filbert—that had been the only way she could

151

see to saving the situation in those impossible times. When she turned her head only momentarily and allowed fate to do its work—the same fate that had brought the car creaking up the driveway with that painted woman inside—she only meant it to be a couple of seconds. But Jonathan's screaming seemed to paralyse her, freeze the life inside her, and it was only when the screaming became frantic that she seemed to have any power to move her limbs at all.

When she saw in her head what happened after that, she was watching another person: someone reaching into the cold water, trying to hold the arms—watching the hands waving, the face staring up, the wide-open eyes seeing back from their future.

None of it was how she'd planned it to be. Jonathan didn't live, to be cared for by her for ever; Mr Sangster went out of his mind, and only Miss Seymour was able to make contact with the man, in his terrible mad despair. The police came, and they didn't commend her for her bravery in trying to rescue the child, for her years of careful love, for her skill in giving a 'right atmosphere' to the beautiful house and its lawns rolling down to the river. The police officers stabbed the air with their index fingers and they made telephone calls to all the towns she'd ever worked in, and they referred to her among themselves as 'Filbert' without the saving grace of a 'Nanny' or even a 'Mrs'. It was the woman who came to see her, Miss Seymour, not Mr Sangster himself: she wanted the woman to rail and rant at her, but she wouldn't, she seemed determined not to give her a reason for hating her. But she hated her all the more: for what she'd threatened to do, to turn 'The Spinney' into a modern home with a father and mother and a child and probably another child, like a pledge to the marriage—a surety—and no room in their neat, bright, tidy, up-to-date arrangements for a uniformed nanny who'd been the best housekeeper 'The Spinney' could have had. That suddenly hadn't mattered any more: that while Mr Sangster was in Africa and India and everywhere else she'd exceeded her duties and managed the place as if she'd been born to the rôle. She'd hated the woman for wanting to cancel out the past, the best part of the past that didn't have to do with Rob, who'd decided to never come back. She'd been so sure she knew how things should be managed in the future:

how the woman could be made not to count, just to disappear, how Rob had disappeared. But the child's staring eyes—while she looked helplessly down—she was conscious they were seeing from another time, and it hadn't to do with this muddled, troubled, haywire one. Jonathan was safe behind glass, and it was the house and garden that were disappearing, and the blue sky, till they would only be a speck in the far, out-travelled distance.

Nanny Filbert twitched awake.

It took her a few seconds to realise she was in another person's house, Mrs Mason's, and the house was in another shire, not in Surrey, not in the jurisdiction of that police force which had lent her such an unsympathetic ear.

She looked down and noticed, vaguely, smoke rising from between her legs. She blinked and leaned forward and saw the cigarette lying smouldering on the hearthrug.

She knew exactly how to deal with it and did so with that same 'brisk efficiency' her earliest references always used to speak of. When she'd stopped the smoke she tried standing still for a few moments; she closed her eyes and felt the room—her own room—spinning round her. She leaned her hand out and touched the mantelpiece. She opened her eyes again: she saw the familiar furniture, the bed with the brass rails, the chintz armchair, the table, the upright mahogany chair with the balloon back, the dancing diagonals of fleur-de-lis on the walls.

Carefully she eased herself back down into the armchair and felt the comfortable reassuring pressure of its arms on her fleshy hips. In another ten or fifteen minutes Susan would be awake.

Nanny Filbert glanced down at the burn-hole in the rug. Mrs Mason was bound to notice, of course: that woman missed nothing. She would try leaving the armchair a few inches further forward, with the drape of the covers just concealing the mark.

It had been a less perilous accident than some: that was Nanny Filbert's consolation. She would tackle Mrs Mason with just a little bit more assurance for knowing that.

Susan was smothered in this place, Nanny Filbert also knew. Mrs Mason with that smooth-as-cream Jean Metcalfe voice thought only *she* had the right to understand the child. It was

153

almost one position too many now for Nanny Filbert: she'd passed the extreme point of loving—first Rob, and then Jonathan Sangster. Sometimes she wondered—not sure how her confused, bedevilled mind was reaching to such profundities—do we experience one, or two, most intense interludes of feeling in our lives: and then, after that, everything else is a sort of third-best, we enter a shadow life where things can never be so real again?

This, she knew, was like a retirement: a premature running-down. Partly it was her, and partly it was the times she lived in. Rob wouldn't have gone off if the War hadn't been making holes in everyone's life. If the War hadn't finished and if Mr Sangster hadn't had to come home, he wouldn't have found Miss Seymour waiting for him, and none of the other things would have happened either.

You live in your own history and also in other people's, the one that's made by great events. But it was too bamboozling to think about. When she went up to the church, the Reverend Aldred tried to tell his congregation in their fancy Sunday hats that Almighty God was in charge and everything was following a pattern.

Again Nanny Filbert glanced down at the burn-hole. Mrs Mason was bound to notice, with her all-seeing eye. 'Oh, Nanny Filbert, whatever has happened?' If she needs me enough, thought Nanny Filbert, then she won't complain too much. Such an unimportant thing, but Nanny Filbert had seen from her experience in different households how the most trivial matters can escalate out of all proportion.

Outside, through the glass, she heard a wood-pigeon chortling. Some days all Surrey had seemed to resound with their throaty cries. They'd always seemed to mean safety, the familiar, things never changing, life like the stories she kept for Jonathan's bedtime and knew by heart.

Jonathan Sangster wouldn't have grown up, not in the sense that mattered: she would always have lived there, and not Miss Seymour, and Mr Sangster would have continued to come home from abroad on his leave, lean and tanned and so distinguished-looking. But the War had ended, too soon, and nothing in the long time since had ever been one tiny hundredth part as perfect as her once-upon-a-time.

'Tilly, dear, have a haystack cake.'

Miss Vane offered the girl the tray of sponge drop-cakes.

'I couldn't resist baking them. I should really have been continuing with my novel. Somehow the "mood" didn't seem right. Do you know what I mean? And I thought, after all *this* is life too, isn't it, baking cakes, and behaving well at "life", now that might be an art—mightn't it, Tilly, don't you think? And I thought . . .'

Tilly accepts a cake. They're still warm, and the girl seems to recognise the taste from a time before. Miss Vane indicates that she should sit down at the table on a stool, and she does so.

'I heard on the news that Mr Hemingway may have been killed in a plane crash in Africa. What a sad loss to literature that would be.'

Tilly sits and eats her cake modestly, watching the crumbs fall. Miss Vane doesn't correct her about the crumbs, as do one or two of the girl's other hostesses in the town. She likes Tilly to feel at home here, in her kitchen, because she does quite genuinely have a surfeit of good feelings. She is happy for the girl to come in and out, and just at this moment it matters not a whit to her who knows and what they think. This is the most positive and attractive face of the multi-faceted Miss Meredith Vane. She doesn't even attempt to remove the half-completed letter to Rose Macaulay she was penning (always in the hope of receiving a fuller reply than she ever receives) on the table-top, where momentarily the elbow of Tilly's cardigan brushes against it.

'Gulls! Do you hear them, Tilly? It's not the gulls here I'm remembering, you know, although I've been here so long. It's Cornwall I see—with my mind's eye, Tilly—where my family used to take its holidays, when I was a gel. It's strange, isn't it, your mind leaps to then—across time, and what's here and now.'

Miss Vane reached for her notepad to write down the remark. Then she noticed she was scribbling it on the back page of her cookery book. She smiled.

'Life and memory. Living, what sustains us. Food for our bodies, experience and memory for our thoughts. Imagination, dreams.'

She sighed.

'Perhaps I should try a few more currants next time? What do you say, Tilly?'

Tilly Moscombe said nothing.

'Of course I'm interested in trying something of that kind. Stream of—what's it called? Conciseness? Ha-ha-ha. No, not that. Dash it, I can't remember. Was it—yes, unconsciousness? I do believe it was. Stream-of-unconsciousness. Maybe I should be thinking of that. Maybe that is what the English Novel is waiting for. Do you really think so, Tilly?'

★

man lady, trousers, cake, kitchen, fire, cup, tea, book, cake, fire, Tilly tell, man lady, trousers, photo-graph, lady smile, dress, finger, hay-stack cake, cup, tea, book, friends, you, me, friends Tilly, hair, car-digan, friends Tilly, kitchen, fire, Sand-mouth, cake, cup, tea, Tilly tell, photo-graph, lady smile, dress, Tilly tell, please, man lady, trousers, friend, friends, you, me, Tilly tell, secrets, you me, friends Tilly, Tilly tell, kitchen, fire, secrets . . .

★

Cordelia Whitgift Spencer. Born 1892, in St Albans. Younger daughter of Mr and Mrs Edward Crawfurd. Educated at St Margaret's School, Totnes. Married 1917 Captain Ronald Spencer, Coldstream Guards. Husband invalided in final year of war; thereafter engaged by Lowe and Hinshelwood, London, Tea and Coffee Importers, as overseas company representative. Lived variously in Kenya, Ceylon and Darjeeling. Widowed in 1947. One daughter, Marcia.

The sight of Mrs Spencer—walking along the sea front or posting a letter in the box in Heywards Road—was enough to set the more active imaginations of Sandmouth hypothesising. She was very rarely seen *with* anyone, so there were few people to work on for information.

Colonial, obviously, that they knew. The face confirmed it, even wrapped in a headscarf and with a raincoat collar pulled up to the chin. The skin always acquires a leathery look, however pale it remains: even with the best precautions taken, the sun and heat will lure veins up to the surface and there they stay. Her clothes had a 'vulnerable' look to them: probably it had less to do with their outdated style than with the washed and faded colours and the lightweight materials. In autumn and winter the patterns of printed cotton frocks were visible under the hems of her overcoat or mackintosh. Her experience of hot climates still meant that she confined physical movements to the minimum, and Sandmouth was intrigued at first (before it later became indifferent) by what might have been her lazy insouciance. Mrs Spencer acquired the reputation of being 'uppity', but it was based on ignorance of her character: people merely presumed from the externals . . .

For her part Mrs Spencer didn't find Sandmouth a very friendly community of souls. After six years she still felt she was considered an outsider. Maybe it would have been the same anywhere else? Sandmouth had been a random choice. Her married daughter lived thirty miles or so along the coast and Mrs Spencer had thought she was placing herself relatively close by but also a discreet distance away. In the end she suspected that her proximity and distance, the two combined, were an irritation to her daughter and her enterprising businessman husband: she wasn't close enough for babysitting purposes and the car journey used up time as well as petrol (not that they couldn't afford it, but Mrs Spencer in widowhood was conscious of such matters), and she knew she wasn't far enough away for her daughter's conscience to be clear on her account—hence the obligatory festive and bank-holiday visits.

They all managed to keep up the pretence of courtesy at least. Her son-in-law, she believed, found her rather amusing as a representative of a breed. She wasn't sure what Roy's exact employment was; she never had been. Marcia wouldn't offer to discuss the subject, and she didn't like to raise it with her. Trade, something in the wholesale supply line, possibly to do with cars. They lived comfortably, in a mock-Jacobean house (detached) on an avenue with verges and alder trees, and there was always a shiny new car parked on the half-moon of gravel driveway outside. Mrs Spencer sometimes felt there was too much comfort, and she found it difficult to adjust to after her own more spartan experiences abroad: gas fires always turned full up, thick Axminster carpets, velvet curtains and pelmets

157

which held the cigarette smoke, brightly-hued and heavily-varnished oils on the walls of swan-upping and Berkshire riverside pubs on sunny days, the cloying, medicated smell of disinfectant in the downstairs bathroom. Of course she must be glad that Marcia was settled, but the mystery pertaining to the source of so much enveloping comfort kept her from greater contentment with the situation.

Her daughter Marcia had become very much more confident and practical with the years and with her altered condition, and Mrs Spencer's responses were a little mixed. Now there were three children, and Marcia seemed to cope more ably with the trio than her mother had with one. Recently she'd begun to advise her mother about little things, the details of her life, as if she too required the patient, tolerant attention which a child demanded.

'You shouldn't wear these dresses, Mother, they're far too skimpy. Get something warmer. You really don't look as if you're eating enough—'

Mrs Spencer didn't care to say that new dresses cost money, quite a lot, and she didn't have enough at her disposal to re-equip herself merely for a change of climate. In the summer she was quite all right; for the rest of the year she had her old overcoat and her even older mackintosh. (Thankfully for her dignity, her daughter had never volunteered to buy her any of the hypothetical new dresses she referred to every time they met.) And as for her thinness, Mrs Spencer esteemed eating sparely a moral virtue as well as an economic necessity: it upset her to see the wastage that passed for modern living in her daughter's house, rations still a threat while plates were taken away from the table with only half the food eaten and the rest picked at and promptly emptied into the dustbin. Her daughter and grandchildren had inherited her own fastidious, modest appetite, only they didn't seem to see that.

Mrs Spencer's visits were only once every three weeks or so. For the rest of the time she was on her own.

'Why don't you play bridge?' Marcia would ask. 'You used to. Get out and meet people. Do you go to the W.I.?'

Mrs Spencer did neither, but she had her housework, and she read the newspaper every day, and she listened to the radio, and she had her tapestry, and occasionally she received short letters from people she'd known in the far past and to whom she wrote back her lengthier replies.

Her past was the problem. In Kenya and India she had forever been hearing or reading the names of women who'd been at school with her or men her brother had known at his school and at Cambridge: there had been so many coincidences and she had quite accepted them as a normal part of her life. Ronnie too came to be haunted by his past, by encounters with fellow-soldiers he'd trained with or served with. Abroad, *they* were all KARs, DOs, ADCs, subahdars or jemadars, ICS or IPS or IFS while Ronnie and Cordelia Spencer, being trade, lived as blockwallahs (everyone had to incredulously ask for the information to be repeated) and thereto had attached the critical problem: they'd found they now belonged to a quite separate social class from the others.

Efforts had been made to include the Spencers, but the results were disastrous: at parties other guests they were introduced to stared at them as if they had blue faces or some terrible contagion, and for the rest of the afternoon or evening would steer a very wide berth round them both. Mrs Spencer's women acquaintances had seemed in perpetual obeisance to their husbands' opinions, and were gradually persuaded to drop the couple socially; Ronnie's former colleagues appeared to have two standards of behaviour, a laugh-a-minute jocularity when there was only Ronnie and themselves and a po-faced, aloof grandeur when they were all brought together in a roomful of people.

More and more Mrs Spencer had begun to see the flaws in people. The women kowtowed too much, to everyone, and gave themselves impossible airs with servants which they could hardly sustain, and lived a quite philistine existence. Their menfolk had little to say that was worth hearing, and the purpose of *their* existence seemed to be to constantly discriminate between people by means of every inbuilt prejudice possible; more than that, they drank too much and expelled too much air without apologising for it.

Also (which complicated the matter), Mrs Spencer had begun to suspect—disloyally?—that some of Ronnie's friends had turned out to be second-raters, or even third- or fourth-raters in the Civil List social pyramid, and their consciousness of it was

159

why they were so obsessed by class and colour in such pettily minuscule detail. Some of them hadn't been to the right schools, and they were living on past regimental glories that had little to do with their own efforts; their accents started to waver after the third or fourth drink—'chotapegs' were two fingers of whisky, 'burrapegs' three—and their faces lost their hoity-toity expressions.

The Spencers were given less and less opportunity to mix with that questionable company, however. In addition, the Europeans and natives Ronnie did business with seemed to suspect them of social ambition, and the couple never felt very comfortable in *their* circles either. The wives concentrated too much on what the Kenya 'stiffs' and the Civil Service maharanees and the Willingdon Club set did, and spoke unendingly of their children; if the hen-house mentality was bad, the men were worse with their sleazy suburban golf-clubhouse manners and conversation, their antipathy for the country they lived in and the scurrilous comments they made about its people.

During all her years abroad, Mrs Spencer often felt that, one way or the other, the two of them had fallen upon the Yahoos.

Mrs Spencer rented her house in Sandmouth. Marcia and Roy were forever telling her she should buy somewhere of her own, put her money into bricks and mortar.

She wasn't sure that she could afford the upkeep on a house, in the unlikely event of her managing the initial outlay. The accountants at Lowe and Hinshelwood had behaved rather oddly since Ronnie's death, as had the rest of the firm: she had the impression they were actually expecting her to feel *grateful* for every payment of the widow's pension that came to her, as if she received it in default of her husband, like cold charity. But even in his lifetime they'd shown signs of stinginess, penny-pinching. Ronnie had sometimes told her he wasn't sure he shouldn't have stayed on in the services; after the first War, though, he'd just wanted to get out, to stand on his own two feet (his walking wasn't affected by the injury, which had caught him in the back), to make what he felt then—after seeing the carnage of Flanders—was a more honest living. Maybe he'd started to doubt the working practices of Lowe and Hinshelwood in the places where they went, although he hadn't confessed his doubts to her; indeed he discussed the details of his job less and less with her, he seemed to become almost lackadaisical about it, latterly he was punctual to the minute about stopping work at the end of every afternoon.

Of course the memories of green England had sustained her in their foreign climes, as they sustained everyone. A cousin sent out three-month-old copies of *Country Life* and the *Illustrated London News* and every Christmas a calendar arrived with photographs of quintessential English scenes, a little the worse for wear after its long journey. Occasionally they came back on leave, to coincide with Marcia's summer holiday from school, and they were vague and approximate when people questioned them about how they were enjoying the life. They always found England rather dirtier and more discontented than they remembered it, but when they were back under baking skies and saw the mad dogs rolling their eyes and foaming at the chops under the noonday sun they forgot again about the lesser aspects of English life and concentrated on what was enduring and uplifting about it. They listened to records of Elgar and Bax which Mrs Spencer bought in London, and to others by Ambrose and Jack Buchanan. Very few books came out—they were expensive after carriage—but Mrs Spencer tried to borrow where she could, and read *David Copperfield* and *Sinister Street* once a year without fail, hearing the din of the rookery and the silvery pealing of Oxford bells.

She'd returned for good from India in its Independence Year, looking for that England. She discovered it was still to be found, in the glories of ancient cathedral cities and nestling in the lea of the chalky South Downs or Devon's red clay undulations or the damp green wooded hills of Shropshire. There had been no reason why she should have chosen Sandmouth rather than anywhere else: she had seen a photograph in a *Country Life* years ago—showing the beach and Britannia Terrace and a Saint George's flag fluttering on a pole—and she remembered it when she was studying the railway maps during one slightly fraught Easter of hospitality in Marcia and Roy's house. In some respects it proved to be rather a characterless town when she walked about it for the first time: there was no maypole, no bell-hung morris dancers and prancing pagan 'obby-'oss, very few thatched cottages or houses with half-timbering to speak of. But the atmosphere seemed to make no particular demands on her that first day; several of the locals smiled politely, and she was left alone. 'The Wishing Well' (rather than Lavezzoli's) seemed to be exactly the sort of tea-shop she was expecting to find, based on an old memory of 'The Maids of Honour' out at Richmond. She'd drunk the tea and not once thought of its method of manufacture, all the various processes of its journey from an Indian hillside to an Indian Tree cup and saucer in a tea-room in a quiet, English backwater town.

Her house belonged to a terrace of other houses in Grenfell Road. They were simply laid out inside and had been reliably built at the end of the third George's reign (the mad king, she occasionally reminded herself); their only pretension or extravagance was a dainty little ironwork portico over each of the seven front doors. The houses had small gardens front and rear, which could be easily kept tidy. Mrs Spencer's neighbours were middle-aged or elderly; two pairs were retired, there was a woman (widowed) with a draper's shop and a spinster called Miss Templeton who worked in the millinery department in Crockers', there was a self-employed house-painter and his wife, and a tetchy, North Country master of sports from Minster Court who shared his rooms with two black labradors. The terrace was of middling status in the town, architecturally and socially: it looked virtuous and decent, as if there was no opportunity for secrets to dwell *here*. Mrs Spencer's house was the only one that was let. Her landlord was a family man of about Roy's age, who had inherited a commodious bungalow on one of the Avenues from his mother. He was a little lax in the matter of repairs; to be fair, although he was prompter in the matter of rent, the sums involved were no more than the house truly merited. Even so, it consumed about two-fifths of Mrs Spencer's total monthly pension payment from Lowe and Hinshelwood, and the proportion was causing her unease.

Marcia suspected boredom was her mother's problem. She had no especially vivid memories of India and England to complicate *her* life: she took events pretty much as she found them, and anyway she hadn't a minute to spare in her waking hours.

'The newspaper doesn't last you all day, though, does it?'
'I read it quite carefully. I like to be thorough—'
'I don't think you need to know *all* that's going on.'
'Knowing a little helps.'
'It'll happen if you know about it or not, Mother.'
'One should be *prepared*, Marcia—'
'Frankly it isn't here or there to me. Still, you've got your own mind—'
'*You* have a family, Marcia dear.'
'Do you see your old friends?'
'I write letters.'
'You should go off and see them, Mother.'
'Well, maybe.'
Maybe nothing, Marcia thought—knowing her mother.

Mrs Spencer had started to find conversation with her neighbours difficult, just as it had started to seem less 'natural' than it ought to have been with her daughter. So many of her thoughts and ideas and even the images she used in speech were drawn from the countries where she'd lived, and when she attempted to weave them into her conversation she was conscious of other people's faces stiffening and their eyes catching other movements behind her. She tried to make what she said sound as interesting as she could, but it still wasn't able to hold them. She began to think people must find her rather tiresome to listen to, boring even. The countries themselves had been *important* to Britain, one way or another: even if the Spencers' own personal contribution hadn't been.

When she'd first come to Sandmouth and settled into her house, her neighbours had invited her in for tea and she would begin the conversation by talking about the beverage itself: they'd smiled patiently as if she was being rather silly, making a topic out of what they never gave a thought to. 'Very interesting, I'm sure,' or something like it was the general response, but Mrs Spencer knew it was emptying the word 'interesting' of all its meaning. People presumed she'd been intimate with the pukka governmental side of things, the colonial service with its flamboyant, halcyon social life, and they made certain deductions on the strength of that: she'd learned from harsh lessons to correct their impressions as little as possible, to save them from disappointment, not to weary

163

them with stories about the plantation compounds and the inferior quality of life there. And in the process she felt she was somehow cheating on herself, and on Ronnie too, as if she was trying to upgrade them when she'd always had so little respect for those other husbands and wives who'd believed themselves obliged to give the Spencers the cold shoulder. She remembered details of life in Nairobi or Bombay or Allahabad she'd heard about or read about in *The Statesman*, or occasionally seen for herself, and she tried to make them sound colourful when she re-told them: people smiled patronisingly at her accounts, as if the experience had been quaint and rather ridiculous and most certainly outmoded, not at all how men and women must go about their lives now, in this new England.

Tentative offers were made that she should play bridge, but the only time she'd had the courage to say 'yes' and make up a foursome and had found herself seated at a green baize table eating miniature sardine and egg sandwiches and drinking dreadful tea from the bottom of a caddy, she'd soon discovered to her horror that the conversation was fraught with all manner of interlacing trip-wires, people who knew people who knew people and where had she lived and what was her husband's name, funny that they'd never heard of him, they would ask so-and-so.

Mrs Spencer had stopped playing bridge. 'Patience' was her game now and she laid out the cards listening to Bax recordings on the wind-up gramophone, crackly with the travelling they'd done, the buff cardboard sleeves occasionally revealing a secret occupant, the faded petal of a flower, or a tiny dead insect which had been lured through verandah doors by the lamplight and had mistaken the lush layers of edible cardboard for a refuge.

★

People were always confusing her with Adele Astaire.

'Adele *Adaire*,' she would repeat, pronouncing the surname quite distinctly so that there was no possibility of its being misheard. Faces inevitably fell after she'd corrected the mistake. Questions about 'Fred' would die away on eager lips.

A chance, she was always telling herself, would be a fine thing: given the dumps you were expected to perform in. She'd never even heard of Sandmouth, so—doing as she always did—she had imagined the worst of the Alhambra Theatre. That normally meant it could only be better when you finally got a butchers on it.

As she inspected it just after a late lunch (a leathery omelette at the 'Camelot' Guest House) it proved marginally better than the very worst she had imagined it to be. It smelt of disinfectant, and had two hundred and thirty seats, and four letters were missing from the name above the front doors—all of the 'bra' and an 'r'—so that it read 'Alham   Theat e'. When she made her entrance and asked to see Miss Adaire's dressing-room please, a surly girl told her there wasn't none.

'Who am I sharing with then?' she asked, knowing it was best to get straight to the point and not insist overmuch on your dignity.

'Everyone,' the girl told her.

'I beg your pardon?'

'You want the players' room.'

'*Room*?' she repeated, removing the constraining beaver hat with its too-tight headband.

'You want to change, don't you?' the girl asked her quite indignantly. 'Before you do it?'

The actress gave the girl a haughty Margaret Lockwood look and told her she wished to speak to the manager of the establishment. 'If that isn't troubling you too much.'

The man smelt of mothballs and wore an eye-patch. The hand he offered stung with cold. She immediately thought of a pirate put into cold storage. 'Captain Kydd', she mentally christened him.

He called her 'Miss Astaire'.

'*Adaire*,' she repeated, pronouncing the surname so there was no possibility of him mishearing.

'Oh. You're not—'

'No,' she said quite definitely. 'No, I'm not.'

She asked him, of what precisely did the actors' accommodation consist? Very commodious, he said, and led her up a narrow, dusty staircase to a narrow, dusty corridor. He opened a door. She looked into a long, narrow, very dusty room. It was furnished with a cheval-glass on a stand, a wardrobe rail, a few chairs grouped round a table.

'Dear God,' she said, and withdrew.

'I beg your pardon?'

She shook her head.

'Gives you room to spread yourselves,' the man said. 'There's a sink in the corner. Lav down the corridor.'

She turned away. She led the way down the rickety staircase, like a ship's ladder.

'We've had a troupe of poodles taken up these stairs not so long ago,' the man was telling her. 'What a mess.'

'Really?'

'Ponies are worse.'

'Are they indeed?'

'We've had everyone here, of course.'

'Which famous—'

'Acrobats, jugglers, fire-eaters, panto horses, the lot.'

'Drama,' she said in a loud voice. 'Do you ever give actors and actresses the honour of performing *drama* in your theatre?'

The man moved closer to her. Leerily, she thought . . .

'That's better,' he said. 'I can hear you now.'

'Well?' she asked, pulling her coat tighter about her.

'Gilbert and Sullivan,' he said. 'That's very popular. The amateurs are just as good as if they were getting paid.'

'Yes, I'm sure they are,' she said frostily, and made a mental note to phone London (reversed charges) to check up on the financial arrangements.

'And how many of *them* can you accommodate at once?' she asked.

Captain Kydd moved closer.

'I missed that,' he said.

'How many pirates of Penzance can you get upstairs?'

'Oh, they come dressed up for that.'

Nothing was capable of surprising her any more. Today had proved what she'd suspected about her career for years, that it was in a downward spiral, doomed to plummet with the centrifugal force of a vortex.

Turning her back on the leery Captain Kydd and the awful girl she walked outside into the fresh air. She imagined picking an even worse moment to arrive in the town and being greeted by the sight of men in bandoliers and cummerbunds swaggering through the streets, dragging cutlasses.

'Dear little England,' she said aloud and meant it to sound

bitter. With bloody places like this: it was like getting to the end of the world.

It must have been a mistake, of course, being booked here, and she ought to have been in a flood of tears about it. It was almost too ridiculous to believe, though: that after the years of tours—even the 'ENSA' and 'Maids and Masks' experience during the War—it had taken this particular day to reach rock-bottom.

Ahead of her she noticed a gangling, lopsided girl waddling mechanically down the hilly street, and she sucked in her breath sympathetically. She was reminded of the wizened old man she'd seen shuffling about the garden of a cottage she'd passed on her walk up, as helpless as a drugged tortoise. The girl looked as if she was missing some slates: but she was walking quite quickly.

The actress in her pre-war burberry, trailing the scent of her toilet-water (Max Factor of London, Paris and Hollywood), set off after her. Perhaps what was in her head was the memory of Shakespeare's wise fools. Or maybe she was thinking that, landing in a town of fools, she might as well go the whole hog and sink all the way down.

★

Mrs Trevis started tidying up after her husband.

She always stood at the front window watching him as his head rolled along the top of the hedges of Walnut Avenue. They exchanged a wave as he shut the latch-gate behind him, but he didn't look back after that. She always turned away when he reached the cherry tree in the Turners' front garden.

Her thoughts could turn to supper now, and plan ahead. Two o'clock was her physical low point in the day, and she needed a short respite then; she would lie down on top of the bed for ten minutes or a quarter-of-an-hour, charging her brain to do its work, and when she surfaced again the answer was usually provided: tripe, or mutton stew, or whiting from Beresford's.

The preliminary was the tidying-up.

Today Howard hadn't finished his scrambled eggs. As a rule he didn't eat very much in the middle of the day, but he usually managed to accommodate whatever it was she made. She wondered why he hadn't enjoyed it, if it had been her fault. She

167

knew he liked to keep himself trim, in good shape, and that he didn't care for food to 'lie' in his stomach: that was why he had his walks in the evening, and went off at the week-end on his solitary rambles round Sandmouth. (Several times she had offered to go with him up on to the cliffs, but she knew he was a much quicker walker than she was: she felt she held him back, she defeated the purpose of the outing which was for him to get exercise and fresh air pumped into his lungs after his week closeted in the bank.)

She tasted the egg on the tines of her own fork. It seemed all right: perhaps a little oversalted. She hadn't asked him what was wrong: she should have. She would ask tonight.

She filled the washing-up sink in the kitchen. The hot water had all been used up in the morning, and she sank her hands into cold. It made scraping the egg off a difficult operation, but—as in every other department of her life—Mr Trevis's wife had taught herself to adjust.

She coped.

★

Sometimes Mrs Dick imagined she *did* hear something, rumblings, far beneath the surface of life. The churning of the arterial channels under the hillside.

It was frightening and comforting both together: knowing there was that potential violence of nature there, ready to surge up—and a solace to know that people had lived on top of it for dozens of generations, that they'd been able all this time to live with the knowledge of it in their ordinary, still-water lives.

★

Dear Steve, Just a scribble. Are we still talking, by the way? Couldn't resist this pc. 'Old Crones on Hill Street, c.1934'. What a dump! Adele's been a hoot, unintentionally. She opened a scout fête in the back streets of Salisbury, a sight to be seen. She took off her hat, laid it down on a table, and a couple of ticks later found someone had stuck a 9d label on it. Endless stories about Mona, Madge, Fay, Mary Ellis. She got her cape caught in the door getting on the train at Salisbury. She's making heavy weather of Rattigan, we all are. Jokes are wearing thin, like Thelma Hurd's hair, he says like the bitch he is.

love, Guy.

★

'Dilly Mushroom,' she thought the girl was saying.

'Hello, Dilly. I'm Adele Adaire.'

The girl rolled the words on her tongue, till they lost their shape and any resemblance to the real sound. Their owner felt as if she'd suddenly had something very private stolen from her. Yet *she'd* stolen 'Adele' from a novelette and 'Adaire' had been her mother's maiden name, supplied in the theatrical style with a final distinguishing 'e'.

'Never mind that,' she said. 'You live here, I expect, do you?'

Up close, the girl wasn't wildly odd. And not at all mongoloid, praise the Lord. Her eyes did have a fixed look that some people's take on when they've drunk too much. She held her head in a queer way, and her sense of direction seemed wonky: it was as if she was wanting to walk away from her body. She had good hair, though, and nice hands and a clear complexion. Her face was a little pushed in, but not too badly. It was tragically unfair, not being right 'upstairs'. Everything begins and ends there. If, as they say, you play the hand you're dealt in this life, then Dilly was a non-starter.

'I'm new here, Dilly,' she said. 'A stranger.'

The girl received the word and squeezed and mauled it out of recognition.

'Yes, that's right, dear. I'm an actress. I'm here to perform in a play. You must come to see me.'

The girl looked at her vacantly.

'The play is by Mister Terence Rattigan and is called "Harlequinade",' she explained, settling the folds and pleats of her cape-coat. 'I play an actress playing an actress. It's very confusing!'

She thought the girl was going to career into a lamp-post but, as if she had a sixth sense, she steered clear at the very last second.

'Careful now, Dilly.'

169

The girl moaned something. It put her in mind of 'The Hound of the Baskervilles', which she'd once played along the coast in Eastbourne, with Liam Trope. Trope—with the proverbial luck of the Irish—had been spared all this: he'd gone down in the War, he was outside Fortnums talking to that Celtic bore with the fey brogue, Lisbet O'Mara, and as he blew her a good-bye kiss and stepped off the kerb he disappeared under a red double-decker. Irony of ironies, the bus had 'Depot' written up on its destination board. At least there was a lovely service for him in the actors' church, and she was able to wear her tulle and the black pill-box with the veil, and talking to Max Milligan she was able to fix up a date for a read-through on 'Heartbreak House'. It was an ill wind . . .

'You *must* come, Dilly. And see me. It's a super play.'

Fairly 'super', although she suspected some of the humour was a bit 'in'. A play about theatre people talking about theatre people wasn't the easiest fare to put over. In the West End you could have managed it, and here and there about the provinces. In this place there wasn't really any point in trying, it was a dead duck. The trouble was *they'd* all be dead ducks too, and she hated having to die a death on stage. At least she'd never have done it in front of such a small house. She would damn well give Mewes a piece of her mind when she put that telephone call through to him. If her days were done, he might as well be a man about it and tell her straight out. An end-of-the-pier would be better than this.

'Yes, Dilly,' she said in as sprightly a tone of voice as she could manage and repositioning her beaver hat for greater comfort, 'it's quite an opportunity to be performing in this play.'

Oh, you took what came—rule number one—and you enthused about it and tried to persuade everyone else involved with you that it was manna from heaven. For some reason she found Rattigan's lines hard to learn and lodge in her brain, and she'd dried several times already on the tour: it seemed to her that the looks of alarm on the others' faces were starting to turn to scowls of impatience. It was difficult to wax so enthusiastic about the play when you nightly caused these little panics around you.

If the girl hadn't been simple, she could have made *her* hear

170

the part: presumably she had nowhere else to go, nothing could be of any urgency to her. The thought of going back to the guest house and having to report later to the others depressed her so much she found herself taking the girl's arm and turning her in the direction of the street-plate marked 'The Jubilee Promenade'.

'That sounds perfect. Fresh air, Dilly! I've been cooped up in a ghastly train all morning. Did you know there are four hundred and twelve telegraph poles on the line between here and Salisbury?'

The girl's eyes stared. Adele Adaire thought, if she'd been born normal instead of like this she might even—possibly—have been half-way to pretty. *If* . . . Someone attended to her, obviously, and had given her a nice tortoiseshell hair-clasp, and the cardigan was rather good quality. A filigree brooch like that would have cost you a few pounds.

Carefully, with her fingertips, Adele Adaire lifted back some strands of hair that had blown forward on to the girl's face. Immediately the girl jumped back, as if her fingers had conducted a charge.

'I'm—I'm sorry, Dilly—'

Adele Adaire smiled. How could she have guessed, waking up in Salisbury this morning, in the 'Rydal Mount' Guest House, that she would spend her day confronting the sad fact of her decline in an out-of-season resort she'd never heard of, playing sophisticated Rattigan in the smallest theatre she'd ever seen, convinced she wasn't going to remember her lines, minus the rabbit's foot which must have dropped out of her handbag between here and Salisbury, leered at by a man in an eye-patch (and showing, she'd noticed with revulsion, an unsightly bulge in the front of his trousers), holed up in a guest house called 'Camelot', absolutely gasping for a drink, chatting pleasantries (as if she was squandering her time and bon mots at a cocktail party, pearls before swine) with a defective girl who—Jesus Christ help her—hadn't the simplest God-given capacity to understand her?

★

Howard Trevis's dreams at night are populated by dockland stevedores and good women. The stevedores are burly, sweaty, their shoulders are stickily damp as he runs his eager fingers over their muscles. The good women are those who raised him: an imperious grandmother in regal purple and hair clasps, twin great-aunts in lace collars and long tweed skirts who exude the perfume of lily-of-the-valley toilet water, and his widowed mother who had no alternative but to return to the matriarchal fold. He was brought up to understand that men are the much-vaunted providers but too good to be true because they are also perpetual disappointers: they promise salvation, but somehow always renege on their promises, and consequently women become distrustful and gradually embittered about the chances lost. Forget mystery, forget enslaved enchantment. Suspicion breeds dislike, and men and women finally fall back into nothing less than that primal state of mortal enmity.

He smells the women, who are all still alive, their soap and talcum and toilet water and (from his mother) the once-a-month odour; he hears the sounds they make, silk and satin and shantung rustling, the loud ticking of masculine watches, the rattling of complicated gold bracelets with locks, the businesslike tapping of low heels on the chessboard tiles in the hall. They envelope him with their concern, the women, they never want to let him go, except to another of their sort. But how could he ever have allowed himself to lift a woman's skirt, her underskirt? Maybe he has grown too like them?—his eyes shift as theirs do, he notices the tiny details that make up an exchange between two people, an emotion betrayed in a single gesture of a hand, a momentarily-too-long leaning on a particular word. He wonders if he feels objects—literally, their touch on his skin—in quite the way they do, and he suspects he probably does, that he is as conscious of his body and its workings as they, even the manner in which it's held to the earth, literally, that he has become as cow-sensitive to the weather as them.

In his dreams he relives the years of growing up. He doesn't have for himself their social sureness, their stillness, yet he also knows that *they* know too much to be quite innocent in the world. Yet why should they be innocent, as if they're dwellers in one of those terrible early novels by that woman they sit laughing at, Miss Meredith Vane? They have suffered too much to be as quietly limited as that woman makes out their kind to be. He lacks the household's steadiness, their commitment to goodness: they have overcome the belittling obstacles because they have standards, because as much as possible their outsides and insides match; perhaps for a negative reason they have always committed themselves to the right and true middle-path, because goodness is easier, tidier, it leaves less mess, it lives in orderly rooms with antimacassars and crocheted tray-cloths and neatly pressed netting, it eats up all its food and says thank you and causes no possible harm.

Asleep or awake, he carries the loyalty of his family, and the technical definition of gender is no impediment to that.

In his most tortured, ecstatic dreams he is lying on a dirty floor with his mouth open to receive while a stevedore in working overalls stands over him and delivers an arc of hot piss. Sometimes he's lying on the floor in Mr Braddock's office and the stevedore is standing on his desk with his trousers round his knees and the fountain spurting on to his face . . .

He wakes sometimes, hanging over the edge of the bed, with his mouth open and pyjama jacket unbuttoned and sweat breaking out all over his body. His eyes stare into the darkness.

Behind him, Maureen doesn't move. It makes him suspicious as the dream clears, that she should seem to be noticing nothing.

He gets up, staggering under the load of an iron-hard erection, and blunders out of the room and along the corridor to the bathroom where Maureen always so carefully attends to her ablutions. He switches on the light, blinks helplessly, then opens his pyjama trousers and aims at the lavatory bowl. Hot semen crashes into the porcelain. Sometimes his right hand is too damp and in his haste he misses and then he has to clear up afterwards with wads of toilet paper. Down on his knees he feels like a penitent, grubbing before God. Once he found one of Maureen's used sanitary attachments and discovering it at that moment turned his stomach and he had to sit stooped over the bowl, staring at his own semen runs on the white porcelain.

Maureen never comes looking for him, she lies without stirring until he has finished and has sometimes relieved himself of his dreams a second time. Perhaps that is suspicious too. Living in the matriarchal home he occasionally used to forget to flush the toilet and he knew someone had seen the writhing frog-spawn swimming in the water and wasn't saying anything. He isn't able to believe in the unblemished innocence of women. Hasn't Maureen guessed?

He can see better in the darkness by the time he makes his way back through to the bedroom. His wife is lying with her back turned to him; she is still solid, rigid. He listens for breathing and can never hear it, not the abandoned sort of sleep.

In such respects she is disavowing her innocence, doesn't she realise?

He loses no more sleep over their little deceptions. When he's worked himself into the hollow on his side of the mattress, it only takes seconds for him to lose consciousness again.

In his second phase of sleep he seldom travels the same wayward routes. His sleep is deep and—in retrospect on waking—dreamless. Or perhaps his subconscious has really been saving him—the dreams were too awful to remember?

We live with the safety catches cocked, he knew that. It's the only concession in life this mischievous, flinty-hearted God allows us.

★

Lady de Castellet was Old Money.

That was one of Sandmouth's credal points of social and moral reference, an article of faith. The Misses Vetch in the dairy conceded her condition of grace. The local branch of the grand family had never permitted the blue blood to be diluted or sold cheap. The de Castellets married and bred with equals. Even a rise in the social ladder at that degree would have been noted by the scrupulous Vetch sisters and thought not quite appropriate: as it was, the Sandmouth de Castellets were spared any censure—through the centuries this scion of the noble family had continued true to their ancestors and to their destiny.

Sadly, however, the town's one surviving (only *just* surviving) de Castellet, Lady Sybil, had no heirs: she had never married, and now in the middle years of her seventh decade she was slowly, discreetly dying in the white Georgian dower house that crowned Moscombe Hill, which she had inherited from her maiden Aunt Juliana. So it was that, in vulgar parlance, the Old Money might now be considered 'up for grabs'. De Castellets patently not of this locale were making their weekly pilgrimages down to 'Hallam House': each single clansman or brace of kin attempted to persuade the others that the Sandmouth expeditions were in the nature of sentimental journeys, how glad—but of course sad—they were to be able to get down, etcetera.

Mr Macey opened the door to them and closed it behind them and, for all his unprepossessing 'below stairs' appearance and his local burr which mystified the house's guests, he was canny enough to have tumbled the present company, as if they announced their intentions to him as well as their names when they arrived. 'Take this, my good man,' some of the wives would command, handing him a coat or gloves, and he knew by their manner what the purpose of at least three out of the four couples was, and how easily the guise of friendliness with one another would be disposed of, just to ensure that they got their hands on what they wanted.

At the last count twelve separate parties had presented themselves, all using the pretext of blood. A couple of them had left visiting-cards; 'Mr Everard Whipple and Mrs Whipple (née de Castellet)' and 'Piers A. de C. O'Neill Esquire, Ballydunroe House, Cork Town'. Lady de Castellet had looked at the cards, blankly, and let them fall among the untouched items on her luncheon tray.

The situation was threatening to get out of hand. The telephone would ring, and sometimes the caller would show up in person later, and sometimes not, and the Maceys were left wondering if her Ladyship's slow, protracted death wasn't turning into a social jamboree: when they were just themselves in the kitchen Mrs Macey would tell her husband she felt they were presiding at a lucky-throw hoopla stall. The newspaper in Bournemouth had been 'holding' her Ladyship's obituary for the past eleven weeks, and had now—thankfully—stopped ringing the house to enquire if they could go ahead and print for this week's edition, or would the Maceys please give them 'a likely date' for publication. Her headstone lay under sacking in the caretaker's yard, a certain Mr Selwyn of 'Arbuthnot Antiques' telephoned regularly on Miss Arbuthnot's behalf to offer a free consultation, and Mrs Macey had heard that the two Tierneys were hoping she'd hang on till the first of the summer blooms appeared. (Which, Mrs Macey guessed, cost them less to buy in, but for which they charged at funeral wreath 'winter' rates.) All in all it was becoming a rather ridiculous and distasteful business, everyone only out for themselves, and the Maceys were both ashamed.

If Lady Sybil realised—and no doubt she did—she was being bravely stoical about it all: about dying, and the last-minute jostling for favour. Only she and her lawyers knew positively what the outcome of events must be. That confirmed the Maceys' faith in old-established institutions—none older or more established or more venerable than the Law—and also their trust in the almost mythical allure and power and presiding genius of the Old Money.

*

Penelope Prentice was discussing the afternoon's business with Mrs Lenny from the town. Groceries had to be ordered and delivered; some of the upstairs curtains had to be taken down for cleaning; a man was coming to look at a leaking pipe in the kitchen.

Mrs Prentice inspected the list she had compiled. After her marriage she had chosen to make a methodical person of herself. She liked to write down everything in her own hand. That way the order seemed to be a more ascertainable commodity, somehow more tangible. Otherwise one day's housekeeping was cancelled by the next by the next by the next and there was never any sense of anything worked for and achieved. She needed markers: even a handwritten list sufficed. Above all she needed to believe that her actions had some lasting effect beyond the span of a single day. She thought, maybe it was a common want of women who find themselves in their thirties, secure and given to one particular way of life: it has to do with stemming the flow of time, not presuming that the *possibilities* of your life have all been taken account of. Even the illusion of something lasting has some worth. Permanence and purpose may be too much to hope for, but a tidy mind is a start. In some ways, she would think, I have become a very *impermanent* person.

Mrs Prentice left Mrs Lenny and went upstairs, to the bedroom. She changed out of the dress she was wearing and put on another, grey jersey-wool with a lower neck and full sleeves. She opened the jewellery box and took out her gold link bracelet and the three strings of pearls and fitted them to her wrist and neck. She pulled a pair of shoes from the back of the wardrobe, stepped out of those she had on and wriggled her toes into the good Rayne's pair. She turned in front of the dressing-table mirror to examine the effect: her face was serious and concentrated, she wasn't the sort of person who needed to smile at herself to drum up confidence. She decided she looked as she always did on those Wednesdays when she went out: so, for that reason alone, she was satisfied.

Cosmetic attention always came last. She hurried over it, as if to convince herself that her face—her most personal attribute—had nothing to do with the afternoon to follow. She opened the drawer and took out a lipstick and drew it across her lips. She undid the lid of her talcum box and dabbed at her cheeks and chin in businesslike fashion.

She found her burberry in the wardrobe and put it over her arm, then decided it was unnecessary: the less she took with her—to forget about and leave behind—the better. She lifted down her crocodile handbag. She gave one final glance at the smart, sanguine woman in the oval of mirror on the front of the wardrobe.

Mrs Prentice closed the bedroom door behind her and paused on the gallery to consult her watch. She had a timetable for these days, a kind of mental check-list she operated by. The intention this time was different from the 'Things to be Done' inventory: it was meant to impersonalise the process as much as she could, to make it seem automatic, unthinking.

She made her way downstairs, one hand on the banister as if nothing was remotely untoward. Mrs Lenny was standing in the hall peering at the list of jobs she'd written out.

Mrs Prentice stopped at the console table and, transferring

her bag to the other hand, casually rearranged some of the flowers in the spray.

'I'm going out now, Mrs Lenny.'

The woman turned round. 'Very well, Mrs Prentice.' She gave her employer an admiring once-over from head to toe. 'I'll just do what needs doing, shall I, Mrs Prentice?'

'Yes,' Mrs Prentice replied, managing to sound distracted. 'Do that, please. I won't be back in time to see you before you go.'

'No, Mrs Prentice.'

Mrs Lenny commented on the cheerful weather as she followed in her employer's wake towards the front door.

'Today's Saint George's Day,' Mrs Lenny said.

'Oh.' Mrs Prentice had forgotten Cedric's information; she allowed herself to sound surprised. 'It'd quite slipped my mind, Mrs Lenny.'

She was reminded of the sameness that had taken over her days. Momentarily she faltered, as if realising there was nothing she could do about that: least of all in the way she planned for her Wednesday afternoons.

'Everything's clear, Mrs Lenny?'

'Your list, Mrs Prentice? Oh yes.'

She asks the question every Wednesday or second Wednesday, whenever she can get away, and she receives the same response. Maybe she could walk out for ever and the house would run itself? Cedric would receive his meals on time from someone paid to serve them precisely on the dot. After her training Mrs Lenny would ensure that not more than one day's dust was allowed to settle. The tradesmen would receive their orders and continue to deliver at their appointed times. By reason of her own efficiency over the past four years Mrs Prentice was on the point of making herself dispensable. For a few weeks after she'd gone a little legend might persist, that Mr Prentice's wife had run the house like a ship and worn Charles Creed suits and Mattli dresses and jewellery out of a satin-lined velvet box and, every Wednesday afternoon or second Wednesday afternoon after lunch, she would leave the house and successfully disappear out of the sight and hearing of every vigilant watcher in Sandmouth. Not a very good woman, in God's and the vicar's and the newspapers' final scheme of

178

things, and not a happy woman either: but cleverer than anyone suspected in the very extent and depravity of her treachery.

★

Dear Colin, Remember me? Just a scribble. Couldn't resist this pc. 'Old Duffers on Promenade, c. 1934'. Is that dog lifting a leg? What a hole! Adele—I've told you, remember?—a walking disaster. Her case fell open getting on the train at Hastings. She screams at me not to help her and starts throwing everything back in. Something solid, long and very pink—and not a stick of rock—rolls to the edge of the platform and drops down on to the tracks. Stunned silence from the party. She behaves as if she hasn't noticed, old pro that she is, and slams the case shut. It used to be that Timothy White's was the only place I believed in The Human Condition. Now Hastings Station. Thought of you—why?—as the gravel flew up from the tracks.

love, Guy

★

Why was it everyone had become so concerned for their own safety and security, why had they let selfishness have a free rein? Had the War so unnerved people that they could allow the baser, ignoble elements of all too human nature to take them over?

Mrs Dick would ponder the question but she could never come to any positive conclusions. In the War she had worked and then she had seen the distinctions that used to keep people apart from each other ceasing to matter as they had. (Wasn't it said that Lady de Castellet had shared her London home for one night with two strangers she later discovered were convicts?—one a mild-mannered thief, the other a man who had strangled his fiancée's boyfriend.) She'd never been sure what the ends were which they'd all supposedly had in common: it hadn't been like the First War, when the enemy had been a beast to be slain. At least you *saw* that enemy if you were a fighting man, you saw his eyes, over the top of a mud trench. The Second War was political and idealistic in an abstract way. In one sense *more* people—the ordinary people

179

going about their business—saw the enemy, on its bombing raids: but it was an unintelligible, almost random violence that came to them, which knocked out buildings like teeth or could reduce a High Street, *their* High Street, to just rubble and waste. Then the planes were gone again, and somewhere else in the country men sat in bunkers planning retaliatory raids on vast table-top maps, plotting on radar.

If there hadn't seemed to be a proper 'cause' (the newspapers personalised and trivialised, made joking fun of the raving Hitler and his schoolboy bully gang), there hadn't been any noticeable benefits accruing either. Freedom's worth is only appreciated when it has been lost, and no one had had to liberate the British: maybe freedom today was costed too cheaply? In the First War too many men were killed for their widows and families to believe they had been taken from them for any purpose less than the country's glory; in the Second it was buildings too that were lost, and the gaps they left made a mental landscape—one where hope might have seeded itself, but for the most part hadn't. Many of the holes were still there, because the Government wasn't able to decide what to do with them. They made a dismal scene.

By now most people had fallen back into their old ways, or tried to, but not all of the old ways sufficed. It was also the case that Britannia's minions were looking for ready assurances that the years of wanting and going without had been for some end after all: victory deserves its reward. To some there was no reason why everything should again be how it had been: they were either the ambitious ones or, conversely, those with a surfeit of jealousy but without any saving confidence and belief in themselves. Hearing the word 'freedom' so often spoken persuaded some that they hadn't been wholly free before, and that now they should have some more say in determining the sort of people they were going to be, rather than allowing birth and circumstances to decide it. They were still a minority, though. The characteristic of the majority continued to be its docility: material things, the covetable accessories of life, could provide them with some temporary consolation. But till when . . .?

Mrs Dick didn't know. In Sandmouth they saw less of the world: and yet, she was aware, they were as much a token

180

sampling of the population as anywhere else. She viewed it from a position of advantage, from her kitchen in the comfortable home of a middle to upper middle-class household: but she sensed that the angles of vision were as clear to her here as they would have been anywhere else, that it was on the middle ground that another phase of conflict was preparing itself: in times to come she or her children might find they were caught up in spite of themselves and ranged on the front line.

★

Mrs Tierney's son, it was said by some, had a screw loose; others were of the opinion that he had survived his upbringing with less damage inflicted than might have been expected.

He wasn't altogether 'right', but communities of the Sandmouth sort *can*—in that one respect—be forgiving.

Certainly he had no friends. There was a school of thought that believed his mother, his only (known) flesh and blood, was his own worst enemy. Maybe he was to be pitied. Only . . .

It had something to do with the way he *watched*: watched young girls. Even when they were only a couple of feet away from him, he stared with awe, as if they weren't really present but somewhere else: in the other world of their childhood. When he opened his fingers to exchange money with them, or to offer them a little posy of primroses or anemones, he performed the gesture with great tenderness and tact. And yet . . .

He stood in the window, among the pails of flowers and maidenhair, and stared at Tilly Moscombe as she lolloped past.

His brow creased into folds. He saw an outsized child, in sandals and ankle socks, but she wasn't carrying herself as the others did. She shambled, and —perhaps the thought was in his head—she only made fun of herself and all those others.

His mother spied him watching from the back of the shop. She noisily dipped her hand into the cash box to sort out the silver. Like mother like son, her brow creased into folds, and she seemed—should anyone have been there to see— disturbed.

But the shop was empty of customers: there were only

themselves. Sometimes she would have chosen to shout at him, to take his mind off them, the pretty little girls who caught his eye, turned his head, caused him to think only of them.

The Moscombe girl was different. She saw his anxiety; she saw that he didn't understand. Maybe she suspected what was true enough, that for her son the girl from 'Hallam House' defiled by her existence all those others in the very prime of their loveliness.

*

Lady Sybil de Castellet has been dying for the last eight months. Latterly, after the initial sadness at her imminent parting, the town has been provided with its winter entertainment—and the members of her family have had to live in an almost unbearable state of tension.

She received the doctor's prognostication after she had started to re-read her favourite novel, *Middlemarch*. She bravely continued, not imagining she would progress beyond the first volume. In the event, she not only finished the four volumes, but managed to tackle *Adam Bede*, followed by *The Mill on the Floss*; since then she has completed *Felix Holt* in its entirety, and *Scenes of Clerical Life*. A copy of *Daniel Deronda* now lies beside her bed, with a bookmark inserted two-thirds of the way through its eight hundred pages.

The delay in her death has caused Lady de Castellet to speculate aloud to her bedside vigilantes about just when in life we do in fact start dying. As they view the immediate circumstances, she has formed a sinister attachment to the writings of Saint Paul and to the Book of Common Prayer; she is fond of quoting *sotto voce* the 'Burial of the Dead', 'In the midst of life we are in death' et al . . . She has made the members of her family quite impatient with her cranky theological theory. While she lingers in the breathing state, bills have to be paid on house repairs, items languish in the better class of pawn-shop, and—for the younger parents—school bursars become less gentlemanly with their requests for prompt payment.

The dying woman was previously unaware that the remoter limbs of this branch of the de Castellet family were so fecund in producing further offshoots. Cousins' cousins abound. Her principal visitors ('supplicants', she is astute enough to understand) have been her closest living kin by definition, three male cousins with their wives. Further cousins have appeared from the back woods of Cheshire, Westmorland, Southern Ireland, and—so far to the north—Ross and Cromarty.

In its desperate way the situation is quite amusing, Lady de Castellet accedes to herself. Money is behind it all, but so it ever was and will be, for those born with a silver spoon in their mouths: in the case of these lesser de Castellets, the silver spoon has had to be loaned back from the broker for the occasion, or promptly sold after the birth to pay the hospital bills, or the nanny, or to fund the replacement of the roof-guttering.

Only her brother had the properly improper, time-hallowed de Castellet manner: bluff, gruff, wilful, cavalier, and decadent to the last. Tilly Moscombe was the outcome of a dalliance with his and Lady de Castellet's much younger half-sister Prudence (formerly, Prudence Kavanagh). The child was born three months prematurely in the lavatory of a first class carriage on a train, the 'Cornish Riviera', while Prudence was attempting to escape to St Ives and avoid scandal. Accounts of the birth had begun to assume a Lady Bracknell touch: that is, until Lady de Castellet travelled down to St Ives to see for herself the extent of her niece's deformities. Of course an endless succession of doctors and surgeons were consulted and no expense was spared, but apparently there was nothing that could be done to correct the damage. The infant was the creation of her parents' sin and must bear their punishment all her life. The only solace to them all was that little Elizabeth would never discover how far from grace she had fallen.

Her life expectancy was guessed at about four or five years by so-called experts. The know-alls were duly confused when the child reached her tenth year. Now nearly seven years later the housekeeper told her Elizabeth was healthy, she ate well, walking about the town put colour into her cheeks. Lady de Castellet wondered how much walking was good for the girl: but no purpose was served by confining her here or anywhere else, and she had enough of her brother's go-as-I-please attitude not to be concerned by public opinion on the matter. She had skilfully resisted the advances of the new community do-gooders who'd come calling, beaming at her with their short-sighted intentions as she aloofly received them in the morning-room. About that time she was re-reading the first chapters of *Jane Eyre*, and her resolve had been all the firmer.

Tilly—or Elizabeth, as her aunt preferred to call her—had had nothing in life. Which was why, by a secret amendment to her will performed in the early days of the peace, Lady de Castellet had arranged that approximately half her estate, including property she had inherited from her late bachelor brother and two spinster sisters, was to pass to her niece (unless the said person was to pre-decease her). The worth of the half-share was close to half-a-million pounds; a trust was to be set up and administered by lawyers (and a Harley Street consultant) acting on Lady de Castellet's specific written instructions.

In a sense it wouldn't give Elizabeth any more comfort than she had at present. But Lady de Castellet had witnessed the despair that had overtaken her brother, especially when the young Prudence had dropped the child and fled to the flesh-pot towns of the French Riviera. She hadn't wanted to blame Prudence, even then: she was still in her twenties, she had her looks, and the life of pleasure she was giving herself to would only dull and deaden her senses in the end. She hadn't expected to forgive her brother so easily for the deed and its living after-effect, but she had. The awfulness of what had happened to Elizabeth seemed to turn him inside out: and for the first time in her own rather self-absorbed life she found the gift of compassion and charity in herself.

Every second or third evening in those lost seasons of full health, she and Elizabeth had eaten supper together. They'd had candles on the table. She'd given her decent things to dress up in. Elizabeth would look at her reflection in the silver salver-domes and seem to ponder on the convex truth of what was there.

The girl took in more than people presumed: only it became trapped inside and didn't register as it did with other people, in their expressions and the words they spoke. Elizabeth wouldn't see her future windfall as charity, which was one excellent reason why her elderly aunt should have arranged it so. It fascinated her to know that the money was eventually to pass to someone uncorrupted by desire: the old money of generations would be purified in a sense, landing by rights with the person who was going to live and die a terrible, mute victim of the family's choice blue blood.

★

'And did I ever tell you about that literary fancy-dress party at Leopold's?' writes Miss Meredith Vane. 'You had to come as a writer, not a character. Writers require more initiative, don't they? There's a thin line between "real" and "fictional", I know, especially in writers: they haven't a clue about themselves, some of them, dreadfully over-the-top, as they wouldn't allow themselves to be with their characters.

'There were some men there. One wore long drooping tweeds and had a pocket filled with little pebbles; he told me he was Virginia Woolf. (Rather bad taste, I thought.) Another told me he was George Eliot, although it was hard to catch the resemblance; he wasn't such a bad-looking young man, and even George Eliot's friends said she had a face like a horse. (Do you think he was confusing her with Georges Sand, who must have been rather prettier if more masculine in her interests? Poor George Eliot was just plain plain! Which reminds me, I read that someone who visited her house said it was furnished in the most execrable taste. Not exactly ascending ducks, but you can imagine what it must have been like, and Victorian too, which is bad enough at its most restrained. George Eliot lived too much in the mind for her own good, I expect.) Of course Marcel Proust was there, looking languorous and appropriately non-Gentile, swooning about with a white buttonhole. I've always imagined him to be rather a—what's the vulgar term?—rather a *prat*! Jane Austen was mooning around too, most untypically given her industrious nature: but rather a plain gel, *that* was quite in keeping. (Apparently dear Miss Austen was a dab hand at apple pies: instructing the cook what to do, at any rate. I wonder if she tried to pass them off as her own, like Mrs Melville here with Sorley's veal-and-ham pie?) Evidently there was a George Gissing, but I wouldn't know what he looked like to save my life. Charles Dickens was pretty unrecognisable; it was only because he was carrying a

185

World's Classics *Great Expectations* under his arm that I did. One of the eighteenth-century lot was there, but I haven't a clue who he was passing himself off as, and I'm not so sure he did either: his breeches weren't properly buttoned up, I couldn't help noticing, so it must have been one of that set. (Very lavatorial. Smollett probably.) Of course Zelda Fitzgerald got in, even though she wasn't dead, but that was cheating; and I think the prop was just an excuse anyway. I don't think Extra Dry sherry was quite her tipple, was it?—unless she wasn't a very fussy woman, but I rather guess that she was, don't you? And I can't believe even tragic Zelda flirted to that extent. There was an Oscar Wilde, but that was another excuse, I think: he came with, not Lord Alfred, but with a very lazily-got-up E. M. Forster (he loudly told me he was), who was distinctly conceited and pompous. (Didn't Forster think quite highly of himself, as all old dons do?) . . .'

★

Dear Jack, Just a scribble. Couldn't resist this pc. 'Lord and Lady Shagwell taking the air, c. 1934'. Drinking, as usual. Staying with my girl-friend, Adele Adaire, at the Right Hard Inn, Upper Pewsey. Guess who I met in Salisbury? Trevor!! Went to the quaintest tea-room we could find. Kept his hat on. He was being very Mildred Pearce, with little Tallulah rumblings. Then a huge hairy spider appeared from nowhere and chose to walk across the tablecloth. T. of course behaved like the perfect queen he is—threw up his hands in horror and shrieked, 'Oh my *God*!' Young waitress full of apologies. 'Well, I never did.' She apologises and copes, wiping perspiration from her forehead. Tea-room in turmoil, T.'s flung himself back against the wall. More apologies from waitress. 'And now, gentlemen, if you'll excuse me—I'll just go and—pull myself together.' T. hears, screams with laughter.

Rattigan's a farty, middle-aged bore, isn't he? Didn't you say you'd met him at someone's party?

love, Guy

★

'I presumed you'd attended to it.'
    'I thought—*you*—'

186

'Why *me*?'

'No,' the Headmaster said. 'It was a misunderstanding.'

'Didn't you order him a taxi?'

'*I* didn't—'

'He didn't deserve one anyway.'

'Well, that's not really the point, dear.'

'Isn't it?'

Mrs Symington-Berry looked daggers at her husband.

Several seconds of silence followed.

'Maybe—maybe—' The Headmaster stalled.

'Maybe what?' his wife demanded.

'Maybe Harry—I mean Blake—drove him back to the station. Or he's going to.'

'He's not still on the loose *here*, is he?' Mrs Symington-Berry asked with a horrified expression. 'Ye gods!'

The Headmaster smiled, faintly. 'Ye gods' was one of his favourites among the expressions his wife used. It came from a world to which he hadn't belonged: which he would never properly belong to, although he had the charge of those who were bound to join it automatically, who had already been proposed for membership of the club. Often he envied the boys for what they took for granted.

'What are *you* smiling at?'

'Oh. Nothing, dear.' Mr Symington-Berry immediately straightened his mouth.

'It's just been a farce, today.'

'I—I wouldn't worry about it,' he said.

'I'm not. It's *your* problem,' his wife said dismissively. 'I couldn't care less. After what *I*'ve been through.'

'Yes, dear.'

'The gloves are ruined. Mrs Patten'll have to work wonders with the coat. There are grass stains all down the front.'

'It was most unfortunate.'

'That horror. For all I know he did it deliberately.'

'I don't think—'

'Just to make a fool of me.'

Mrs Symington-Berry's jaw locked into place.

'He should be reported,' she said after a dark silence.

'Who to, my dear?'

'To *whom*.'

'To whom,' the Headmaster repeated.

'For heaven's sake, it's simple grammar, Philip.'

'I'm sorry, dear. You had a better education than me.'

'Than *I*.'

'Than I,' the Headmaster repeated.

'Well, don't start all that again. About how you've missed out.'

'I'm sorry.'

'It's not *my* fault if you did.'

'I didn't say it was, dear.'

'But you make me feel I've had something *you* haven't.'

'Well—I suppose, dear—you have.'

'But we're in the same boat now, aren't we?'

She made it sound like an accusation.

'Well—well, that's one way of putting it, I dare say.'

'I dare say nothing. We *are*!'

The Headmaster realised it was not proving to be even one of his wife's middling days, even though he'd presumed the worst of it to be over. He also realised he was giving in to her rather more than he was accustomed to doing. School functions tended to knock the stuffing out of him; he felt the presence of the parents intimidating him rather than doing what he knew it should, confirming his professional success and status. They reminded him of the responsibility he now had to the growing community of the school, which went beyond the accident of having sixty boys as paying guests in a house that he and his wife happened to own. Or perhaps he'd never properly had total faith in the person he purported to be? Whenever he felt the pricks of conscience about his university degree or its non-existence, the problem seemed to centre itself in his study; it was almost an abstraction, which didn't have to do with actual people. The parents—mothers in their finery and the fathers in professional pinstripes or easy in tailored tweeds that indicated an attitude and tradition he would never naturally have—invariably unsettled him. On public days he also lost the capacity to think of answers to give back to Lavinia: she seemed to belong to *their* ranks as much as she did to him. Inevitably on these days he felt cornered, and most uncomfortably alone.

★

Mrs Lenny watches from the drawing-room window as Mrs Prentice in her grey dress and no jacket or hat walks down the sloping driveway, past the banks of laurels, and out on to Hill Street.

Mrs Prentice has never said where she goes on these Wednesday afternoons. Perhaps it's to have tea at the Clarence Hotel or 'The Wishing Well'. She has asked her daughter Denise if *she* has seen her, but Denise has little patience for the Prentices and their doings. People like Mrs Prentice (Mrs Lenny has served in various persons' employ) receive a lot of letters, which suggests to her a lot of friends: maybe one of her old schoolfriends meets her, or one of the cousins who sometimes ring up. Mrs Lenny has no reason to suspect any worse of her than that. There's no atmosphere of something 'wrong' about 'The Laurels' as she's sometimes felt with houses she's worked in: you recognise that straight away, it's as if the curtains hang stiffer and the flowers wilt sooner because of it. (Denise laughed out loud when she told her once, a cold laugh like a scoff—'Mum,' she said, 'you're going soft in the head.') But Mrs Lenny liked to think she'd learned a thing or two, that she hadn't paddled up the Channel on a tea-biscuit.

Also, she liked working for elegant women, even though they might be more demanding—niggling—about the smaller details: more particular, more fastidious. It gave her work more worth when they noticed tiny things. Mrs Prentice was quite grand-ish and also quite practical, at one and the same time. Mrs Lenny suspected she'd had to do quite a bit of work herself in her old life, before she married. She'd lived up-country, Winchester-way. Occasionally relations called, in battered shooting-brakes, and gun-dogs jumped out the back and ran demented all over the lawn; the women and men wore similarly unflattering tweeds, and everything was loud ha-ha laughs and whistles to the dogs until they'd had their tea and gone. They belonged to the life she'd come from, and it satisfied Mrs Lenny to discover that much: it allowed you to know where you stood with people, what was what. Of course she fell to wondering about the marriage more than once in a while: Mr Prentice was at least twenty years older than his wife. She had fine, race-horse looks—but, unlike her cousins, wasn't 'horsey' to look at, quite the opposite—while her husband might have been not at all bad-looking once, but he'd started to

189

stoop a little now and his hair was grey and thinning. It was what some women looked for, of course: a husband who was like a father, solid, secure, rather set in his ways. He was quite well-to-do, which was another thing to be said in his favour, but no one could claim that the bargain was all hers: he had a smart, pretty wife, well-connected, who never seemed to be at a loose end as some women gave you the impression, although there were days when she did seem more distracted than on others, distracted and remote.

Mrs Lenny fully intended staying on here as long as she could. Since the War, people of a certain kind had started cutting down, they hadn't all gone back to their old habits: now it was the people with the new money and money always coming in, like the Pargiters up at the 'Rectory', who were trying to take on the old ways and make them seem their own. But Mrs Pargiter, the mother, was supposed to be a tartar in the house and more niggardly than the most tight-fisted woman *she'd* ever had to work for.

Mrs Lenny now considered herself part of those old ways and—theoretically—had pride in her own position as well as those of her employers. She knew things were a bit more complicated than they appeared to be: *Mr* Prentice's background was less clear to her than his wife's and his ability to buy his wife new dresses and pieces of jewellery every so often distinguished him from any of her previous employers. Also, her pride and satisfaction were occasionally subject to 'influences', when it wavered just a little. They had been dull years since the War in many ways, even though everyone had started out trying to enjoy themselves again: it was the go-getters who showed you that you didn't have to 'do without' all the time. In some households she'd heard about—the Fieldings', for instance, and the Lavezzolis' and the Pargiters' of course—there had never been any trouble with the rations and making-do. Someone like Norman Pargiter wasn't anybody's man and he'd shown Sandmouth you didn't need to go to the right school and have tweedy relatives with complexions the colour of beetroot to be able to live in a house like the 'Old Rectory'. Their lives had colour of a different kind, literally: he drove a white car and his mother—so it was said—had some American clothes for best in sunny, summer-bright tones.

At least she was working for Mrs Prentice, though: she had the background but she didn't look like the women of her age-group who came in the shooting-brakes with the steamed-up windows and muddy running-boards. She had her hair cut smartly and she wore neat suits and she didn't depend on the company of other professional wives in the town.

To Mrs Lenny that independence was wholly admirable. She didn't see anything suspicious about Mr Prentice's wife's choosing to hold herself apart. She didn't see anything suspect in her own thinking: her allying herself with the old ways and also admitting to herself Mrs Prentice's fascination because she seemed to belong somewhere mid-point between the old-traditional and the brand-new. Maybe it was because she herself couldn't decide that she lived through every day with her rather blurred notions of money and class (just after the War it hadn't been so important, all that mattered was having fun); she believed she served the old order while she knew quite well that Mrs Prentice was even more complex than her husband—a kind of maverick, a woman who didn't meekly accept the rules and conventions of her kind, who seemed now to need to spend more time than she ever used to inside her own head.

*

The white Lagonda swung between the gateposts at the end of the 'Old Rectory' 's grand driveway and out on to the Sand-mouth road.

The engine throbbed and the chrome radiator grille and bulbous front wings seemed to rive the air and leave it sighing. The car had the mystique of some great white sea bird floating through the streets. Children would run after it, businessmen looking through the windows secretly coveted it, the old men walking on the esplanade admired its grace and their eyes filled with rare tenderness. When it was parked teenage boys rubbed a hand along its white flanks or caressed the emblem on top of the radiator grille. Teenage girls and young women imagined riding low in those white leather bucket seats. Older women envied Pargiter his car and its comfort, but knew the dangers of travelling with a single man.

When he would marry and whom was a gossiping matter.

191

(There wasn't any doubt that he *must* marry eventually. There was no reason why not, if he wasn't out-and-out handsome his looks were fair-ish and nothing to be ashamed of.) The gossip had reached Pargiter's ears too: there was very little that didn't. He also knew that it was only a question of time—and applied thought—before a younger Mrs Pargiter was established up at the 'Rectory', alongside his mother.

It was difficult for him now even to look into the driving-mirror without seeing in it the fate of an unmarried man. The prospect of 'who' and 'when' was behind most of the remarks his mother addressed to him in the course of a day: the subject was referred to indirectly, because after one particularly heated exchange of views on a certain young woman's suitability as a spouse an understanding was reached between the two of them that the issue would only be broached when the situation was deemed 'serious' enough.

Grudgingly he'd had to admit to himself that his mother's instincts had been correct on that occasion, and that he wasn't always able to appraise women as cannily and shrewdly as he took the measure of his business colleagues. Maybe he'd improved since then. He had a premonition that the issue was going to have to be broached again soon, and he knew that his mother knew from the Sandmouth tittle-tattle.

She was called Gloria Barlow; she lived at home with her family in the best area of Bournemouth. He hadn't even had to chase after her, they seemed to be thrown together, it was as if their paths had been meant to cross. Her father—like him—was in the construction business, but called himself a 'property developer'; he had a reach of half the south coast, from Weymouth to Hove. The family—father, mother, two daughters, two sons—were Jewish: the gossip principally had to do with that fact, not with the Barlows' wealth.

Gloria Barlow wasn't the sort of girl he'd originally had in mind for the vacant situation of 'Mrs Norman Pargiter'. He'd presumed it would be filled by someone from old stock, who had been brought up in the old ways: it wasn't going to matter to him if there wasn't much money, so long as there was plenty of what couldn't be undone—manners, good taste, a good accent, an instinct for what was fit and proper. Looks would be an advantage, but not a prerequisite: set against the rest, it was comparative. In his mind's eye he'd always imagined someone dark-haired, slim, thin-faced with high cheekbones, green or grey eyes, long fingers and slender wrists, speaking in a slightly drawly accent that had doors opening for you and people turning round to see who was speaking.

In contrast to all of which he had settled on whom he had. Gloria Barlow had dyed blonde hair and was a little plump, from what he could see through her clothes, which he hadn't yet requested her to remove. (And which probably wouldn't be removed until their wedding night, so he hoped in his more dispassionate moments.) Her fingers lacked length, she had thick wrists and sturdy ankles, but her eyes were a delightful cornflower blue. She wore a lot of jewellery, so there was little he was required to give her in that line. She had been educated at an expensive boarding school, but her early years in Golders Green and her Jewish nasal twang had proved to have a more lasting influence than the compulsory elocution lessons she'd told him about.

What appealed to him about her more than anything else was a sort of innocence, which could include little forgivable vanities like wanting to dye her hair. When she told him about herself, she did so in a completely open, quite guileless, breathless, schoolgirlish way. Hair dyes apart (they were borrowed from her mother's collection), she seemed to lack worldliness. She wasn't stricken by the difference between her early years in much more modest circumstances and the cushioned life she now led on Branksome cliffs. When he was with her, in his favourite outfit of double-breasted Simpson's blazer and pleated charcoal flannels and hand-made suede shoes, he tried to imagine that he was a dapper third brother to her, and it appeared to do the trick: it kept his own thoughts pure, and it made her want to treat him as someone close to her own age, nineteen, with the same interests and enthusiasms as hers.

Mr Barlow was welcoming, as was his wife; the sister and the two elder brothers were less at their ease with him but didn't show him any marked hostility either. He drove over to the house with its green-tiled roof every Sunday; he stayed to have tea with the family on the glassed-in sun-terrace. Beforehand he and Gloria went walking about Branksome with the two Borzoi's and a clipped and ribboned black French poodle. Gloria dressed in a white fur jacket if it was chilly, in a white cashmere cardigan and Hollywood-style Hermès headscarf if temperate. Pargiter enjoyed when she produced crumbly biscuits out of her pockets and made the over-bred dogs stand on their hind-legs and beg. He liked listening for her hearty laughs, he liked the cheerful rattle of her gold charm bracelet, he liked the trace of French perfume he caught every time she turned her head to see where the dogs had gone.

He could have bought these things for her: perfume, charms, bracelets, headscarves, dogs. Because his money wasn't what impressed her—she seemed to have no real sense of its value—he presumed that it was himself she cared for: the first time in his life that his company position and his money *hadn't* had a bearing on his relationship with anyone.

She didn't ever refer to his white Lagonda as she waved him off from the front terrace. (Her swarthy brothers, who wore formal suits for tea, affected not to notice it, but he knew they did.) She trilled when he phoned to tell her he was safe home in Sandmouth and he heard the gold charms on her bracelet rattling; he felt he could have listened to the two sounds all evening, and he conveniently forgot that in the morning he would be back behind his desk first thing, entertaining certainly highly unethical practices to ensure that Copplestone's and he both remained top-dog.

Having to continue under the name 'Copplestone's' irked him. In another six months he would suggest an alteration to something 'neutral' like 'The Sandmouth Construction Company Limited'. He discussed his own business affairs only very guardedly with Gloria's father; he wasn't sure if Barlow suspected he was a bit of a young innocent in a man's world. Barlow's empire was building all the time, but Pargiter wanted to keep Copplestone's independence in the meantime. He was gradually buying more shares from Archibald Copplestone's widow as she discovered the pleasures of the casinos in Deauville and Biarritz, and he wanted to have a tidy stock first before he got down to discussing mergers.

Gloria was her father's favourite child. Louis Barlow wished only for what would be best for *her*; at the same time he was cautious about disapproving of any of her enthusiasms. Pargiter believed his full acceptance into the household was, if not a dead cert (what ever was?), a very favourable odds-on bet, and he was staking hard on it. Even if Barlow Senior was tempted to under-estimate him at the moment, he probably realised what his full potential would be in time.

Bizarrely, the tough, unprincipled, knife-sharp Pargiter sometimes felt that Barlow might become the father—a very Jewish, very rich father—he'd wanted and missed having all his adult life.

★

'Ruins, dear,' the actress said, pointing with a gloved hand towards the archaeologists' dig. 'I think Mortimer Wheeler looks such a distinguished man, don't you? A bit of the actor about *him*, too, of course.'

She piloted the girl past the protective ropes.

'It just looks like a midden to me, Dilly. Do you think anybody *really* knows? They say it's important we find out about our past, don't they? In history, I mean. To know where we're going to. Watch out, dear!' she warned, reaching forward. 'We don't want you falling in, for heaven's sake!'

They passed on. They had the rest of the town to see, and couldn't spend their time dwelling on the past.

'You must show me where you live,' the actress said. 'Where your folks stay.'

She wondered if that couthie term was quite suitable. She tried to be adaptable with people: all of us, she liked to say, are social actors and actresses. (And now in these times more than ever, she had the impression.)

'What a steep hill, Dilly, however do you manage it? I feel I'm quite winded.'

The girl continued walking and the actress had to quicken her step to keep up. She could have let her go, of course: would it really have mattered? But more than anything else in her life what she feared was loneliness, having no one and being seen to have no one: if she was to be friendless in Sandmouth, she knew that this time she might finally go under without trace.

★

Guy Pennicote had business to attend to at the bank.

195

It chanced that Howard Trevis was standing in for young Wainwright. He noticed the stranger enter; he lowered his eyes and sensed the man taking his place behind the customer he was attending to.

'I think you've given me too many notes, Mr Trevis,' he was told by Miss Phelps.

'Have I, Miss Phelps?'

'Please check again.'

He re-counted, conscious of her eyes on him and the man's gaze travelling over her shoulder.

'Quite right, Miss Phelps. My apologies. I don't know how that happened.'

'I'm sure you're normally quite correct, Mr Trevis. Otherwise why should this bank continue to employ you?'

Trevis returned a chilly smile.

'It's very honest of you, I'm sure, Miss Phelps.'

'Well, I should hope so.' She sounded quite indignant.

'I'm sorry, I didn't—'

'It's not a matter of my *choosing* to be honest or not, Mr Trevis, you quite misunderstand.'

Trevis stammered. 'I—I—'

'I was brought up to behave in a certain way, Mr Trevis. My responses and my instincts are the same.'

'Like Pavlov's dog,' Pennicote said over Miss Phelps's shoulder.

The lady turned round sharply and conferred one of her famous stares on the man. The handsome stranger didn't flinch.

Miss Phelps walked off in high dudgeon. Pennicote smiled at Trevis and lifted his eyebrows. Trevis saw and forgot the possible unpleasantness resulting for him. He smiled, with a certain reserve.

'Can I help you, sir?'

'Yes. Yes, I'm sure you can,' Pennicote said.

Trevis thought he smiled and hesitated fractionally too long for the remark to mean quite what it purported to mean. He lowered his eyes to the counter and felt his face flaming.

Pennicote pushed some notes and a postal order under the grille.

'Singles, please.'

Trevis watched the fingers and took care that his own didn't make contact.

'Tough birds, those old dames, eh?' Pennicote leaned his elbow on the counter. 'Can't make your job very easy.'

'Usually I'm in the office,' Trevis said. 'I'm spared it, you see.'

'Same old faces?'

'Mostly, yes.'

Trevis tried concentrating on adding the figures.

'Trouble is,' Pennicote said, 'you never have the money when you're young. Then, when you're like that old bat, you've got it but you're too old to enjoy it.'

Trevis smiled at the disrespect in the words.

'Single notes, sir?'

'If you'd be so kind.'

Trevis thumbed through the notes clumsily. Then he handed them across.

'Suppose I should count these and tell you they're not enough, shouldn't I?' Pennicote laughed. 'Must try to think up ways of getting a bit extra, mustn't I?'

Trevis smiled and felt his eyes turning glassy.

'Glad you don't have *me* as a customer?' Pennicote asked.

There was a pause. Trevis read it as meaning the man wanted to hear an answer.

'I don't think I would say that.'

He hoped the words sounded of a general application.

'Sir,' he added, looking full-square into Pennicote's face.

Underneath the counter he was conscious of himself stiffening, alarmingly. He shifted his balance from one foot to the other.

Pennicote's mouth widened to a matinée-star's smile. Trevis didn't think he'd ever spoken to a handsomer man in the line of duty, and probably wouldn't have another chance like it however long he stayed in Sandmouth.

The stranger didn't seem eager to depart.

'You—you don't come from these parts, sir?'

'No. I'm an actor. Peripatetic.' He said it in a fol-de-rol voice. Trevis smiled.

'Are you at the theatre? Appearing there?'

'I have that good fortune. I don't expect it's *this* place's good fortune anyroads—'

'Mr Trevis?'

A face was looking over Pennicote's shoulder: Mrs Armitage's.

'I'm sorry?' Trevis said.

'I haven't much time today. I should be grateful if you would serve me.'

'Another of the good ladies requiring your servicing,' Pennicote said. He stood back and performed a mock bow. Trevis watched his profile and felt his cock harden against the back of the counter.

'You *are* a popular chap, aren't you?' Pennicote said, and walked off.

The rest of Trevis's shift passed in a kind of joyful daze. Several times he swelled to an erection. It was a delicious sensation as he pushed forward and rubbed his groin on the wood. Once he thought he was going to come and quickly debated if he should allow himself.

Thereupon Miss Phelps reappeared. He heard her barking from the door. She'd mislaid a glove, had anybody seen it?

The moment for a climax was gone, and much of the delirium. Not all, though: Trevis wondered if he could ever replace Wainwright again and not have the memory of the man like Montgomery Clift filling him like a sudden sickness and seeming to throb a hole in his best Bradford cloth trousers.

*

Beneath the golden head might lie other, further layers of—as yet—undiscovered time.

The area has yielded many older remains, accidentally turned up over the years by ploughs and horses' hooves and workers' spades. Among those was the skeleton of a young woman from the Bronze Age: only when an attempt was made to remove the bones from the clay was it discovered that her head had been neatly severed from her body, and the find became an even grislier one than it had at first appeared. The woman lay on her front with her hands held behind her back: once her wrists must have been bound, by some rope or hemp that had rotted away to nothing.

If the 'how' was guessable (beheaded by an axe), the 'why' was lost. Many questions suggested themselves. Had the victim been a traitor, or an unfaithful wife, or a brazen flirt, or merely one of the chosen ones, selected to do the will of the priests of the gods? Might she have volunteered herself, believing she did a noble good? Was she the sacrifice meant to win from the all-seeing, all-powerful ones the prosperity and safe-keeping of her people? Had her death brought that vantage and security to them? Were further sacrifices offered, as gestures of gratitude?—or else in expiation, to appease the gods for some inexplicable anger that had cast the tribe into disfavour?

There used to be a story that Thomas Hardy had found the inspiration for his 'skimmity-ride' in the town's annals from the century before last: the straw effigies of two adulterers were strapped to a sledge and dragged at speed through the streets by the lovers' masked, howling, unforgiving neighbours.

In 1937, one bright and breezy Monday washday morning, a housewife in Town's End Lane rose early and, using the vegetable knife out of the drawer in the kitchen table, calmly proceeded to slit the throats of her snoring husband and their three sleeping children.

No reason was ever alighted on why she should have committed such an outrage on human decency. The woman was unnatural, and base beyond words. A London newspaper called her a 'modern-day Medea'.

The beheaded girl with her arms bound by nothing is kept under glass, in a town a couple of dozen miles from Sand-mouth.

The Dicks once took their children to see it. Mrs Dick bought a postcard of it and she finds it this afternoon as she searches through a drawer for a telephone bill she has to pay.

She takes it out and looks at it. She wonders what the girl had to suffer for, if there was strictly a reason—or was religion to blame, sticking its nose into human affairs where it didn't, and doesn't, belong?

Doctor Dick's wife smiles. Gods are only man-made; men *choose* to scourge themselves as they do.

Or maybe the girl broke some tribal law, or some taboo. Pity her, then, that her instincts were made for another age and she was born a couple of millennia too soon. Perhaps her body lusted after another man of the tribe than her husband. (Or a woman even?)

Mrs Dick has another fancy as she stands at the bureau in her sitting-room, supposedly looking for a telephone bill she has mislaid. An imprudent fancy that the woman was a rebel: for some reason, or maybe for no reason, she decided she didn't want to carry on doing the things women were expected to do. She wasn't going to accept a ritual simply because other generations had, just accept it and not think about it.

Maybe her hut had been a particularly dirty and unkempt one. And the trouble came, as it always does, when other people objected. Maybe *she* didn't care, but it was the others who compelled her to care. Could keeping—or *not* keeping—a slovenly home have merited a punishment of that kind? Quite possibly. An act of disobedience like that might have been considered tantamount to murder: it was a forward thrust with the point of a blade at the collective morale, and a most insidious enemy. She would have been told she was a danger, to others and to herself, she wasn't right in the head and there was no hope of curing her.

Maybe. Mrs Dick returns the postcard to the back of the drawer. She finds the telephone bill, quartered over. She must have pushed it away, not conscious of what she was doing.

She shakes her head. Maybe she's losing her touch, losing the thread. All is not quite as it was. She wonders if she should be compunctious on that account, contrite: or mightn't it rather be a cause for private joy and celebration?

★

In Mrs Prentice's bedroom Mrs Lenny finds the dress she's looking for—the label says 'Susan Small'—and she stands in front of the wardrobe's oval mirror holding it against herself. She pirouettes, as actresses in films do.

She returns the dress to the rail. Quickly she sorts through the other dresses hanging from their wooden yokes. Every few weeks another one appears, two sometimes. Today there's nothing new to arrest her attention.

She opens the jewellery box on the dressing-table. She takes out a thick, silver filigree bangle and passes it over her wrist. The opal ring is too tight for her fingers. She unties her apron strings and throws it behind her on to the bed, then she picks up the four strings of pearls; she undoes the catch at the back and places the pearls round her neck, then fastens the clasp. She gently fingers the four rows of pearls, how she's seen women in films do it to show their anxiety or their powers of conniving design.

The watch in the box reminds her of the time. She carefully removes the pearls and the bangle and lays them in the box just as she found them. She closes the lid.

She picks her apron up off the beige satin bedspread. She eyes the bed in a worldly way and tries to imagine—vaguely—what might go on there at the end of an evening. She's seen the nightdresses and stroked them in the drawer where they're laid. She can imagine it of Mrs Prentice but not of her husband. Although you never can tell, still waters run the deepest and all that . . .

It's a beautiful room. Sometimes Denise at home looks at her with a proud look and she doesn't know where she got it from (there's more than the awkward age to blame): how can you do it, she's asking her, waiting on *them*? The job's not all like that, though: and the Wednesdays when Mrs Prentice is away are better than the other days, she can let herself go a bit then. She can work at her own pace; she has the house to herself for three hours, and her imagination makes the time fly. She drinks tea in the drawing-room, from one of the cups in the china-cabinet. She just sits in the silence and breathes in the wax polish and the flowery smells and lets the sunshine warm her, like a cat. It's only for a quarter-of-an-hour, but they're the sweetest fifteen minutes of her week, almost worth battling through the thousands of others to get to and call her own.

★

'Did you take the Major back to the station, Harry—Mr Blake, I mean?'

'No, sir.'

'No?'

'Was I supposed to, sir?'

201

'I—I thought— Who took him, then?'

'Dunno, sir. Dunno *what* happened to him. Just went off.'

'Oh. Oh, I see.'

'Should I have, sir? You didn't say. And Mrs S-B didn't give me no orders about it.'

'No?'

'Orders is orders from her. So I didn't think—'

'It's all right, Harry. I expect everything has sorted itself out by now. Somehow.'

★

The white Lagonda stopped in a lay-by beneath some trees. About a hundred yards away were the first houses you passed driving into Sandmouth.

Norman Pargiter undid the chrome buttons on the front of his blazer and turned on the wireless set in the walnut dashboard. A woman was giving instructions on how to clean silver. He lit a cigarette and listened for a few minutes. He leaned back in the seat to ease the bunched stiffness in his trousers. He felt a damp surge of anticipation and looked down at the cloth to inspect for damage.

The woman spoke very properly, in clear, confident boarding-school educated 'county' vowels. She advised on dips of solution and how to make your own polishing wax. Pargiter felt another little spurt of dampness and shifted about in the seat till he was more comfortable.

He heard her approach, heels stabbing on the tarmacadam. Through the sagging branches of the trees he had his first view of her. She always looked smart, slim, cool as could be. Attractive. She might have been walking out of a photograph in a magazine. Nice legs, nice hair. They would have looked good together, if anyone could have seen them. Maybe it was a clumsy arrangement, picking her up like this, but it gave him this minute or so to watch her: their rendezvous required a faintly sinister, definitely illicit feel which put him properly 'into the mood' as he relaxed on the white leather.

Mrs Prentice smiled—a cold, narrow smile—as she watched the driver through the reflections on the windscreen. She walked spryly. In the middle of the afternoon there were usually few cars about, but if ever one did pass she pointedly ignored it and continued walking as if she was simply out for a clearing breath of fresh air in her finery.

Without a word she got into the front seat and pulled the door shut behind her. She leaned into the back and laid her handbag on the seat. Looking through the shadow-dappled windscreen, up at the sky, she tried to empty her mind. Tried.

Pargiter turned on the ignition, the engine growled to life, and off they drove.

★

Cordelia Spencer walked upstairs towards millinery. She rested for a few moments on the corner in the staircase. Her heart was thumping against the walls of her chest. Sun-spots passed in front of her eyes.

She wished she was at home: at the same time she knew that was the very last place she wanted to be. She needed air to breathe and she didn't get it there, in those small, confining, closeting rooms.

She climbed the last flight of stairs to the second floor. She saw there were a couple of women already inspecting the wares on their stands.

A girl smiled over to her. Rather automatically, Mrs Spencer thought as she smiled back and walked on purposefully.

She heard the head of the department buttering up one of the two customers, easing her into the right mood to commit herself to a purchase.

'No lady's wardrobe is complete without a cloche, madam.'

'Don't you think it's . . .?'

'Yes, madam?'

'Just a little old-fashioned, Miss Templeton?'

'Oh *no*, madam. The cloche is timeless. But it's not everyone who's so discriminating, you see.'

'I'm not so sure, really. My face—'

'Madam has the *French* face, of course.'

'Have I?'

'Oh, yes, madam.'

'I don't know—I just feel—'

The woman sounded much less certain about the virtues of the cloche shape. She distracted attention from herself by indicating the second customer.

'I think—*that* lady—'

'Yes, of course. Will you excuse me for just a few moments, madam?'

Mrs Spencer turned away and cast an eye over the new straw hats perched on their stork's leg stands. Thank goodness the world was coming out of black and grey. All that darkness was like a bad dream.

'Can I help you, madam?' she suddenly found the junior was asking at her shoulder.

'Oh. No. No, thank you. I'm just—looking round.'

She watched the girl as she walked off, hands demurely folded in front of her. She thought the briefest look was exchanged between the head of the department and her underling.

The hat came off the stand quite easily when Mrs Spencer reached across. She turned towards a mirror and carefully placed it on her head. She adjusted the angle of the brim.

She'd gone out on the *Viceroy of India* the first time with boxes of hats from Herbert Johnson. Everyone had warned her to be very, very careful with the sun. Ronnie had smiled indulgently at the pile of boxes as they travelled over: later, off the boat, his smiles had become more anxious as the nature of their future life was revealed to them. In the end she'd only had the heart to use two of the hats, one for her everyday life and another to wear on her more and more infrequent visits to those friends she could still persuade to see her.

The hat she was wearing now hadn't the style and swank of any of the ones she'd bought in such girlish anticipation of what was coming to her. It might have been made for a mayor's wife.

'*Very* smart, madam!'

Mrs Spencer spun round. The head of the department reached her hands forward and deftly, surely, removed the hat with the outstretched tips of her fingers.

'Is it for a garden party, madam?' she asked, looking inside the crown as if she was searching for a hatter's label or a price and not for signs of damage.

'I thought—I thought it looked rather—'

'Rather chi-chi? Oh, yes. All our hats—'

'—fetching—'

'These come quite expensive, madam. I feel I should warn you.'

'Yes.'

'Very nice, though,' the woman said, replacing the hat on the stand. 'Madam likes hats?'

'Yes. Yes, I do.'

'I thought I had seen madam here before. Several times. Am I right?'

Mrs Spencer heard the serrated edge in the woman's voice.

'Madam should tell us what she is looking for and we will strive to oblige. Meanwhile—' The woman flashed a look at the assistant. '—meanwhile I'm sure Miss Willis in my absence will advise madam on any purchase she might want to make.'

Miss Willis came forward on cue. Mrs Spencer found it hard to smile at her. She knew quite well when she was being put in her place. She'd had all her life with poor Ronnie to tell her that. She hadn't thought it was going to happen here too.

She hadn't come to Sandmouth to flaunt herself, she explained to herself for the n-th time as she walked round the island of hats in the middle of the room: only to lead a decent, respectable life and not to feel she was a certain sort of person because she'd lived where she had, married to a decent, loving husband who'd done one job of work and not another. She didn't want revenge for her life on the tea-slopes.

It was still hard to find her level, though. Now people either talked about India, *that* India, and nothing else—the 'Koi-Hai' life, jackal-hunting, the Tollygunge Club set, polo at the Calcutta Race Course with the heaven-born, the Simla seasons—otherwise they just weren't interested, they wanted to forget about it, the sun had risen and set. If she'd announced when she came that she'd also lived in Kenya and, briefly, Tanganyika, people wouldn't have presumed so much of her and then let her see the disappointment working on their faces. Without meaning to, it was as if she'd miscalculated every move in her life since the day she decided to accept the Wickhams' invitation to their midsummer party, where it was she set eyes on Ronnie, who was only there because his escort's intended young man had a summer cold and couldn't come . . .

But Ronnie was also the one saving grace of her life. It was because of Ronnie that she didn't find herself afraid to think of the past. It was such an old-fashioned word, but truly she had never stopped loving him.

It was Ronnie against the rest. Standing in the middle of Crockers' millinery department, shadowed by the grave-faced girl, Cordelia Spencer saw herself as a victim of circumstances: the sacrificial offering of people's combined pride and indifference, unimportant people who shouldn't have mattered but did. And yet, even at this late point of her life, she didn't feel bitterness. She just wished she had a little more money when she saw other people with it, and that they wouldn't read her as if she was a character in a book who had no power of determining her own thoughts and feelings. (When they spoke to her it was as if she only served to confirm all their expectations and prejudices: because she hadn't lived in a government compound, that fact alone decreed how they should treat her.)

Yet—she looked sideways at the girl, who met her gaze without flinching—wasn't that always the way of it? She wasn't a snob, like some of the women in the town. She didn't want to proclaim where she'd lived before she married, whose daughter she'd been, how she was educated, the houses she'd been invited to visit in her early life. To people she knew well—never a great many—she had allowed those things to be offered. Even now, she felt, if she were to let the information slip in the Misses Vetch's dairy then she might find that doors were being suddenly—cautiously—opened to her. But it was enough to damn her and damn Sandmouth that the place hadn't taken to her. Such, she thought, is pride—theirs and mine.

The result was a terrible sameness about some days, which made her despair when she walked along the promenade on her obligatory twice-daily constitutionals and she had the town on one side of her and the open sea and sky on the other. She'd gone home some afternoons and, quite calmly, smashed this plate or that cup—one she especially liked and had taken care of—because it seemed to her on that particular day to have no more reason to exist: it served no purpose in such a dull, routine existence that had no hope to it. (Maybe—she would ponder the question—throwing fine porcelain against the wall was easier than doing an injury to herself?)

In Crockers' millinery department Mrs Spencer looked down and noticed that her fingers were bunched into fists. The knuckles were white.

She walked away from the girl, from the watching supervisor. She had tried their hats on before, and in all probability she would again. She was drawn to them, and it was as if she had no say in the matter.

Now, though, it was only instinct and sound common sense not to arouse any more suspicion than was necessary.

Sometimes she longed to assuage these violent feelings of vexation on something inanimate that *didn't* belong to her: she could have collided with one of the hatstands and toppled it and, like dominoes, they would all have gone falling.

In her perverse and incorrigible way it was because Mrs Spencer valued Crockers' as a refuge and a diversion that she wanted to discredit herself here too. It was a feeling she was darkly conscious of but couldn't get a grasp on to understand. Doing herself down, she saved other people the task: offering herself as a victim, as a person to be disapproved of, she guaranteed that people would treat her in the way they always did eventually, after their initial smiles and expressions of interest, when they realised she was only 'tea' and not Government service.

She did need the refuge, though: she was quite conscious of that, and she couldn't contemplate life in Sandmouth without it. What she wanted was simple enough maybe, and she very dimly perceived what it might be: just a little something to excite, to take her out of herself. It would lift her mind out of her body on a day just like any other, it would give her a momentary elation of height—soaring detachment—in the stillwater flatness of her life of genteel economy in Sandmouth.

★

Betty Messiter was sitting in curlers perusing an article about Anne Gunning when the woman's head was raised wringing-wet out of the basin and swathed in a towel. Mr Gutteridge himself was attending to her.

Mrs Messiter crossed her legs and sucked in her mouth to give her cheeks sharper definition: her observations had taught her that the better class of woman tends to have clearly boned cheeks.

Not that the woman she was watching above the page of the magazine was quite *that* kind. She'd heard her telling Mr Gutteridge she was an actress. It didn't explain why she'd brought in that preposterous Moscombe girl with her; while the hairwashing was in progress the silly lump sat side-saddle on a chair staring at the other clients as if she had no conception of decency and manners. Betty Messiter realised she did not look her best under these conditions: the rollers showed what a narrow brow she had, and made her plucked eyebrows appear too severe and lacking length. She wished her legs weren't so thin, and she hated how the girl seemed to be obsessed by them. You never knew what the girl was thinking or was capable of thinking. Sometimes, when she didn't wriggle and slouch, she might almost have been normal, and you saw the shadow of sense on her face: at other times she was totally uncoordinated, all at sixes and sevens, and it was curious how she made you conscious of your own physical *dis*advantages, not the things you should have been grateful for.

The actress advanced across the room, managing to resemble an eastern sultana in her pink turban instead of the ruddy Poole whelk-seller Betty Messiter felt herself to be when she was steered from the basin to the wall seats. The actress looked round the room with her eyes wide and unseeing, over the heads of the other women rather than looking *at* any of them.

Mrs Messiter turned to another page. '*It is a feminine need to be told that you are loved.*' She tried following the sense of the type on the page. The woman's voice carried across to her, loud and bell-clear.

'All right, Dilly dear?'

Mrs Messiter raised her eyes as the girl mumbled, then spluttered saliva.

'Excellent, dear.'

Mr Gutteridge did the honour of personally combing-out. He was better than any of the girls, but he kept his services for his favourite clients. He always smiled to Mrs Messiter (in the salon, that is), smiled politely but also distantly, as if he could see right through her. He unsettled Mrs Messiter: yet she couldn't have considered taking her custom anywhere else. This was *the* hairdresser's in the vicinity. Even that aloof, faintly supercilious smile conferred its own third-hand gentility and Mrs Messiter could put up with the unease.

There was only one conversation in the room thereafter, and strictly speaking it was a monologue rather than a conversation. The usual little bits and bobs of chatter in all the corners faded away. Mrs Messiter fixed on a photograph of Rock Hudson, under the heading 'Rock's Manly Beauty'.

'I had such a good coiffeur when I was in the films. He was very naughty, the things he used to tell me. He did everyone: Margaret L., Martita, Ann Todd, Constance Cummings. He used to say "Miss Adaire, you knock them all into a cocked hat, you really do". For hair, he meant. Because it was so thick. Of course it's thinned a bit since then. Women so hate being seen like this, don't you find? They somehow think everyone'll forget when they're outside, and you didn't really see that woman's bald spot over there, did you?'

(Betty Messiter flinched and recrossed her legs. She readjusted the height of her magazine.)

'He used to tell me'—the voice dropped to mention the name—'she wouldn't show her bare arms on the screen. Her husband was churchy, you see, and she was so much under his thumb. Of course it all fizzled out for her, but then it *would* if you weren't going to 'show'. It's just like women in hairdresser's, you imagine no one's going to remember you looking like this if they see you in real life, at a party, or in the street even. With actresses, it's a different person in the film, up on the silver screen. Not that I 'showed' much. I read for Anna's part in the Nell Gwyn thing, the woman with the oranges. Terrible tart really, of course, Nell Gwyn I mean: it was all cleaned up, she was like a national heroine the way they'd written it. She was very good in it, Anna, did you see it? Margaret would have played it differently, but she would have been far too young. Women love those wicked ladies of hers, I expect all your customers do. That's who they'd *really* like to be, for a little while at least. I don't mean the whiplashes—'

(Betty Messiter flinched again and felt an uncomfortable rash prickling in an embarrassing spot.)

'I suppose if you worked in a munitions factory or something, it must be difficult, not having it any more. If you had responsibility, I mean. I don't see why it *should* be a man's world, unless God told Moses. Of course, in *your* position it's different.'

Gutteridge laughed respectfully, and asked her why should that be?

'You're—well, not a threat. A man in your job can get a woman's confidence. You're more sensitive than her husband. It's so odd, have you thought about it, how girls and boys are brought up so differently and maybe they're not educated together, and then at some point it's presumed they can get married and set up home together and everything'll be perfect because they're husband and wife. They don't really know the first thing about each other, do they—as people, or as someone of the opposite sex.'

(The last word caused Mrs Messiter to jolt in her seat, how she jolted in her bed at night when cramp took hold of her.)

'Better like us, single and out of it, I say. Don't you agree?'

After a moment's pause Gutteridge spoke through a smile, in the imitation of a BBC accent he reserved for his own customers.

'I don't know if that's a sentiment my wife would agree with.'

Another longer pause followed. Mrs Messiter put down the magazine and picked up another, *Woman's Journal*. The actress's mouth was drawn back into a pained, embarrassed smile and fixed in place: she was taking care to direct her attention on to the daft Moscombe girl.

'Well, I suppose Dilly's spared *that* way, aren't you, dear? How patient you are. Am I boring you terribly, talking with this gentleman?'

'Head just a fraction up, please, madam. That's lovely, thank you.'

'I'm often told I should write my memoirs,' the voice continued, overcoming the embarrassment and catching a second wind. 'I've had so many proposals from men, you see. For marriage. I believe you can pay people to be your "ghost", it all sounds very sinister. I don't think I'm really an Ethel Mannin or Angela Thirkell, though. My education was very— interrupted. Just so long as you can read a script, and you can

210

work out ten per cent of any sum of money, you're all right. But you never know—life's always turning up surprises.'

'Almost finished, Miss Adaire.'

'Even for Dilly, I dare say. I hope life still holds a few surprises for you too, Dilly. It'd be too tedious without them, I think.'

'Coming to Sandmouth, was that a surprise?'

'Oh yes. I think I can say that. I don't think I would ever have expected a booking at the—I've forgotten the name.'

'The Alhambra.'

'Is it?'

'It's seen better days.'

'Well, probably we all have. They'll come again, I dare say. You've got yours planned, I dare say?'

'I'm sorry—?'

'Your better days. The trouble is, we never know when we're living them, do we? I mean, if I'd known when I was called to read Anna's part . . . I've done other things, of course. Just as good. "Mrs Kennedy of Kensington", "Pimlico Secrets".'

Betty Messiter lowered the magazine. She'd been to see 'Mrs Kennedy of Kensington' once when Beryl had come over to Essex to visit. She and her sister had been on friendly speaking terms then: now Mrs Messiter felt they were socially sundered as they must be. Beryl's husband had come back from the War and decided he liked Navy life better than the land: unfortunately he was on the technical side, not in the officer contingent. He was a signals operator, which Mrs Messiter didn't consider an occupation fit to discuss in polite company. She didn't care to seek out opportunities to discuss her own husband's trade connections either, but at least she knew she wouldn't be shamed through a proverbial hole in the floor if the subject should ever be raised.

They'd sat in the picture-house, she and Beryl, watching the film, both of them imagining they were looking at Fred Astaire's sister. 'Adele, what a name!' Beryl had said as the credits rolled up. Even on that point her sister had felt ready to disagree with her: 'Adele' made her think of *Jane Eyre*, her favourite classic, and the little French girl in the nursery, and she considered the name refined and distinguished. Beryl seemed less and less capable of appreciating these things.

'Still, you can't help wondering. I was invited to go to Broadway to do a play. Not the main part and *very* unsympathetic, but you never know.'

Mrs Messiter watched the actress cross her legs.

'The television's the new thing over there. I can do cameo, and that suits the small screen. I've heard interesting things recently, how they're looking for people—'

Betty Messiter almost roasted under the drier, listening to the one-woman performance. She wished for once she'd had slow, clumsy, vulgar Brenda instead of pert Angela, who was so brisk and sure-fingered at the unrolling.

'There you are, Mrs Messiter,' the girl said. 'Bet that gives your husband a treat.'

Mrs Messiter's smile vanished.

'Is he coming for you today?'

'I am expecting him,' she informed the girl in the county voice she kept for best.

The girl leaned across to the window and lifted the netting.

'I don't see him,' she said.

No, well you wouldn't, Mrs Messiter told herself. She'd only allowed him once to park the Hillman outside the window. She preferred that he park just round the corner, in Albert Road, unless the weather was (a Mrs Messiter word) 'contrary'. When it was raining he drove up and down the street; she stood in the doorway when she was finished and waited for him to draw up at the kerb and get out with the golfing umbrella and raise it over her to keep her dry.

Today was clement, and after she'd paid she daintily threw a cobweb-light, lime-green chiffon scarf over her perm to protect it from any puffs of breeze.

'Thank you so much,' she said, returning sixpence change to her purse and leaving the other sixpence as a tip.

'Much obliged,' Angela said, in what sounded to Mrs Messiter a decidedly off-hand tone of voice. Angela with her efficiency rather intimidated her, and she was afraid of not tipping her and tipping well.

She was left to open the door for herself, as usual. It had a tight spring, and her weak wrists had difficulty holding it open. Letting go the handle, she always had to exit quickly before it caught the back folds of her raincoat.

No service again at the door as she was leaving (*some* customers received it) put her into a bad mood. Her smile for Sandmouth as she picked her way along the pavement on her heels was tight and taut. She realised she hadn't checked the condition of her lipstick, as she always did, covertly: the actress talking had distracted her out of her routine. 'I've seen Adele Adaire' she could tell Brian.

She saw him sitting in the car. He'd had to park on the opposite side of the road today. She was annoyed at having to stand on the kerb waiting for cars and bicycles to pass. Her smile wavered. Then the last car drove past, and she ventured on to the road.

Her husband was looking ahead of him, drumming his fingers on the steering wheel, and he failed to see her at first. The passenger door was on the road side, and it was locked when she tugged at the handle. She hammered at the window with her bony knuckles. Her husband jumped, then reached across to unlock the door. She had to pull it open herself, with her left-hand wrist, which she always felt was the weaker of the two.

She glared at her husband, and lowered herself regally on to the seat. The unvarying and silent ritual followed, of storing her handbag at her feet and unknotting the lime-green scarf and folding it over on itself three times. She pulled down the visor and consulted the mirror she'd had Brian glue on its obverse side; expensive cars included them among their appointments as a matter of course, and it seemed to her a necessity rather than a luxury. She always patted the nest of hair very carefully.

Usually Brian commented on how nicely her hair had been done. He did so today.

'That looks very nice.'

Usually his wife agreed, indirectly. This afternoon she chose not to reply.

She pushed at the sun visor. It wouldn't budge, and she had to apply the strength in both wrists. The visor clattered back into place.

Mr Messiter started the engine. His wife attempted to smile, for the sake of anyone who was looking in through the glass and seeing her.

Once round the corner, past the hairdresser's and the last of the shops, she didn't need to smile any more. Her face invariably soured: that was another of the customs of the weekly expedition.

'That tom next door got into the garden again when you were out,' her husband told her.

Really she wasn't wanting to interest herself. She'd been listening to a conversation that had had nothing to do with Sandmouth, or with the normal lives which normal people lived.

But she abhorred the tortoiseshell tom-cat, and always kept the leavings in the tea-pot to aim at it.

'What did it come in for?' she asked, knowing the answer.

'Must have sniffed our Tara,' her husband said.

It was a disgusting animal. Even so, Mrs Messiter jibbed at the uncouth words.

'I wish we didn't have neighbours,' she said. 'Not those ones anyway.'

'It looks as if we're stuck with them—'

'Well, I don't intend putting up with that cat of theirs *any* longer.'

The conversation on the subject always took the same tack. Events never progressed beyond Mrs Messiter's declaring that she refused to tolerate any more of the cat's behaviour and its owners', and 'that was that'. Today, though, she'd had quite enough of the Drews and their wretched cat, even before they'd properly got going on the subject.

'Adele Adaire was in the hairdresser's.'

'What?'

' "*Pardon*".'

' "*Pardon*",' Mr Messiter corrected himself.

'Having her hair washed and set.'

'Fred Astaire's sister? What's *she* doing in Sandmouth?'

Mrs Messiter sighed. 'Adele *Adaire*.'

'Oh.' Her husband realised his mistake. 'I don't know her. Is she like Kay Hammond?'

Silence descended. It lasted till they were turning up into Windmill Road, to reach the bungalows in 'The Wyldnesse' at its other end. Mr Messiter pointed.

'There's old Thingummybob.'

His wife looked in the direction of his finger.

'I don't know anyone called "Thingummybob",' she said grandly.

'The Major chappie. Fitt. He got his leg shot off. He was up at the school.'

Mrs Messiter's eyes focused. It was a day for famous names. Out of the ordinary indeed.

'He looks lost,' Mr Messiter said. 'Or looking for a bird's nest.'

The man was standing in front of a hedge, with his back to the road. Seconds too late Mrs Messiter's husband made out what it was the old man was doing: that he wasn't lost, or searching for a bird's nest. He was relieving himself through a gap in the hedge.

Mrs Messiter noticed too, and her expression turned glacial. She sank her top teeth into her lower lip and averted her head. Her husband looked in the driving-mirror and saw a urine arc shooting through the hedge. He also saw rather more than that, and was astonished that it could grow to such a length on a day of just so-so temperature.

Mrs Messiter passed from a condition of shock to telling herself—with grim satisfaction, mouth pressed tightly shut— that fame is a tainted bauble indeed. Beside her, her husband was silent: not (as his wife presumed) out of affronted decency, but because of the fleshy object he'd glimpsed in the man's hands, which seemed to make a mockery of what was acceptable and which suddenly revealed to him one of the likely reasons why he'd always felt the so-called 'private' side of their marriage was a bit of a let-down, never taking them blissfully 'out of themselves' as he'd once read that it should in an American book of 'clinical psychology' flicked through in a bookshop.

She—the other woman—had never suggested that he was in any way 'lacking'. But that was years ago, and in her arms Mr Messiter had felt himself capable of prodigious feats he would never have achieved with his wife in holy wedlock, if she had ever been so forgetful of herself as to express any interest in his performing them.

★

215

Nanny Filbert and her charge also saw, approaching along the junction with Windmill Road along Linden Road.

Nanny Filbert forgot about the danger to the child's morals, so rapt was she in the memory of her departed Robert.

Susan tugged at her hand.

'Give over, will you?' the voice scolded from on high.

'What's the man doing?'

Good God, Nanny Filbert thought, she probably doesn't know. She never plays with any little boys.

'He's making an exhibition of himself. As your dear mother would say.'

'But what's he doing?'

'He's pulling his plug out, that's what he's doing,' she told the child.

'Why is he?'

'He—he likes to make shapes in the air.'

'Can *I* make them too?'

'Not like that, you can't.'

Nanny Filbert was remembering waking to see her husband—it was a frequent occurrence in those years when he used to come home—standing drunk at the window, relieving himself by moonlight into the little lane that ran up the side of the house. She'd missed that animal coarseness in all the time since.

'Who is he?' Susan asked.

'Who's who?'

'*Him.*'

'Some poor old man. How should *I* know?'

'I thought you might—'

'I'm supposed to recognise him, am I?'

'Does Daddy do that?'

'Not through hedges, I expect. I don't know what your Daddy gets up to with his rubbery bits. I wonder sometimes.'

' "Rubbery bits"?' Susan repeated.

'Never mind.'

She'd missed the coarseness, and she'd missed the sudden shock of his weight landing on top of her and the hot ramrod of flesh lying along her belly. He used to be like a goat some nights. Even when he was roughest with her and she was still only half-awake, she instinctively opened her legs to take him.

216

It was as if the roughness would make her want him more. In the War she never knew when she was going to see him again, and she'd let him do more or less anything he pleased with her. Sometimes he called it 'fucking', and hearing the dirty word only made her readier to let him have what he wanted from her.

'Don't tell your mother you saw him,' said Nanny Filbert, who was smelling different this afternoon from her usual self.

'Why not?'

'She'd go spare, that's why.'

' "Spare"?'

'Old men piddling through hedges.'

The child pronounced the word carefully.

' "P-pidd-ling".'

'Going wee-wee.'

'What's that?'

'You don't know *anything*, do you, Susan? Even with all those books your mummy gives you.'

The child looked confused.

'Waterworks, Susan.'

'Oh.'

It was the only word the mother allowed to describe the business. Nanny Filbert guessed that the mother was bottled up, like gas in a jar.

The thought of 'gas' prompted another thought in Nanny Filbert's far-from-befuddled head. Indeed she felt she was thinking with particular clarity this afternoon. Most illuminating, she decided, the enlightening effects of two drams after lunch.

They passed opposite the spot where the man stood, on the pavement on the other side of the road.

Yes, a little gas would do the trick, and very nicely. It was an old custom in the trade, and Nanny Filbert took a snobbish delight in her professional's knowledge of these things. She believed she descended (metaphorically) from a long and noble tradition of child-watchers: she'd had her training in the 'twenties, when the last of the Victorian and Edwardian battle-axe nannies were still in the game, in the days before those la-di-da agencies had opened up with their look-alike, talk-alike impeccable misses for hire, all theory and no experience. You didn't just have to know how to be firm with children but also how to let *them* know you weren't going to allow them to run your life for you, *they* had to fit in with *you*.

'Don't dawdle!' Nanny Filbert called to the child.

'What's the man doing?'

'Drying off his rubbery bit,' Nanny Filbert said, turning to see. It was like a length of rubber tubing; he made even Robert look small. Unless showing himself stiffened him up.

'Are you turning into a willie-watcher or what?' Nanny Filbert asked.

The child looked up at her, unable to understand the peculiar language she was speaking this afternoon.

'Come on, miss, we can't hang around making an old man happy.'

Gas, the idea was gradually taking hold of Nanny Filbert's mind. All nannies used to do it in olden times, like lacing night-time milk with brandy or rum. Then nanny got her shut-eye too and everyone was happy. Who could say it was the milk that turned a child into a drunkard in later life?—there were lots of frustrations in people's lives to drive them to the demon bottle.

'Where are we going?' Susan asked.

'*You*'re nosey today, aren't you?'

'This isn't the way we came—'

'We hardly ever come into Sandmouth, Susan Mason.'

'—last time—'

'This is *today*, m'lady.'

'Where—'

'To see a friend of mine, if it's any of your business.'

The child mumbled something. The word 'Mummy' was just audible.

'Yes. Well, this leaves the coast clear for your dear old mum as well,' Nanny Filbert said, feeling extravagantly irreverent all of a sudden, recklessly so. 'Not that she'll take advantage of it, will she?' Nanny Filbert asked, talking over the child's head.

'Who is your friend?'

'A man who giveth succour.'

The child laughed: in a high, very silly way, Nanny Filbert thought. But suddenly she too was feeling lighter-headed, not so clear-seeing as she had done earlier: but still collected enough to know this was her opportunity to try what she'd never tried before in Sandmouth.

They continued walking; Nanny Filbert held Susan's hand and steered her.

'Where are we going?'

' "Where are we going, Nanny Filbert—if you please wouldn't mind telling me?" ' The doyenne of Sandmouth nannies shook her head. 'Whatever would your mother say to hear you, Susan?'

The child shrugged.

'Nanny deserves respect.' She gripped the hand tighter. 'Nanny is to be spoken to properly, young miss.'

Nanny Filbert marched along the pavement, brimful of confidence and deceit for the moment. Every time she felt the child dragging, she applied more pull.

'You're—'

'Are you talking to me, Susan?'

'You're hurting—'

'Always say "please" when you're speaking to Nanny. "Please, Nanny—" '

'Please, Nanny Filbert—please—you're hurting my hand—'

'What? That's nonsense, Susan.'

'No, you're—'

'I know, Susan, you're making up stories now. That's naughty.' Nanny Filbert waved a finger. 'Very bad, do you hear? Definitely shows a turn for the worse, I'd say. They'll be stoking up the fires for you—'

With that Nanny Filbert gave the child's arm an especially rough jerk. It caused a shriek, but no one heard: by adroit, skilled timing Nanny Filbert had diverted them both off the broad pavement where Sandmouth went about its business and down a narrow back-lane with high walls and flint cobbles underfoot.

The child cried out with the hurt of the stones through her soles.

'People used to walk about on these and they never grumbled, never said a thing about it.'

'It's sore—'

'If cobbles are all that makes you sore in life, m'lady, you'll be lucky.'

Nanny Filbert heard her voice echoing between the dark walls and she wasn't quite sure what she'd meant by the remark.

'Where are we going?'

' *"Please"*—'

' *"Please"*—where are we going?'

'Curiosity killed the cat.'

Where they were going was the back door of the 'Spirit of Good Hope' Inn. Nanny Filbert stopped outside. She kept her grip on the child's hand while she rapped her knuckles on the old blistered wood.

A bolt was pulled back and the door was slowly opened several inches. A man's stubbly face appeared in the gap.

'Sweet Jesus Mary!'

'Try again.'

'What the hell—?'

'*There*'s a welcome!'

'What're *you* doing here?'

'Come to pay you a visit, of course. What does it look like? Collecting for the Seamen's Mission?'

'Why didn't you tell me?'

'I *did* say. Last time.'

'You've brought the child.'

'Well, your sight's all right, even if your hearing isn't. I said I'd drop in. One Wednesday, remember, when your dear beloved wife's gone off to her mother.'

'But what about—?'

Another sharp jerk was applied to the child's arm.

'Don't go bothering yourself about Susan. I've plans for her!'

The man's eyes widened. ' *"Plans"*?' He sounded aghast.

'You're a milk-sop sex, you men, aren't you? Here, let us in—'

Nanny Filbert pushed against the door with her foot. The kitchen inside had a sweating stone floor and grimy walls with flaking paint the colour of tobacco. The child stared into the gloomy corners. Strands of dust shifted in the draught as the door was closed. A gas bracket on the wall shed a weak white light through the gauze; the flame flickered out of kilter momentarily.

Placing herself between the man and the child, Nanny

220

Filbert stood studying the bracket with most particular attention. Her brow furrowed. She took the child's hand and gave it a squeeze. It might have been a tender gesture, inspired by kindness and conscience: might have been.

'You're not used to this old-fashioned gas, are you, Susan?'

Susan shook her head.

'Pretty, isn't it?'

The child whispered, 'Yes'.

'Do you—do you know how it works, Susan?'

Susan shook her head.

'Would you like me to show you? Since I can't show you at home?'

The child didn't respond. Nanny Filbert gripped her hand tighter.

'Well, Susan, *would* you? Remember, you give Nanny her proper respect from now on. No silly sourpuss stuff with *me*, missy.'

'Yes,' the little girl said despondently.

' "Yes, *please*".'

' "Yes, please".'

'You *would* like to see?'

' "Yes, please",' was repeated with equal despondency.

'Well, now. *That*'s easy done, isn't it?'

Nanny Filbert hesitated before stooping down. In the kitchen, dark as a cave, her knees cracked with a sound like pistol shots; crouching, her breath came to her in short, troubled puffs and the girl smelt its sourness. For a couple of seconds the child and the woman, breathless and orange-faced, looked into each other's eyes. Susan opened *her* eyes as wide as the man had done earlier, staring into the fiery face of Nanny Filbert, now filling the whole space in front of her own face; she peered at its curious geography of tiny speckly veins on the cheeks and the shiny pimples shading the sides of her nose. After tea, being put to bed and having only the lamp-light on top of the chest to see by, she was normally only aware of the straggly grey hairs brushing against her face like an insect's legs as Nanny Filbert straightened the counterpane. Sometimes then her breath would have a smell, like the smell that came out of the bottles which her father kept on the sideboard like a line of sentries, like the smell that came out of the glasses he handed to the guests who came to the house. Was Nanny Filbert really one of their guests too?

The arms held her tight, then she was hovering above the ground and rising, like Jane and Michael Banks in the P.L. Travers books her mother read to her, about Nanny Mary Poppins. She looked down as she floated at Nanny Filbert's knee height—then she was lifted higher. The arms holding her shook and Nanny Filbert seemed to be wobbling.

'Steady on, old girl!' the gruff man said behind them.

Susan thought it was a very odd thing to say: in a funny low voice, that didn't speak the words how she was used to hearing them said. 'Old' and 'girl' didn't belong together, not by any concept of the world she was capable of understanding: she thought he must be referring to *her*, the man.

'Now look, this is how it works,' Nanny Filbert said, taking hold of the little key. 'Like this, you see. You turn it—'

The flame spluttered, it sank to almost nothing. Then the light went out, with a little hiccup. The child smiled at the sound. She continued looking at the bracket in the murky daylight from the one window on the other side of the room.

The flame had left a pleasant odour behind it. Susan sniffed through her nostrils. Then that odour became another one—Nanny Filbert's—and in turn it became another one, stronger and making her eyes start to nip.

'Listen,' Nanny Filbert said. 'Listen, Susan.'

The child felt the touch of the loose, coarse strands of hair on her skin. They were rough like wire, Nanny Filbert was always announcing they were her heart's despair.

'Can you hear, Susan?'

'What're you up to now, you mischievous cow?'

'Can you hear, Susan . . .?'

The child smiled again. The words didn't fit. Over the words she heard the sweet hissing of the gas and smelt it cramming itself into her nose. She felt herself smiling as she watched for the flame to reappear. Nanny Filbert was gently bumping her up and down and singing the words her mother had first taught her, 'Home again, home again, jiggity-jog'. Susan felt how heavy her head was on her shoulders and wondered why she didn't notice more often, and didn't know how she was going to hold it up much longer. And why didn't the flame come

222

back when they were all waiting, where had it gone? 'For Johnny will work for a penny a day,' Nanny Filbert was singing under her sticky breath, 'and Jenny will have a new master.'

The child closed her eyes and the man stepped forward with a lit match.

'Susan?'

She heard Nanny Filbert's voice from the top of a tree, from as far away as Bournemouth, from the bottom of the sea. The flame's heat passed across her face and she was scarcely conscious of it, scarcely conscious at all.

'Nanny's tricks,' Nanny Filbert turned and said to the man, nursing the child in her arms.

'God, you're a sly one. How'll she—?'

'She'll be all right. Won't you, lovey?'

'God help her—'

'It's thirsty work, this.'

'What d'you fancy?'

'Your best tap, landlord.'

'*You're* fussy.'

'Not with you I'm not.'

'What does that mean? You'll take what comes.'

'I should coco.'

'You don't know what's coming yet.'

'I've a good idea.'

'Wishful thinking.'

'Hark at you, then.'

'One thing at a time. This glass do you?'

'Is it clean?'

'Well, *I've* just been drinking out of it. Should be.'

'Doesn't follow. Any road, that's not how you treat a lady.'

'Where's *she*? Been and gone? I must have missed her.'

'Down you go, precious little Miss Mason. What *would* your mother say if she could see you now?'

'Put her through in the public. Or the parlour. Will she . . .?'

'Stop asking me about her. Nanny's tricks, I said. *I* know.'

Nanny Filbert was familiar with the corridor through to the snug. She'd paid several visits already to the back quarters, always when she had advance warning that the portly Mrs Gribben would be doing this or that in some other place. No

223

one up on Linden Road or the Avenues would have had any dealings with the 'Spirit of Good Hope', except the staff, and she'd been careful to monitor *their* movements. More careful than she'd been elsetimes in her long and varied life as Nanny Filbert or Nanny Graham or Nanny Meek or Nanny Hicks, but that was water under the bridge or under the boardwalk, only she didn't want to think that way just now, or ever, if she could only get the message through her thick skull to her brain . . .

'Put her under the window,' the man said, following her into the dark front room. 'On the bench.'

'That's stupid, anyone could look in and see her.'

'By the fire, then. On the settle.'

'If you'd any manners, you'd do the lifting *for* me.'

'Thought *you* knew best? *You* said, *you* said . . .'

'I've done enough carrying in my time.'

'You're in your prime, girl.'

'Not for this millarkey, I'm not.'

'I thought it was millarkey you come for.'

'*You* know what I mean—out the way.'

'You've done this dozens of times, I'll bet.'

'What? The gas flame trick?'

'No, Nanny's little outings.'

'Not dozens.'

'Remember all their names?'

'Not their names.'

'I'll bet—'

'If you *must* know—' Nanny Filbert sighed. 'I *wasn't* like that. Not till you-know-who bolted. Into the blue beyond.'

'A good girl, were you?'

'In my way.'

'What was that?'

'There's good and good, Dave Gribben. Depends on where you're standing, doesn't it? How you see it? Depends on the deck you're dealt.'

Nanny Filbert drank from the glass, soberly at first. She looked at the child and considered. She looked round the room, at the dust in the corners of the ceiling and the dirt runs on the windows and the trampled sawdust on the floor. She reflected on her history. She'd started out as an under-nanny in a house in St John's Wood: then came responsibility in the household, and her own charge from the brood: then a house in Rustington, followed by the one at Virginia Water: then marriage, and no marriage: followed by 'The Spinney' where the Sangsters lived: then—all the time since then—wherever there would be no one liable to have a suspicion in their heads.

'Someone stepped over your grave?'

'What's that?' she said.

'I've seen undertakers look cheerier than you.'

'I'm thinking,' she said.

'Feeling guilty now?'

' "Guilty"?' she repeated.

The man nodded at the child lying on the settle, quietly singing senseless snatches of songs to herself as she looked up at the ceiling. They both watched her twitching hands and feet.

'What no one sees,' Nanny Filbert said.

'Another one?' the man asked, studying the level of drink in her glass.

'Hold on,' she said. 'Give us a chance.'

'I'll join you.'

'When's *she* back?' Nanny Filbert asked.

'When? I don't know. Five-ish.'

Nanny Filbert raised the mug in a toast. 'Here's to *her*, then.'

'Don't waste your breath.'

'Is that how a husband speaks about his wife?'

'I don't speak about her.'

'How d'you stand it?' Nanny Filbert asked. 'Why d'you put up with it?'

'What else *is* there to do? Tell me that.'

'Do a bunk.'

'We've been married too long to change.'

'Ho-ho.'

'It's just how it is.'

Nanny Filbert frowned again, into her drink. Somewhere in England Rob was still alive. Or maybe he'd gone abroad. Found himself a Spanish wife, or he had a girl—a fancy piece—he was forever promising to marry.

She had failed him, and she would never be sure quite why. It was too late to ask. He'd dumped her: it was the word she chose to humiliate herself with, she'd been 'dumped'. Bloody *dumped*. She wanted to feel humiliated: to believe there must

225

have been a reason for what had happened. and if someone had to be blamed then *she* deserved all the blame that was going.

She hated the thought that he'd just been able to get up and go and, because he was a man, that meant he was free. She needed to believe *she* was the reason and that the faults had been developing over the years—that it wasn't a new idea occurring to him one evening. An ordinary Thursday evening, she remembered with just a hint of autumn in the air . . . There couldn't have been *no* reason why he'd thrown his jacket over his shoulder and then walked out the front door as if he was meaning just to walk to the corner of the street, how he'd done so often, and after that so coolly having nothing more to do with her and probably not for the rest of his natural.

★

'Would you believe it, Dilly—'

Adele Adaire stopped in her tracks and re-checked her pockets.

'Good God, I'm senile. I've gone and left my gloves in that crimper's.'

The actress slipped her arm through her companion's and turned her round.

'Come on, Dilly, back we go—'

The high heels set the pace and the girl shambled to keep up.

'They're blue suede, you see. The colour's to match a dress and coat and court shoes I've got, puff blue. I once had an invite to Leslie Harrold's, a Blue Party. Everything had to be blue. I don't think that was meant to include the witticisms we got. Celia's face—his wife—*it* turned a kind of blue, which I don't suppose was the point either. Poor thing, she wasn't cut out for the life really. She liked dogs, and horses: breeding them. Of course you can imagine the fun people used to have about *that*. I expect it was because she didn't have any children herself.' The voice was lowered. '*Couldn't* have them, actually. Someone said she'd never had the curse; that always sounded a bit odd to me, but—' She looked at the girl beside her. 'Anyway, Dilly, that was poor Celia. Found she'd married a man who produced films for his living. Some people seem to blunder their way through life and it does them no harm. Maybe it's an asset, not to have too much upstairs, in the attic. And precious

226

little to look at in Celia's case, although I shouldn't be catty, she was perfectly nice to me and she did have taste. Old Money, you see. *He* paid for everything, of course, so she wasn't using hers. And then he also had his other little peccadilloes, everyone knew about *them*, but he could afford to do whatever he wanted—with all *his* money. After he died I heard she had the horses in the house, they went up and down the stairs, leaving their visiting-cards everywhere, but I don't know if it's true. She was rich, so she could do it and it was only being eccentric. Anyway, that's the story of my blue suede gloves, Dilly. And now—' She reached for the door-handle. '—here we are.'

There was no one in attendance at the desk. The owner himself had dealt with them as they took their leave.

'Wait here, Dilly. I'll pop in and rescue them.'

She pulled open the second door and stood surveying the salon and clientele.

The long narrow corridor had a third door, at its far end. The re-arrival went unnoticed by Mr Gutteridge, who was in the store-room up-ended over a half-filled carboy of shampoo: he had inserted a filter-spout into the glass neck and was adding water from a milk bottle he customarily used for the purpose.

As he bent over, his right buttock caught the handle of the door and the impact swung it slowly and noiselessly back. The business of dilution was too engrossing for him to notice the witless girl standing there staring until it was too late. He'd placed himself directly under the bare light-bulb on its flex and didn't have a shadow of an excuse.

The girl gawped. Mr Gutteridge straightened himself, blinking out at the girl and holding the empty milk bottle in one hand.

The girl continued staring. Mr Gutteridge tried smiling. No response came back.

Of course it shouldn't have happened but Angela and Elaine had said they would both need more shampoo by the end of the afternoon and he'd planned on supplies doing them till the end of next week. His wife bluntly told him that he stinted but it was the habit of a lifetime with him that buying more than you immediately needed meant, not sensible husbandry, but *using* more than you needed. He liked every last drop to be used.

He'd never knowingly been caught in the act before. He smiled again, as he smiled to his best customers when he spotted them in the street.

A wasted smile. The girl's expression didn't alter. She continued staring at him with her eyes like saucers.

Mr Gutteridge lost his smile. He recognised the indignity of being discovered by a frightened, cowering girl reputed in the town to be brainless, and the stupidity of behaving as if he was intimidated by her.

The smile was forgotten. He assumed a cowboy pose, hands on hips. He was also asking himself in all grim seriousness, *how much has she seen*?

The danger that Tilly Moscombe presented to others—could she have but known it (perhaps it was better that she didn't)—lay in their inability to make the usual calculations about her. So much of human intercourse relies on our expectations and suppositions about others: in part we work to create the responses we receive back from them. Tilly in that respect was like a cold star: unpeopled, transmitting none of the usual signals of intelligence by which we regulate our own. She conveyed a vacancy, and nothing else: and so too, of course, she had become a vessel for other people's pity and their wilder imaginings. If the eyes *are* the windows of the soul, then there was a distinct possibility that her soul was not a blur of moral confusion: her eyes showed no less intelligence than those of many of the inhabitants of Sandmouth. But the eyes in their sockets communicated helplessly: they alternated between interludes of either staring or of ceaseless flitting about, so that most people felt they never knew where they were with her—and those who *did* feel that they knew and could sympathise failed to acknowledge to themselves the degree of guesswork that was invariably involved in the business of 'making contact', with Tilly or with anyone.

For some reason determined by the quirks of human nature, a good number of those good folk of Sandmouth had a tendency to presume not only that Tilly Moscombe 'knew' more than she was letting on, but also that she 'knew' the things about themselves they least wanted to have imparted to others. She had thus become the focus of their fears, their self-righteousness, and their own distrust of themselves. Because she was too much of a variable and because she didn't function by any of the legitimate standards of communication, Tilly Moscombe received back the raw, ungilded reflections of people in their natural condition: they didn't 'try' for her, they made no effort to play up to the socially received image of themselves. Maybe there was even a kind of frisson of daring, as if while she looked at you you were holding up a curtain and displaying what was never seen . . .

She was viewed with suspicion, because it couldn't be known for certain just what had fixed in her memory, and the suspicion revealed itself in ordinary conversation as either snide mockery or, more often, as head-wagging and eyebrow-raising and mirthful smiles for the girl's most unfortunate condition.

cupboard man, back, bottle, milk bottle, gloves, blue, not milk, water, cupboard man, door, not shut, back, cupboard man . . .

The door of the salon opened and out walked the barmy actress.

'Ah, faithful Dilly!' She held up a pair of gloves. 'I've got them, see . . .'

Instinctively Gutteridge retreated a few steps into the box-room; he reached out his hand and switched off the light at the wall. When the actress turned round to see what the girl was looking at, the chances were that she wasn't able to see him. In any event Gutteridge knew that women like her—so self-absorbed—only notice what they're interested in seeing.

'It's a broom cupboard, Dilly. Where the seductions are done, I dare say. There's always a broom cupboard, isn't there?'

They stood in the empty hall, looking down its length towards the open doorway. Gutteridge imagined what his eyes must look like if they were visible, like a cat's eyes in a coal-cellar, yellow and bright.

'Into the broom cupboard with the crimper. *Not* the high-light of any woman's life, I should have thought.' The actress turned her back on the cupboard. 'Even for his wife . . .'

The door opened into the street and then sighed shut on its spring behind them.

With a stern face Mr Gutteridge pulled down the light

switch and picked his way over the carboys and cardboard boxes. Had she caught sight of him, had she meant him to hear? What was the point of the last words?

At the moment he was preparing to come out of the store-room, empty milk bottle in his hand, the street door opened and the breeze blew in his wife. Pulling at her gloves, she tottered forwards on the new high heels she favoured. Her face carried an indecipherable smile, it widened as she stopped in front of the mirror behind the plinth. She stood lost in contemplation, not even feigning to attend to the posy in the swan-shaped vase. She wet a fingertip with her tongue and lightly smoothed the arc of one eyebrow. Her mother had always taken the same care with her appearance, believing that even modest circumstances didn't preclude being able to take pride in how one looked.

Mrs Gutteridge was well known for 'making the best of herself', an often-paid compliment which—her husband realised—had a little knife-twist in it: several knife-twists. She made an impressive-looking wife for himself and mother for Christina (named after her) at Convent functions. There was something rather Latin about her appearance which seemed to appeal to the nuns and certainly did to the svelte lay headmistress. Her skin had an olive tint, she had shiny black hair and naturally-round doe eyes with brown pupils and long, dark lashes; luckily she had the know-how to deal with an inherited swarthiness on her upper lip, and brassieres supplied through a stock retailer in Southampton gave her a Silvana Mangano outline. Sometimes her husband questioned his own good fortune—why me?—then he would recall that, without the success of the business, she wouldn't have looked quite how she did: his own acumen had assisted in her manufacture.

She stood in front of the mirror, holding her gloves in her hands as Margaret Lockwood might have held riding-gauntlets. She lifted her head high and considered herself grandly. It was the look her husband received occasionally, when he was impious enough to remind her of some event in their shared past life which she was determined not to remember. On the whole, though, she gave herself few airs with him: when she did, it was always for a reason. He was closer to her than he had been to anyone in his life. He admired her ability to change her outside to suit circumstances, and to behave with him very much as she had always done: they even shared an accent in private, the one they'd grown up in Gosport speaking, and he felt that that bonded them in a positive way rather than shamed them: it reminded them of how far they'd both come, in each other's company, and how far they might still go.

In the business, that was. Kenneth Gutteridge believed hairdressing to be one of the new professions. (Most definitely a profession: he dealt directly with people, partially in an advisory capacity, so it couldn't be a trade.) The women of Britain wanted to look and feel different, and now they would have everything to look and feel different *for*. Kenneth Gutteridge and his wife were standing by to take full advantage of the situation.

Only—at this precise moment Mr Gutteridge, with empty milk bottle in hand, felt apprehensive: for some reason that eluded him. His wife was smiling charmingly at herself in the mirror and he thought that properly she shouldn't be: that she was looking very fancy for a run-of-the-mill Wednesday afternoon. (They'd eaten breakfast listening to the flying church bells pealing Saint George's Day, but Mr Gutteridge considered it a middle-class festival: one he alluded to in conversation with clients but which didn't touch him or Christina.) When she wasn't at the desk in the salon in her honorary capacity as 'Paul's wife', she dashed about the town in a very convincing imitation of a busy middle-class life lived to the full and plied with demands. In both their books, that was fulfilling the terms of a modern marriage, one like theirs.

Only . . . He couldn't explain it to himself. If she made herself so attractive to him after their years together (just as *he* did his best for *her*, keeping himself slim and fit), he wondered how it was that *other* men must see her. Sometimes she allowed the impression to be given that how she looked was of little concern to her: but now he had the evidence in front of his own eyes that she realised perfectly well the effects her appearance was likely to have on others.

For a moment, stupidly, he wasn't looking at Christina, he was remembering the Moscombe girl. She walked about the streets with her head full of dangerous knowledge probably: she ought to watch herself. She wouldn't be welcome here again, he would tell the girls: in the company of a down-on-her-luck actress or not. He had rules about these things: just as he never gave a girl a second chance if she'd done a wrong, he didn't mind seeming uncharitable if it ensured the salon's reputation: if the dismissed girl said anything, people would presume it was a case of sour grapes. You had to be firm on matters of principle.

It had been his own bungling, letting his guard fall, which had brought the situation about. He had only himself to blame, which was the provoking thought.

Such a half-witted girl, so why then was he standing embedding his nails into the soft flesh of his palm as he watched his wife turn in front of the mirror, casting herself an admiring sideways glance and squeezing out a Mona Lisa smile?

★

cupboard man, back, bottle, milk bottle, gloves, blue, not milk, water, cupboard man, door, not shut, back, crim-per, eyes, bottle, cupboard man, sed-uc-tions, water, plant, bulb, lightbulb, not milk, door, open, clearglass, gloves, crim-per, back, eyes, cupboard man, eyes . . .

✳

Norman Pargiter's white Lagonda lies hidden in its covering of trees and undergrowth behind the golf course. Not quite a sylvan glade, Mrs Prentice realises as she prepares herself for what is to come.

He likes them both to be naked. There is little tenderness in his thrusts although he pretends it. He reaches as far inside her as he can. He is a tight fit, much more so than her husband, and he hurts her; but that is part of the ritual too. She doesn't look at him. He has to assist himself to a climax. He withdraws before she is ever ready. She says nothing, she doesn't complain. Her only satisfaction is in saying nothing, not admitting to him that he abuses her.

She has a dark notion in her head that one Wednesday he will demand something different of her—that other thing—as they lie in the back of the car: that he will point her head at his lap. She has no experience of what the act would entail, but she has an instinct that she is destined to open her mouth for him.

232

It's a feeling, a vague weight in that part of her anatomy, like the one she was aware of when she was eleven years old and knew nothing of the adult world, that the fork between her legs was made to receive. Every Wednesday that passes without it happening she feels relieved, and more anxious because she knows it has only been postponed.

She will comply, however, when the demand is finally made. She can do what she is required to do because she believes that, doing it, she is another person. It's like putting on a coat and taking it off again: she doesn't allow it to matter to her any more than that. She hardly as much as looks at him, even when he's kissing her. She is aware, though, that certain women might happen to find suave, rather characterless looks appealing. She doesn't.

Previously they used to frequent an out-of-the-way hotel along the coast. The last time they'd used the fusty, airless bedroom he had produced lengths of rope from his briefcase. She'd failed even to raise an eyebrow and merely obliged him by binding his wrists and ankles to the brass bars at the head and foot of the bed. It crossed her mind to leave him there, stark naked and spread-eagled on his back, but she had no other means of getting back to Sandmouth except in the white car. He had expected rather more of her that afternoon and she was unsure how to do the deed he requested. She did it because it wasn't really *her* pumping him with her hands. Standing over him with her arms taut she felt she was doing penance for her material comforts at 'The Laurels'. Choosing not to think that she was performing an unnatural act couldn't be any different from not having to think whenever a bill or invoice fell through the letterbox and was whisked away for Mr Sutton at the office to take charge of.

And anyway, she had argued with herself on that last drive back along the coastal road in the white car—wearing a headscarf and sunglasses for some kind of disguise—how could an act be 'unnatural' when she was able to perform it: she was sitting here in the car physically unharmed—and, she imagined, mentally unscathed. Another interpretation which she didn't allow herself to consider in too great detail was that she couldn't be corrupted by it any more than she was already. Maybe that was closer to the truth of it.

She was perversely attracted by the notion that, in her Susan Small dresses and her Hardy Amies suits and her Jacqmar separates, she was actually beneath contempt: that she was too numbed in her own mind to feel the shame that she *should* be feeling. She told herself that Mrs Cedric Prentice and Norman Pargiter's mistress were strangers to each other: that neither should know anything about what the other was doing, that to all intents and purposes they were dwellers of different towns, of different countries.

Now Pargiter preferred Sandmouth for their Wednesday afternoon sessions—an isolated site in shrubbery fifty or sixty yards behind the rough on the thirteenth green of the golf course, at the end of a grass track, under cover—and Mrs Prentice mutely and impassively accepted the situation.

★

'Dilly, dear, I have an idea.'

Adele Adaire had the 'Camelot' Guest House in view.

'I'm having dinner with a fr. . .—with a young colleague of mine. At an hotel. Why don't you join us?'

The girl looked bewildered.

'Dinner, Dilly. Can you come? Dinner at the Clarence Hotel.'

She wasn't sure why she was asking. Certainly she didn't think she could endure another evening of Guy on his own. But she'd been touched that the girl should have stuck with her for the best part of an hour-and-a-half. Towards the end she'd found she was actually making sense of a few of the things she was saying.

The actress opened her handbag. She tore a page out of the back of her diary and scribbled down the name of the hotel and a time. She added her signature with a wild flourish.

'Show this to your friends, Dilly dear, *they*'ll remind you.'

She folded up the piece of paper and slipped it into the pocket of the girl's cardigan. Good quality cashmere, her fingers told her, must have cost a pretty penny.

'Do come, Dilly.'

The chances were against it. But if fate meant it to happen, the actress decided, then it would happen.

She thanked the girl for showing her around.

'And you brought me back where I wanted to get to.' Then she qualified the remark. 'Well, not *wanted* exactly. But I have to get a little shut-eye, and a little practice, dear. For tomorrow.'

The girl nodded, as if it was all quite intelligible to her.

Adele leaned forward and gave her a kiss before she could back away. The girl looked astonished.

Adele smiled.

'I've known some very famous people,' she said. 'Very famous. *And* good-looking.'

Which fork of the road had been the wrong one, she would often wonder, the first wrong one? And how many forks after that had been the wrong ones to pick? Till she was travelling further and further from where she had been in the first place, and there was no going back . . .

If she'd known where she was wanting to go, she might have tried harder to find her bearings. But from day one, arriving in Mr Berner's office, it had been guesswork. She'd presumed that everyone else knew best what was good for her, until she discovered too late that none of them was especially bothered. After that it was hit-and-miss, pitch-and-toss, and the most parlous days had always been those when she felt that what was happening was *meant* to, that she didn't really have any say, and the downward pull was as natural and irresistible as gravity's.

*

'Penelope, Penelope!'

He repeated her name over and over. He always repeated it, making it sound like a charm instead of the embarrassment it normally was to her.

'Penelope!'

He whispered it into her ear. A silly name, but to him it seemed to suggest class, hauteur, a gift worth coveting. It went with the Swiss dress and the Rayne's shoes and the bracelet of gold links and the three-strings of pearls with the heavy clasp she could feel sinking into the back of her neck as he leaned over and covered her with kisses.

He spoke her name into her ear.

235

'Penelope!'

With 'Norman' it was difficult to reciprocate. His ear wasn't very shell-like either: the lobe was covered with a fur of tiny black hairs. As he nuzzled closer his face felt rough with stubble, although she knew he made a point of shaving after lunch on the days when they met. It grazed against her skin and she determined not to let his face drop any lower, to the exposed top of her chest, in case the beard pulled on her dress.

'Penelope!'

He must have seen lovers in films mouthing names to each other, over and over. The habit had come to seem unreal to her. Every time the whole performance had an air of unreality for her. Even her own mute complicity was an attitude she persuaded herself into: for one thing it seemed to satisfy *him* that she should say so little and at the back of her mind there was a genuine dread that she might do something to cause him displeasure. After the ten or eleven times they'd met like this she felt she was no closer to him than she'd been at the beginning and not any better able to comprehend. Pleasure seemed confused in him with anger and hurt and the need to *do* hurt. Sometimes he said curious things to her which would suggest to her he was in possession of certain—incriminating?—information about her; at other times it was as if he was implying that *she* had total command of *him*, the best cards were all hers. But for herself she had no doubt which of the two of them would suffer more if the relationship between them chanced to come to Sandmouth's notice and the talk started.

She humoured him, as if he was a child: but knowing too that this was a dangerous child, who might wreak some terrible harm on her for no reason she would be able to understand. Even humouring him was an element in the ritual game. He 'expected' and she 'supplied'.

She didn't pretend there was any affection in it. She made that very clear to him. She guessed there was no real affection on his part either. Any affection he showed was of a warped, depraved kind, and it was only for the double deed of worshipping her and defiling her. She did allow herself to speak at certain points in the proceedings, but very sparingly, parsimoniously—to excite him more: she knew he enjoyed the sound of her voice—with a puritan, church-school boy's pleasure—the way she pronounced her vowels. She could see in his eyes that he delighted in how she looked, and part of his pleasure was unwrapping her like a very expensive parcel, fingering each of the layers of clothing, covertly sniffing at them, making beautiful things sordid with his contact.

That's what it was all about, of course: pretending he wasn't good enough. *She* knew that *he* knew that *she* knew. They were pretending that money didn't matter, certainly less than breeding. They had sexual intercourse on the white hide back seat of a beautiful white car and they were feigning to forget that beautiful white cars cost a small fortune.

Perhaps it would have served the joke better if Cedric hadn't had his own considerable means, then she could have been the sorry victim of circumstances: but Cedric's being well-to-do added an edge to the danger of his discovering—to a poor man it might actually have seemed understandable that his wife should fall for a man who drove a fast sports car. This way she appeared to be condemning Cedric for his kindness (the name had always evoked the image of avuncular, unfailingly respectable Cedric Hardwicke): while in her own thoughts she knew she was condemning herself for having married a man for money, to save herself from not having any. Somehow she objectified the guilt by behaving adulterously: instead of having to live with the phantom of that guilt, the phantom became a constant threat just beneath the surface of ordinary life and she abused herself two times over.

What they both wanted was punishment: she for suspecting that she had given herself in marriage for base reasons, her Wednesday lover for advancing out of his class. He wanted her both to welcome him and resist him. He affected to be unworthy, while all the time he must know he had brains and guile to outdo them all.

'Penelope!'

She let him unhitch the straps of her underskirt, first one and then the other. That silly name, what on earth had her mother been thinking about? When *he* said it, he managed to make it sound vulgar—which was surely the very opposite of her mother's original intention.

His hand cupped one of her breasts. Through the white satin

237

he plucked at the nipple. He liked hurting. He was like a schoolboy torturing a fly (in her own case, a slightly more exotic specimen of prisoner, a butterfly, to make the outrage on her kind worse), discovering how much pain it could take.

A lot, she knew. A lot of pain. As much as you can give me. But what about you, Mr Pargiter, don't *you* also require your hurt, physical and hard? When are you going to ask me to scratch your back, bite those hairy lobes, sink my teeth into your shoulder?

It would come, another day—his requesting, her complying—between the long interludes of foreplay and, at last, the vital, explosive act of brute sex.

★

Tilly Moscombe went stamping her way down George Street, promenade-wards, at quite a lick. She leaned into the walls like a crab steering itself. The tips of her fingers touched stone and glass.

Howard Trevis watched her from the window of his office in the bank. Sometimes a darker and deeper thought than any of the others stirred in the murk inside him; it was even hidden beneath his tormented, racking adoration of the Bendall boy.

Maybe Trevis himself didn't properly understand the impulse. It was savage and cruel. Just once he would penetrate a woman properly and make her cry out to him with hurt and desire. He would give his best as a man, and it would be to someone he knew didn't deserve it: that way he would exact his revenge on Maureen for the goodness of her character which he couldn't find a flaw in, for the antiseptic domesticity that seemed to stifle and smother him.

It wouldn't be Tilly Moscombe. But somewhere a woman was waiting. He imagined a pudendum even though he couldn't brace himself to look at Maureen's under its quiff of soft chestnut curls. He saw its raw red mechanics, lips pulled back like some obscene tropical man-eater in a hothouse. She would never know, the Moscombe girl, because she would never grow up. But why should *she* escape, more or less—with her ignorance—when the rest of them were in the thrall of such desire and loathing?

★

Cedric Prentice stepped back to let the girl pass. He lifted his bowler.

He knew the story, of course. It was an open secret in Sandmouth. The best way for it to be.

The girl stared at him as she paddled past; her mouth made loose shapes but no recognisable word came out, only dribbles of sound. He smiled, just a little uneasily, realising she wasn't meaning to speak for politeness's sake. Rather, it was as if she was making some association . . .

And then she was gone. Mr Prentice watched her: stood watching as she hurried along the length of Britannia Terrace, past the town's first and last building, the Clarence Hotel, making for the break of trees and shrubs that shielded the ninth, tenth, eleventh greens on the golf course.

★

In his idle moments, at his desk or driving in the car, Pargiter dreams of sex.

It isn't Gloria Barlow's maidenhood he's breaching this time. Always it's Prentice's wife who's his partner in these manic games of lust.

In his imagination's scenario, the white Lagonda is parked in the same place it's parked on Wednesday afternoons, behind the golf course, just out of sight of the thirteenth green.

Bondage and humiliation are the stuff of Norman Pargiter's fevered, pepper-hot, daytime dreams between business appointments: Penelope Prentice wearing only high sharp heels, and himself buck naked with no defences. She teases him, demeans him, subjugates him, perforates him with her heels, then whips him to a very lather of self-disgust for what she makes him suffer when really, all the time, he has the knowledge and evidence to drag her down, her and her kind, as low as himself, lower, if such a thing could be conceived of.

★

Mrs Melville was organising a charity musical evening under the auspices of the Ladies' Circle. It would take the form of a 'Victorian Evening' on this occasion: period dress was not obligatory, but 'would assist in lending the evening authentic atmosphere'.

239

Mrs Dick turned over the notifying letter, as if the blank white back could convey anything more to her.

The Victorians hadn't learnt either, that charity isn't so easily disposed of, reserved for a certain Thursday evening in a certain place, the 'Prince Regent' Room of the Clarence Hotel. She knew how great and manifold were the intrigues and jealousies of the Mrs Melville Set. Good deeds had become the final end and justification of everything. (Proceeds to—where?—'missionary work in Papua New Guinea', she read.) *We know this will be regarded as a most worthwhile venture. Charity will begin here in our own homes!'*

Oh, not so, Mrs Melville, not so.

★

hat man, car people, bird car, trees, grass, green, greens, hat man's wife, no hat man, bird car, car people, trees, road, lane, trees, under, bird car, far, trees, car people . . .

★

Pargiter tells her 'Again!'

She rolls under him. He pushes into her. There is no tenderness in that department.

Mrs Prentice turns her eyes away and looks up through the back window. The branches of a tree, still leaf-less, are like cracks in a blue plate.

He mauls her breasts as he works himself to a climax. He curls his tongue round her nipples. She dreads that he will start sucking on them. She couldn't have a child, not now, letting it share the same teat. Cedric would like a son, but she's afraid that by some accident it would be this man's seed and not her husband's that would fertilise the egg in her. It's what she deserves, but she doubts if she has the mental and physical strength to endure.

Pargiter is frenziedly grinding to a climax, rubbing his sweat on to her stomach, when she glances up towards the side window. She sees—*someone looking in*—and, not able to help herself, she lets out a scream. In the next moment Pargiter's full weight collapses on top of her as the hot condom balloons.

At first he thinks it's her ecstasy, or what books are always saying is a mystery for a woman, an orgasm. She tries telling him, into his shoulder, she's just seen a face at the window.

He pushes himself up on his arms and stares at her. He freezes for a couple of seconds. She can feel him starting to hang slack inside her.

'I saw someone,' she whispers, her heart thumping. 'Oh my God!'

His withdrawals are always abrupt: this one is rough and painful. He continues to stare at her. His head is in line with the window.

'Who?'

'A face. Watching.'

'I don't believe you.'

'It's true.'

She knows he doesn't doubt her.

He makes a decision—he lifts his eyes and looks. His mouth is turned down at the corners.

'Can you see anyone?' she asks.

He doesn't reply at first.

'Maybe they've run away,' she says.

'If there *was* someone.'

'I didn't make it up.'

He seems determined not to believe her—but that's in the way of a game too.

'Funny I don't see them.'

'They've run away,' she says, looking up past his shoulder, to the sky.

'Get dressed,' he tells her, stripping off the condom.

Even with the backs of the front seats pushed forward it's always a struggle. Were she in the throes of passion she wouldn't notice: but passionate is the last thing she ever is. Today her stockings won't slide, she can't find the buttons on her suspenders, her brassiere won't hook, she pulls her knickers on back to front. She watches how surely he does up his trouser buttons, in record time, and steps into his shoes; it's as if the danger inspires him.

They crouch forward and open the front doors and step outside. She knows that she saw a face, nose pressed against the window looking down, the mouth steaming the glass, then the face disappearing. It was only there for a second, but she knows she's not mistaken.

They sit down in the front tub seats. He winds down the driver's window. She opens her handbag and takes out her

241

compact. As she lifts the lid up there's the sound of a branch breaking. It might be a bird plummeting into undergrowth. She catches the worry-lines around his eyes crinkling in the driving-mirror.

She looks at herself in the compact mirror and wills her hand not to shake. She lets the mirror swing off her face and range over the bushes eight or ten yards away. In those seconds she sees it again, the face: Tilly Moscombe's face, staring out of a bush.

She can't believe it. The 'arrangement' has invited their discovery—that has been its purpose. But she can't believe that it's happened at last.

He sees too. He opens his door and clambers out; she watches him set off at a run in pursuit.

The face has disappeared. Again there's the sound of breaking branches. One of the bushes shakes. He hurries into the brake.

She opens her door and gets out of the car. He's gone for half-a-minute or so while she stands motionless, compact open, lipstick poised between her fingers.

When he comes back he doesn't say anything to her. His face looks grim. A tic pulls in his right cheek. His eyes are tight and intent but seem not to see her or the car.

He walks past them before he realises. He turns back. He looks across at the bushes and trees.

She steadies the lipstick between her fingers and draws it over her lips. In the compact mirror she fixes on her mouth, not on her eyes, to see what they're giving away.

car people, bird car, white fast bird, eyes, not the lady smile, bushes, hat man, hand wave, lady smile, clip heels, hill, trees, white car, no hat man, silver buttons, not the lady smile, eyes, hat man, no hand wave, lady smile, clip heels, trees, white car, no hat man, silver buttons, white car, white skin, eyes, eyes, 'Pen-el-ope', eyes shut open eyes, hat man, hand wave, not the lady smile, eyes open OPEN, O-P-E-N, God, God sees, hat man, no hat man, white car, white skin, 'Pen-el-ope', 'Pen-el-ope', eyes, white skin, white car, s-s-shh, silver buttons, no hat man . . .

Normally they sit for a few minutes, listening to the radio in the dashboard. Then he starts the engine, it growls to life; he reverses, they drive off.

Sometimes they pass a solitary farm-labourer, or a rider on horseback, or a sturdy walker from the town, but the windscreen of the Lagonda is more raked than most other cars' and it's difficult for people to get a glimpse of who is inside.

They usually speak then, a little, about this and that. She isn't interested in his businesss affairs, and he is only indirectly interested in her husband: you never know when an extra outside accountant might prove useful.

Every Wednesday they meet he returns to the lay-by under the trees where he collected her and she gets out there. They don't kiss, or make any demonstrative parting gesture. He tells her if he is free next Wednesday, for more of the same, or if she will have to wait for the following one. She never offers any objection to what he decides. She doesn't attempt to make him think the prospect offers her any delight: any pleasure she gets is from behaving like an automaton who gives nothing of herself away.

Today it's not quite the same.

Pargiter presses his foot too hard down on the accelerator and the wheels spin in the soft earth. They're both thrown backwards in their seats as the car lurches forward.

This afternoon that silence has a different meaning, other than to express their indifference. They've been seen: caught in the act. By Tilly Moscombe, which is the only decent card they hold in their hands.

She doesn't reproach him for something happening that they should not only have foreseen but which was inevitable. She has knowingly engaged in these fantasies of non-desire and non-fulfilment, and for her this is only the same game continuing. The guilt is now directed outwards, to include the shambling girl who isn't able to help herself: she has watched her scrambling up and down Hill Street for six years, ever since she became Mrs Cedric Prentice of 'The Laurels'.

They drive up the back road, behind the golf course. Unusually, she looks at him: this afternoon his expression is lowering—his eyes are dark and hooded, his mouth set in a determinedly straight line. She notices the grasp of his fingers on the steering wheel. The car engine groans and whines on the inclines and corners.

He draws into the lay-by, although today he almost over-shoots it and he has to press hard down on the brake pedal. She sits for a few moments with her handbag on her lap. He says, perhaps they should leave it a few weeks? He says it with an anxiety that lets her know the fault has nothing to do with her—that they have to lie low for a while. Yes, she replies, I think we should.

She waits a few moments more. She stares ahead of her through the windscreen. She assumes the guilt back on herself: it is no more than she deserves, she thinks. She senses that he perceives the situation quite differently: that the girl and her knowledge are a danger, a danger to *him*. Considering the predicament in such a light, she begins to see the harm that might also come to *herself*.

Now she starts to feel sick in her stomach. Briefly she turns and looks at him and sees that his face is white, drained of its colour.

For the first time in all these many weeks, she touches his wrist with her fingers. He jumps as if he's been stung, then he turns and stares at her. She looks away. With her other hand she pulls at the handle of the door and swings her legs out. She knows that they don't require to say anything more to each other.

She walks away. Her handbag slaps on her hip: she concentrates on taking normal, even strides on her heels. She is conscious of his eyes on her back, on her bottom, on her legs, the seams of her stockings.

She hears the engine starting up and the wheels turning on to the road—with more urgency than usual, she is aware.

She never looks back at him. Today will be no different in that respect, even though she knows that they end this afternoon not as the same people who began it.

★

'Very nice, Miss Adaire. Very nice.'

The proprietress of the 'Camelot' Guest House looked round the bedroom with less satisfaction on her face than her voice pretended. She didn't like it when guests cluttered the surfaces

244

with what didn't belong in the room. She'd never come across photographs before, in frames, with soppy messages scribbled on them.

'You *have* made it seem just like home, haven't you?'

'I feel they're with me. My theatre friends and colleagues. Wishing me well.'

'We like to think that's what we are here, a guest house: a house for our guests. By the way, I meant to tell you, the hot water comes on at six o'clock. Leaving ten minutes for it to heat up. But Mr Shrimpton always—'

'*Six*?' the actress repeated, sounding incredulous. 'But that doesn't suit.'

' "Doesn't suit", Miss Adaire?'

'I'll need to have a bath no later than five o'clock tomorrow.'

'Couldn't you wait a bit, dear?'

'But I've a performance at seven-thirty!'

'Oh, the theatricals.'

'Yes, "the theatricals",' the actress echoed in a very queenly tone.

'Couldn't you eat first?'

'When?'

'Half-past-five-ish. We do high tea.'

'But I have to prepare myself, Mrs Cleggs. I have to—get into the mood.'

'Our regular guest, Mr Shrimpton—more a member of the family, really—he likes to have *his* bath at six anyway. Or just after, not to tell a lie. Ten-past or so.'

'Well, I'm not waiting about for *him*—'

'Oh, he's pretty sharp-ish about it. Quick in, quick out.'

'There's no possibility of my going in *after* him.'

'He's a creature of habit, Mr Shrimpton. And I suppose he does have first say-so.'

'He doesn't have *my* say-so, Mrs Cleggs.'

'Maybe you could sort it out with Mr Shrimpton yourself? He's a very accommodating gent. He's terribly quick about it, really. He doesn't slosh about or lie there.'

Adele Adaire eloquently pressed a hand to her forehead.

'Does he clean it out?' she asked.

'We leave that to our guests. We prefer to think we're—well, a sort of democracy here.'

'Can't you heat the water up earlier?'

'It's the expense, you see.'

'How much? I'll pay.'

'I'm not sure.'

'One of the quaint customs of this "democracy"—as you call it—is bribery, I suppose?'

'Oh, what a word, Miss Adaire!'

'Bribery. I'll repeat it. *"Bribery"*.' The actress scowled. 'This is blackmail, Mrs Cleggs. You might have known I should require a bath before I make up and dress for my performance.'

'You'll watch your talcum on the carpet, won't you? And not in the bathroom, please, Mr Shrimpton is allergic to—'

'Bugger Mr Shrimpton!'

'Really! Miss Adaire! Language! I'm quite shocked. Mr Shrimpton is—'

'I can imagine *exactly* what Mr Shrimpton is. Kindly instruct him from me that I must have the use of the bathroom on the dot of five minutes past six for the next three days. If earlier is utterly impossible, which apparently it is. If you are to be believed. *And*—'—Miss Adaire drew herself up to her full height—'—unless I alter my plans in the meantime.'

'Oh—oh, Miss Adaire, I'm sure there'll be no call for that. We like to think all our customers—guests, I mean, our *"guests"*—are fully satisfied while they're with us.'

'They would be *more* "satisfied"—if that word is applicable—if the hot water would be put on *before* six o'clock.'

'What about quarter-to-six? And give it ten minutes?'

'It's not very convenient. But it's better.'

'And Mr Shrimpton could still—'

'He can get in when I'm finished. Thank you, Mrs Cleggs.'

The actress held open the door. Quivers of frustration pulsated up her arm. She stood like one of the characters she'd played in the past, pulling a french window open to let out an unwelcome visitor, a forward and over-earnest suitor.

Mrs Cleggs smoothed her skirt. Miss Adaire smiled—an arctic, lethal smile—then pushed the door firmly shut behind the departing back.

'Scenes' upset her. But just as well to discover today rather than tomorrow, when it could have jettisoned the performance. As it was she was less than confident about some of her lines. She'd struggled during the first days in Hastings, and then dried in Bognor and Salisbury. (A fourth time it would be a case of not drying but dying. Death in Sandmouth.)

She picked up her script. She sat on the edge of the bed, not caring if she was creasing the bedspread. She closed her eyes and tried to remember.

'I know it's difficult for you to grasp, but the theatre of today has at last acquired a social conscience, and a social purpose. Why else do you think we're opening at this rat-hole of a theatre . . .'

The bedroom smelt infernally of mothballs. Sod that stupid woman.

'I don't see why you should skulk about in romantic moonlight while I'm on my balcony, being burnt to a cinder by Eddystone Lighthouse.'

The girl could listen, Dilly, when they had dinner. If she remembered to come. At least she had the scrap of paper, folded and tucked into the pocket of her cardigan. She wouldn't have to respond: all she was needing was another person sitting in front of her and looking at her, to help her concentrate her thoughts.

'Oh, Arthur, it's not in my nature to . . .'

She consulted the page.

'. . . to reproach you for what is past and done, but I . . .'

She looked again.

'. . . but I do think you've been terribly, terribly foolhardy.'

She read ahead in the text, then flicked back through the pages, trying to cue herself off other lines.

'Edna, I've thought of an entirely new way of dying.'

She was trying to remember whereabouts in the story they occurred even.

'They're true theatre, because they're entirely self-centred, entirely exhibitionist, and entirely dotty, and because . . . because . . .'

She lowered her eyes—read—closed them.

'. . . because they make no compromise whatsoever with the outside world.'

★

'The customer is always right, Mavis Clark, remember that.'

Miss Spink spoke quickly, taking care that Mrs Fisher's daughter was out of earshot.

'If you don't understand that, you might as well not bother.'

Mavis Clark lifted an eyebrow, cocky as you like.

'Bother with your career, I mean,' Miss Spink explained in an ominous tone of voice.

Mavis Clark shrugged.

'Some career!'

She spoke quietly, into her ample bosom, but Miss Spink heard and drew a sharp intake of breath.

'I beg your pardon, Miss Clark?'

The older woman struggled for composure. Whenever she lost her bottle (as Mavis Clark termed it out of her hearing), she had difficulty holding on to her front-of-shop vowels.

'You think there's something to be ashamed of, do you?'

Mavis Clark pulled herself up, looking down at the peaks of her breasts as she did so. She said nothing.

Miss Spink watched her sullen defiance. Momentarily her eyes alighted on the pert, thrusting breasts under the straining blouse. Her eyes flitted back to the face and, to show the insurgent the full measure of her displeasure, she sucked in her cheeks.

'I suppose it's all just a joke to you, Mavis Clark?' she said.

The girl pouted. Cheekily, Miss Spink thought, and as if she was remembering the remark to laugh over later, with her cheeky friends she met up with after work.

'Every job deserves to be done well,' she rattled out to the girl.

Mavis Clark stared at the glass top of the counter and the gloves underneath. There was nothing in her face to suggest repentance.

'Well, can't you say anything, Mavis Clark?'

In another year or two it wouldn't be like this, the girl would be brazenly impudent.

'Cat got your tongue, has it?'

Mavis Clark shrugged again.

'I don't know, Miss Spink.'

Quite right: she knew nothing. With her big bullet breasts and her heaving blouse and her turquoise skirt, she knew nothing. Nothing at all.

'Your nails are too long for another thing,' Miss Spink told her.

'No, they're not,' the girl said indignantly, holding out her hands.

'Yes, they are.'

'*Why*?'

'Because I *say* they are. That's why.'

The two of them stood looking at the red lacquered nails.

'They're too long,' Miss Spink said decisively.

The girl took a deep breath. Her brassiere squeaked.

'Too long for what?'

Miss Spink bit her lip. She made her eyes into slits.

'I beg your pardon?'

'*You* heard—'

'What did you say?'

'*You* heard—'

'Very amusing, I'm sure, Mavis Clark.' Miss Spink's voice quavered.

'My nails. What're they too long for?'

'Isn't it—isn't it enough I tell you they're too long?'

The girl looked at her; she shook her head.

'Just because they're too long for *you*, Miss Spink?'

'It's the principle,' Miss Spink snapped back, and saw her own spittle flying. 'The *principle*, girl.'

'You can't say that to me.'

'Say what?'

'Say I'm a girl.'

'Well, you *are* a girl.'

'No, I'm not.'

'Yes, you are.'

'Only compared to you.'

Mavis Clark pulled herself up again. Her breasts were the size of plate domes in big hotels.

'I—I—' Miss Spink was lost for words at the impertinence, the outrage. 'I shall report this incident. To Mr Cheevy,' she announced, in as solemn a voice as she could manage.

Mavis Clark shrugged. 'Suits me.'

'Yes,' Miss Spink retorted. 'Yes, I'm sure it does.'

Miss Spink didn't understand the remark, but she had a glimmering of what it might mean. The harsh truth was that she had come to doubt Mr Cheevy's final loyalty in just such circumstances as these. She'd seen how he studied the girl when he made his rounds of the departments, waiting till he had a chance of a profile view. Then the girl would turn round so her breasts were pointing at him, and she would smile: such a sickeningly empty smile, for the girl was incapable of feeling, wasn't she?

Miss Spink bit her lip again. The girl stood looking at the floor; she put her weight on to one hip. *Hostile*, Miss Spink decided: she's actually daring me, forcing me . . .

'Very well then, Mavis Clark. You leave me no opportunity.'

She turned her back on the girl. Now she would have to do it. She wasn't at all keen on their assistant manager Mr Cheevy, with his small, wet mouth and his dandruffy moustache. She suspected the feeling was mutual: he distrusted her because of her famous experience in London. He thought all there was to his job was staring at a girl's over-sized bosoms and dunking Bath Olivers in his tea, a habit which her ally the accountant had told her about.

What would he do if she confessed everything to him? She would have to go through with it now: tell him, lay out their dirty linen. Maybe he'd summon the girl up to his office?

She paused on the stairs with her hand on the shiny brass rail. She felt herself shiver as time seemed to stutter and she was thinking that she'd lived through all this before: in another shop, in another set of circumstances. She closed her eyes to remember.

'Are you all right, Miss Spink?'

Miss Templeton from millinery was looking up at her. She blinked back at her.

'Yes, I'm quite all right.' Miss Spink smiled, not very warmly. 'Thank you ever so.'

Miss Templeton smiled the same tepid smile and sailed away.

Miss Spink's face fell. She knew everyone considered Miss Templeton and herself undeclared rivals in the staff hierarchy. It would have been impossible for anyone to inform a junior which of the two was more senior. She couldn't allow Miss Templeton to think she was going to chalk up any little victories against *her*.

Up another flight, on another angle of the staircase, Miss

Spink put a hand to her brow. She'd passed the awkward age of flushes and tears and hurried exits to the Ladies: that had been like a dark tunnel which every woman has to travel through with as much grace as she can muster, but in her own case she wasn't convinced that she'd fully emerged at the other end: she wasn't living in golden daylight anyway, not yet, if she ever would.

She read Mr Cheevy's name on the door at the top of the staircase, the brass nameplate screwed on top of old Mr Dinsmore's underneath. *He* had been a gentleman, trained in the Army: she'd known where she was with him. *He* wouldn't have peered at the front of a woman's blouse. In Mr Dinsmore's day they'd all worn modest black pinafore-dresses: women staff didn't smoke in their rest-room, they didn't refer (however discreetly) to their intimate bodily functions in one another's company. Oh, for the days when stock had been in such short supply that the seniors on the floor had been Personages in this otherwise dulling, unattractive new world.

In a mirror at the top of the staircase she saw herself looking strained and pinched and tired: positively grey with tiredness.

She tidied the ruff of her jabot and pulled at her starched cuffs. She was standing near an open window and heard the squawking of gulls wheeling above the promenade.

Every so often, caught out like this, she would think of what might have happened to her if she'd stayed in London. She used to say it was the travelling that would have worn her down, but it was the sprawl of London away from its heart that had always unnerved and dispirited her: the terraces lined on steeply sloping hillsides, smoky, jolting, boneshaker trains at the end of the day with destinations like Romford, Dagenham, Penge, Lee, the trudge home on hard pavements.

It would make her puzzle what the advantages of Sandmouth could possibly be. In winter she coughed and became bronchial, and on blustery wet days with chimneys smoking and the sea splashing across the esplanade it was like the very end of the world. She would have given anything then to be walking along Piccadilly or up Regent Street, watching the other people: being drawn into the underground stations with their advertising hoardings as if she was being pulled into a vortex, into the very centre of things, the 'here' and the 'now'.

In the raids she'd slept on underground-station platforms—slept as well as she'd ever done since—and now she would dream on her rare nights of long, easy sleep of fitting elegant, slim-hipped women in a modern salon that would be her own, in a cosy country town, with flock-papered walls and cheval-mirrors that didn't wave and a rosy-patterned carpet and a willing, presentable girl to run and fetch, with long arms to reach into the window and a tidy bust and a sweet face that would continue to smile in the short, very short lulls between customers.

★

One day, thought Mrs Dick, I shall rise early and set out their breakfasts and go up on the 7.17. I shall take the underground and visit the shops in Knightsbridge; I'll have lunch at the Hyde Park Hotel; in the afternoon I shall visit the Royal Academy, then cross Piccadilly and have tea in Fortnum's; I'll look round Fortnum's, and Simpson's, and Burberry's, and walk up Bond Street and down again, then I'll saunter through the Burlington Arcade, and maybe I'll dare to have an aperitif in a hotel before I head for the underground and back across the river to the station and the train and the journey home.

It will have to be a sunny day; warm, but not hot. Memories of bright, cheerful days are always the clearest, and I shall need to have them to sustain me—all the good memories I can muster—in the months and years as they come to me.

★

A dark-blue Alvis coupé follows the slalom curves of Hill Street. The observant notice, and wonder if it has anything to do with Mr Pargiter who lives in the 'Old Rectory' and drives a famous white Lagonda with white upholstery. The sun-visor is pulled down against a grey metallic glare from the sea which is a hazard when driving downhill. It obstructs people's view of who is driving the car if they are looking straight into the windscreen: but as the polished Alvis purrs past it is possible for anyone watching from the side to distinguish that the driver is, in fact, not a man but a woman.

The hands pull carefully at the steering-wheel on the corners, as if the driver is used to coping with hairpin roads with

252

twists and loops. She must be unfamiliar with this particular road zig-zagging down through the town, however: Sandmouth memories are long and given to the specific and no one is able to recognise this woman driving.

The more attentive eyes follow the car's brake lights, blinking red on the next corner. Sandmouth roads are sufficiently quiet for the *sound* of a car to register, and heads turn to look over shoulders as the car seems to cleave the air with an expensive whisper.

The reaction is old-fashioned curiosity. Material jealousy has yet to nibble at the Sandmouth disposition, although the young are showing the first symptoms of the condition. The car will be safe where the woman finally parks it, in the yard behind the Clarence Hotel on the esplanade. Some of the town's rotarians will peer in through the windows, shading their eyes against reflections, and they will be admiring rather than envious.

Not that the woman now finds herself in a town unacquainted with the demeaning, least honourable aspects of human character: culpable emotions, nefarious instincts. She is already aware of the sinister undertow to genteel life, and she knows for a fact that it affects Sandmouth just as it does London where she has come from. She realises Sandmouth is just as modern and primitive as anywhere else: aspects of an age's behaviour may take longer in reaching such an out-of-the-way place and in revealing themselves, but reach it they will. People presume on the innocence of these backwater towns: wishing that it could be so. What is it they so distrust about themselves that they require that innocence in others?

The woman driving the car and parking it in the yard of the Clarence Hotel doesn't view Sandmouth so rosily. She knows her car is safe as it might not be in London, because here it is too conspicuous for anyone to contemplate stealing it. But she also knows that that is the least of it. What people are capable of constructing in their imagination and living with for years is the real test: in that respect, a town's smallness is no guarantee that a mind won't go beyond itself and that a thought won't become a deed. Quite the contrary: thoughts become obsessions, obsessions need their outlets—anything to upset the custom of one day seeming like every other day in the allotted twenty-six thousand between starting and finishing.

The woman in the fur coat and headscarf has no delusions. She knows the worst that Sandmouth is obliged to conceal— worse than the piracy of cars—and she knows how she herself is implicated in the wrong and has to suffer the guilt of it.

★

Susan surfaced as a key blundered into the lock of the door. She raised her head, then leaned it against the back of the settle as she saw, first, a wedge of sunshiny street and, blocking it, the outline of a stout woman huffing and puffing who might have been Nanny Filbert but who wasn't because she wore a hat with a long feather in it.

The woman took a few steps into the room.

'What on earth . . .?'

The door stood open behind her. A car drove past, then Susan saw the old man who'd been making waterworks through the hedge go walking along the pavement on the other side of the road. She stared at him, then at the hat with the quivering feather.

The child smiled. She wasn't sure where she was or who she was or why she should be here—wherever she was. Perhaps she hadn't been properly asleep, or she wasn't properly awake yet, because her dream still seemed very vivid: Nanny Filbert pulling hard on her hand as she led her down a lane of cobbles and then stopped to knock at a door. The door creaking open. Being taken inside. The man talking nonsense in a deep, rumbling voice. Being held up high to inspect the gas flame.

'Lost your tongue, have you?'

No one outside the garden spoke as her parents' friends did inside it, Susan was thinking. Nothing was quite the same beyond the walls and hedges as it was in the warm greenness behind them. She didn't recognise any of the smells here. People wobbled a lot, even Nanny Filbert.

The woman had taken a few steps further forward. *She* seemed to be swaying on her heels too. Susan closed one of her eyes to see against the sunshine streaming through the doorway. That way she could make out the woman's face a little better. It was white and pudgy, and had tiny chinaman's eyes, which were staring at her through the slit lids. Nanny Filbert was nicer to look at: Nanny Filbert reminded her of the china doll Uncle Adrian had brought her back from Spain, with its round face and red cheeks and wide eyes and (her mother called it) a little bud mouth. She preferred unpredictable Nanny Filbert to this person, who didn't have good manners to stare at her as she was doing.

'So, it's a secret then, is it? Is it? Oh, yes. Yes, Lady Muck, I'll *bet* it is—'

The woman was talking to her but didn't seem interested in hearing a reply. She suddenly straightened up and stood with her head cocked, listening hard for sounds in another part of the building.

The child felt with her feet for the floor. She imagined her legs like the weighted pendulums in the case of the grandfather clock at home. For a few seconds—while the woman stood motionless, holding in her breath—a terror seized Susan that she wasn't where she should have been, and she wouldn't be able to make her own way back, and her mother would never find her again.

'Where—where's Nanny Filbert . . .?'

Then, curiously, the alarm passed and her ribs stopped hurting with fright. She watched the woman creep towards the shelves of bottles and glasses: tip-toeing forward without so much as a sideways glance at her. The child's eyes opened wide—as wide as the doll's—as the woman directed all her attention to one particular corner of the ceiling. The feather in the hat trembled. There was a far-away sound, and the woman tipped her head like a blackbird.

Susan smiled woozily. How odd to discover that women wore feathers and had blackbird habits. In the garden at home her mother was always telling her polite little stories about Nature but, according to Nanny Filbert, Nature isn't so sweet and simple after all. She'd told her that birds and animals don't have feelings, and they don't know about things like prettiness, all they do is look for food and eat and eat to keep alive. 'Everything's life and death to them.' Nanny Filbert would tell her that kind of thing on days when she wasn't smiling and when she couldn't even be polite to her mother. (So why then was she always instructing *her* to be polite?)

Susan blinked at the sunshine and found herself walking

towards it. Trying to walk towards it, trying to concentrate on it as the woman in the hat with the feather was concentrating on something else. She stopped at the point where the dark flagstones strewn with sawdust met the others brightly white with sunlight. The glare made her blink again and she smiled. She loved heat whenever the sun fell through the thick trees in the garden and mapped the grass with hot little pools in which she could dabble.

Carefully, superstitiously, she stepped across the boundary between shade and light. She looked down at her sandals and saw the scuffed leather on the toes taking on a shine.

The sun drew her to the doorway. A holly hedge gleamed on the other side of the road. A car drove past slowly and she watched the greasy sun reflected in the black paintwork of its roof. She smiled again.

After she'd ventured out on to the sunny pavement and experimented with a few shaky steps, she found she was smiling at everything and everyone she encountered. Smiling and smiling.

Indeed she wasn't the same Susan Mason. Today the child's disposition was sunny, having total command of her movements for the first time she could remember and not having the inevitable burden of two eyes turned on the back of her head or the small of her back. Repeatedly she looked over her shoulder, as if to check that her freedom was real and no illusion and that no one stood watching.

The child had almost no conception of Sandmouth at all. She half-recognised some buildings from journeys in the back of the car, but her mother had as little to do with the town and its creatures as she could and she was her mother's child rather than her father's. In the car she was chiefly familiar with the turns and inclines on the roads—the feel of the roads transmitted to her through the tyres' contact with the tarmacadam and the juddering of the chassis cage—not with their names and functions. Sometimes she stood at the railings in the wall under the cypress tree, where the garden was skirted by the lane, but she never spoke to the people who walked their dogs and who tried to speak to her and she didn't greatly care to know anything about them, the sort of lives and gardens *they* returned to when they'd rounded the corner and she'd lost sight of them. It was the sunshine and the shade that she was conscious of, the quality of different kinds of shade in the garden: the touch of colder air on her skin, and the degrees of coldness on her brow, her arms, her knees, the colours of shadows.

It had become her sustaining concern in the garden: to appraise her own reactions to all the sensations that acted on her in the course of a day. Mrs Mason didn't understand this, but Nanny Filbert—in her rather confused, winey way—did. Shortly after taking up her position at 'Linden Lodge' with the Masons she had realised the specimen of adult her charge was likely to grow up into. While much else remained wraithed in a fog to her, she saw Susan's future with exceptional clarity— she would become a woman who only thought about herself, who made every judgment through her senses; much later she would become impatient and sometime in early middle-age she would surrender her dignity too easily as she went hunting for new and more pleasurable sensations. Nanny Filbert had forgotten much, but she knew not a little about the social types on whom she depended for her living.

Bloody poor cow she would be too, she thought. Who was going to save Susan Mason from her fate?

The child is mercifully unaware of the trouble to come to her in the first half of the 1990s as she strokes a smiling passage for herself along the pavement, trusting implicitly to her own feelings for the goodness of certain paving stones and the badness of others. She scarcely looks up at all, so intent is she on saving herself from malevolent sprites baked into the concrete.

She follows the sun, meeting other objects' and people's shadows but never her own. She measures their effect on her pale skin, she stripes her arm with them like bars; in simple *jeu d'esprit* she waves her hands like the fronds of seaflowers. She forgets Nanny Filbert, and a little later she also forgets to think about her mother, who never allows her to see the shadowed side of human nature. For this interlude of one afternoon she even forgets the garden where she spends her days, which she has once overheard her mother telling her father will seem to have been the very happiest of her life. (It happened that Nanny Filbert also overheard the remark, and that the child caught the queer little signal she knew was meant just for her—a slow, sly, knowing conspirator's wink.)

Sometimes he's 'Arthur Brown', when he's not 'John Jones' or 'Geoffrey Crane' or 'Philip Todd'. His transport is always the same, a sedate black Standard, which blends anonymously with most of the backgrounds his commissions take him to.

He's on home ground or near enough in six or seven South Coast towns but Sandmouth is new to him, and untested. He's usually quick to taste the flavour of a place. Sandmouth, he's decided, is too small to give proper camouflage to his prey. He recognises its potential virtues. The hotel where he's staying is comfortable, there are half-a-dozen guest houses, a couple of appealing tea-rooms, there's a department store for women to put off their time in and, for the men, a chandler's window and the tobacconist's (and the golf club, of course, but he hasn't enquired about the arrangements for temporary membership).

There are many disadvantages too. While the beach is bracing and good for walking on (i.e. for purposes of rumination or the very opposite, mind-emptying), it's overlooked by the promenade; the clifftops have lovers' lay-bys, but the coastal road to Bournemouth is only three yards away. The truth is that there are too many eyes in Sandmouth to see and not enough places to escape them. Personally, there's also something in the brisk sea air he finds disconcerting: the town has an unhealthily neurotic feel to it, and he can be no more specific than that in describing it to himself. Normally in his job he's vexed by the very ordinariness of things, sucking people in. A sense of history—obstinate, unfriendly history— hangs over this place, while in other resorts he frequents the past is almost lost sight of in the welter of distractions. He prefers the distractions. (They're professionally expedient, for both parties. Towns like Sandmouth—white gloves and doilies—should entail a higher tariff, in his opinion.)

He's got another job the day after tomorrow and a fair drive along the coast to Hove. In Hove he's on familiar and favourite territory, among the funereal Edwardian villas with sunless lawns shaded by cedars of Lebanon and monkey-puzzle trees, owned by persons (he's discovered) of frequently opaque intentions. Hove is the home of contested wills: it's a town of the rich and dying. The dying are just as slippery to anticipate as anyone else, but he prefers them—their last-minute intrigues before lights-out in musty rooms in that menacing town, and all the venomous revenge instincts of their blood relations—to any of this fraught small-town gentility: people too dull for infidelity or the adventure of running away, living by the code of everyone else. That's how it's struck him after—he looks at his watch as he nimbly takes the front steps up to the hotel—after less than a couple of hours in the most respectable borough of Sandmouth.

He walked into the hall of the Clarence Hotel, instinctively moving as close to the wall as he could. Even here though, he thought, there must be secrets people would choose not to have disclosed. Such was only human nature, after all. That was his confirmed and tested opinion after the best part of a decade in the business.

He'd begun nine or ten months after he was demobbed, laying like a ghost the memory of twelve years' graft as a clerk in an insurance office in Holborn. The times had created his new vocation. His first cases were of missing persons, assumed identity, forged papers: clever types taking advantage of the muddle to become someone else. He admired cleverness. In all his cases—even those which had to do with infidelity, the commonest sort now—he did his best to think himself into the mind of his quarry: lovers were less likely to have a cool, intellectual, dispassionate approach than those with a *cause* to disappear, but even they on occasions could be cold and contriving and downright cunning. He would think himself into their situation: he followed every conceivable turn of their fevered fancy, he crossed and re-crossed their tracks so often that he was able to anticipate their next move one step ahead of them and—usually figuratively, once or twice literally— jump out and astonish them. Sometimes, just now and then, he would feel bad about doing the very thing he was being paid to do.

You couldn't have had a life like his with 'ties': that's where some others in this game made their mistake. They imagined that having a wife and kids gave you a 'balance'. That was balls. You had to exist on *their* terms: the hounded. Maybe living with a nagging wife and screaming kids could convince

259

you *why* people did it—making themselves invisible or just slouching off for a dirty weekend—but it didn't make you a better sleuth. For that you needed total attention, 'involvement'.

He never told anyone his theories: they were a private philosophy and wouldn't have been worth having if he'd spoken them aloud and passed them around for approval. He'd learned to live his life secretively, trusting who he was and what he did for money—and no one and nothing else.

He moved round the walls of the hall. He'd trained himself to do it in the most natural-seeming way. How you appeared was of the greatest importance: you should never needlessly invite people's attention.

The maid had the room-key he wanted, but he would try a bit later. It was the advantage of a smaller hotel, smaller than the Clarence: if you were pushed for time, you could stretch across a counter and snitch a key from a hook. Doing it with a smile: that con-man's smile he sometimes surprised in a lit dining-room window of an evening.

Hotels like the Clarence were worst for his purposes: not so small that he could be certain of a regular staff (he couldn't get the faces of the maids fixed in his mind), and not big enough to allow him to be faceless himself. An elderly dame had tried to enlist him as a listener: 'Good afternoon, might I introduce myself? I am Miss Austen. Yes, a descendant. And you are Mr—?' She'd come up to him just at the moment when he had his object in his sights: a woman in a black sable coat and headscarf who'd been sitting on a bench on the pavement directly opposite the hotel and who was hurrying back up the flight of front steps into the vestibule.

The old woman had turned and looked too. 'What an attractive woman,' she'd said. 'Attractive' wasn't the word *he* would have used. She was striking certainly: she strode towards the desk with great purpose and confidence, her coat and scarf and shoes were the real articles, but her face was rather too fine and sculpted to be 'pretty' in the way he liked women to look. She would have turned heads on Piccadilly or Kensington High Street, but in London looks also had to do with manner.

The old woman had taken a few steps towards the lounge

door and stationed herself between him and his quarry. He'd caught sight of the sable coat and headscarf hurrying past, in the direction of the staircase.

'Perhaps another time, Mr—?'

He'd nodded his head, oblivious to the sense of the words.

'We can have our little chat then?'

He'd smiled: a professional smile of expediency, one which gave off no heat. It must have satisfied the woman, because he was conscious of her smiling up at him before she turned away.

This was threatening to develop into one of those cases where, no matter how much thinking you staked on it and kept plugging in, you got no change back. Just occasionally a mystery refused to 'yield': to Brown/Jones/Crane/Todd it was as if some eternal principle was being established, that not all matters were finally reducible. Or maybe he was just plain unlucky in these instances? Whatever was the cause of it, the result was the same: he felt he'd failed to get the final vote of confidence in himself and his methods that would have made him more content with himself and more self-assured at his job.

The years to come would probably be exactly the same as the ones since the War. He might be able to treat himself to a car with a bigger engine and plusher comforts, a Zephyr or even an A70, the next suit he bought himself might be better-quality cloth and have just a little more dash to it (sometimes hotel staff in the superior class of resort looked askance at him). But he felt that it was probably his fate to always operate in this comparative backwater of the complex English psyche: the kindest way of looking at it was, that this was what he was suited for best.

Perhaps—just once— he *would* strike lucky and unravel a tangled plot and sub-plots much more complex than anyone might have suspected, and the consequences would reach to include the great and worshipful. Maybe a political sex scandal, or a murder-for-lucre case in the higher echelons of society: no group could be considered above criminal intent or capability, the need to guarantee our own safety and well-being—a caveman urge—cuts across any barrier of class and money. That was how upper middle-class life in particular— his own 'speciality'—was conducted: by a system of truces it negotiated with conscience, so that it would be able to enjoy its material comforts undisturbed.

*

At her post in the kitchen Mrs Macey was cooking milky porridge for Lady de Castellet. There wasn't much she could eat. She would hazard a few spoonfuls, then abandon the attempt. She would be most polite about it, as ever.

'I'm so sorry, Mrs Macey. I really don't think—'

And somehow she survived from one day to the next to the next.

Mrs Macey had come to the house when its glory days were already over. She had grown up in the town in the 'twenties, hearing the stories about the fancy dinners in the house with Lady Sybil's Aunt Juliana still holding sway: candles in silver brackets, all the plate out on the table, the food carried in on salvers under shiny silver domes.

The silver was tarnished with neglect by the time she and her husband were taken on. Lady Sybil had more or less stopped the entertaining by then; the wholesale abdication of staff after the War had decided that anyway. She had become much frailer and what she really required was simple looking after, and to have proper attention for Elizabeth, who lived in her own room in the house.

No one knew positively what the girl's history was. Everyone speculated: her life had become public property in a way, especially since Lady de Castellet wasn't in the least possessive about her and let her spend her days as she wished, going into different houses about the town. If her history had been so very disreputable, was it likely that she would have allowed her such freedom? Not that it was possible to get a straight reply to anything from the poor chit anyway. Mrs Macey considered Lady de Castellet's treatment of her ward not at all as indifference, as some people insinuated to her that it was: you could claim the opposite, that it was even quite enlightened. The girl suffered as little as possible for being how she was.

Sometimes when she was sitting at the opposite side of the kitchen table from you, you could almost imagine she was normal: at those moments she seemed quite quiet in herself, when she wasn't jerking her shoulders and her face didn't have a tic and it settled, and she could lay her hands up on the table in front of her. Mrs Macey believed that she could respond to your kindness then: somehow or other she perceived your good intentions and she became still. It was other people who upset her, Mrs Macey believed: they stared at her or, worse, they let her see what they were thinking, and she picked that up, at her own level of understanding.

She had her own language and all you had to do was educate yourself: in time you learned a smattering. After a few years it would have been curious if you hadn't. People presumed having her there was one of the disadvantages of the job, but Mrs Macey believed you created your own disadvantages in these circumstances. The same people made the girl more of a problem than she needed to be: she was as simple as a mirror in some respects, and if you were confused about her in the first place, then naturally that was the image that was returned to you.

What would happen after Lady de Castellet passed over was anyone's guess. Mrs Macey suspected some of the visitors were helping themselves, although neither she nor her husband had caught any of them at it. No one would want the girl, of course. Maybe she'd be made a condition of someone's getting the money? There were none of them who looked as if they would know what to do with her, or even care. Lock her away maybe. They turned their noses up at her, or they avoided looking at her altogether, or if they did acknowledge her presence it was by staring her into the panelling.

Mrs Macey was sorry she'd missed out on the house's best and favoured years, but that was the way of it. Those times were over. She guessed there were a few undiscovered skeletons on the premises but the true-blue de Castellets took everything in their stride, and that was how you needed to be to have charge of a house like this one, in this day and age. She'd never had cause to feel done down by Lady de Castellet: all business was conducted in a civilised, commendably fair fashion. In these depleted times the house could—just—be run by two pairs of hands, and Mr Macey had made himself quite a favourite.

Mrs Macey laid the tray. Lady de Castellet would help

herself to a few spoonfuls of the porridge, then apologise to her when she returned to collect.

'I'm so sorry, Mrs Macey, I really don't think—'

Mrs Macey sensed that in the background of their four lives in 'Hallam House' all sorts of surreptitious shiftings and alignments were taking place. She could only hope that they were all treated gently, and that the vipers and adders and the other crawling, snapping things hadn't come to over-run them and destroy them like a pestilence.

*

People looked with excusing fondness at families like the de Castellets. Even if they hadn't held on to their money, they would still have been looked on with excusing fondness. When people sat down in their homes to eat off crockery transfer-patterned with glorious Georgian houses in stately grounds, deer cropping at the grass in the park, they viewed the scene with a softer eye, reason temporarily went into abeyance, today became a better day because of it. Antiquity was enough, and a certain condition of wealth and comfort. The *dis*comforts were forgotten: puddles in upstairs bedrooms, birds shattering windows and flapping dementedly from room to room with no way out. Everyone knew their place in the pyramid and that was sufficient. Why should this be, the doctor's wife wondered, in an age when people had begun to dispute the expectations they were born with? In a previous age most of them would never have been allowed inside somewhere like 'Hallam House', unless they'd been employed to carry trays and stoke fires and wax and polish boots.

Mrs Dick would stand considering the shelves of china on the dresser while the children filled the house with their noise: a bow scraped scales on a violin, 'Sur la glace à Sweet Briar' was being performed on the piano at breakneck speed, a bath ran upstairs and was probably steaming the landing.

Even the worst deprivations of those far-gone days could be included in the cozy, halcyon picture. The croup, and the cancers, and the infant deaths that no one was spared: she'd heard on 'Woman's Hour' that the chances of a fatality were only slightly reduced if you delivered in a four-poster, with attendants and clean hot water. In that sense there had been an equality about people's conditions so long ago, albeit of a desperate, tragic kind.

Or perhaps there was a simpler and cruder explanation to account for the revived appeal? People—however impossibly—wished themselves there: lording it over their demesne, strolling around the policies, watching the spotted deer feed contentedly. A fall of money—only that—and it could have happened. Money was the impossibility remover: with it might come the magical elevation to leisure and gentility (responsibility forgotten) and to the happy-ever-after, but even without it hope could fill that space of waiting and want.

★

Alistair Meiklejohn de Castellet, of the twice-removed Caledonian clan of the de Castellets, pushed open the door of 'The Wishing Well Tea-Rooms' and headed for the nearest vacant table. He pulled out the wheel-back windsor chair and dropped on to it.

A waitress in starched linen corrected the set of her cap and advanced towards the table. De Castellet observed her with hostility. The girl appeared to hesitate, then she smiled the special smile for difficult customers.

'Good afternoon, sir.'

The words sounded clenched.

'What—what would you like, sir?'

De Castellet grimaced. 'That really *would* be telling, wouldn't it?'

'I beg your pardon, sir?'

'Tea.'

'Yes, sir. A pot of tea? And something to eat?'

De Castellet nodded.

'What—what would you like to eat, sir?'

'It doesn't matter. Anything.'

'We have—' the girl took a deep breath— '—fruit scones, cheese scones, soda scones, empire biscuits, Bakewell—'

'For God's sake, it doesn't matter, woman. Anything, I said.'

The girl stood with her mouth wide open. Every so often 'The Wishing Well' received rum customers, and this one promised as bad as the worst of those—the woman who'd

265

crammed the contents of the plate of cakes under her hat and the old man who'd dipped his dentures into the hot-water jug.

De Castellet glared after her. He'd just put through a phone call to London for the information that he'd been anticipating for days. His contact at the other end had given him the news he'd least wanted to hear: the old woman's brother really had sired a child, and the birth had been registered by a doctor in St Ives, in Cornwall.

He guessed the rest: that the bastard child and the idiot girl who lived in the house were one and the same person, if 'person' she really was. Of course the old woman, who was technically her aunt, might have seen the gross stupidity of leaving anything of the estate to a walking vegetable like that. On the other hand, they were a devious lot on her side of the family, and straight thinking wasn't a faculty they'd inherited. She'd never been very warm to him when he sent off his occasional letters (written with blood); he would eventually receive back a curt postcard to acknowledge the letter's receipt and to communicate her 'regards'.

Everything possible had gone wrong. It should have been an easy enough business, dying. Instead the pig-headed woman had decided to make a full seven-course meal out of it, extracting all the drama she could from her going. Things were getting pretty desperate with him, and the chance to buy stock in the stables syndicate would be gone by the end of the season. Probably she was trying to hang on till the summer now, Jesus Christ help them all. Bloody old actress, hamming it for all she was worth. Was there nothing that would hasten her exit from life's stage and get her dragged off into the wings?

A plate bearing a buttered fruit scone appeared in front of him, then a tray of tea things. Dejectedly he tilted the teapot. The old woman was hanging on for dear life by her fingernails. Somehow he—all of them—they had to find the means of making her loosen that fierce grip.

He spooned sugar into the tea abstractedly and stirred. He glanced up and saw the waitress staring at him. Out of the darkness of his thoughts he shot her a smile. It stuck on his gums, like a werewolf's. He watched the girl's eyes widen with fright. He felt his top lip sliding down over his teeth and the skin on his face returning to its hangdog folds.

266

He could try to waylay the idiot niece and pump her for what she knew. Chances were she wouldn't know anything. Maybe she wouldn't even realise he was talking to her: only advantage of that was, afterwards she wouldn't be able to remember him from Adam.

What happened next was a matter requiring careful thought. No more information was likely to be forthcoming on the terms of the will unless the old girl divulged it. If he was left alone with her he might manage to get her talking and trick it out of her. He wasn't her favourite relation, though, Jesus only knew who was: probably that cretinous girl. She might not let him be left in the room alone with her, those buzzards she paid to guard her would bar the way.

Unless, he thought, unless *they* knew and could give him the information he was wanting. A couple of pounds each might do it; a fiver all told at the most, between them. And if they confirmed the worst, then what?

That left them all with the bloody girl. What sort of farce had he landed himself in this time? It was questionable which of the two of them—the aunt or the niece—was more alive. No one had expected the girl to live. Why *had* she, except to spite all their prospects?

Thus considered the hapless Alistair Meiklejohn de Castellet while, unbeknown to him, the waitress watched from the service hatch. She didn't appreciate that the details were registering and she only realised later, when she had reason to go over them again: how he'd poured four teaspoonfuls of sugar into his tea, how he'd stirred and stirred and wouldn't stop twisting the stem of his spoon, how he'd been dressed very smartly—as if for a visit—in flannel trousers and a tweed sports coat with leather buttons.

He drank cup after cup of tea and, when he'd finished, she went across to ask him if he wanted another pot. He didn't seem to hear her but he nodded. She stood stacking the pot, water jug, depleted milk jug, and side-plate on to the tray. She wasn't sure whether to leave the cup and saucer or not. She decided to bring a new one and when she leaned across, the oddest thing happened. He grabbed her wrist: roughly, not even looking at her, as if it was just an instinct. She tried to wriggle free out of his clutch. At last he did seem to understand what he'd done and his fingers loosened, they opened. He looked up at her, for the first few seconds he didn't appear to recognise who she was or what he had done.

She stood in front of him holding her wrist. The skin was quite white and bloodless where his fingers had dug in like claws. She rubbed at the numbing pain but didn't dare to speak.

In the kitchen Mrs Froggit inspected the hand. The white marks were turning an ugly red.

'Mr Froggit gives him his bill,' she said. 'He goes *straight* out of here.'

The girl watched through the crack between the hinges of the door as Mr Froggit gave the man his bill. The man said nothing—as if he wasn't expecting any more tea; he screwed his eyes up at the amount and paid out of the change in his pocket, rather grudgingly.

Then he stood up and left: slouching a bit, the waitress noticed, although he looked quite a bit better than that, nobbier than the usual. She said so to Mrs Froggit, who told her 'nobbier' didn't come into it, and 'better' didn't either, for there was no comparing 'worse' with 'worse'.

★

'Tilly Moscombe, for the last time *give me that child*.'

Nanny Filbert snatched at the child's hand. Susan let out a little whine of pain.

'Shut up, Susan. I'm not in a mood for one of your bloody—your sulks.' She shook her arm. 'Buck up, for any's sake.'

Susan didn't appear inclined to buck up.

'What d'you think you were up to, running off? Tell me that.'

Nanny Filbert, winded after her run, stood breathing fiercely. Like a dragon, to Susan's limited sensibilities.

'I didn't.'

'Yes, you did,' Nanny Filbert corrected her crossly.

'No, I didn't,' Susan replied, just as petulantly.

'Yes, you *did*.'

Nanny Filbert gave an almighty tug to the child's arm, and she howled with the hurt of it.

'Just be quiet, Susan . . . I've had more than enough for one sodding—for one day. Of you and everyone else.'

'You weren't there.'

'What? What did you say?'

'You weren't there.'

Nanny Filbert stared at her charge.

'Wasn't there?' she repeated. Anger fired her face to the colour of the boiled lobsters in Beresford's window.

'To take me home.'

'*You* ran off.'

'*You* weren't there.'

'Holy Mother of God,' Nanny Filbert oathed under her breath.

'Nanny Filbert—'

'What?' she growled.

'Who's God's mother?'

Nanny Filbert tugged again on the arm and anticipated the cry that came.

'You're asking for a strapping.'

'No, I'm not.'

'Shut *up*, will you?'

The single whelp became howling that wouldn't stop.

'Be quiet, Susan Mason, we're going home now—back home, do you hear me? You want that, don't you? Say nothing to your mother, I'm warning you. If she thinks you've been talking—'—Nanny Filbert nodded to where Tilly Moscombe stood watching—'—to someone like *that*, she'll have your guts for garters. There'll be fireworks.'

The howling stopped, quite suddenly.

' "Fireworks"?'

'I'm just warning you. You'd better keep it buttoned, if you know what's good for you.'

' "Buttoned"?' the child repeated, looking at the chrome buttons on Nanny Filbert's front.

'Keep quiet. About what happened. You going off like that, with no reason.'

'But—but where were you?'

'What?'

Nanny Filbert might have ignored the remark, but she knew the girl too well: she wouldn't let a question be.

'You'll die of asking too many questions, you will.'

She pulled the child away from the demented girl.

'How will I die?'

'Asking too many questions, Susan Mason.'

'But I couldn't find you.'

'You couldn't find me because—because I was—discussing something—with my friend. Having a confab.'

'What's that?'

'Jesus wept! What's what?'

'What you said.'

'I was *talking* to him.'

'To who?'

The arm was tugged again, after Nanny Filbert had checked there was no one in the vicinity—Tilly Moscombe apart—to see.

'Oh don't—'

'Don't *please*!' Nanny Filbert roared.

'*Please*!' Susan pleaded.

'Just remember, Miss Smartyclogs, I'm not to be treated as if I'm some bleeding—some bit of the furniture you can come along and do as you like with. Just kick and scuff!'

Through her anger Nanny Filbert sensed she wasn't explaining herself at all clearly.

'Why are you hurting me?' Susan asked her. 'Please?'

'I'm not.'

'You *are*.'

'Don't—'

She wanted to thrash the child. She wanted to inflict the most terrible injuries on everyone who had imagined they knew better than Wilma Filbert. Which exempted nobody, not even long-departed Rob—that sod of a husband.

'Don't tell your mother or I'll bl. . .—I'll hide you, Susan Mason.'

'*Hide* me?'

'*Tan* you, then.'

'Tan me?'

'I'll give you a lesson you'll *never* forget.'

Rob had always favoured 'coitus interruptus'; it took a bastard to be able to do that to you. At least when *he* did it (or, more to the point, didn't do it) she'd known the 'interruptus' was coming. It was a different proposition to look over a man's shoulder and see his wife standing smiling in the doorway, removing a long sharp pin from her hat.

270

'So don't tell your mother, miss, do you hear me?'

'Yes.'

And then to have that dimwit Moscombe girl to contend with, who lived in a dream, but you never could be certain just how much she was taking in. She was a menace, she ought to have been shut away years ago.

'We've been for a walk, Susan. A nice, long walk.'

'There! Look!'

'What?'

'It's the man.'

'What man?'

'The man we saw.'

For a moment Nanny Filbert thought it must be Dave Gribben, and he'd come running after her. But it was just an old man.

'What's *he* got to do with anything?'

'We saw him.'

'Where?'

'Doing his business. In the hedge.'

'Oh.'

She'd forgotten about that, and seeing him. Dirty old bugger.

'Ignore him. He should be in a prison, that's where.'

'Why?'

'No more questions, Susan.'

She tried to be less violent as she grasped her hand and shook her arm.

'We've had enough of them for today. All of them.'

'*Them*?'

'Men, Susan Mason, men.'

This was another day in her life she just wanted to forget about, drowning it in Nanny's cure-all which she kept in the back of the second drawer in the tallboy; it was secreted beneath the silk nightdress she'd appropriated as her own from the house in Sweet Surrey which Mr Sangster had bought for his bride-to-be, thinking there was to be a marriage, little suspecting.

★

blue woman, red face, hands off you!, little eyes, Susan Mason!, blue woman, no hat, red face, little eyes, grab, wrist,

271

*thief!, red face, blood-y thief!, little eyes, little sneak!, blue
woman, no hat, red face, no hat, blood-y thief you!, grab,
wrist, little eyes, say nothing you!, or else, red face, not hat,
fingers, wrists, you hear!, fingers, nails, twist, wrist, red face,
little eyes, teeth, breath, say nothing you!, teeth, breath, red
face, no hat, fingers, wrist, you hear!, little eyes, red face, no
hat, little eyes . . .*

★

Mrs Spencer walked down the central staircase of Crockers'
and into the paired Haberdashery and Ladies' Accoutrements
departments at the front of the ground floor. Glove-less.

Before she married she used to go up to London for the day
with her older sisters and together they would frequent the
better class of stores: looking, buying occasionally, drinking
tea in the restaurants and listening to the orchestras and
watching the mannequin shows. Then it had seemed as if the
rest of her life would be like that, even when she would be
married and have children: perhaps meeting up with her
sisters, scouting round the good shops, drinking tea and listening to the songs of the moment, the songs subliminally
becoming memories.

Now Letty had passed on and Evelyn lived with her son in
Vancouver and she felt she would have been rather an interloper if she'd dared to haunt any of those grand emporia in the
West End. The snooty assistants would have tried to put her in
her place. Her daughter continued to go, but mothers are an
embarrassment when you're still young-ish and pretty. Anyway, shops bought for a different generation from hers and
everyone else just had to fit in with *their* taste as best they
could. She didn't have the means anyway, not on Ronnie's
pension.

The saucy young assistant was sitting at the counter, engros-
sed in reading a magazine. There were no signs of the older
woman. Not like my friend upstairs, Mrs Spencer thought, that
girl couldn't care less.

She moved behind a display of scarves and gloves, where the
girl couldn't have seen her even if she'd wanted to. The scarves
were draped from a hatstand, like a maypole. Some of the
gloves were laid in a fan on the counter-top, others contained

plaster dummy hands—the fingers were spread in impossibly genteel contortions.

One of the pairs of gloves—actually white chamois—reminded Mrs Spencer of white lace ones she'd taken out East with her on the boat. She had thought they might have done for the coolness of a bridge evening out of the hot season. In the event they'd stayed in the trunk like so much else she hadn't been able to find a proper use for.

One glove of the pair caressed the counter-top—Mrs Spencer laid her scarf down on the wood and picked up the white lace souvenir of bridge evenings that had never happened—the other glove was fitted over a plaster hand.

Therein was the problem. When she tried pulling the second glove off the dainty fingers, she simply couldn't budge it. She slipped her handbag on to her arm and lifted the plaster cast with one hand while she struggled to ease the glove over the fingers with the other hand. It still refused to come off.

Then, in a single moment, she'd done the deed: opened her handbag and dropped in first the hand, and after it the loose glove, and quickly snapped shut the gilt catch.

For a few moments more she stood tidying the loose ends of her hair. She was barely aware of what she was doing, what had just happened, why she should have wanted to take, to steal . . .

In one of the mirror-stands she didn't recognise her reflection for several seconds: the eyes didn't seem like hers, not at all, not with that wide-awake look.

Then she turned her head and saw Tilly Moscombe through the window. She was standing looking in: staring at her, with her silly mouth hanging open.

Mrs Spencer grinned back at her. The girl's face didn't change: it didn't show surprise, or ignorance, or anything else, it just looked and looked. Mrs Spencer felt the grin stranding on her face as she realised what she didn't want to, that the girl had seen. She *must* have seen. Why else was she standing there?

Mrs Spencer's eyes stared at the girl staring back at her. She could open her bag and tip out what had gone in. But that would only have been confessing the deed, to a silly gormless girl. What if she *hadn't* seen it? But why was she gawping if she hadn't?

273

Mrs Spencer thought quickly. She would pretend the girl was imagining it: she must show her that if she chanced to blurt it out she must deny it *because it hadn't happened*. Unless the girl at the counter saw her staring with her mouth fallen open . . .

Mrs Spencer walked forward. She didn't look over at the counter. She tried to set the features of her face.

Then, at that instant, the assistant was speaking from two feet behind her. Mrs Spencer's heart missed several beats, it seemed to be up in her throat.

The girl in the turquoise skirt was talking to her and Mrs Spencer didn't know what she was replying with. Inanities. She smiled. She thought, I'm not really here: the words are speaking themselves. 'Madam', the girl called her, and she started. Then it was the weather they were discussing.

Mrs Spencer coughed, had a little fit of coughs. When she was able to stop, the girl was gone.

With nothing said about it. She couldn't have noticed after all.

Mrs Spencer stood seeing spots in front of her eyes. For several seconds she just stood. The blood was swilling around in her head, rushing, it drummed inside her temples.

The worst of it passed. Mrs Spencer reached out for the brass door handle and pulled. The bell rang and the door swung inwards. She smelt the sea in the bay. 'Good-bye,' she heard herself saying very quietly.

Then the girl in the turquoise skirt and the tight blouse spoke again. Rendered immobile, Mrs Spencer didn't think how she could keep standing. 'Haven't you forgotten something?' Something about a scarf. It was put into her hands. Mrs Spencer felt the burning heat on her face. Something else she didn't hear. A parting smile for the girl. Nothing said. Her joy to be going, to be able to move her limbs again, to be escaping.

Quite calmly she pulled the door shut behind her, firmly enough for the glass to rattle. She paused on the mosaic letters in the paving, blue and green chips like bottle glass which spelled out 'Crockers'.

It was over. Over. Almost.

Except that Tilly Moscombe was still standing a few feet away and—Mrs Spencer sensed—was turning round to look at her.

In the interlude of silence neither of them spoke.

Quite calmly and quite deliberately Mrs Spencer removed the handbag from her arm and let it hang by her side, the side closest to the girl.

The saucy piece inside the shop had said nothing. In those few seconds she dared Tilly Moscombe to give her away. *Dared* her.

Mrs Spencer continued to stand in the entrance-way, looking straight ahead, to the ironmonger's on the other side of the street.

The door didn't clatter open behind her. The simple girl still didn't speak.

With a steady, dignified gait Mrs Spencer moved off the shop's lettered paving and walked to the kerb's edge. She paused to let a van pass. At the last second of waiting, watching out of the corner of her right eye, she thought she caught a clumsy, staggering movement from the idiot girl.

Mrs Spencer stepped off the edge of the kerb and nimbly, speedily, made for the opposite pavement in a straight, no-nonsense bee-line.

Reaching it, she searched in the ironmonger's window for Tilly Moscombe and saw her staring after her. She saw herself, looking the picture of respectability, how she'd always imagined herself during the years on the plantations: doing English things in an English town, the 'other' Mrs Spencer she might have been.

★

rain-coat lady, eyes, hand-bag, Irene, mag-az-ine, hand-bag, eyes, hands, scarf, gloves, eyes, mag-az-ine, hands, scarf, hand-bag, white glove, Irene, white hand, fingers, eyes, hand-bag, Irene, Somer-villes, white hand, fingers, hand-bag, snap, smile, smiles, garden, Ralph, Pearl, trees, rake, Lon-don, smile, Tilly tell, Irene, tell Tilly, Sand-mouth, you me, cross-heart, friends, hope to die, Tilly, you me, Irene, Tilly tell, mag-az-ine, eyes, white hand, hand-bag, cross-heart, secrets, rain-coat lady, white hand, hope to die, hand-bag, snap, eyes, secrets, apples, Irene, mag-az-ine, hope to die, eyes . . .

★

Mavis Clark is sitting behind the counter reading an article about flying saucers in *Titbits*, quietly humming the tune of 'I See the Moon', when she hears heels approaching the department from the direction of the staircase.

She raises her eyes from the page momentarily and sees Mrs Spencer. She wouldn't normally pay her any more attention than most of the customers who pass through in a day but something in the woman's manner catches her attention.

She doesn't show herself; the magazine rests on her lap. She looks again and sees the woman casting an eye round what she must presume to be an empty, unguarded department. The girl is used to calling Mrs Spencer a 'cold fish' to her friends in the town, but this afternoon it strikes her that she is behaving in an (even for her) unusually furtive manner.

The reason becomes clear when Mavis Clark catches sight of the woman putting her handbag over one arm and tugging at the white glove on one of the dummy hands. It won't come off. She stops pulling and, quite suddenly, drops the gloved hand and the other loose glove from the counter-top into the hold of her bag.

Mavis Clark is confused in the first instant. Then she's conscious that she's smiling at what she has just witnessed.

The realisation quickly comes to her that she alone has seen what has happened, that it establishes a different relationship between her and the woman from that involving any other person in the town. A strangely intimate relationship, it *could* be, if she—Mavis Clark—chose it to be so. She, Mavis Clark, has the command of choosing.

She notices the Moscombe girl standing outside, but ignores her. She crosses the floor.

'Hello, Mrs Spencer.'

Mrs Spencer jumps like a scalded cat. Her eyes swivel: she *looks* like an intruder apprehended. One hand reaches up to her bun of hair, the other closes over the clasp of her handbag.

'I didn't—I didn't—'

'Miss Spink's away. It's just me.'

'Oh. Oh, I see.'

'All on my own.'

'Yes.'

Mrs Spencer smiles: very awkwardly, it occurs to the girl.

'Can I be of some assistance, Mrs Spencer?'

The woman's eyes roam round the department in alarm, above that strained, rather manic smile. She has never smiled to Mavis Clark before. Her mouth is quite dry, and it's less a smile than a grimace.

All this Mavis Clark is taking note of for further consideration later.

'I was just—'

'Looking round, Mrs Spencer?'

'Yes. I wanted—just to look.'

'Feel free, do,' Mavis Clark says, in the style of Miss Spink when she speaks to her favoured customers. 'Feel free, madam.'

'Thank you.' Mrs Spencer appears to start at the 'madam'. Regular customers of the shop—Mrs Spencer is one—are aware that 'madam' is not a Mavis Clark word.

There's a silence between the two women. Mavis Clark realises that her knowledge is suspected by the other one.

'Wind's getting up,' she ventures. 'Don't you think, Mrs Spencer?'

'It's blowing, yes.'

'Better keep yourself wrapped up. Put something on your head.'

'Yes.'

'Four-fifths of the body's temperature is lost through exposure of the head,' the girl says, speaking Miss Spink's words but uncertain about the fraction.

'Yes, I'm sure.'

'So I think you should—'

Mrs Spencer smiles nervously in the silence.

'—look after yourself,' the girl continues.

'Yes.' Mrs Spencer coughs. 'That sounds—it sounds a good idea.'

Nothing further happens. Mrs Spencer walks towards the door. She turns the handle. The door-bell rings.

'Good-bye,' she says quietly, and coughs another frog out of her throat.

'I think—' Mavis Clark pauses.

'Yes?' Mrs Spencer is obliged to ask.

'—haven't you forgotten something?'

'Have I?'

The girl crosses the aisle, to the denuded display-stand, where other long-fingered hands continue clutching at empty air.

'Your scarf,' she says and picks it up.

'Oh. Yes.' Mrs Spencer manages a very hollow-sounding laugh. 'How stupid of me.'

The scarf is returned to its owner, who looks only at her battered lizard-hide handbag and doesn't lift her eyes to the girl.

'You should be more careful, Mrs Spencer,' Mavis Clark tells her, imitating Miss Spink's talking-to-the-customers voice. There's a very deliberate 'tone' in her delivery, which she hasn't practised before on anyone: she fully intends it as she watches Mrs Spencer's face reddening.

'You'll be forgetting your gloves next, Mrs Spencer.'

She knows she has carried this little encounter on her own terms. She wonders how many more there will be.

The door closes. Mavis Clark has time to think and she is less clear what she can win from doing the thing she has: letting Mrs Spencer walk out through the door with the booty of the stolen hand and gloves in her handbag. I have to get something out of it, she thinks, but she doesn't know what.

In films she'd seen at the Alhambra people would say, 'But this is blackmail' and you were meant to reply 'That's an ugly word' and play the scene quite casually, very contained, smiling all the time. But maybe since the War good and bad had become more muddled?

When her father was still alive but away on duty, her mother had become very friendly with a man up the street and she'd been told that she read to him in the afternoons because his sight was bad—'it's this War's doing', her mother would say and nod her head in the knowing, solemn way adults always nodded their heads, with brows wrinkled. Things had never sorted themselves out for her after that. When her father came home he didn't speak so much about the night blitzes he got the planes ready for, and the killing: and her mother, dressed in heels and fancy clothes, didn't tell any of them where she was going when she went out. 'Can you get me this or that?' she would ask the eldest daughter, Lilly, and it would mean she had to ring up one-and-sixpence on the till in the shop where she worked while she bundled the blouse or jumper into a paper bag.

Mavis Clark stood at the counter watching Mrs Spencer hurrying across the street, into the teeth of the wind. The stupid Moscombe girl had turned round and was staring after her. A drainpipe hung loose on the building next door and it rattled dismally. Not as bad as those cats-and-dogs days when it pissed down.

The elation she'd felt left her.

She felt almost sorry for the woman, and she also despised her for her pettiness. Suddenly too she was hating *herself* for not knowing what to do; and she was hating Mrs Spencer more, for making it more difficult for her than it should have been, and for using her nob's voice on her. She hated that idiot girl: and she hated the rattling drainpipe hanging loose from the wall, and the wind seeping between the door and the lintel, and the whole bloody rotten place.

★

This is a stranger assignment than the investigator's usual. A husband has asked him to trail his wife: nothing out of the ordinary in that. The presumption is infidelity. But, as yet, Brown has no evidence of a man involved. He has made enquiries in London, and can find no trace there either of any impassioned gentleman.

His quarry is more enigmatic than he is used to, but professionalism is the issue here, and 'Brown' prides himself on getting to the bottom of each mystery. He takes every pain and precaution to ensure that nothing and no one should be able to escape him. Only a handful of times has he been left stumped. This lady isn't wholly enigmatic, though, not to Arthur Brown/John Jones/Geoffrey Crane/Philip Todd.

Something about her face—glimpsed beneath a Grace Kelly headscarf and behind her white-framed sunglasses as she attended to her shopping on Piccadilly—had struck him as hauntingly familiar. Luckily he has a photographic memory for faces, even those noticed in newspapers for a couple of seconds. He made enquiries. The story had appeared four or five years back: it had to do with a villa party at (of all places in the world most unlike Sandmouth) Cap Ferrat. The woman was captioned as 'Miss Kaye' beneath the photographs: she stood on the terrace of the house holding a champagne glass, surrounded by the rich and famous. In the background of the group was a younger version of the man who had hired his services: Mr Alexander Lambert-Flitch, a house-guest of the industrialist villa-owner.

'Miss Kaye' was possibly a well-preserved forty-year-old now, or just a little older: in the photographs she must have been in her mid-thirties. The chances were that she hadn't been '*Miss* Kaye'. Usually an unmarried woman of that age who had the good looks of a 'Miss Kaye' was either a liar or a lesbian. The latter was possible, although that kind normally gave off a chill he picked up easily. (There was more than a touch of the refrigerated about the sorry-looking assistant he'd seen staring out of Crockers' window at lunchtime, and definitely more than a suggestion of the deep-frozen blasted off the woman in the cape and fur hat breezing along the promenade with a defective in tow.) If there wasn't a man *or* a woman involved, he was on much less predictable ground. Dealing with love (if it ever truly was: Mr Brown was a sceptic) or with 'lust' perhaps, the victims were burned splendidly, and frequently perished in the flames: dealing with the criminally inclined, you were required to set traps to catch them—but first of all you had to gauge the nature of their intended crime.

Brown could conceive of the likelihood of crime in this case, if not the specifics: the background of the case was notoriously anonymous and dubious at the same time—the ritzy Corniche, plush Mayfair (where the couple lived), a hick seaside town out of the season. His suspicions were that, as so often happened, the woman was hampered by conscience: her comfortable, luxurious life without wants in Mayfair unsettled her, she felt no more assured there as a married woman than she had as a glamorous visitor called 'Miss Kaye' at a Sunday alfresco lunch beside a Riviera swimming-pool. To Brown, the cast of her face and her soigné poise suggested she wasn't a stranger to money itself, it had always been a familiar habitat to her. (Instinct invariably told you if someone was living out of their habitual element, they had the marks of slow drowning or became ether-drunk.) The nature and source of that original wealth had probably been very different: 'Miss Kaye' might have had a North Country upbringing, or been born into moth-eaten, inbred gentility. Her mother might have been widowed and re-married or the family might have had Asiatic holdings and lost them in the War: money was also the least stable and predictable of elements to depend on, but it brands for life.

Brown badly needed a strong lead, but Mrs Lambert-Flitch (as she now was) appeared to have covered her tracks very well: a private wedding in Paris with the minimum of company present, a vague account of her history told to her husband (home in Ireland, an education in Cumberland and Belgium, not a single mention of the old favourites—Hove or Budleigh Salterton), no relatives, no friends salvaged from the past.

What caused Brown's perplexity was the fact that the woman didn't seem particularly concerned about concealing herself. She wore her long fur coat and her French silk headscarf and dark glasses inside the hotel as well as out, which did as much to draw attention to her as to eliminate her presence from the scene. If she wasn't known here, if she was going to risk people's noticing her, why had she come? He'd watched her remove her sunglasses to consult the map in the hotel's foyer, looking not at the stretch of coast but at the plan of the town's streets, tilting her head to read their names. But why had she driven down *now*, and why did she need to familiarise herself with the town from a map? Of course she'd used a false name to sign the register (Mrs Grosvenor), but the midnight-blue Alvis was the one she used to drive about London, and her clothes couldn't be confused with any of the forms of local costume in these parts.

When the old gossiping dame had called her 'attractive', he'd blamed her eyesight. Catching sight of her in the hall as he came downstairs, he'd noticed the shapely legs positioned with a decided crook, like a model's: a stance designed for use at Cap Ferrat cocktail gatherings, not for the delight of Sandmouth's rotarians and elderly couples taking cheap pre-season holidays.

He'd stepped sideways at the bottom of the staircase, to make sure she didn't see him. He was presuming that she still didn't know who he was, and that she wouldn't suspect—unless she was more used to this cat-and-mouse game than he imagined her to be.

A cluster of men with sociable, outward-going faces stood discussing rotarian business: a midsummer pageant being organised for charity. The floats seemed to be giving them some problems. They were discussing the wisdom of having a pageant queen, and should she have something to do with the goddess said to be buried under the excavation site?

One of the men paused when he caught sight of the woman in the three-quarter-length sable coat and headscarf and the sunglasses pushed up on her brow. She was asking the man at the reception desk a question. Brown/Jones/Crane/Todd strained to hear what was being said. He saw the other men turning or looking backwards. They stared at her quite innocently. Probably she *was* attractive to them, all contentedly married men with wholesome and passably pretty wives waiting at home. From side on, the thinness of her face was certainly less noticeable: perhaps her nose in profile was just a little too sharp for the eye's comfort, but her audience were only viewing the composite image, and that was impressive by Sandmouth standards.

Attractiveness, of course, was a purely academic concern to a man like Brown/Jones/Crane/Todd. Those who had it tended to squander it rather than capitalise on it, and those who didn't have it coveted it. How could it possibly affect this case, that was the matter for debate. Where was the man who was lusting for her? Where was the plain, lemon-faced woman attempting to bribe her with some secret knowledge? Where was the handsome, feckless lover who had distracted her from her husband—a man in his sixties with white hair and a yellowy parchment complexion and the means to buy her whatever she wanted, a black sable coat and a Paris headscarf and a midnight-blue Alvis car to give her the illusion of her independence?

★

Perhaps the fault was in being single? Adele Adaire would frequently perpend the matter. She'd read once that married people live on average eight years longer than the unmarried. 'What the hell?' she'd persuaded herself. 'I have my independence after all.'

But, after all, what was independence, convincing yourself

282

there was nothing to hold you, no staying ropes, when it always seemed to be the wrong person you were attracted to time after time after time, who respected you least of all for this foolish pride of solitude and self-determination which wasn't that at all?

A child might have made the difference, Mrs Messiter would tell herself. It was the reason for a house, a home, a routine: the propagation of the species.

She didn't wish for herself that there might have been someone to whom she would have continued as a memory, after her mortal days were done. But she felt she'd let *Brian* down, because she hadn't been able to conceive.

Long ago that guilt had become something else: she'd tried to argue to herself that Brian didn't even deserve her pity and compassion, just as she was certain she didn't merit his. She knew she was impatient with him. She couldn't help it. She couldn't explain 'why' to him, didn't know how to, how to begin.

Children excused everything, Mrs Dick knew. Everything.

They supported a marriage, they justified it. The Bible said so, the Bible the five of them sat listening to on Sunday mornings in the church of St Andrew and St John.

A marriage survived on piano scales, and violin exercises, and steaming baths, and lost socks, and a rabbit called 'Thumper' running loose in the garden.

More bother than they were worth, Mrs Lenny thought, remembering home.

She paused, holding the tin of Silvo in one hand. She shook her head.

Children should give *back* to you, not suck out of you all the time. Sometimes she felt she'd given away something precious of herself she shouldn't have, spawning her kids. Denise was going to take years off her in the end.

Mrs P. was lucky, for just now. But it would come to her too. It was what *he* wanted, she could see that. The child would be sent away to school, though, and it would be much easier that way, worth any money. They could all go on being polite with each other, because they wouldn't be getting under one another's feet every hour every day of the week.

Money shielded you from so much. A house could never be big enough to hold all the feelings it was required to. Even this one, 'The Laurels', it could start to shrink in on you, start to suffocate you if—against the odds, right enough, but possible, just—if life decided it was going to take you on the famous switch-back ride.

She'd quite enjoyed it sometimes, the sex business with Rob, but not as much as *he* did, of course.

While he heaved and humped away she'd be looking at her uniform hanging up on the back of the bedroom door. She'd always have the uncomfortable notion they weren't using it properly, the sex, that really it should be for kids, and just a few times you could do it for pleasure's sake, for the hell of it.

She'd had to pretend a bit, of course, that she was getting as much out of it as he was. Except she was never very sure what she *should* be feeling.

In the houses she worked in, the double-beds would creak busily on their one or two nights a week—she had an ear for it—and she'd lie in her own prim narrow bed wondering what it was the wives were thinking of while it was going on. Apart from England. If they endured it, or if they ever dared to *enjoy* it. If they could ever contemplate *asking* for it.

Your polite, brisk satisfaction was as much as men expected of you, and the right word in their ear now and then. Men liked good girls. It didn't stop them going to the pix and ogling Jayne Mansfield, bursting out of her bra, but it was you they came back to. A blushing girl in your 34B cup. 'Don't let them go too far', 'no man wants you shop-soiled', 'he won't respect you'. And all the time by that second or third outing he's pleading with you, 'Just a finger, please!'

It was complicated, a muddle, too much for Nanny Filbert. She was glad she'd got her youth over with, behind her. Well behind her. Today the standards weren't so different from the 'twenties, only the temptations were worse and there were more opportunities. She'd never known a man with a car to take her places, no one well enough off for that. And if she had, she could guess where, the two of them snug on the back seat, his final destination would have been.

284

What if *she* could hear me thinking, Nanny Filbert often asked herself. Bloody Mrs Mason. She'd blow a gasket. Knowing I see through *her*, that married life at 'Linden Lodge' isn't happy ever after, and they're like a couple in a weather house, they're stuck here with each other, together and apart, and it's foul after fair, fair after foul. Foul after fair, Mr Sangster, you should have been grateful, *grateful*, didn't I spare you all that?

She'd left Tommy Dorsey's orchestra in the living-room playing 'Anything Goes' when she discovered the marks on the bathroom linoleum, under the lavatory cistern. Lots of white spots. Mrs Trevis was puzzled why she couldn't get rid of them.

Momentarily a thought—a very troubled thought—had come into her head, as to what they might be, but she'd immediately banished it and hadn't entertained it again.

She sensed things weren't quite as they should be in 'Lyndhurst', although she had no experience or knowledge of life otherwise to judge the situation by. It'll all come right in the end, she would tell herself: having this nice house, and Howard having his good job, and Mr Braddock having such high hopes for him. On Hill Street and George Street people smiled at her and she smiled back, but a little hesitantly.

One day there would be a child: a boy, she hoped. She'd be able to smile back with confidence then, with bright confidence, knowing the Trevises were shipshape and sea-worthy, they'd found the proper course at last, they were floating now on an even keel.

*

Mrs Gutteridge just happened to look across George Street at the very moment Mr Jope from the Clarence Hotel (Sandmouth's next Mayor-elect) was making his exit from the premises of Thos. Bendall, Accountant. She saw his eyes notice her, concentrate on her for three or four seconds, then shift their gaze elsewhere.

The three or four seconds were crucial, she felt. When Stephen Jope looked at her—scrutinized her—she was conscious of his attention as she was of no one else's in Sandmouth. Maybe she imagined a particular interest that wasn't there: or maybe it was.

She had only been introduced to him a couple of times. They'd exchanged a few words. His eyes had had an intensity she'd never encountered before. She found those craggy, rather careworn looks appealing in a man: by comparison, she sometimes felt Ken's trim, well-cared-for appearance and the ready tan he picked up on the golf course must be making his job and its responsibilities seem easier to people than she knew they were.

Stephen Jope's footsteps slowed after a few yards. Mrs Gutteridge turned away before she had a chance to discover if he was going to look back at her or not.

Better perhaps if she didn't know. Better perhaps if, for a while longer, the mystery remained just so.

★

Mavis Clark is not really Mavis Clark but Irene Sweeney. She'd always liked the name 'Mavis' and 'Clark' made her think of Petula, so she picked her moment and she changed.

No one in Sandmouth knows that. No one in Sandmouth knows anything about her, but that is exactly as she wishes the situation to be. Not even Miss Spink realises that her London vowels aren't affected, but come to her quite naturally. She betrays herself, of course, a dozen times a day; however, Miss Spink has her own dignified appearances to maintain, and is usually too busy concentrating on those to notice. Sometimes her eyes do suggest recognition: but Mavis Clark as she now is can shrug her off, she is never going to give anything of herself away to someone like Miss Spink.

No one in the town remembers her, although she was here in another life before her reincarnation as 'Mavis Clark'. In the War days a trainload of child evacuees brought her and deposited her on the 'down' platform of Sandmouth Station; then she and the three others in her group were driven in a car to the 'Old Rectory'. That was in 1941, when the house belonged to Mrs Somerville and her husband. The couple had good intentions and a lot of room to spare and although the house badly needed repairs and redecoration, it was like nothing else on earth to little Irene Sweeney and she felt she'd woken up inside a dream.

The Somervilles had volunteered to have them—four children from London—and tried to cater for their every whim and fancy. The others quickly learned to take advantage of them; Irene Sweeney did try her very best not to, not if she could help it. Jocelyn and Eunice Somerville were a tall, willowy pair, who wore out-at-elbow clothes and down-at-heel shoes, but they had great—so Mavis Clark appreciated now— refinement. Their behaviour was unfailingly courteous, their goodness quite unforced; they wanted their charges to feel they *belonged* to this house and its garden for the duration of their stay. Certain drawers and the sitting-room bureau were kept locked, but the child had the impression that the Somervilles had probably only lost or mislaid the keys and it wasn't a house of secrets, like other people's. The only secrets were the children's, taking an extra spoonful of something when the Somervilles' stooped backs were turned and when they weren't at all hungry for it, lifting the telephone when there was no one to hear and listening to the woman in the exchange asking 'Who is this speaking, please?' The Somervilles took them on outings in the car, and made up picnics and teas for them all to eat in the garden when they were at home, and borrowed bicycles from their friends in the town so that the four of them could go off exploring the countryside.

She'd had to go back to London eventually. Nothing there was as she was expecting. Her mother told her that her father was dead: her father who had turned morose and silent with the War, and who'd started to spend as much time in 'The Pewter Pot' as he did at home. Even more men came to the house than in the long-ago before she left. There always seemed to be money now in her mother's purse, quite a lot of it, but she never used it to buy any of the things that had made the Somervilles' life so special. She missed the good things, and the Somervilles' excellent manners, and she forgot that the house, even to a city child's eyes, had seen grander days. As the years passed, the memory of Sandmouth became even happier, summerier, and more and more seductive. She hated London by comparison. She missed the simplest pleasures of daily life at the 'Old Rectory', the warmth of the thick blankets, the smell of soap in the bathroom and wax in the downstairs rooms, the rich shine of the silver on the sideboard, the deep lustre of the mahogany dining-table, the echoes her feet made on the wooden floorblocks, the weight of the panelled doors when she turned the brass knobs and pushed with all her strength against the wood.

What had finished her with London was walking down Clerkenwell Road one Springtime Monday lunchtime in 1951 and seeing her dad, as alive and like his old self as could be, stepping quite dapper and jack's-the-lad out of a pub, whistling 'I got plenty o' nuttin' '. She'd stopped in her tracks, stood frozen on the spot, clueless what to do. Every second she lost was taking him further away from her. But that day she'd just let him go. By the evening, with a clearer head and an uneasy conscience, she decided she would go back to the pub the next day and look for him. She went back, and searched, but there was no sign of him: no one knew what—or who— she was talking about. She returned for the rest of that week, and on the following Monday, but she never saw him again. Maybe he'd been tipped the wink and he'd scarpered?

It settled the matter about where to live and who she really was. She didn't want the past that had to do with her dad and her mum, and she didn't want the name they'd given her. She went home early one afternoon, at a time when she wasn't due; she found a man's jacket hanging up on the hat-stand in the poky little hall and heard groaning noises from behind her mother's bedroom door. She packed a suitcase while all the business was still going on—the bedsprings creaking, feet or arms slapping on the thin walls, gasps exploding—then she emptied her mother's purse and walked out without a backward look.

She couldn't have thought of going anywhere else except Sandmouth. Waiting for the train in the station she ransacked her case to find the silver teaspoon she'd stolen from the 'Rectory'; she dropped it into her coat pocket and stood turning it over and over and over, like a lucky charm. It was on the journey west, staring at the sepia photograph of white cliffs and a pretty town that might have been Sandmouth above the opposite seat, it was then that she settled on the 're-adjustment' of her personality: Irene Sweeney became Mavis Clark and by the time she jumped down on to the platform at journey's end, she was in an even surer frame of mind.

It was as well that she was, because she very soon learned

that the past hadn't survived intact, as she'd been presuming it must have. She was intensely disappointed when she discovered that the Somervilles had gone and the house was up for sale. For the first few afternoons of her new life in Sandmouth she took to walking round and round the garden of the uninhabited 'Rectory', now even wilder than it had been in the Somervilles' days when she and Phil and Raff and Pearl and (sometimes) a queer girl called Tilly Moscombe had played their running and chasing games there. The glass in the cucumber frames had shattered, and birds were roosting in the old summerhouse; all the vegetation seemed to be conspiring to trip her up, to lay her low, and she needed her wits about her just to keep upright and walking.

She found herself a job in Partridge's ironmonger's shop, then a better one in Miss Craxton the Milliner's, then about eight months later a position fell vacant in Crockers', in the combined 'Haberdashery' and 'Ladies' Outerwear Accoutrements' departments, usually referred to by the shorter name as 'Haberdashery'. The man who interviewed her smiled at her how the men she used to find in the house would smile at her mother, and she played the scene in his office with what she could remember of her mother's forced sunniness on those occasions. She found out through the grapevine that Miss Spink wasn't half narked because she hadn't been allowed to have any say, but what the hell, she could cope. Now she was quite popular in the town, even with the natives like Dolores Drinkald: she was in a set that could share a laugh together, she was accepted as Mavis Clark who didn't let things get her down and who gave men a bit of what they fancied if they set about it the right way and who knew someone in Bournemouth who'd shaken hands with Max Bygraves and claimed to know his telephone number, and she believed that, all told, she'd really masterminded this new life not at all badly.

Mavis Clark shifted on her stool. She laid down her magazine on the counter-top.

She was being watched through the window again by Tilly Moscombe. She'd got to know the girl, sneaking into the old orchard of 'Hallam House' with the others to steal apples. (The 'Rectory' had had its own orchard, tumbledown and with a glut of red apples, but an apple always tasted sweeter when it came from where you weren't supposed to pick them.) The funny girl of six or seven used to sit with them under the trees, and they would all tell her tales—the most shocking ones they could remember—about life back in London. She'd taken less relish in the tale-telling than the others: they spoke as if that was the 'real' life and somehow this one in Sandmouth wasn't, but she knew differently. She talked to the daft girl more than the others did. In return she liked to be told garbled bits and pieces about the town, and these gave her a feeling that she 'belonged' in a way the others couldn't, in her imagination she could go weaving in and out the houses with Tilly Moscombe on her daily round. People in Sandmouth accepted the odd girl and she felt *she* must too if she wasn't to continue to be an outsider like Phil and Raff and Pearl. She'd never known anyone like Tilly Moscombe. In her foreigner's cockney she told her things about herself no one else knew, lots and lots of things, because—at eight years old—she'd felt she should, so she could trade one life for another one. The girl in London she was telling her about wasn't really *her* any more. Sandmouth was the nicest place she'd ever seen, with the sea and the gardens behind their hedges, and she felt she was telling secrets on someone else, another person who just happened to have the same name as herself, 'Irene Sweeney'.

She was never very sure what Tilly Moscombe was taking in of the things she said. Sometimes she looked so stupid, with no expression on her face: at other times all the feeling she had seemed to be there in her eyes, trapped inside. In a spooky way it was the *risk* she enjoyed, never knowing how many of her confidences were going into the girl's head and sticking there and how many of them weren't, but just floating away into the blue.

Mavis Clark shifted fretfully on her stool.

She felt a cold shiver pass down her back, from her neck to her bottom sitting on the cushion. She had always been careful to keep out of Tilly Moscombe's way. She had supposed she would remember nothing from a decade ago, and anyway she knew she looked nothing like the London kid she'd been—but she did it out of superstition: and maybe because she still had such a vivid memory (stronger than any of those of London) of the changing phases of intelligence behind Tilly Moscombe's eyes.

The girl was mouthing something through the glass: like a fish under water, behind an aquarium window. Mavis Clark looked away, at her own hands holding the magazine, and she saw they were shaking.

The bell rang above the door. Mavis Clark lifted her eyes. She watched, horrified, as the girl crossed the threshold and took a few steps into the shop, shuffling one foot in front of the other.

The magazine fell on to the floor and Mavis Clark stiffened. There was a queer, screwy expression on the girl's face. She was shaping the words like bubbles: sounds twisted out of all recognisable shape. What was it she was trying to say?

Mavis Clark shook her head at her. The girl was pointing. At the street—then at her. Then she shook her head, how Mavis Clark was shaking hers.

'I don't know you,' Mavis Clark said, remembering the words from somewhere else: her mother saying it to her the first time a man had ever come to the house, before she was sent away—her mother repeating the words and then whispering to her as she closed the front door on her, 'I'll tell you later, Irene, just go away now.'

'I don't know you,' she repeated, more definitely. Tilly Moscombe gawped at her.

'This is a shop. What do you want?'

She saw the confusion on the girl's face, like an image of her own, not knowing what to believe and what not to believe.

For several seconds they watched each other, both of them fixed by the other: Mavis Clark rigid on her stool, Tilly Moscombe stranded between two counters.

A movement appeared in the corner of Mavis Clark's eye. She looked over—it was a customer—then her eyes swivelled back to Tilly Moscombe and she stared at her very hard. Very hard indeed, so it was the stupid girl's turn to flinch.

The woman asked a question from one of the display stands. Mavis Clark tried adjusting her voice as best she could but it came out sounding hopelessly London. She felt herself burning red. The customer didn't reply, as if there was no obligation to engage with inferiors.

'Get out!' Mavis Clark hissed at the girl. She caught another

291

movement in her eye as the customer turned her head.

She glanced at Tilly Moscombe. Just get out, she wanted to shout at her, go on, piss off, you: clear out of it.

And, magically, Tilly Moscombe retreated: some word still unspoken in her mouth, heavy as a stone maybe.

Orchard conversations. The bad shining out of the past, like the bloody watermark it always was. Mavis Clark wanted to shout the foulest word at the girl. 'Just bloody fuck off, you!'

The customer walked round the edge of the department. Mavis Clark felt she was on fire. The woman didn't look at her; she was fluttering her fingers at one of the displays.

Tilly Moscombe had stopped on the pavement outside the window and was looking back into the shop. Mavis Clark might have looked away, but she was drawn to the watching face and shook her head.

The girl was holding up her hand; the fingers waved, like fingers fitting themselves into a glove.

Mavis Clark shook her head again.

Apples.

She shook her head a third time and realised she shouldn't be. Stolen apples, Cox's orange pippins and bright red Worcesters and sour green Prince Alberts, and stomachs too full to eat.

She saw the woman looking across at her, then at Tilly Moscombe standing outside the window. Mavis Clark smiled at the customer, a brilliant, frantic, unforgettable smile to put the connection out of the woman's mind. *I am just as you see me, Mavis Clark. My life is clear and untroubled. Except where did the Somervilles go?—the girl at the window knows nothing—the past is never done, it tugs and tugs on a chain.*

*

'So really, Miss Spink, hard as it is for me to say this—'

Miss Spink wanted to hold on to the edge of the desk but was determined that she wouldn't, she mustn't appear to be weakening.

'On our side, it's been a very happy relationship—'

She stared over his head, out the window, across the rooftops of Sandmouth. The wind had got up. A Saint George's flag flapped from a flagpole and seemed an unconnected fragment of the day.

'—but all good things, don't they say, they have to come to an end sometime—'

She couldn't believe it was happening, any of it.

'Crockers', of course, would be generous in, er, showing their—*our*—appreciation—'

A jumped-up little rat of a man: right off they would have been wise to him in London.

'—our appreciation of your fine service over the, er, past, er, nine years—'

'Ten years,' she immediately corrected him.

'Yes. Yes, of course. Ten years.'

She should have stayed in London.

'Of course I was going to discuss the reorganisation with you. I *would* have done, in fact, very shortly.'

What had she got from this place?

'A smaller department certainly makes more sound *business* sense. It's what we should always be thinking of—'

How could she have lived here?

'Miss Clark has given me a few suggestions.'

'What?'

'Oh, just one or two. Her ideas. They're, er, very fresh, very novel.'

The slut.

'Of course it'll be a while before we can reorganise ourselves. Modernise ourselves, I should say.'

The two-faced slut.

'It's my hope, Miss Spink, that we will be one of the most modern stores in this region within eighteen months or, let's say, a couple of years.'

Behind my back.

'I hope you'll approve when you see it. And that you'll continue to, er, support us, to be a good customer. Just as you were—as you have been—a loyal member of our staff—'

He was fumbling for the words. She hoped they would stick in his gullet and choke him. The sly, deceitful pig of a man.

The door opened. Miss Naylor didn't notice at first what was happening and stepped into the room. Then she glanced over and saw Miss Spink. Her eyes went out on stalks.

Miss Spink lowered *her* eyes to the girl's modern, stream-lined breasts pushing through the front of her blouse. The

293

common tart. Like Mavis Clark, she would be on her back for that man—the goat—and ne'er a thought in her head for what she did. 'Red hat, no bloomers' they used to say in London. She wondered where they did it: on top of the broad, sturdy desk?

'Er, a glass of water for Miss Spink perhaps, Miss Naylor—'

'No, thank you,' Miss Spink replied in her chilliest voice.

She wanted to hold on to the desk top but she wasn't going to allow herself. She didn't want to touch anything in this squalid, vile room. She only wanted to be gone, to be out of it, away.

'You're, er, going, Miss Spink?' Cheevy asked her.

'Apparently. I think we—you—have said all there is to be said.'

'I hope we part—'

'Of course,' she said impatiently. 'I shall fulfil my duties until the end of the month.'

'We needn't say any particular day—'

'How *very* generous of you, Mr Cheevy,' she replied corrosively.

'I—I represent *Crockers'*, of course, Miss Spink,' he told her in a justifying tone of voice.

Oh no you don't, Miss Spink knew. I remember the other Mr Crockers, the father and the uncle: not this poor substitute of a son *you*'ve got under your thumb. Does he have an eye for the girls too, the busty kind with lots of 'it' bursting through the fronts of their blouses?

She flounced out of the room, without a backward—or even a sideways—look. Regally, majestically, like Bette Davis in 'Elizabeth and Essex', she was thinking as she did it: or like Flora Robson in 'Fire Over England'. My proudest moment.

She left the door standing open. It was closed behind her, rather abruptly: that girl, who else? And now what?—they were going to have a good laugh about her, were they? She had half a mind to stand at the door and listen. But tears were bubbling up into her eyes.

She looked behind her. She hated the name on its plaque on the door. Just damn Leonard Cheevy, she thought: if God has any justice, He will surely damn Leonard Cheevy. *And* Mavis Clark, damn the pair of them. Please, God.

How else, she thought as she started walking downstairs,

how else can I believe that there truly *is* mercy? But how—the tears floated in her eyes—how does *this* fit into the godly scheme of things: all that happens being for the best?

★

Cedric Prentice paused as he sifted through the letters for the afternoon post.

He was remembering the remark of the early morning. 'Gang warily with Mr Pargiter'.

What had made her say it? What did she know, his wife?

In a small town morality was a more (or less) complex affair than an onlooker—even Penelope—could appreciate. He preferred to think they had reasonably enlightened views about such matters in Sandmouth. They lived in colour, not in black-and-white: they didn't judge by extreme contrasts of wrong and right, that was how people became victims and were sacrificed to the system.

Pargiter survived—they all survived. It was like being at school (even though the younger version of Pargiter couldn't have had any experience of the proper kind), everyone being required to shake down.

Penelope didn't quite comprehend. But he was content with all her other virtues—made more than happy—and he left it at this, that there are certain aspects of human conduct concerning which a husband cannot expect his wife to have any true conception, one of them being trapped in the ring, in the din and dust of the fray, and the other looking down from the trees.

★

Eric Selwyn hesitated, then stood up as the girl in butterscotch colours walked into the shop.

'I'm looking for a present,' she said with her habitual coolness.

'Any sort?' he enquired as he always enquired of her.

'It's for a birthday present. I'll be staying with the person, so I *have* to get something.'

'I see.'

'I don't care, really. Anything'll do.'

'*I* see,' Selwyn repeated, with a shade less respect in his voice. The girl—as he was able to anticipate—was sensitive enough to notice, and he watched her eyes return to him from the corner of the room.

She came in occasionally, sometimes just to browse, sometimes to taunt him with the possibility of a purchase. She'd bought a few things, nothing very expensive, always 'for presents'.

The air sparked, he knew, whenever they came into contact with each other. His first impression had been the right one: she was a rich Iti bitch, turning up her nose at his corduroy trousers and mustard waistcoat. He'd convinced himself she was a tease; every time she came into the shop, he was able to catch her out, looking at him in mirrors and the silver backs of the dressing-table sets he laid out.

Maybe she came in with the specific intention of *being caught* sneaking a look at him?

Why *him*, though? Unless it was because he appeared to have a pedigree she didn't?

Appearances can be put forward to deceive: or did she realise that? Was the situation even further complicated? In other words, she knew for a fact that she was being conned?

'How much is this?' she asked in an Oxford-y voice she probably practised on the assistants in Elliston's.

'What's that?'

'This.'

She picked up a silver mustard pot.

'I—'

He hadn't meant to leave it out; someone had called on the telephone just before the shop bell rang and he'd left it lying on top of the gesso table.

'It's *quite* nice,' she said.

He still had to consult the silver hallmark tables before he could date it and price it. He had a hunch it came from Hester Bateman's workrooms, or from her sons', but his magnifying glass hadn't been to hand.

'I'm afraid—Miss Arbuthnot is holding that one back. For another customer.'

'Oh.' Lavezzoli's daughter nodded. 'The fabled Miss Arbuthnot,' she said.

Her tone sent, literally, a shiver through Selwyn. She sounded, at the very least, sceptical.

'Aren't *I* a favoured customer, then?' she asked.

Selwyn felt himself, against all his principles, blushing. He was aware of her smiling in his direction, running one hand through her hair.

Hacking jacket and mustard waistcoat notwithstanding, the young man knew that without the moral bulwark of the fabled Miss Arbuthnot he lacked the confidence he ought to have, which he *appeared* to have, and he hated himself for the failing and for the obligation of deception.

A movement outside the window arrested his attention. It was the gangly Moscombe girl: she was walking past—louping past—and gazing in.

He ignored her, turned his head away: *tried* to ignore her as he looked round the room for something else to offer in place of the mustard pot.

He pushed a thumb into one of the pockets of his waistcoat. He wasn't going to let Sandmouth's ice-cream heiress—even if she *was* at Oxford—get the better of him.

'What about . . .'—he pointed with the other hand—'what about the figurine?'

'Where?'

'On the dresser.'

He watched the corners of her mouth turn down.

'It's too—pretty,' she said.

' "Too pretty"?'

'I want something useful. Useful-ish.'

She'd spoken the word 'pretty' with a sneer in her voice. Her tone was always adversely critical. He was starting to plumb the depths of her dislike, not just for his trade, but for the values she saw it representing. Beneath the toffee-coloured top layer (he envisaged the pleasurable undressing) she had the disposition and commitments of a—a socialist perhaps? Her famous, much-envied social life was a blind to the truth of that: she was a viper in the unsuspecting bosom . . .

yellow waistcoat man, shop house, lady lady, mirrors, chairs, tables, china lady, yellow waistcoat man, shop house, open door ring bell, lady lady, yellow waistcoat man, eyes, mirrors, chairs, tables, plates, china lady, yellow waistcoat man, eyes, lady lady, mirrors, eyes, not friends, but, lady lady, eyes,

*yellow waistcoat man, mirrors, brush, silver, lady lady, open
door ring bell, but, not friends, lady lady, mirrors, shop house,
china lady, yellow waistcoat man, eyes, lady lady, mirrors,
eyes . . .*

'I prefer the mustard pot.'

Selwyn watched her pick it up again.

'I . . . I don't think . . .'

'I know, you've told me. All about your Miss Arbuthnot.'

Her eyes met his, quite frankly. It was a look he interpreted
as inviting him to share in a conspiracy: their mutual, double-
deception on the town.

'On second thoughts,' he heard himself saying, 'perhaps . . .'

'For a good customer—good-*ish*—I'm sure she wouldn't
mind.'

'No,' he replied. 'No. I'm sure she wouldn't.'

'It's what I want . . .'

And what you want, Selwyn knew, you will most certainly
get.

But, perfectly, a bargain should implicate two in the pleasure
of the transaction.

He smiled: something more than his 'Best Customers' effort.

She didn't return the smile: but he saw that it had been
understood, with the oft-discussed intelligence that had taken
her all the way from Sandmouth to Oxford. No doubt, he'd had
no part apportioned to him in Angela Lavezzoli's gilded
scheme of things: however Sandmouth likewise was only a
starting-point for *him* (which she must have guessed for
herself, it was what brought her to the shop), and who in this
day and age was so simple as to think the princes wouldn't
have to fight it out with the village boys for the princess's
hand?—especially when the village boys might know a thing
or two above their station, and ply a trade in silver mustard
pots.

★

Miss Templeton was describing to Miss Linmer of foundation
garments a séance she'd once attended in the town.

'My brother had just passed over, and naturally I was
distraught.'

298

'Oh *naturally*—'

'Something about bereavement makes people so terribly—careless—in what they say to you, have you noticed? Someone actually told me she'd always thought Jack had been—I quote, I tell you no lie, Miss Linmer—"a dead good sort".'

'She didn't—'

'She did.'

'Well, I never—'

'Someone else we'd known as children kept going on about how awful I'd been to him. Someone we'd known in Sandmouth,' Miss Templeton added for emphasis. '*Old* Sandmouth, that is. I say that because *you* know how suspicious it is when someone says "Oh, *we*'re Sandmouth people", and you can guess they don't belong even if you didn't know it for a fact. Anyway, we were talking about Old Sandmouth, and she kept harking on about the past and when we were all children, playing. And I'd done this or that, or so she kept telling me. The threats I used to make to poor Jack. How I'd nagged him and so on. Quite a beast she made me sound.'

'Oh *no*—'

'Oh yes. And then—can you credit it?—Jack not dead a week and she says, "Remember such-and-such. I bet you really felt you could have put a knife in him!"'

'She never —'

'She did too. Anyway, to get back to my story, Miss Linmer. Where was I? Oh yes, I said I'd go, to this séance thing. Miss Donohue was going, you see, and she'd invited me. Very interested in anything spiritual she was. Not quite right in the head, poor thing, but that's neither here nor there.'

'She wasn't, was she?'

'Mind you, *any*one who has any truck with séances and the like isn't right in the head, if you ask me.'

'Oh, I couldn't agree more.'

'Anyway, I went.'

'Did you? What on earth was it like?'

'Oh, you've no idea. "Queer", it's the only word I can think of. Lights out and hands on the table. It gives me the willies just to think of it, all of us sitting there in the dark, having to hold hands and link fingers. "Spooky"—you know? Waiting for a "message from beyond". But Mrs Holbrook, *she* says it's a trick, and Miss Harter is only knocking herself up under the table.'

'I—I beg your pardon.'

'That's what she said. I know it's hard to believe, isn't it?'

'Are you sure—that's what she said?'

'Oh yes. It was something like that. She doesn't know how she does it exactly, because she's got her hands up on the table all the time. She thinks she must have something between her knees.'

'What's—what's between her knees?'

'Something long. That can reach up.'

Miss Linmer of foundation garments had turned very red.

'Then she gets everyone to press down on the table-top, you see, and she just knocks away.'

'Oh.'

'No one sees what her legs are doing while the banging's going on. That's where the art comes into it, I expect.'

'Yes. Yes, I expect so.'

'Anyway, what a to-do, I must say.'

'Yes, *what* a to-do.'

'Then another time I heard—'

At that moment a movement caught Miss Linmer's eye and she turned her head. One hand went to her throat.

'I do believe . . .'

'What, Miss Linmer?'

'Isn't—isn't that Miss Spink?'

Miss Templeton had meanwhile dextrously placed herself behind a hatstand.

'Is it? I can't see. No glasses. Oh yes, so it is.'

'Don't you think she . . .'

'Yes?'

'She looks a bit—well, affected?'

'*Does* she? I can't see, I don't know. I need my spectacles.'

'*I* thought so. Oh yes. Definitely—affected.'

'I wonder what's happened? What do you think—?'

'She's been upstairs.'

'Yes, she has.'

'Do you think she's been to see Mr Cheevy?'

'I couldn't say.'

'Why should—'

'I've no idea.' Miss Templeton shook her head. 'Mr Cheevy, did you say?'

'I suppose that's where she *must* have been.'

'Not much change there.'

'No love lost.'

'I *thought* she'd been looking a bit out-of-sorts recently.'

'*I* hadn't noticed that—particularly—'

'I presumed it was—well, you-know-what,' Miss Templeton said.

'Isn't she past that?'

'It can go on for years. I read, "Age is no respecter of a woman's convenience". Or something like that.'

'Convenience? Do you think she'll have gone to the rest room? I could go and—'

'Maybe *you* should be getting back, Miss Linmer, no? Myra can hold the fort for me here, and I could see if I—'

'Without your glasses? But she might need us *both*, poor Miss Spink. *Very* affected, she looked.'

'Of course,' said Miss Templeton, 'I've always thought her highly-strung.'

'Highly-strung, yes.'

'I don't think she eats enough.'

'They say if you don't eat enough your nerve ends rub together.'

'That could account for it, then,' Miss Templeton said.

'Mr Cheevy gets on better with the younger ones any road.'

'That's one way of putting it.'

'The walls here have ears, Miss Templeton. I say no more.'

'Well, I'm not keen on men with moustaches. And I don't care who knows it, Miss Linmer. I really don't.'

'It's just a little one.'

'Even so.'

'Do you remember when he first came here?' Miss Linmer said. 'Looked so wet behind the ears. Remember that time Old Mr Crocker found him after closing-time?'

'Not at the moment, I must confess—'

'Caught sight of him and barked across the shop at him, "Isn't it time you were going home now, sonny?"'

'Oh *no*!'

'Oh *yes*!'

'It sounds familiar, now you say it. What a to-do!'

'That's when he started growing it, you see. His moustache.'

'It's a bit scrubby. They just don't suit some men, moustaches. Most men, *I* think.'

'Usually it's to hide something, that's my theory.'

'An—' Miss Templeton struggled to find the term. '—an inadequacy maybe?'

'Well, yes,' Miss Linmer said. 'That could be it. What do you think Mr Cheevy's inadequacy is, then?'

Miss Templeton blushed to the tips of her ears to be asked the question. 'I—I'm sure I can't say, Miss Linmer.'

'I dare say—' Miss Linmer lowered her voice. '—that Miss Naylor upstairs would know if anyone does.'

Miss Templeton merely nodded, with a regal mien she'd based on the example of Miss Spink's former superior, Miss Mansell. Because of it she was often compared, favourably, to the late Queen Mary, for bearing as for dress.

'*I* also heard,' Miss Linmer said, 'he has plans for this place. Crockers'. Why haven't *we* been consulted about it, I'd like to know.'

'No thought,' Miss Templeton replied. 'No consideration at all, that man. It's all just straight in and bang away.'

A sound suspiciously like a sob carried up the staircase. Miss Linmer, looking in that direction, stretched out her hand and touched her colleague's arm.

'I think, Miss Templeton—perhaps—on reflection—we should allow her a little time to herself, don't you agree?'

'Maybe—maybe that *would* be best. In the circumstances.'

'In the circumstances,' Miss Linmer repeated.

'We wouldn't want to rush in—'

'Where angels fear to tread.'

The two women stood nodding their heads in sympathy with each other, mutually satisfied at their quiet but worldly wisdom and the old-fashioned principles of considerateness and decorum.

★

Lady Sybil de Castellet rose from the sea-bottom of sleep, felt herself floating to the surface where dreams make contact with the air and bubbles go flying off upwards . . .

From further away still, high above the bed, above the white plastered ceiling, she heard sounds.

Footsteps?

Still sipping at the cold air—with the same dull wonder that she'd risen at all, that she wasn't dead and in the beyond—she even remembered printed lines in a book, a Henry James story. Which one was it? About a man who's dying, he's lying on his death-bed in an empty apartment. From above him he hears footsteps. Footfalls in the empty house. Who goes there? They call me 'Death'—

How Death clatters! Does Death make the light cord twitch, rattle the fitting? Death's rattle, perhaps?

Lady de Castellet smiled, knowing coy, stealthy Death was never so cumbersome and leaden-footed as this. She opened her eyes fully. The footfalls seemed to echo across the joists. There was a heavier sound, like something being dropped: some tiny parings of plaster were shaken from the ceiling and blew inconsequentially hither and thither, like winter snow.

Lying supine underneath, Lady de Castellet slipped loose the anchor of memory and let her mind journey back to the snowfalls of yesteryear. Somewhere in the Tyrol—the Paris streets one New Year's morning—a sprawling house on a Yorkshire moor. Single tracks of footprints, or a pair, or as many as a dozen. A flurry catching in car headlights, London in the 'twenties, lit shop windows smearing the pavements yellow, tea at the Ritz, a *thé-dansant* at the Berkeley, supper with naughty cousin Rex at the River Room, walking home alone when she had the little flat in Cranley Gardens, old dried snow lacing the railings, footprints leading up to the front door which had turned and walked away again, a man's.

Movements grazed more particles of plaster from the ceiling. To Lady de Castellet's eye they appeared to hover, float, like more infinitessimally lightweight, featherlight snowflakes; she watched entranced, spelled out of the ordinary and the demanding into all her waiting past life.

The movements continued, more loudly, above another corner of the ceiling: but the dying dowager, mesmerised, failed to hear. She was considering the snow: not inclined to re-compose her life—in a separate compartment of her head where she saw more clearly she realised the folly of wishing things had been otherwise. Instead she reflected on the completeness and irreversibility of what had been, and she knew—knew positively—that she now did a good and honest thing in setting it against what was still to be, the coming to fortune of Elizabeth Moscombe, to whom the past had never acknowledged its rightful and legitimate due.

★

Mrs Spencer made herself a pot of tea. She seldom had a taste for it now; she only took it when she was in the after-throes of some little 'incident', an unpleasantness.

This afternoon she thought a fresh, hot pot made double-strength might help to steady her nerves. Instead the opposite seemed to be the case: she felt she was only agitating herself more, turning her brain—as the expression used to be out east—'oolta-poolta', topsy-turvy. She couldn't stop thinking about what had happened, how it had happened. The assistant saying nothing about it, and the girl outside seeing through the window. The girl's eyes following her as she crossed the road, watching her watching in the ironmonger's window.

The tea had strength but no true flavour whatsoever. The British imagined they kept the tea plantations of the world in business but wouldn't have known if they were drinking the sweepings off the floor or not. The British imagined everyone everywhere respected them and looked up to them as the model civilisation, but she'd seen how sloppy the locals had got in their manners latterly and she'd caught the aggrieved, embittered looks on the settlers' faces when they'd begun to realise that they weren't protected any more by their pose of the godlike. The locals made fun of them, and didn't wait till their backs were turned.

Mrs Spencer thought of the girl watching her, and the assistant who couldn't have cared less, and the banging drain-pipe on the wall, and Ronnie driving her up-country in Kenya once and parking the car under some trees and leaving her to go off and talk to two of the workers he trusted about some labour crisis in the offing. She'd been sitting in the car with the windows closed against the dust and insects when, from different directions, a tribe of monkeys had descended on her. There must have been thirty or forty of them. She'd sat bolt upright, unable to believe what was happening. In seconds they were swarming all over the car, they were gawping through the windows at her and baring their teeth and their rumps. They jumped up and down on the roof and she started to panic. Leering faces and red buttocks were pressed flat against the windscreen, paws slapped at the side windows. She hid her face in her hands, too terrified to look. Over the demented chatter she heard the metalwork warping, buckling under with the weight of them. The car started to sway, gently at first, then she could feel it rocking. When Ronnie and the others finally saved her, she was screaming into her hands. There was a touch on her arm—and she shrieked hysterically.

'It's over, it's done,' Ronnie kept telling her. 'It's me, Cordelia. It's Ronnie.'

Over his shoulder, through the windscreen, the men and women villagers out of the huts seemed bemused as they looked in at her, some of them even shook their heads.

'Oh God, Ronnie!' she said. 'Oh God, Ronnie!'

Over and over. Sounding like a silly Englishwoman in a novel, speaking words someone else was making her say, which the common experience of 'Abroad' was supposed to have prepared her for.

'Oh God, Ronnie. What happened, what happened?'

'Monkeys. A family of monkeys . . .'

'Why?'

'They were curious. Curious, that's all.'

'They knew I was terrified. They *knew*, Ronnie.'

'Calm down, Cordelia. It's over now, they've gone.'

'It just happened. Like that.'

'Well, we've chased them away. Shoo'd them away. They've all gone.'

'Have they? Are you sure?'

'They've all gone.'

'I hate this place.'

'It's all right. I'm finished now.'

'No, *all* of it. Africa. Not just here. I don't understand, nothing about it.'

'Well, we don't need—'

He hadn't finished. He couldn't have been going to tell her 'We don't need to stay here', because he knew and she knew

305

that there was no other life for them. Perhaps he'd meant to say 'We don't need to make sense of this place'? But Ronnie had tried to, better than anyone she'd known, tried to make sense of the land and its people, and she had admired him for it, these scares apart: if he'd failed to understand it as he wished to, it was only because that must be the way of things, always. They'd both tried, she too, and even though their way of life (commercial, civilian) laid no strict obligation on them, not like the colonialists. They'd collected whatever native wares had appealed to them both, the bits and pieces people in the villages were willing to sell to them or barter, and she'd doggedly held on to them all and still had them with her in Sandmouth: carved masks, skins, beaten copper trays and pots, little clay gods, a leather knife-sheath and an ornamental wicker shield, a gong to beat, dyed cane baskets, bird feathers she kept in a tall glass jar. They surrounded her, they comprised the furniture of her life, and still she didn't understand them, she couldn't have begun to. Once the man from 'Arbuthnot Antiques' had paid a call on her and given the rooms a once-over and said that what she had wasn't the stuff that sold.

'I'm sorry,' he told her. 'I have to sell what I'm forced to sell, what people want. Supply-and-demand, you know?'

The visitors to the house either smiled at the mementoes or else they viewed them with something like alarm, finding themselves out of their depth, imagining she must be an expert.

She wasn't an expert, not on anything. Except knowing when tea didn't taste as it should.

She pushed the cup away from her. Everything had lost its taste, its freshness, its life.

It was as if, now, she had to *make* these false concerns for herself. When really the world was quite imponderable as it was, past her patience and reason.

*

Christina was in tears. Mrs Gutteridge immediately presumed the trouble was menstrual.

'Christina, darling. Please don't—please don't cry.'

'I can't—can't—help it.'

306

'Tell me, darling. You can tell *me*.'

'No, I can't. I—I *can't*.'

'Yes, you *can*. I'm—I'm a woman.'

Christina, still wearing the convent uniform, turned herself over on the rucked bedspread, opened her palm and revealed a crumpled ball of paper inside.

'What is it, darling?'

'I—I—'

More tears. Mrs Gutteridge made comforting gestures.

'I—I—found it. In my bag.'

'What is it?'

'Someone—put it there.'

'Who? A nun?'

More howls.

'A—a—girl.'

'Oh.' Mrs Gutteridge's face hardened. She prepared herself for the discovery of something unpleasant.

'They're—they're—snobs.'

Mrs Gutteridge forced herself to smile.

'Snobs? Oh no—'

'Oh *yes*.'

'They can't be. It's a convent. Our Lady of the Sacred Heart.'

'They're—they're—snobs.'

Mrs Gutteridge held out her hand.

'Here, Tina.' The diminutive was only spoken in time of crisis, in private. 'Give it here.'

The girl held out her hand; her mother picked up the ball of paper and opened it out.

On it was copied, in the wide cursive hand the nuns taught all the girls, the verses of a poem. Habit even in these malicious circumstances had been hard to break and the poet's name had been written underneath:'LOUIS MACNEICE'.

'Christina' Mrs Gutteridge read, and the sight of the christian name—her own as well as her daughter's—caused her to start. She swallowed drily, reluctant to read on. She felt her eyes glazing as she tried to keep her face composed.

> The doll was called Christina,
> Her under-wear was lace,
> She smiled while you dressed her

And when you then undressed her
She kept a smiling face.

Until the day she tumbled
And broke herself in two
And her legs and arms were hollow
And her yellow head was hollow
Behind her eyes of blue.

'How silly,' Mrs Gutteridge said.
'It's—it's horrible.'
'Gobbledygook.'
'It's a *poem*.'
'A nonsense poem,' Mrs Christina Gutteridge said. 'Some-
one's playing a prank, that's all.'

She smoothed out the creases in the bedspread and asked
herself if this was all you got for behaving yourself in Sandmouth and shelling out what they had to every term to the
nuns, and whatever might be coming to them next?

★

Cox, Dovey, Quinn . . .

Mr Braddock's 'Senior Cashier' closed the book where the
bank's clients were listed, returned it to the drawer, turned the
key in the lock.

Every few days he would check the columns to see that the
names hadn't been added, none of the three ghosts was about
to materialise out of his past.

From the window in his office, over the frosted glass, Trevis
watched the new heavy-footed young constable trudging along
George Street: probably thought he had a cushy billet here all
right . . .

Once a couple of policemen had called at the house. They'd
stood in the doorway with their helmets on, filling it, eliminat-
ing the daylight. Something to do with the bank, it transpired,
but for the first few seconds he'd thought his legs were going to
collapse under him.

The alarms had become worse with the years, as he grew
more set—and craftier—in his deceptions. Long ago he'd read
it was merely a phase every man went through. Marrying
Maureen Gray had been meant as his initiation into adulthood:

he would learn a husband's ways, marriage would cure him. Marrying Maureen, his worst fears for himself couldn't be true.

Instead of which . . . Quinn had read the wedding notice in the *Telegraph* and thought fit to write to him, a few words scribbled on a blank greetings card. 'Welcome to the club!' Loyalty rewarded with his attention, for having kept his mouth shut all those years. Join the club of self-deceivers, Trevis, but needs must, old widow Justice having her eyes blindfolded as she does . . .

The plodding constable tramped along the street, under Crockers' awnings, and out of Trevis's sights.

A well-put-together young man too, probably married himself. Closer to fair than dark, the way Quinn had always preferred them.

The worst of it was how his days had come to be consumed with these thoughts. Married life only intensified the feelings he'd previously been able to control: it multiplied them, it was like a magnifying-glass applied to what at twenty years old had been a minor private embarrassment.

Trevis stood at the window clutching the top of the lower sash, craning his neck to see through the small panes of clear glass, as far along George Street as he was able to.

The constable wasn't required to understand his duties, he should merely accept them, like a faith: absolutes. Homosexuality was one of the absolute sins, beyond most decent people's pity. Again, understanding had less to do with it than the need to hold to a dogma of values, to have 'standards', to protect the sanctity of the status quo, the *via media*—England's safe and sure middle way.

And where in the land was more dedicated to the preservation of the middle way—the average, the median, the mediocre—than pretty Sandmouth introverted on its arc of bay, without a single extraneous thought beyond itself?

★

man, suit shirt tie, eyes, window, police-man, eyes, window, suit, stick arms, fists, suit shirt tie, police-man, boots, window, eyes, suit shirt tie, washing rope, police-man, boots, window, white collar, tie, window, eyes . . .

★

Nanny Filbert reflected on the events of the afternoon from the window of her room. She reflected on her reflection in the window glass through the sides of the tumbler in her hand.

Bloody Mrs Mason telling her off as if nannies grew on trees and all you had to do was shake a branch and down one would fall ready and ripe. You'll be lucky to get another one to come to *this* dump of a town, she'd almost told her. Bloody little piddling Sandmouth, it was the worst thing that had ever happened to her.

Almost.

Another swallow, and another . . .

The woman had just stood in the doorway, Gribben's wife. But for a moment she was in another place, another woman was standing in a doorway with the same smug sureness on her face.

'Oh, you've come back, Freda,' he'd said at her shoulder, sounding so casual about it.

'Not before time, I see.'

'I've got to explain, Freda—'

'Oh, *you*'ve got to explain nothing, I can see just what's what.'

'Please, dear.'

'Don't "dear" *me*, Dave Gribben! I'm not giving you a chance to explain *any*thing.'

She'd jumped out of bed, grabbed her clothes and fled: run like the clappers. Now—Jesus wept—she realised she'd left her hat behind. And buggeration, who should have chanced on the brat like a bloody saint but the half-witted Moscombe girl, who only had to open her mouth and Sweet Jesus alone knew what would come tumbling out of it. It was as if Fate, dear old Dame Fortune, had caught up with her again and decided to give her a very unladylike boot in the crotch. Or roll her tits through a mangle.

Nanny Filbert had another taste of her cure-all. It stung in her throat and she felt her eyes nipping. She had the additional solace of reminding herself that—because funds always ran down at the end of the month—she'd tipped this re-fill out of one of the crystal decanters on the drawing-room sideboard downstairs.

If 'solace' was the word, which she doubted. Not with her

hat missing and that girl on the loose. She couldn't afford to let this job go as well. It was getting difficult finding references, and people like the Masons did their own checking-up on you, as far as they were able to. (She already depended heavily on a 'Miss Barnett' in Exeter, who was a nanny at a posh address, and they used each other as referees—no reference being made to Miss Barnett's status in the house, of course. But sometimes the world seemed a shrinking place to Nanny Filbert, threaded by the most unlikely coincidences and connections.)

So, why not ... —Nanny Filbert swallowed from the tumbler—why not *use* the girl, apply a little physical force on her to find the hat and bring it back to her? The threat would be to tell her that, unless she did, dear Susan's mother would go to the police and file a charge of abduction.

Nanny Filbert smiled at her own ingenuity: at her ability to keep calm and level-headed in a fraught situation. A man might have been able to do it too. On the whole Nanny Filbert didn't care for women as a race: they were a weak-willed lot who never took any chances: pretty women were the worst, thinking that how they looked was enough to save them from being put upon. Silly cows!

She had to find the girl first; she had to explain to her what the hat looked like. Mrs M. had made such a brouhaha about the new uniform, as if she was joining the ranks of the blessed and elect. Fuss and more fuss. She didn't think a beefeater's outfit could have involved more bother for a fitting, or the bloody Pope of Rome's Swiss Guards in St. Peter's. The hat had come from Savile Row, in a box, with the price receipt left inside, no doubt purposely. It was the worst of working for amateurs and arrivistes, they never left you any leeway, they felt they had to get every single last penny's worth out of you. God save her from them! (But God, if He was at home, didn't appear—old snob that He was—to give a monkey's about nannies.)

Nanny Filbert toasted her intelligence, with no one to hear but herself, and emptied the glass. Then the feeling started to pass from her legs, as it often did, and she flopped backwards into the ample hold of the armchair.

It was *their* bloody loss if they couldn't see beyond the ends of their effing turned-up noses.

Thought Mrs Dick as she stood in Beresford's the fishmonger, last customer of the day, watching the weights drop on the scales: there is no such accuracy in the apportioning of human deserts.

The sight of Tilly Moscombe standing on the promenade, staring after the Masons' daughter and her nanny, had touched her. How could it ever be said that you get what you deserve in this life? The punishments maybe, but never the rewards. What had Tilly Moscombe ever done that, in the divine scheme of things, she was judged to merit the condition that had been meted to her? Maybe she really *didn't* know how much it was that she suffered, and how far she'd been allowed to fall from grace: but why should that excuse the fact of her suffering, and permit people like Norman Pargiter to continue living their diabolic lives?

There were lesser degrees of suffering: her husband had steeled himself to those instances of a man's career or a wife's usefulness in the home cut short by illness and disease, but *she* never had. Her husband attended church every Sunday (and so did she, for shared appearances' sake), and he lustily sang hymns to God's wisdom and bounty. All the time she was mouthing the words she could only think of what Quentin's patients were having to endure.

Of course if that was what could happen to you, why should you feel obliged to heed the Reverend Aldred's words, his urgings to goodness, and not just go your own way and do exactly as you dared to?

Standing in Beresford's, watching the boy sluicing down the slabs, no convincing argument to the contrary occurred to Mrs Dick. Maybe 'integrity' came into it, and faith to oneself, but they sounded too suspiciously like words and rhetoric in her current frame of mind. And in Sandmouth she had quite enough red herrings to contend with as it was.

Saint George must have known all about it, canonised for goodness. Yet who could be certain what his true motives were in slaying the dragon, which she'd heard on the wireless last year might not have been a dragon at all, just as the Wooden Horse of Troy may never actually have existed. Perhaps there was a woman behind it, a damsel in a tower, and George had done his tricks for *her*? A social climber indeed? Or if the dragon was not a living creature but a metaphor for devilish obstacles, maybe George was inspired by vainglory and the hunger for reward?—if the dragon represented impure thoughts, then it had badly mauled the young adventurer. But George had won, hadn't he, and gone to join Heaven's elect for his efforts?

Round and round Mrs Dick thought the matter. In the end, though, it was the young man's own end which puzzled her. How bizarre that eternal rest should be the guerdon for bravery and virtue; couldn't it then be that, for some, goodness becomes a questionable means to an end rather than an inspirational quality directed away from 'self'?

'Five and tuppence, Mrs Dick, if you please.'

Mrs Dick smiled as she paid the teller.

'Were you up at Minster Court this morning, Mrs Dick?'

'Yes. Yes, I was.'

'Lovely, I expect, wasn't it?'

'Yes. Very pleasant.'

'A good idea, making Saint George's Day special. Memorable for the boys, I mean.'

'Yes.'

'*And* their parents!'

'Yes.'

Mrs Dick smiled again. Often she felt her mouth operated independently of her will. She was turning into the new kind of Sandmouth person she liked least of all; in the book of Shaw's plays she'd read, hadn't Doolittle the dustman spoken out against middle-class morality, living-for-other-people in a way the Reverend Aldred didn't mean at all: the temporal philosophy of appearances.

She wished she knew more about the dragon, and what the story signified. There must be ways to discover, but she didn't feel confident about asking. She didn't know *how* she could ask, how you began. Maybe if she'd had a chance to go to a university, it would have been second nature to her. But no one, least of all herself, had calculated that she would have had any reason to spend three years at the end of her teens reading books in libraries and memorising reams of notes for examinations. Now she was beginning to understand better what were the arrant lacks and wants in her most respectable life as Mrs Quentin Dick.

★

'Cap Ferrat'. The name floated up from the deeps. Lady de Castellet lay staring up at the ceiling.

On the Riviera, somewhere. Had she been, to that place—Cap Ferrat—or was she imagining she must have been?

She couldn't distinguish it from—where?—the towns. Beaulieu (was it?). Antibes. Menton . . .

Had she been? Or dreamed she'd been? But dreams are clearer . . .

Hadn't she heard it claimed, waking is really being asleep and dreaming at night is our waking life? She was becoming confused. Was she now making up a past for herself? Or is that what we always do, and—never mind things 'happening'—the 'real' past is what we forget? We live between experiencing and imagining,—or, it might be, between a fictitious past and a remembered future—and no one has ever told the story of all our lives properly and recorded the confounding sensation of living in print on a page.

Once in Cambridge, when she was visiting George, they'd all gone out on the river in a punt. Something happened. Surely it had. She'd fallen over the side, or she had a recollection of falling out and into the river. She'd looked up and seen their faces from very far away. They don't do anything, she'd been thinking: or maybe she'd been operating on another level of time from theirs? Eventually hands and arms had come crashing through the water to reach her but, she'd thought, by now perhaps it's too late, the damage has been done and you haul me back screaming as if this is a second birth into a world in which I no longer belong?

She'd lost all her impressions until now. Always it had just been 'that incident', which she would hardly ever discuss. She'd forgotten that she'd *seen*, she'd been looking back from the other side. How had she managed to forget, unless this too was an invention?—or had the knowledge simply been too much for one person to bear alone? All the years since then, perhaps she had been living them underwater, she had experi-

314

enced sixty years in the trice of an eye? Did everything really happen as she'd imagined it had happened?—did her mother remarry, a man half her age?—did George commit an indiscretion with his pretty young half-sister Prudence?—was Tilly born or had she been aborted, did she live to have her own room in 'Hallam House', which was really her rightful home?—could the family money purchase any good and recompense so late in the day?

Lady Sybil felt she spun on her axis, upside down on the fulcrum of fallacious knowledge and profound ignorance. Maybe this was what the Reverend Aldred and his kind meant by the return: losing nothing at all, it was like a going home at last.

★

'You're late, Mum.'

'I know I'm late.' Mrs Lenny dropped her shopper on top of the draining-board. The wireless was on, playing that silly 'Cherry Pink and Apple-Blossom White'.

'I thought you must have had an accident.'

'Do I look as if I've had an accident?'

'Wouldn't she let you away?'

'Who's "she"?' Mrs Lenny asked sharply.

'Her. Mrs Prentice. Did she keep you?'

'That wasn't it.' Mrs Lenny removed her hat.

'Bet it was,' her daughter replied.

Mrs Lenny put a hand on her hip.

'What's it got to do with you anyway, might I ask?'

'I thought you weren't coming and I'd have to get Dad's tea, that's why. But I knew it was *her* fault.'

'That's enough, d'you hear? You think you know everything, don't you? Better than me.'

Denise didn't speak. She put her tongue in her cheek.

'You've really got it in for her, haven't you?' her mother said. 'What's she ever done to *you*, I'd like to know?'

Denise removed her tongue from her cheek.

'Nothing personal.' She shrugged her shoulders. 'She's not going to have anything to do with the likes of *me*, is she?'

'So? You don't know most of the people in this town, do you? Not to talk to.'

'Oh, I wouldn't talk to *her*.' Denise sank her hands into the pockets of her cardigan. 'I don't see why you've got to work for *her*. It's skivvying. It's humiliating, that's what.'

'No, it's not.'

'Why can't she do it herself?'

'She can afford not to, that's why.'

'*She* can't afford it. It's her husband does the affording.'

'You don't know what you're talking about, Denise Lenny.'

'*And* I bet you call her "madam".'

'No, I don't.'

Mrs Lenny dumped her hat on top of her shopper, then reached across and turned the wireless knob to off. Denise made a face.

'Anyway, it's none of your business what I call her. Keep your comments to yourself, my girl.'

'It's *you*'s getting embarrassed.'

'No, I'm not. And that's enough.'

Denise looked at the floor. Then she lifted her head and stared at her mother, hard.

'What d'you know about her?'

Mrs Lenny opened the cupboard door to fetch down the caddy.

'About who?'

'That woman you work for.'

'She's got a name, you know. "Mrs Prentice". And she's not a woman, she's a lady.'

'She's *his* wife, that's what. "*Mrs* Prentice".'

'Every wife has her husband's name.'

'He's older than her.'

'Your father's older than *me*.'

'That's different.'

'How? How's it different?'

'Dad's just a *bit* older. Anyway, you and Dad are the same.'

'How the same?'

'Well, you—you just *found* each other.'

'So?'

'But she must have gone looking for *him*. And *he* must have been looking for *her*.'

'I don't know what you're talking about.'

'You can tell, it's dead obvious. They'd never make a mistake, their kind.'

316

'Mistake? You don't know anything about it.'

'But don't you *see*?'

'See what?'

'How they are. With each other. Unnatural.'

'It's *Mrs* Prentice I see.'

Denise paused.

'Does she give you orders?'

'It's not orders. Not like that.' Mrs Lenny put down the tea caddy.

'What does she do then? *Suggest*? "Please do this—" '

'I'm not discussing—'

'I don't know why you—'

'Denise!'

Mrs Lenny snatched up her shopper and her felt hat. Her face was red.

'You've no respect.'

'Yes, I—'

'No respect for me *or* for her.'

'I didn't—'

'Denise!' Mrs Lenny shouted the name. 'That's enough, I told you. You've no respect at all.'

Denise stood, and put her weight on to one hip.

'You should remember everything that's done to give you a decent home. You and Raymond. If I didn't have a job, *you*'d know all about it. You'd be the first to complain about it.'

Denise's shoulders heaved under her cardigan.

'Oh yes, you would,' her mother told her. 'I know *you*.'

Denise's tongue rolled around inside her cheek.

'Young people think they can just say whatever they like. Any tosh. They think they know everything. When you've been married twenty years you'll know all about it.'

'Not likely! *I* won't be married for twenty years.'

'No?' Mrs Lenny's eyes tightened in her face. 'Well, no husband would put up with you for twenty years, would he? But you're not *getting* married, I suppose. You're too good for it?'

Denise shrugged.

'Oh, *you*'ll get married all right. It'll be the first thing you do, Denise Lenny, to get you out of this house. It'll be straight out of here and into some place of your own. And just you watch, my girl, it's not to have his baby.'

Denise scowled.

'I've heard about some of the boys outside the "Spirit of Good Hope". And I've heard they talk to *you*, Denise Lenny. If talk's all they do.'

'You can't say that to me.'

'Oh yes, I can. I *am* saying it to you too. Just you watch yourself.'

Denise continued to scowl.

'No sitting on the front with them, d'you hear?'

'But it's just talking—'

'That leads to other things.'

'What things?'

'You know quite well. There's time for all that, and babies, later. When he's got a decent home set up for you.'

'Everything's "decent" to you.'

'Of course it is. It has to be. If I hadn't wanted to have you when I did—then Raymond—what sort of pickle would we have been in?'

'Worse than this?'

Mrs Lenny drew in her breath. She took two steps forward, raised her arm and slapped her daughter across her face. The girl reeled, then put her hand to her cheek.

'Don't you ever—*ever*—speak to me like that again, Denise Lenny.'

Mrs Lenny clenched the straps of her shopping-bag with both hands.

'This is a respectable house. We've done everything we can to make it a proper home. Just now I wish I could tell you to clear off out of it. But don't think you're leaving, because you're not. I'm going to make you regret everything you've said, every single word of it. And for a start you can *do* something for a change. Go through and set the table. Your film stars don't, but you're not a film star yet, so just do like everyone else. When you can afford to pay someone to do the job for you, then just you wait, you'll get it all back, that nonsense about Mrs Prentice.'

Mrs Lenny slammed shut the cupboard door.

'What're you waiting for then, girl? You know where the things are. Jump to it.'

Denise sighed, then pulled open the cutlery drawer and

noisily rifled through the knives and forks and spoons.

'You're just going to have to put up with us, aren't you?' her mother said. 'This is your life till Prince Charming arrives. I hate to disappoint you, but I don't think he comes to Sandmouth very often. So maybe you should start changing your plans, madam.'

Mrs Lenny threw the tablecloth on to a chair.

'And just remember what Mr Aldred said. Everyone serves, from the lowly to the great. *Everyone*. There's things go on in people's lives, deep things, and *you* can't even half-suspect what, Denise Lenny. You don't *really* know, no more than Rover next door knows. So you put that in your pipe and smoke it.'

Mrs Lenny glowered at the clutch of cutlery in her daughter's hand.

'We do use side-knives in this house, Miss Know-all. You may have forgotten. It's above our station in life, of course, but when the Princess Royal drops in—and your Prince Charming, or your Dick Bogarde—it's nice to think we're going to be ready for them.'

★

He practised first on the lock of his own bedroom door: he found he could open it with a looped hair-grip.

Brown was standing at the window when he saw his prey in the black sable coat and headscarf emerge from beneath the canopy over the front steps and turn left and set off at a brisk pace along the pavement towards the town. His natural instinct was to run to the door and follow her. He needed to know if she had a particular destination in mind: she was walking too quickly for someone who'd decided to take a harmless stroll. But he also had to see inside her room: it had occurred to him that if he left it till later, till dinner-time, there was the risk of one of the maids interrupting when she came in to turn down the bed.

He undid the catch on the window and pushed up the sash. He listened to the stabs of her heels on the pavement grow fainter.

He found the hair-grip, remembered to put his own room key in his pocket, and walked smartly along the length of corridor from his room to hers. He paused as a precaution before he slid the crinkly wire into the keyhole. It 'gave' with almost ridiculous ease. He looked over his shoulder before turning the handle and slipping into the room.

She'd bought herself better accommodation than his. She had two armchairs, and prints of local landmarks on the walls, and the gas fire was set into a boarded-up fireplace; the basin was broad and had its pipes and workings concealed by chipboard painted white.

First of all he looked inside her suitcase, but found it was empty. The next place to look in a bedroom was inside the drawers of the chest. These proved much more fruitful. Under some underskirts he discovered a guidebook to the area: he turned the pages, his eye caught a cross in a margin and he turned back to the map of the town. Edgehill Road had been underlined in red pencil, and a question mark occupied the junction with Goodwin Road. Between pages in the front portion of the guidebook he found a return railway ticket to—of all places—Hove. (He'd followed her from Mayfair to the station booking-office: presumably the purchase of the ticket had been in the way of an alibi? Everyone either has a maiden aunt in Hove or can confect one.)

He opened the other drawers, but she'd only used the top two. In the second was more underwear: he weighed its soft silkiness between his fingers. At the bottom of the drawer he felt the corner of an envelope, and pulled it up to the surface, with his fingertips.

It hadn't been sealed, and he realised his luck hadn't run out on him yet. He opened it and let the contents fall on to the top of the tallboy.

They were photographs. They obviously hadn't been taken with a box camera—with something much more expensive— but the results were still amateurish. (They usually were.) Two of the photographs showed a woman very like 'Miss Kaye' in much the same social territory: a house with blazing white walls and spiky bushes in its garden, and a knot of people drinking from long-stemmed glasses. In one, someone held up a newspaper—a Continental *Mail*—with V.E. headlines. The other photographs had darker backgrounds: British probably. The garden (or gardens) had cedar and monkey-puzzle trees. In a couple of them a younger 'Miss Kaye' (or a pseudonymous young woman) stood poised beside a man much older than herself. In another two they were grouped with various formally dressed persons very ill-matched by age, who stood awkwardly in a semi-circle; they all seemed intimidated by the camera lens, as if they'd been brought together by some necessary, unavoidable event which required them to be polite and sensible with each other. 'Miss Kaye' and her mature companion managed to smile in them all: the man a little sheepishly, she with her brazen charm. A few grainier shots showed a beach and cliffs, perhaps the Cornish coast: in one there was a high-gabled villa with pebbledash walls and deck-chairs on a lawn, and—just visible in the distance—a hunched, seaside town like some of those he'd visited, on the trail of intrepid young adulterers. In the remaining two photographs, taken in the same seaside garden, the background revealed a nanny wearing a white uniform who was pushing a pram with a sunshade. A newish-looking, pre-War model of car was parked on the gravel driveway: the year might have been 1937 or 1938, Brown guessed. In the last photograph the pram was placed under a tree: a man in uniform with the same thin face as 'Miss Kaye' stood stiffly beside the older man: neither of them was smiling, and the garden seemed unkempt by comparison with the earlier scenes.

Mrs Lambert-Flitch (as she now could legally call herself) wasn't an adulteress, or if she was it wasn't the matter at issue here. Why did she carry around these photographs?—why should they have accompanied her on this expedition, to 'Hove' which wasn't Hove at all, nor even St Mawes or Fowey or St Ives, but a tedious little town without a single claim to distinction?

He replaced the photographs in the envelope and returned the envelope to the drawer, beneath the covering of sheeny underwear. He opened the wardrobe door and looked inside: there were a couple of dresses and a cashmere jumper on wooden hangers and, stacked beneath, several shoeboxes. He checked the other storage places in the room—the little wall-cabinet above the toothmug stand, the bedside cabinet, beneath the bed—but there was nothing of interest to him in any of them.

321

Clearly she was tidy and neat, systematic, but he had already guessed as much from the evidence of the house in Upper Grosvenor Street, which she appeared to oversee for her elderly husband and ran with clockwork efficiency. She was also discreet: except, notably, for the photographs. These suggested to the investigator nothing positive as yet for the purposes of his search, but they did confirm that Mrs Lambert-Flitch was a woman with secrets. Apparently her husband was jealous of her fidelity, which was why he'd contacted him: since the age of Chaucer elderly husbands have had that reputation, and the lady had indubitably favoured the 'mature gentleman' in her time. Of course that pretext for Mr Lambert-Flitch's concern was only a side-issue now: maybe he was really seeking information about his wife's past, or her sanity. He would surely get it. If a pram was involved in the story—however many years ago now—there was certainly the possibility of an Achilles' heel in all that frosted, most English deportment.

Proudly Brown/Jones/Crane/Todd never allowed pity to interfere with his dispassionate working methods and professional principles. Most of the people he found himself dealing with brought misfortune on themselves, just as much as they were the victims of uncontrollable circumstances: you live inside history and you also make your own. Most folk had an instinct to turn a bad situation into worse.

Feeling sorry for the hard luck cases was one thing. But how could you ask your own little measure of pity to cope with all the mortal stupidity in the world?

*

Death over Lady de Castellet's head had assumed the form of Mrs Westropp (née de Castellet) for the afternoon. She had persuaded her husband to stage a diversion in the driveway to draw out the Maceys, so that she could have an opportunity to see the old woman alone.

Unfortunately for her purposes she had taken a wrong turning at the top of the back staircase and she quickly became confused; she couldn't find her way back and by some further accident she came to a second staircase, steep and carpetless, which only led her further from where she'd intended to go.

Another floor up, she discovered she was in another kingdom altogether; she followed various dog-legs and angles of passageway, then stepped into a long echoing corridor with doors opening off it. She found herself looking into maids' rooms and dusty box rooms with piled tea-chests and mildewed cardboard boxes. Everything smelt of dust, neglect, the past. Dirt made little drifts on the bare wooden floorboards and against the chipped and gnawed skirting boards. Where pictures had hung on the walls there were only patches of dirty apricot paint outlined in grime.

Intrigued, Mrs Westropp walked on. Then, remembering her object, she started to retrace her steps but at the end of the corridor she realised she'd lost her bearings, she didn't know through which door she'd come in. The deadly silence seemed to seize her throat as she looked round in all directions for a way of escape—the stillness, and the fog of dust she walked into whenever sunlight shone in through one of the high, barred windows.

She resolved not to panic, to take her time and to try to calm herself. Look on the positive side, she told herself: maybe this is my chance to discover something. Somewhere up here, she was aware, must be the clues which the family had speculated on for years: in one of the cardboard boxes or buried deep down in a tea-chest or secreted beneath a serving-girl's mattress. If she'd been reading about herself in a book some instinct would have drawn her into one of the rooms rather than any of the others and there she would have found the secret knowledge she required: folded letters bound with blue ribbon, a morocco album of fading photographs, a birth certificate tucked into an envelope and lost sight of.

Mrs Westropp stopped at one of the windows and raised herself up on her toes to see out. Far beneath, her husband stood on the gravel driveway, pointing to the car and explaining something to the Maceys. He was forever telling her she had too much imagination, it ran away with her: now he was learning for himself that it had its uses, in certain situations.

She reminded herself she was wasting time and turned away from the window. She walked out of the room into the corridor. She suddenly realised how loud her heels sounded on the floorboards and went up on her toes for the next few steps.

323

Looking into another room on the other side of the passage she saw a trunk with initials stencilled on it. *'G.E.O.S.deC.'* It must have belonged to that dreadful brother . . .

Some of the floorboards in the room were missing, and she realised she would have to pick her way forward with care. She reached the trunk and tried to lift up the clasps. She tried several times. Locked, damn it. That silly old woman, just teased them all . . .

She forgot about the missing floorboards in her exasperation and, as she stepped back, her right foot disappeared beneath the level of the floor. Her heart jumped, a hammer swung in her head. She had nothing to reach out for and her right leg dropped between joists, there was a light cracking noise and then her foot and ankle broke through she didn't know what, something crumbling and giving.

She sat inelegantly and dizzily straddling the hole, her left leg at the level of the floor on one side, her right buttock just perched on the ledge on the other, and her hands—one planted on each section of the floor—having to balance her.

Her heart seemed to be up in her throat. She looked down, into the darkness beneath her, and saw—yes, daylight, where she didn't expect to, like a ruff around her knee. Particles of some material drifted like snow.

It was only then that she realised the full horror of the situation, that she'd stepped through one of the ceilings.

Curiously her leg felt no pain, which was why she couldn't believe it had really happened. She looked again, and stared.

Slowly she understood. By some terrible mischance her leg had bypassed the heavier timbers; there had only been a layer of soft wood and thin plasterwork between her and the room beneath.

She tried twisting herself round to try to free the foot and ankle, but she felt she didn't have enough strength in her arms to hold herself up. After a couple of minutes of straining her arms ached impossibly at the wrists and elbows and couldn't hold her any longer.

Her whole weight dropped another foot or foot-and-a-half. Her left leg went wide of one of the timbers and the joist rode up into her crotch. She yelped with the hurt of it.

Her arms were now pressed tight against her sides. She

looked down again. From the knee down her right leg was projecting into the room beneath. She moved her ankle and her foot, tried to make circles to test that they had their feeling left.

She shook her head. She couldn't believe it, that it had happened. Not to her.

She knew she wasn't going to be able to get free by herself. She realised she hadn't the strength to haul herself back up.

After a minute or so of stunned misery she started calling out for help. Her voice hardly carried through the room she was in, let alone anywhere else. She took a deep breath and then tried to throw her voice further, but keeping some vestige of dignity in it. That worked no better.

There was only one other possible way of saving herself, she somehow had the acumen to understand: only one choice left to her. So she opened her mouth—and then she just shouted, dignity forgotten. Shouted and shouted for all she was worth.

How long went by? When she hadn't the breath left to continue, she listened to the house settling into silence around her. An unending silence. Later—how much later?—she looked up and saw the blue starting to leave the sky, through the barred window. Some early stars sparkled, light years away. Around her the walls seemed to be sucking the light out of the room. She shivered. Tears rolled from the corners of her eyes. The old timber felt rough against her thigh and her private, tenderest parts. She itched. God only knew what was crawling off the wood, what dirty nibbling little creepie-crawlies. The feeling was leaving her left leg, folded up on her knee. Her right leg too was responding less and less whenever she tried to move it, the part that had disappeared from view. It was going cold, numb.

The lumber room was cold, wintry. The room beneath her, into which she stuck her leg, felt even colder, icy. It was as if her leg was beneath water.

Then from somewhere close to her in the darkness she thought she heard rustlings, scramblings: from behind the skirting board, it might have been. Her eyes opened wide and gelled.

A little later, though, tears flowed, uncontrollably. She couldn't sob: she was too frightened, and her arms were too tightly packed against her sides to thrash hysterically.

What, she said aloud to herself, what if no one ever goes into the room downstairs?

The rustlings grew louder in her right ear. *Inside* her right ear, it might have been. She understood that she could even— yes, she could *die* here—among the mice and rubbish, among these already dead and mouldering de Castellet lives.

★

'Have you changed rooms with the lady, Mr—er—'

'Arthur Brown' spun round on his ankles. The old woman was standing at the top of the staircase.

'I'm next door to you, you see.' She pointed. 'Number fifteen.'

Brown nodded.

'I expect we have the same view, do you think so?'

'I—yes, I expect so.'

'Have you *just* moved rooms?'

Brown assented with another nod.

'The lady must have gone, then. Very interesting face, I thought.'

Brown continued to nod.

'I couldn't help noticing you were looking at her. I wondered maybe—if you recognised her. Is she famous perhaps? An actress on the stage?'

Brown lifted his shoulders, then let them fall.

'Oh well. I'm always pleased to know who my neighbours are. Do you find that in hotels? Someone's sleeping in their bed only a few feet away from you: or a few inches even, if the beds—'

Brown beamed at the woman, but it was a wary smile. He realised he couldn't very well walk past her, along the corridor.

'Are you going downstairs too, Mr—I'm sorry, I didn't seem to hear—'

'Brown.'

'Mr Brown. With an "e", is that?'

'Without.'

'Ah.'

They looked at one another.

'I am Miss Austen. I thought I might sit in the lounge for a little bit.'

'Oh yes.' Brown tried to smile pleasantly.

'What a pity they don't have a coal fire here, or a log fire. Gas is such a—*fussy* heat, don't you think, Mr Brown?'

'Oh yes.'

'Still—' Brown's interlocutor stepped stiffly down on to the first tread, looking up as she did so. 'Are you—?'

'I—' He noticed the door of a W.C. behind her. 'I have to—' He pointed.

Miss Austen turned her head and looked over her other shoulder. Instantly she was offering genteel apology.

'Oh. Yes, of course. I'm so sorry. I've—'

She stepped on to the second tread, and the third. 'Perhaps later, Mr Brown?'

'Yes,' he said. 'Later. Perhaps.'

Brown watched her as she picked her way down the steep staircase, her hand holding the banister rail tight. Not bloody likely, he was trying to assure himself. But he knew from his experience of hotels how persistent these old dames were. What could they have been like when they were younger, when they had their full vigour as well as their nosiness? Or did the nosiness develop with the state of spinsterhood?

He waited till she'd taken the half-landing before he set off for his own room. She'd been a curse, standing there at the wrong moment. Or maybe she was really a warning to him, served to him by kismet; that he should be more careful, there was more danger involved than he'd thought—women in black sable are the most inscrutable, they have too much at stake to risk anyone discovering and telling the tale . . .

★

Mrs Lenny had gone. She had left a few lights on. Mrs Prentice walked through the hall; she looked into the empty rooms, at the perfect order.

Her heart constricted in her chest. She opened the door in the sideboard and took out one of Cedric's bottles. She found a glass and tipped a measure of whatever it was—whisky, she read on the bottle—into the bottom. She flung her bag on to the sofa and walked over to the french windows, drinking from the tumbler.

In summer the view outside was like a photograph on a calendar. A fall of blue wistaria framed the doors; the beds were filled with old-fashioned blooms and the colours were as brilliant as any in a painting, by Renoir or Manet maybe. High-climbing plants and creepers disguised the top edge of the wall. Butterflies shimmered and bumblebees droned. The garden was an idyll, then, in summer.

In April the daffodils did their 'Fluttering and dancing in the breeze' routine. Plants—and, more cautiously, the beech hedge—showed green. At the end of this afternoon there was still some blue left in the sky. Spring was well on the way but she didn't feel her spirits rising.

She uncrossed her arms. Her heart somersaulted in her chest. The breath wouldn't rise in her throat; she felt she was having to will it up.

She swilled the liquid around in her glass. Normally the first thing she did when she reached the house was to hurry straight upstairs to run the bath; she would wash herself very carefully, every part of her, then get out and rub herself dry with a clean towel and apply powder and eau-de-toilette and change into one of the dresses Norman Pargiter had never set eyes on. When Cedric returned home, she would be in the kitchen, wearing an apron over her dress, her face a little flushed—but she would be coping. They would kiss politely, Cedric would go off to help himself from one of the bottles or crystal decanters in the six-legged sideboard; she would join him for twenty minutes or so, and ask him the usual questions about his day and they would sit back and discuss the garden and any little odds and ends that had occurred—a letter, a telephone call—which chanced to make this day in some way different from all the others.

But this Wednesday wasn't like any of those days, it wasn't even like the other deceitful Wednesdays.

She shut her eyes. She felt herself shaking. Shock, she told herself: delayed reaction.

She leaned against the wall and opened her eyes. She pressed her brow on to the cold glass of the door. The blood was thumping in her head as the drink got to work on her.

Through the glass she was seeing the scene in the wood, that travesty of love. Maybe she *had* only imagined it?—the eyes watching, the bushes moving in the compact mirror. But she knew better. Why else had they played that perilous game if it

328

wasn't to dare the conventions, to blast them away—to want to risk someone seeing them and passing on the word?

From the drawing-room of 'The Laurels' the plight seemed too far-fetched, too unreal to be hers, to belong *to her*.

She gulped the drink in her tumbler.

From 'The Laurels' a lot of things seemed far-fetched and unreal to her. There was always a tendency for all her past life to float uncertainly when she tried to concentrate on it. Sandmouth also had the distance of a memory, especially in summer when 'The Laurels' became a fragrant world of its own and was almost too good to be true, smothering her in its scents and sounds, and that terror of slow suffocation made worse and worse—exacerbated beyond all logic and reason—by Cedric's endless patience and good humour with her.

She saw now—looking out at the depleted beds—that she'd underestimated that silent presence on the other side of the boundary walls, its capacity to exert an influence on her thinking. For what else had she been doing all this time, if not trying to deny any possible claim it could make on her? But with the banks of laurels to protect her in all seasons, she'd allowed it to become an abstraction: instead it was made up of people with watching eyes and tongues that moved in their mouths and ears that listened for the tasty tit-bits.

Her stupidity appalled her. Not even stupidity. That girl wasn't so mindless as she had been.

Somehow, she was realising, she'd also made an abstraction out of Cedric and the comforts he allowed her, which he'd so painstakingly, obligingly, smilingly surrounded her with. She'd seen him as her husband in law, 'Mr' Prentice to her 'Mrs', as much one of the fittings she'd suddenly acquired for herself as the six-legged sideboard or the console-table in the hall: not as a man dependent on his own responses, who could be hurt.

He *would* be hurt. And *she* would be totally to blame.

The tumbler dropped out of her hand and shattered on the parquet. She looked down helplessly at the mess, feeling addled in her head. It took her several seconds to realise what must be done with the spiked shards of glass.

She found the cloth and dust-pan and bowl in the kitchen broom cupboard. She hurried back through to the drawing-room. She was crouched on her knees and felt the tears pricking behind her eyes when the front door opened and heels sounded in the hall.

'Penelope?'

Her husband looked over at her from the doorway.

'What's happened, my dear?'

'Oh.' She pushed the hair back from her brow. 'A silly accident, that's all.'

He immediately crossed the room and stooped down by her side.

'I'll do that,' he said.

She wished he would leave her alone, that he would give her some reason to feel this was her duty, her responsibility, her look-out—*only* hers.

'Give me the cloth,' he said kindly. 'I'll mop it up.'

'It's so silly.'

It's *your* fault, *your* idiotic business, she wanted him to tell her, your *own* bloody mess. If you hadn't been rolling stark-naked with a man in a car behind the golf course, none of this bedlam would be happening. Cheap bitch, whoring bitch . . .

She thought of the girl, traipsing through the town, trying to tell her story to whoever would hear. Maybe no one would believe her, they'd tell her it was a tissue of lies?

She sank back on her heels. Tears rolled out of the corner of her eyes. She looked at Cedric's bony neck, his narrow back, bent over the puddle on the floor.

Suddenly she felt the sickness travelling up from her stomach, into her throat, her mouth. She couldn't rise quickly enough before it frothed between her lips: a trail of yellow vomit dribbled down the window glass, the remains of the lunch she'd eaten so calmly, knowing what her afternoon would be like. Not knowing . . .

She felt Cedric's hand on her back. It made the tightness worse.

'Penelope . . .'

What was he thinking, that it must be a baby? A baby to grow up like the girl who couldn't decide in her mazy mind what message her eyes were telling her?

He opened the french doors. She stepped out. 'Breathe in,' he was telling her, so concerned. 'Take deep breaths. Deep breaths, my dear. In, out.'

He gave her his handkerchief. She cleaned her nose and thought she smelt the sea as she tried to breathe more evenly. Her heart grew still smaller. The sea . . .

It was what lay between them and the sea that sent the despair shooting through her again. The rooftops, and the houses, and the rooms filled with people, and people's heads filled with thoughts, and the thoughts filled with mischief and spite.

★

Dear Mrs Lambert-Flitch,

Of course you don't know who I am, and I for my part have never cast eyes on *you*. Naturally I have read about you in the newspapers and seen your photograph taken at social functions. Your husband must be very proud of you. Even a rich man cannot be sure of his wealth buying him a beautiful wife. He seems to have bought exactly that: or would it be true to say that *you*, a beautiful woman, have allowed yourself to be sold to *him*, such a wealthy man?

Commerce is what this sordid life on earth is all about. Financial commerce—and of course the sexual sort. Isn't it strange how we choose—or do not choose—to form our intimate physical alliances?

I am straying from the point. To be blunt, I am concerned to know if your doting husband will continue to hold you in the same esteem which he does—or seems to do—at present. I dare to think that you may not yet have disclosed every aspect of your past life to him.

I know that until recently you lived in Paris, and before that in Rome. You may not realise that some of us in this country have taken a considerable interest in your past history. (You have allowed yourself to become a figure in the public eye, after all.) I should like to believe that *you* haven't forgotten your past life, either, and that certain events and certain places continue to hold particular associations for you: such as, for instance, St Ives . . .

I wonder if you are aware that certain consequences of past conduct—or misconduct—are of longer duration than may be convenient to us to imagine? Owing to your long absence abroad, you may be unacquainted with some of those surviving aspects of past time. It is my strong conviction that if you were

331

to visit somewhere that—strictly speaking—does *not* hold any personal associations for you, you might make certain discoveries. (Although these would not be of an altogether welcome nature.) You may have forgotten that such tedious places as Sandmouth on the South Coast exist: while the town is doubtless unknown to you, certain persons there have not forgotten or lost track of *you*. You are remembered, from another period of your life, when neither your name nor appearance were as they are now.

Perhaps only one person remembers with any exactitude and *her* memory is sadly misted by approaching death. Another person—who is now, it may greatly surprise you to learn, sixteen or seventeen years old—is incapable of remembering with any degree of clarity at all, but she too may be said to have a claim.

I am unsure how to conclude this initial piece of correspondence with you. I trust that you will be gracious enough, or intrigued enough, to accept further letters from me. But firstly might I presume to advise a brief journey to Sandmouth, to acquaint yourself with a small town—admittedly rather dull—that will repay your close attention? Contrary to appearances, it has much to offer that will be of interest to your own fair self, and I do not speak of architectural gems.

I suspect that we might be able to place our correspondence on a more intelligible, purposeful and *fruitful* footing once you have made your visit to the coast. I would further suggest that your husband does not accompany you: I believe he is no longer in his prime, and the journey to such a spot is not advisable for one ill-served by a weak heart or by an over-impressionable disposition. Money, I appreciate—if one has access to it—cannot *guarantee* us our health: nor, for that matter, can it necessarily buy wholehearted peace of mind. Certainly it *can* equip us with other commodities: in your fine home you must welcome the fact that seclusion and *silence* are among those luxurious indulgences which wealth *is* able to provide.

In the meantime—until I again put pen to paper—I shall declare myself, madam,

An Anonymous but Sincere Well-Wisher.

As the woman in the smart sable coat was walking out of the hotel—collar pulled up to her cheeks—Alistair Meiklejohn de Castellet walked in. He held the door open for her and stood looking after her. He sniffed the trail of scent. *Very* nice . . .

The sight lifted his spirits. After 'The Wishing Well' he'd taken the risk and gone up to 'Hallam House'. Predictably the old girl had refused to see him. He'd held a couple of pounds in front of the housekeeper woman, then a fiver, and she'd seemed, not enticed, but quite indignant. What a bloody time to get virtuous and high-minded.

He turned away from the sweet-smelling woman in the fur coat, who'd been a pleasant diversion after his day. Inside the hall he dodged past the awful biddy who cornered the guests and told them she was descended from Jane Austen. She'd found another couple to waylay, and their expressions showed they'd reached that point of disbelief everyone must reach.

He took the first few steps of the staircase at a run, then—approaching the landing—he slowed. His thoughts were of Lady de Castellet and 'Hallam House', and the predicament—one of several—he currently found himself in. The letters he wrote seemed to have no effect: he doubted if they ever passed beyond the housekeeper. If she wouldn't agree to see him, then *he* would have to cook up some means of guaranteeing that a meeting between the two of them *did* take place. Possibly he would have to break in: or else use someone else, completely unknown to her Ladyship and the Macey pair. He'd sleep on it; he was a willing believer in the subconscious, and he would wait to see what plan started forming itself out of the images of the day in his dreams.

It had already occurred to him that the battle with Lady Sybil was probably lost by now anyway: in the light of the evidence he'd had telephoned to him, the tack he'd taken—if the news about the Moscombe girl got around, the brother's name was mud—seemed to have no bearing on things any more. In the meantime he had other vital business to attend to, potentially more lucrative: swanky mothers ought to be more suggestible and responsive than spinster dames in corsets and mothballs.

Upstairs in his room he sat down at the dressing-table. He opened the drawer and took out a sheet of the hotel's monogrammed writing-paper. He undid the top of his fountain pen and sat for a minute or so with the nib poised above the paper. He experimented with a few characters from the alphabet. He had to be careful to disguise his hand. When he got back to London he would pen his fair copy, on the anonymous blue notepaper he'd sent her last time.

He filled one side of the page with random words he might use. All the time he was trying to imagine what she *really* looked like, out of the photographers' range, cocooned by comfort and wealth in that highly desirable new home in Mayfair.

He'd chucked a stone into that quiet pool and he wondered how much upset it had caused. What was still to come was going to make sure that *her* life at least was never quite the same again.

Time for a try-out, he decided. He turned the sheet of paper over on to its other side. He held the nib above the page and told himself that another hand than his own was in command.

How much would he ask for as a first payment? Time to decide that later.

He began to slowly etch the letters, simultaneously cautious and confident like a draughtsman. 'My Dear Mrs Lambert-Flitch . . .'

★

Ruth, treefall quiet, and talk, talk, no one, nothing, mouth, lips, tongue, constants, const-ance, eyes, father, window light, treefall quiet, talk talk, church, steeple, God, God sees, Ruth, treefall quiet, and talk, talk, no one, nothing, window light, mouth lips tongue, no one, eyes, Tilly!, talk talk, nothing, no one, church, father, steeple, steeple God, Tilly!, eyes, not the lady smile, Ruth, eyes open, OPEN, O-P-E-N, treefall quiet, window light, no one, nothing . . .

★

It sounded like 'Ruth talk-talk'.

The vicar's daughter swung round at the slurred words. When she spotted the girl watching her from the undergrowth her eyes narrowed, then narrowed again, shrank to pinheads.

'Tilly Moscombe!'

The sounds were repeated.

'What on earth are you talking about?'

The girl pointed.

'I don't know what you're talking about, Tilly Moscombe.'

Tilly shook her head.

'What? Who?'

The girl pointed again.

'Who is it?'

More words like 'Ruth talk-talk'.

'Stop inventing stories, Tilly Moscombe. I haven't been talking to anyone.'

The girl was about to point again. It was too much for Ruth Aldred. For the first time in years she lost her temper with a fellow human-being.

'If I tell you there was no one here, Tilly Moscombe, there was no one here. Do you understand?'

The words repeated themselves. 'Ruth talk-talk Ruth.'

'You heard wrong then. Do you *hear* me, Tilly Moscombe?'

The girl looked about her, seeming utterly confused.

'And don't go telling people, whatever you do. Do you hear? What will they say about you then?'

Ruth turned away shaking.

Another word followed: it sounded like 'Constance'.

The vicar's daughter spun round.

'What's that?'

She was definitely trying to say 'Constance'.

'What do you mean?'

The girl mimicked someone chattering away, nineteen-to-the-dozen.

'I don't know what you're going on about—'

Suddenly Ruth Aldred hated everything in God's world. The sky, the grass, the cypresses and unclipped yews, the house, Tilly Moscombe. Why had He botched her body and her mind if it wasn't to show He wasn't caring tuppence about this world He'd created? It was a toy and He was bored with it. Killing her mother . . .

The vicar's daughter stood with her hands pressed against the sides of her head. Tilly Moscombe took a few steps forward and held out her hands to her. She spoke a word like 'headache'.

'Go away.'

Headache. Pain. Ruth.

'Leave me, please.'

Ruth. Headache.

Ruth closed her eyes.

Ruth. Talk-talk. Constance.

Shrieking was the only reply she could think of. The sound rose out of her, from layers down: a suddenly light, piercing scream higher than any of the trees in the garden. She wanted it to shatter glass, make a hole in the day she could escape through.

She wasn't seeing Tilly Moscombe standing in front of her, she was no longer aware of her. The scream was all that mattered to her; and then, when it had been spirited out of her, an echo was left, caught in the frenetic geometry of the fir tree's branches.

Only later—pressing her back flat against the tree's rough, scaly trunk—did she remember Tilly Moscombe. A fear seeped through her. It passed up to her throat, she felt it like a little bird trapped in her windpipe. She remembered the moment of hatred, pure and unalloyed; the exact feeling had gone, but while it lasted she'd felt it was explaining the world to her as nothing in this placid backwoods life had done before. In those few seconds she'd had a vision of it—a black, dizzying hollowness around which all their tidy, respectable lives revolved.

The church clock struck six. Her father's women were due at seven.

In the annals of all time that single hour didn't even register. Not even a year did, or the length of a war or the span of life of a generation. Not even two millennia of Christ's teaching.

Thinking these things in her father's garden wouldn't have happened without Tilly Moscombe. She forgot about Constance, all about her better half, picturing that lumpish, corkscrew body—one of God's jokes—limping and stumbling all day long up and down Sandmouth's Hill Street.

★

'What?'

Susan explained again as her mother leaned over the pillow.

336

About Nanny Filbert showing her how the gas worked, and the man in the strange house with so many seats, and walking around Sandmouth, and dodging between the cars and finding her new friend.

Susan watched the eyes above hers opening wider and wider.

'What new friend?'

'Tilly—'

'Tilly Who?'

'Just Tilly.'

'Tilly Moscombe?'

Mrs Mason knelt down, shakily. She drew her face down to the level of her daughter's.

'Tell me the last bit again.'

'There was a man.'

'Where?'

'In the hedge.'

'What do you mean?'

'He showed it to us.'

Mrs Mason hesitated. Suddenly her eyes grew much smaller: very small indeed.

'He showed you—what?'

From her supine position, with her hands on top of the coverlet, Susan mimed what they'd seen. Mrs Mason's mouth fell open.

'Get out of bed, Susan Mason. Get out of bed.' She pulled her by the arms. 'Get out of bed *this instant!*'

Susan found herself airborne—then standing upright on the floor, in her nightgown. Before Mrs Mason could make sense of what she was doing she had smacked her daughter hard on her bottom.

Susan howled. Mrs Mason slapped again, and again. 'Wickedness, wickedness,' she was saying. The wickedness of what she wasn't sure, she didn't know. Of the man, of Susan remembering, or of Nanny Filbert losing her.

'I want you to forget, Susan. Do you understand? All these bad things. These terrible things.'

Mrs Mason pulled some loose strands of hair out of her eyes, snatched at wisps that had fallen down.

'I don't—I don't know how you—'

And Tilly Moscombe too. In times past she'd seen the girl

337

looking through the railings next to the pond, watching Susan as she played. It used to make her flesh creep, seeing her and remembering how many premature children had been born during the War, their bodies and their brains not ready to begin the crazy business of the world.

The wickedness persisted. Watching Susan climb back into her bed, snivelling and shoulders shaking, Mrs Mason sensed she might have been unfair to Tilly Moscombe, that in a way the girl only represented the misfortunes of her own life: the bomb falling on Colquhoun Gardens, the front of the house falling in, the staircase collapsing under her as she tried to make her escape. That was the spectacular aspect of war but it warped in untold ways. Maybe through her her own child had inherited some instinct of sin, seeing the wickedness men cause to be done to other men?

In the future, from tomorrow, she would insist that Nanny Filbert took Susan on no more outings. Positively insist on it. No more. *No more.* She would just have to go everywhere with her herself.

What would that be like, for goodness' sake?—eyeing every stranger with hostility as they went walking for exercise, the faster the better. In perpetual dread of a sighting of the old man Susan had told her about, or an encounter with him. In half a day the worst had happened, she'd learned that Nanny Filbert wasn't who she'd presumed her to be; she'd learned that the old stone walls weren't high enough or strong enough to protect them from what wouldn't be kept out. The old-fashioned garden of tea-roses and japonica and hollyhocks wasn't their own any more.

★

Mr and Mrs Symington-Berry had brought in the left-overs from the marquee and were having an early supper of pickings on their laps.

'I feel,' the Headmaster tentatively suggested, 'maybe we should have offered to feed him?'

'I have little enough appetite as it is,' his wife said testily. 'Let me tell you, I'm having to force this down.'

Mr Symington-Berry allowed himself to look a little puzzled by her reply.

'I'm never clapping eyes on that man again,' his wife

announced, using the leg of a turkey drumstick for emphasis. 'I know the food wouldn't stay in my stomach if he knocked on that door.'

Mr Symington-Berry was trying to imagine the coincidence of events when, at that moment, the telephone rang. They both jumped. Mutual panic crossed their faces.

'Please answer it, Philip,' Mrs Symington-Berry said in a hoarser and shriller-pitched tone of voice than her usual.

Her husband sprang to his feet. A meringue slithered off the plate balanced on the arm of his chair, fell on to the carpet, and shattered. Unseen by his wife, the heel of his shoe trod in the cream and mapped snowprints across to the telephone.

The Headmaster picked up the receiver and let a couple of seconds pass before he spoke.

'Symington-Berry here.'

A belly-laugh rumbled down the line. From the sofa Mrs Symington-Berry heard and her face clouded. She laid down the plate of turkey pieces and spring salad on the cushion beside her. She hissed across the room at her husband.

'Who is it?'

The Headmaster covered the mouthpiece with his palm.

'It's—it's Pinky.'

Mrs Symington-Berry shook her head like a mute. Her husband offered some tepid words of mild good cheer into the receiver. Bright as a silver sixpence, a reply rattled jovially into the Headmaster's ears from Pinky's latest port-of-call.

Mrs Symington-Berry strained to hear. 'Not here, old chap.' 'I don't know, Pinky.' 'I doubt it.' 'Do you think that's wise?'

The question was hissed again.

'What does he want?'

Her husband smiled helplessly at her. It was a look of despair.

'Not here,' she told him in a louder voice, shaking her head. 'Not here.'

She spotted the cream-prints on the carpet and pulled herself up off the sofa to look.

'I don't think so, Pinky. Not really. Yes, a *bit* quiet.'

Mrs Symington-Berry had folded her height in half and was stooped over the worst of the marks. Her husband noticed her face was scarlet.

'Speak to you again, Pinky.'

Words gargled out of the receiver.

'Not—' Mr Symington-Berry found the old riposte hard to say. His face was unsmiling. 'Not if *I* see *you* first, Pinky.'

He put down the receiver. His wife looked up at him like a crouched animal planning its moment to leap for the jugular.

'It was Pinky.'

His good lady ground her jaw ominously.

'Yes,' she said. 'Yes, I *know* it was Pinky. What does *he* want?'

'I'm sorry?'

'That man *always* wants something. What is it now?'

The Headmaster shrugged his shoulders innocently.

'Where is he?' Slowly his wife got to her feet. She spoke with a new suspicion in her voice.

'Pinky?'

'Of course Pinky,' she growled.

'Sounded—I should say—jolly near.'

'*How* near?'

'He's—eh, in our part of the world, actually. Our—our neck of the woods.'

'*Where?*'

'Quite—quite close by. I—I said we hadn't room at the moment. He—he's heard about Ferris's gift shop. It might—it might be up for sale soon. He heard a rumour—'

'*What?*'

'He said he bought some gooseberry fields last year. It was a good year for the gooseberries. So he said. He—he wants to be indoors this year. Under a warm roof.'

'Under *ours*. For heaven's sake, Philip, why Sandmouth?' Mrs Symington-Berry asked, incredulous.

'I—I don't know. Just—just chance, I suppose.'

'*You* didn't tell him about "The Gyft Shoppe" being up for sale, did you?'

'Me?' The Headmaster shook his head. 'I haven't spoken to him. Really, Lavinia.'

'I've just about had enough of everything,' Mrs Symington-Berry said, drawing herself up to her full six feet. 'Today—and now Pinky Taylor. Those awful parents. We just can't get away from it, can we?'

'I'm sorry?'

'You're—you're *sorry*?' A withering laugh followed.

' "We can't get away from" . . .?'

'The past!' Mrs Symington-Berry hurled the word across the room. 'We can't get away from the past!'

The Headmaster stared at her feet, at the cream prints on the carpet.

'Every time I think it's behind us,' she said, 'it jumps out on us. It's—it's like something—with a will of its own.'

'You've got to look on the bright side,' her husband told her, thinking he had to say something. He realised the expression didn't sound right for the occasion.

'I thought this was!'

'I'm sorry?' he asked.

'The *bright* side, of course!'

Mrs Symington-Berry took several steps backwards, away from him, to get a perspective on the creamy footprints.

'I'm beginning to believe all that claptrap,' she said. 'You're born under a certain star and it's lucky or unlucky. Maybe it *is* true.'

Her husband gave her a beneficent, forgiving smile of sage reason. It was too much for her.

'What do *you* know about it?' she asked, forgetting the first precept of the house, that they keep their voices low. 'Tell me that, then.'

The Headmaster winced.

'What makes *you* so superior?'

'Lavinia, please—'

'It's *you* who landed us in it.'

'I don't think,' he said, modulating his voice, 'I don't think we've landed in anything.' He meant his subdued tone to be kindly, encouraging.

Mrs Symington-Berry just shook her head and, looking at him, retreated backwards to the sofa.

By some unfortunate chance she happened to lower herself on to the cushion where she had placed her plate of turkey scraps and mixed spring salad. Her husband anticipated the calamity at the very last second but she misread the expression on his face and his gesture of outstretched arms for more of the same—the man's wretched moral cowardice.

She sank back, realised in an instant that some days defy any

341

manner of understanding, and closed her eyes with sheer, certifiable vexation.

★

'I'm sorry, Maureen, wrong with what?'
   'The scrambled eggs.'
   'I didn't notice.'
   'You normally eat your lunch, Howard. I thought—'
   'I just wasn't so hungry today.'
   'Oh. I see.'
   'That's all.'
   'Too much salt maybe—I thought.'
   'No, I don't think so.'
   'I try to get it right.'
   'Yes. I'm sure you do.'
   'If you don't want it again, we don't need to have it.'
   'I *do* want it again.'
   'Do you?'
   'I just wasn't hungry.'
   'Maybe you would have liked something else?'
   'It doesn't matter, Maureen, really.'
   'I just thought—well, I'd say. I should have said at lunch-time.'
   'It's over now.'
   'I thought you might have been—'
   'I didn't think about it.'
   'At the bank?'
   'At the bank.'
   'Oh.'
   'I'll have a look in the garden, I think.'
   'Yes, dear, do. I hope supper—'
   'It'll be fine.'
   'I'll be ready in twenty minutes.'
   'Twenty minutes, then. The side bed needs weeding.'
   'Yes. Yes, do that.'
   'Right.'
   'Maybe I should be helping you?'
   'I thought you had to get supper.'
   'Yes. Yes, of course I do.'
   'Well, *I'll* do the garden then.'

342

'Yes. That's fine.'
'Right.'
'Right.'

★

The boy was keeping out of his way. Odd, thought Mr Brown.

He stood in front of the mirror above the wash-basin trimming his moustache with a pair of nail scissors. Amazing how a moustache made other people at ease with you. He'd read somewhere that people look into your eyes more if you wear facial hair. He liked to think he could make his eyes appear sincere.

Funny how the boy hadn't responded. But youngsters at the awkward age never gave you much change. The boys envied you your moustache, girls thought every chap was a rapist out to rob her of her virtue. It was a pity they couldn't all be shut away till they were sixteen or so, then let out on the world. Come to think of it, that would be worse. On the whole they were a waste of time: just clogging the world up with their growing pains, their moodiness.

Heads full of flying saucer tripe. Probably jacking himself off, the boy. Sex was at the root of everything, though, never mind money. In the War it was worse, only people had forgotten: the desperate search to lose your virginity with a stranger, or to screw someone stupid or be screwed—flat as a kipper— because you never knew if you'd see them again. Now people were so po-faced about it, or they kept it for weekends. But it was still there, it never went away. And those bloody school parents needn't look so snooty about him, because that was the only reason why they were here, they'd banged each other through the War. And *their* parents must have banged *them* into existence. Unhealthy really, all the po-faced looks. But if people weren't so hypocritical about it, he'd probably have been out of a job long ago. Chinese boxes, wasn't it?—boxes inside boxes . . .

Brown opened the door of his room and saw the old woman turning the key in the door of hers. Her reflexes were sharp and she looked round.

'Oh, Mr Brown,' she said, 'I thought you'd—'

343

He casually pulled the door shut.

'—changed rooms,' she said.

'Oh. Yes.'

'You've forgotten something, like me? I'm always doing that. I reach the bottom of the staircase and I remember. Why can't I remember *before* I go downstairs?'

Brown smiled and decided silence would be the safest policy and best defence.

'I'm sure you've made a wise choice, Mr Brown, changing your room,' the woman said as he walked towards her. 'We get the sun through the day on this side. And we don't have the trees, you see. Are you staying long, Mr Brown?'

'No.' He shook his head. 'Just a night or two.'

'I think I might have a little something before I eat. A snifter, as my dear brother used to say. Would you care to join me, Mr Brown?'

Brown invented a lie, he had to telephone a friend—a couple of friends. Perhaps when he'd finished that, if she hadn't gone in to eat . . .?

'I'm sure we could both be accommodated at the same table, Mr Brown. If you would like that.'

Brown felt his smile sticking. His shoulder twitched.

'I'm not sure how long I'll be,' he said. 'Or if I'm terribly hungry even. Maybe when you're finished?'

'Oh excellent,' Miss Austen said. 'Yes, just whatever you wish, Mr Brown.' She stood wrestling with the lock. 'Dear me, what a carry-on—'

'Just be firm,' Brown said. 'You know, I'm very bad with locks myself. Hopeless.'

'No, there we are, I've done it. No need to call on your expert services,' the old lady said, as if she hadn't heard.

'Oh they're not,' Brown said more quietly, not knowing who was behind the other doors in the corridor, obliged to listen to their conversation.

'Well, till later, I hope, Mr Brown.'

He nodded, and even half-inclined to a little bow.

'Then you can tell me what you thought of our mysterious fellow-guest.' Miss Austen chuckled to herself, perhaps— Brown thought—amused by all these strata of petty deception and hypothesis and intrigue that are possible to those who live their lives in hotels.

'I'm afraid I don't—'

'Oh, I'm sure so, Mr Brown,' Miss Austen told him from the doorway of her bedroom. 'You look a very—perceptive man to me.'

Brown's brow furrowed as a possibility occurred to him, that Miss Austen was less harmless than she appeared to be. In her hands, under the strap of her bag, she carried an Agatha Christie novel, with 'A Miss Marple Mystery' emblazoned across the top of the cover. Maybe she read too many novels for her own good?—it was a commoner fault than was generally appreciated. Or maybe the coincidences should serve as a warning to him—as he often received these little cautions in his work—that he had to be on the alert constantly, to prevent himself making false deductions of character from externals?

'Not really,' he said.

'Oh, you're being too modest, Mr Brown.'

'No, no.'

He shook his head and smiled, as if it was just a jokey conversation after all.

He started walking towards the staircase, shoulders twitching again.

'Good-bye,' he said.

'Good luck, Mr Brown.'

'Good luck?' he repeated.

'With your friends. You *are* about to telephone them, are you not?'

'Yes. Yes, of course,' he said.

Miss Austen nodded and smiled. As she stood looking at him, the book slipped out of her hands and fell, covers splayed and pages fluttering, on to the floor. Brown took advantage of her stooping down for it to make his escape. He hurried down the first few treads of staircase.

She was calling something after him but he didn't look back. She was making him feel uneasy: an old dame he'd never met in his life before. He realised the wrong of the situation. It had always been his professional opinion that the company of strangers *liberates* people from themselves, his quarry; someone has no knowledge but also no expectations of you, and you're free to practise on them your own fantasies and suppressed desires.

Brown believed you needed a bit of psychological know-how

345

for this business. The danger was in comprehending a little about people's psyches but not enough to give you a full professional reading of their characters, to allow you that intimate access to a particular process of thinking you required. What would an expert have made of self-compensating Miss Austen, Brown wondered: he guessed at the inventions she would try to regale him with later—she'd already begun with her accomplished ancestor, and he hadn't believed a word of it. For that matter, what would an expert have made of his own unwillingness to believe? Brown sometimes had the curious sensation that, doing the job of work that he did (as necessary as anyone else's was), he was as much a case for examination as any of the adulterers or defrauders he was hired to trail. It was part and parcel of his line of business to think himself into the minds of the people *other* people paid him to shadow: at the same time he knew he had to feel no sympathy for them—rather, something like cool, aloof contempt.

Occasionally it troubled him that, earning his living in such a fashion, he might also just be turning himself into a victim— of the failings of his own character, its lacks and absences.

★

Mr Westropp sits in the car on Edgehill Road. The garage has replaced the fan belt, which he was obliged to cut through with a penknife before he summoned the Maceys.

His wife hasn't come back. It's a mystery to him where she can be. It's a couple of hours since he watched her run round the side of the house to try the kitchen door.

It was a damned stupid idea in the first place. She's always getting these madcap, feather-brained, will-o'-the-wisp notions into her head. Why hasn't she come back? Have that Macey couple rumbled and surprised her? Or did she decide to go back and see old Lady Sybil, and now they're having a heart-to-heart: the old girl's been able to unburden herself at last?

That must be it. What else could have happened? Unless . . . Unless Myrtle's been trapped upstairs, and there's no way of getting down. Earlier he stood under some rhododendrons for a while, looking up at the windows in the attic for a sight of her, a hand waving, a handkerchief signalling a message—but there wasn't anything for him to see.

He will presume the best: that nothing is untoward, that

everything is proceeding exactly as Myrtle must have planned.

*

'You're still with us, my dear?'

The woman in the fur coat glanced to her side.

'My name is Miss Austen.'

The woman raised her eyebrows.

'Yes, my dear, you're quite right. A descendant.'

'I beg your pardon?'

'Of the other Miss Austen.'

The woman appeared baffled. Miss Austen lightly touched her arm.

'I'm so sorry you've gone, my dear.'

'What do you mean?'

'Well, you're not with us any more, are you?'

'I couldn't be more here.'

'But not staying?'

'Aren't I?'

'Not staying with *us*?'

'Yes, I am.'

'I thought—'

'I'm sorry, you thought what?'

'The man told me—you'd gone away.'

'*Who* told you?'

'You were in bedroom fourteen?'

'Yes. Yes, I am.'

'Oh.'

An explanation suddenly occurred to Miss Austen, not a very seemly one.

'I believe it's a lovely room,' she said. 'Very capacious.'

'I shall be leaving tomorrow. You might have it then.'

'Oh, it's not for *myself*, my dear.'

'I'm not finding this at all easy to follow, I'm very sorry.'

'I'm sure you've thought about it very carefully.'

'Thought—thought about what?'

'Why you've come to Sandmouth.'

The woman's eyes re-focused.

'Oh?' she replied, her voice rising as it stretched the word.

'I'm—I'm a little more—liberal than you might think, my dear.'

The term surprised even Miss Austen. But in an embarrassing situation she was apt to say things she didn't understand.

'How very generous of you,' the woman replied.

'He seemed a very nice gentleman. And easy to talk to, which is a great recommendation.'

'What—what gentleman?'

'Don't you worry yourself, my dear, not on *my* account. The secret is safe with me. Quite, quite safe.'

With that Miss Austen took her leave. The woman stared after her. She was afraid of people like that interfering, coming too close to her—literally too close.

The past was worse, though, you couldn't be rude and pretend to have nothing to do with *it*. The past was infinitely worse. It came after you with arms like the grasping tentacles of plants. It could reach out of years ago, into first-floor Mayfair drawing-rooms, slither up brickwork and stucco into second-storey bedrooms in the dark. It was silent and cruel, it whispered and lashed. Sometimes she thought it was out to wreak a revenge, and it was too crafty and malevolent for her to outwit, not unless—

Not unless she retaliated, paid back in kind. It would take some desperate act of destruction to achieve it, one which her reason must loftily wash its hands of.

But without *that*, she suddenly realised, without proud reason—then, she foresaw, she could become another person yet again: this time *an utterly free, limitlessly reckless agent*.

★

Mrs Mason rapped on the door of Nanny Filbert's room.

'Please open the door, Nanny Filbert, I have something very important to speak with you about.'

No reply came from inside. Mrs Mason knocked again, more loudly. The sound of her knuckles pounding on the wood seemed to be carrying all through the house.

'Nanny Filbert?'

Mrs Mason turned the handle. The door was locked. She stooped down and looked through the keyhole. The key had been removed and the curtains drawn: the room was in darkness. She swivelled her head and put her ear to the keyhole. There were no sounds.

Mrs Mason stood upright, mystified, afraid as she hadn't

been since the dire days of the War: afraid of the things that were happening to them, as if all that bad luck had come back to torment her and do its damnedest again.

★

Mrs Mavor was the first to mention it.

'Can we expect Ruth, Mr Aldred?'

The reverend gentleman had lent an ear to Miss Collinson. 'I'm sorry, Mrs Mavor, you were saying?'

'I was wondering, Mr Aldred—is Ruth coming?'

'I trust so, Mrs Mavor. Has she not appeared?'

'Perhaps she confused the time—'

'Ruth has always been very punctual on previous occasions,' Mrs Marjoribanks interjected.

'She knows where all the tea things are,' the ever-practical Miss Dutton cut in.

'We shall—' The Reverend consulted his watch. 'We shall allow her another ten minutes. Then I suggest we might send out the search party?'

The faces stretched to smiles. It was hot in the room and hands reached up to loosen collars and tug at strings of pearls. Tea would have been very welcome: Ruth was the tea-maker. Mr Aldred was forever making the point that 'we all of us "serve" in our different ways'.

Ruth, so the general understanding was, served the tea.

It was too bad, Mrs Mavor decided: and her friend Miss Conway nodded her head telepathically. It wasn't as if the girl had anything much else to do. She was a bit of an odd bod anyway, she'd always thought so. Young people nowadays— although she wasn't so young any more and old enough to know better—they thought anything was good enough for their elders. A nice world it would be if you gallivanted off doing whatever you wanted and ne'er a thought for anyone else. Looking after Number One.

There was the trickle of several conversations round the room. Mr Aldred circulated: just for a moment, a little anxiously, he tipped back his cuff and consulted his watch again.

The talk was of knitting-wool, and the National Health Service, and the quality of tea these days compared with what it used to be, and a person called a 'teddy boy' someone had

349

seen, and the origin of the expression 'A red sky at night', and the reliability or otherwise of that maxim, and how everybody used to feel more in the pink on rations than they did now, and (*pianissimo*) for heaven's sake where *was* that girl?

★

'What's that you're showing me?'

Tilly Moscombe passed the piece of paper across the pedestal-base mahogany table, the same table where the Judds' elegant guests came to dine and speculate about the marriage.

'The Clarence Hotel,' Mrs Judd read. She looked at her watch. 'You have to be there in twenty minutes.'

The girl nodded.

'Well, then,' Mrs Judd said, 'I'm sorry if you have to go.'

She'd asked her into the house on impulse, standing at the bedroom window upstairs and noticing her walking past from the vicarage end of the road. The girl had shown no embarrassment: almost as if she'd been expecting an invitation.

The girl had told her, in a rushed and very muddled way, about her room at 'Hallam House' and about the Maceys. She had told *her*, quickly, that her husband was in South Africa, on business. She had read out bits of his letter, about the houses and the weather and the beach picnics. She had let her know on which date he was due back. (Charles would never understand if she were to mention to him the visitor she'd had in their dining-room.)

'You must come again, Tilly. When you've time. My husband sometimes goes away. On business. I'm on my own then. He telephones, of course.'

The girl nodded.

'We could have tea next time. A proper tea.'

She nodded again.

'Now you must go.'

They both stood up.

'Is that Adele Adaire the actress? Who signed your note?'

Another nod.

'She's in the play, isn't she? I should go—and see it.'

Why not? She wondered if it was a play with a story. Then you saw people's lives in the round. Incidents added up, everything had its place.

350

In the hallway, standing by the open front door, Mrs Judd touched her guest on the elbow. The girl looked surprised. Mrs Judd smiled: gladdened that the gesture could be perceived, but saddened too that it should be so special to the girl. People said she had no reactions, no sensitivity, but it wasn't true. Perhaps what made her exceptional was that she was able to distinguish between kindness and hurt. People had forgotten how indifference can become a custom, and you become too used to it to know how to live without it. Indifference is less than kindness but it's better than hurt. It was almost as if they became content that they should feel so few emotions colouring their lives, or—if they could achieve it—feel none: feel nothing at all.

★

Miss Spink headed for the lights of the Clarence Hotel, where she knew there was a small licensed bar. She might have gone into one of the three pubs in the town, but she had her standards. She might be seen and a lady would be demeaned in such company. The lights in the white frontage looked, somehow, *discreet*.

She hurried along the promenade. A wind was blowing in off the sea and she could feel it chafing her cheeks under their burning heat, chilling her through her best fitted wool coat (French navy, claimed—without Crockers' discount—as soon as it was unpacked in the back room on the first floor). She fumbled with the impractical, three-sided blue leather buttons.

All the complaints she'd ever had about life in Sandmouth recurred to her. About the location, the weather. The sea here had never appealed to her: for most of the year it was either a dismal leaden grey or wild and frothy and throwing spray, and for the weeks of summer when it was still and blue it had to be shared with an untidy squatter of humanity. The site had seemed a virtue of the place when she decided to come, but she couldn't have said why: perhaps she'd imagined benefits to her health, but the climate had given her bronchitis three winters running, and she always felt lethargic in the summer months as if the sea had fixed her with its dazzle and sheen. When the wind blew it was like a joker set loose in a playground, and out of doors she had to grit her teeth. Britain was an island of

351

sailors, she'd been taught at school, but she had no affection for the brine, nor pride either, only a dim terror for its perils and the purposeless devastation it could wreak.

In the 1930s the sea wall had crumbled in a storm and the sea had washed up over the promenade and into the town. In Victorian times, before a proper stone sea-wall had been built, it had reached the lower slopes of the hill behind George Street; she'd heard that tides had flooded the graveyard and when the rescuers had walked downhill in the morning they'd looked over the wall and, at the height of their shoulders, they'd seen coffins afloat like boats. The wrath of breakers and swell made her blood run cold.

She didn't care for the sea: full stop. She didn't greatly care for the rest of Sandmouth either, but she had made her choice and that was that. After ten years she knew people still saw her as a Londoner come to settle among them: 'a bird of passage', ready to fly off again when the fancy chanced to take her. She noticed them eyeing her London clothes and she guessed that they resented her experience of the world. (In fact she hadn't been back to London since, but she felt it was unnecessary to put anyone right on that point.)

She took the steps up to the portico of the Clarence Hotel as gracefully as she could. A man held the door open for her and she smiled fuzzily in his direction, suddenly maudlin to think that manners had survived in the world after all and not quite trusting herself to keep dry-eyed.

She found the Ladies' Room. She filled the basin; she splashed her face with soapy water and dried it. The towel was hard. She stood in front of the mirror challenging herself not to let the traumas of the day overwhelm her now—when she had no escape except through the lit front hall of the hotel, past the faces she imagined crowding behind the pillars to watch her. She stood looking at the woman in the mirror, with an unsparing, scathing scowl: she blamed her for putting the idea of leaving the house into her head, it was madness when she should have been alone with her unhappiness, either lying on top of the bed or taking her anger out in some violent exercise in the kitchen—washing sheets in the sink, putting them through the mangle, hoisting them up to dry on the pulley. That was her usual method of coping: a kind of self-defence,

352

and normally it would do the trick. Staring at the woman she was reminded that these circumstances were unique—heaving at the handle of the wringer wouldn't have been enough this time.

She blinked and looked away. She remembered Mr Cheevy's face, his lips drawn back into a jackal smile. She remembered stumbling her way downstairs, negotiating the right angles of the staircases with her face ablaze and her eyes blurry, past the shape of Miss Templeton in millinery unnecessarily arranging the hats on their stands and Miss Linmer beside her. Everyone in the shop would know by now. Mavis Clark would tell her circle in the town. The circle would spread the news, and it would reach other circles.

In her head as she stood re-folding the towel she saw circles in a dark pond, circular wavelets endlessly ribbing the surface. She felt sick to the pit of her stomach.

The door opened and someone entered. Out the corner of her eye Miss Spink registered a woman in a cape: someone of her own proportions, but with actressy legs and high heels. She heard her singing the words of a show song, lightly, in tune.

Miss Spink flashed the woman a smile and was conscious of her own blatant insincerity—and hurried past to the door, which was slowly closing on its heavy springs.

Outside, a group of people were laughing in the hall and she turned away from them, towards the modern cocktail lounge.

She heard the ebb and flow of social conversation before she reached the doorway. She paused to listen to the talk but she didn't recognise any of the voices—and she breathed more easily.

She walked into the room, keeping her eyes trained on the floral-print carpet. Full-blown red and yellow summer roses and swirls of green leaves on a royal-blue background.

She removed her coat and seated herself in the window alcove. The chintz curtains had been drawn; she was sorry to have no view. Beside her a gas fire on the wall sizzled, casting a pink glow on the carpet. For some reason the gassy sibilants covered her with goose-pimples. She held out her hands.

'Cold?'

She jerked her head up and saw the owner smiling at her. 'It'll soon heat up,' he assured her.

She shook her head and pulled her hands away. 'No,' she replied. 'It's—it's fine.'

She smiled and unconsciously crossed her legs. She placed her hands on her lap. She hadn't meant to cause offence.

'Hasn't been a bad day. But one swallow, and all that,' the man said.

She nodded.

'No, summer's still a long way off.'

'Yes. Yes, it is,' she heard herself responding in her shop vowels.

The man looked across the room at the businessmen from the town lounging in the corner: they stood in a group, each with one hand in a trouser pocket and the other holding a sherry glass or tankard. They were laughing at a story. She heard the words 'fairways', 'the eighth' and 'the fifteenth'. She watched the owner listening intently to the tale of someone's humiliation.

She lost the final words in the fresh outburst of mirth. She wondered when she'd ever known women to be quite so unselfconsciously demonstrative. Did it happen, but in secret?—among intimates? Were women permitted to shake their shoulders as they laughed?

The owner called some words over into the corner. Such ease, she thought. She'd always recognised the two sexes as being quite separate and distinct: you were assigned to one or the other, and you belonged to it as a member did to a club. This evening she was stressing the separateness, coming here alone: the normal rounds of her life dulled her to that keenness, she subliminally made the distinction in the shop or in the street—men in trousers and women with their legs in stockings and skirts below their knees—and she made her quite separate judgements for the two cases without having to think hardly. In the course of a normal twenty-four hours her judgements were surface, painless, automatic. Now she seemed to be confronting that distinction which she wasn't conscious of ever thinking about, how it was she received the world, as male or female.

She was the only woman in the room. It was a state of affairs which simply never happened to her. She didn't know whether to be fearful, or shocked, or . . .

The owner turned back round and looked at her again. He smiled.

She made her mouth into a smile and aimed her eyes at the dresser on the opposite wall. She re-crossed her legs.

'I'm sorry . . .'

Her eyes flitted back to the proprietor.

'I haven't asked you what you would like.'

'Tea, please,' she said, without giving it a second thought. And then, as the man smilingly walked off with the order, she wished she had thought more carefully. It would go to her head like drink, she would have to find her way home floating on a cloud of theine.

The tea arrived on a tray, with a plate of plain biscuits. She'd been sitting tidying her hair for the owner's reappearance, and was disappointed to see it was a waitress who pushed open the door from the kitchen.

She poured the tea and swallowed gulps from the cup. The girl's subservient position in the hotel had reminded her of Mavis Clark: there was something too about her build . . .

She poured another cup. It was rather bitter tea, so she added sugar. Tea had never tasted like tea since the War. She was used to saying in the staffroom it was India's 'revenge' after Independence. She would deliver her verdict with a sage nod. It had been her own theory and she still held to it.

Stirring sugar into the tea, she thought of the staffroom. Tomorrow the news would be passed around, outdoing flying saucers and Princess Anne's head-cold, the words would be in everyone's mouth. She visualised the room falling silent as she opened the door and tried walking in quite nonchalantly. She saw the triumphant sparkle in Miss Templeton's eyes; she heard the rattle of Miss Armitage's steel knitting-needles, stitching a little weave of impudent, damning thoughts.

She noticed Mr Partridge with his handlebar moustache at the bar. Other people were drifting into the room. She watched them, with what attention she could bring to them: hotel guests, two elderly couples, the women with pearls and cameo brooches and handbags, the men in suits and shiny shoes, waiting for the gong to strike. A stray middle-aged man followed behind: he carried a folded Ordnance Survey map and wet his lips as if he was meaning to start a conversation with someone, if someone could only be found. She could just see, through the doorway, a younger woman, standing reading the hotel notices; she wore a smart fur coat (Miss Spink recognised London taste) and a silk scarf on her head. She looked over her shoulder—rather anxiously, Miss Spink thought—then she sauntered off somewhere, her heels clicking on the tiles.

The guests sat at different points in the room. Miss Spink felt herself encroaching, although no one was bothering to notice her: the man unfolded his map, the two couples separately muttered in hushed voices, only waiting for an occasion to exchange a pleasantry with each other.

Miss Spink looked at her shoes, then at the rather blowzy roses on the carpet with their wide-open buds and petals pulled back—curiously disturbing, for a reason she couldn't quite think of—then at the pale pink glow of the fire.

'May I?'

She looked up from her cup, over the rim. A man in a Prince of Wales check suit and with a little ginger moustache stood in front of her. He was breathing rather quickly; he was holding a rolled-up newspaper and tapping it against his leg.

She meant to shake her head, I don't understand—

'May I sit down? Do you mind?'

She looked round the room—embarrassed—and saw that the three other groups of chairs were occupied. There was another bay with a window seat but the couples sat on either side of it. A cat lay fast asleep in the armchair.

'I'm just going,' she said.

'Don't do that—'

The cup shook in her hand. Why should he say that?

Behind him the woman who had been in the Ladies' Room made her entrance into the room. Heads lifted as she looked round for someone who seemed not to be there. A cheeky-looking young man in a brown suit was staring at her most intently: the new class of rep.

'I have to go,' Miss Spink said, rather wearily.

'I didn't mean to send you away.'

The man sat down in the chair opposite her, with his back to the room. She smiled with closed lips. She continued sitting as he'd found her, with her elbows on the arms of the chair and the cup in her hand.

'Nippy evening,' the man said.

'Yes,' she replied—and thought very fleetingly of the chilly journey home still ahead of her.

'It's not the season,' he said.

356

'No.'

'What brings you here, might I ask?'

'Well . . .' She leaned forward and replaced her cup on its saucer. 'Actually I live here.'

She watched the man raise his eyebrows.

'In the town, I mean,' she said.

From its quite promising beginning the conversation didn't get anywhere. Miss Spink had the feeling that the man wasn't really attending to what she was telling him about Sandmouth, its climate, the layout of the streets, train times to London.

At one point the woman in the fur coat walked back through the hall. Her heels rang on the tiles. The man looked round, saw her, and—while she was in mid-sentence—hurriedly apologised to her for leaving as he got to his feet.

He *crept* away. Miss Spink could think of no other word for it. *Creeping* on the toes of his shoes. What terrible thing was he about to do?

She sat, cup cradled in her hand, watching as he sidled out into the hall. The woman in the fur coat had been consulting the map on the wall; she turned away towards the front door. The man followed.

A woman and a man.

Miss Spink lowered her eyes and stared into her cup. That kind of normality reminded her how much further she had drifted from it in the course of a day.

She opened her handbag to find a handkerchief. Across the modern, brightly-lit room she could hear a woman's voice telling someone the story of her life: how she'd been born in a grand house on Lake Windermere, how her name was Austen, how it was she had descended from the great writer.

Was her story true or false, Miss Spink wondered. Was 'either/or' even the point any more? Weren't true and false probably hopelessly confused to the woman by this time?

The tea leaves at the bottom of her cup might explain all I need to know, she thought, but who is there who will instruct me?

★

'Aren't you changing, Norman?'

'What's that?'

357

Pargiter looked over his shoulder. His mother was watching him from her wing chair where she sat knitting.

'You're not changing?'

'I—No, I haven't.'

'Look after your clothes and *they*'ll do *you* a good turn.'

Keep them good, she meant; only wear them when there are people to see. But mothers, *we* don't count.

'I—I might go out again.'

'Business?' she immediately asked him.

'Sort of. Yes, business.'

She always monitored his movements very carefully. He guessed that she didn't entirely trust him. But then he was never very comfortable with *her* in a room: he'd inherited her suspicious nature. He knew the matter of girlfriends and fiancées obsessed her.

'I just thought you—'

'Yes. All right, Mum.'

'You're snapping today, Norman.'

'I've things to think about.'

To Pargiter the silence seemed to imply that he'd been inferring she *didn't* have things to think about. His mother often stage-managed these silences in a conversation so that he would seem to be putting her down. She liked to suffer, and to imagine she was below respect: that she not only didn't deserve her surroundings, but deserved to be spoken to less well than a servant. It was a complicated game of self-denigration that his mother played: the more he bought for her and provided her with in the way of material comforts—even though he'd given her the best bedroom at the front, for instance, while he slept at the back, facing north—her respect for herself became less and less.

Sometimes Pargiter felt it was too much to handle, certainly by himself: and what wife would want the responsibility?

Inevitably the picture of Gloria Barlow occurred to him, overlaid by another, of the family in Branksome sitting down to Sunday tea. Nothing—but nothing—must interfere with that excellent arrangement of interests: unless he learned something not to his liking about the father, Gloria's dad, which was an unlikely possibility. But what if Barlow chanced to pick up some damning piece of tittle-tattle about *him*?—he must have his contacts, ears and eyes, everywhere. Surely nothing that was spoken in the gossip line could become eternal ether without him intercepting it first?

The thought would perturb Pargiter, menace him, normally the most resolute and unflappable of operators. This evening there was worse to contemplate: much worse.

'Are you all right, Norman?'

'Of course I'm all right, Mum.' He looked over his shoulder again. 'Why shouldn't I be?'

Suffering silence.

In a way he'd been willing it to happen. It was why he'd grown bored with the hotel they'd gone to: no one in the dusty hall smelling of steamed cabbage except a wall-eyed woman at the desk to see the elegant, sophisticated woman who followed him upstairs to have sex with him. Car sex was a bit suburban, but at least he didn't drive a suburban car. At night he dreamed of her heels spiking the thirteenth green, the two of them lying naked on the fairway in full daylight or rolling in one of the sandy bunkers and a pair of good and honest burghers seeing them and turning apoplectic. At the same time that he wanted and required Sandmouth's respect, he wished he could dese-crate the smug, unthinking, self-righteous purity of those contemptible little minds. Sex was the chink in the armour, so it is in every situation: someone had told him about one of Gloria's father's accountants—he made detours in the car to and from work past various junior school playgrounds in Bournemouth—and, working over that piece of intelligence, a plan had begun to form itself in his mind. He'd also heard that one of the assistants in Braddock's bank on George Street where Uncle Arkwright did his business apparently had an eye for the boys . . .

Those two—the accountant and Braddock's subordinate—only merited notice because of the classified information they might provide. It was Norman Pargiter no less who was at risk now: *might* be at risk.

Was it possible that it had taken him this long to discover a self-destructive urge in himself, which he'd been too busy to take account of before? He shook his head at the possibility . . .

'You make a better door than a window, Norman.'

'What?'

'I can't see.'

He took a few steps forward.

'Oh, by the way. Your lady-friend phoned.'

'What?' Pargiter's eyes grew small.

'Your Miss Barlow.'

'Why didn't you tell me?'

'It slipped my mind.'

'What did she want? What did she say?'

'She's planning a party.'

'What?'

'Seemed a funny message. I didn't think anything else about it. Unless it's a code, of course.'

Pargiter stared out at the lawn.

'All right for some, isn't it?' his mother said, wielding her needles. 'Parties! That's the life!'

'For Christ's sake, Mum!'

'Norman!'

'Why don't—'

'What language! *I* never taught you to—'

'You can have a party any day of the week you like, Mum. *Every* day, if you want one. Go on, why don't you?'

'*Me?*' She laughed a bitter laugh.

Pargiter turned his back on his mother and crossed the room; he pulled open the french windows and stepped outside on to the white gravel, desperate for air. Christ, some days he felt he could lift his hand and strike her, son or no son.

Gloria, a party, what did she mean? A surprise? Pargiter puzzled about it for several moments. A party for him to prove himself, an occasion to allow him to prepare an announcement?

He thought ahead. First he would have to beard Barlow, of course. The worry of ever losing Gloria was all he needed to convince himself that he wanted no one else, nothing except that happy ending for the story. Casually dropping in as he drove through Branksome, a request for a few minutes of his time, a conversation that would meander in a certain direction . . .

The two doves flew down out of a tree and hovered above the bird-house, fluttering and twittering in a pantomime of innocence. Pargiter stood watching and nodded his head. He would have preferred more time: to check up on Barlow's financial position, maybe to allow himself to make an offer to Uncle Arkwright and strengthen his hand that way.

It all hung on that half-wit Moscombe girl, Pargiter reminded himself. Staring hard at the white Lagonda, he dug his nails into the soft flesh of his palms, burying them like claws into a kill.

★

In one of the back bedrooms of 'Hallam House' which Mrs Macey prefers to keep locked a light snowfall of plaster lies in a posy ring on the Persian carpet. Directly above, the lower portion of Mrs Westropp's right leg protrudes through the ceiling; it might belong to some inspired surrealist's scheme of decor, if it didn't firstly belong to her. No part of it moves; the generous covering of flesh is unnaturally white through the stocking. The back of the shoe has parted company with her ankle and the whole hangs by the toes.

Night seeps into the rooms of the house: or, alternatively, all the light has seeped out. The leg projects through the plaster-work for what might seem to be no good purpose at all.

The ways of humankind are frequently devious, however, and might not accord to any readily discernible logic. There may be more to this than meets the eye, or maybe not: if it only chanced that an eye were here to see.

★

Mrs Prentice sat with a book open on her lap.

'What are you reading, my dear?'

She looked up, surprised by the voice and the question.

'What did you say?'

'I wondered—' Her husband indicated. '—what it is you're reading.'

'Oh.' She looked at the name on the spine. '*David Copperfield.*'

'I didn't know you were reading it.'

'Oh,' she said. 'No. Only very slowly.'

'It's a wonderful book, isn't it?'

She nodded, not knowing what sort of book it was, wonderful or anything else.

'I'm not sure why it is,' her husband said, 'when you read it again, even though you know what's going to happen, you're surprised by it. Some of the things are a bit far-fetched, of course, but no more so than life. Don't you find that?'

'I'm sorry?'

'The coincidences, how people's paths cross.'

'Oh. Oh yes.'

'It all seems—not forced—but quite the opposite. Quite real in fact.'

She nodded, but she wasn't listening. She didn't know how she was going to last out the evening. The french windows stood ajar. Birds sang outside, too loudly, dementedly; thrushes pecked and pecked at snails in shells, smashed the shells to lance the meat. She had the sense of the town lying waiting on the other side of the walls and hedges, cowering like a hunting animal choosing its moment. She had somehow managed to side-step her conscience every Wednesday afternoon: now she didn't see how she could ever have peace of mind again.

If she ever really had. If she *had* been truly content, she wouldn't have had to make such a game out of her guilt at marrying Cedric. One way and another she'd been living on tenterhooks ever since her father died, realising that every choice from then on in life had to be the right one.

'And what about Heep?'

She looked up.

'I'm—I'm sorry?'

'Uriah Heep.'

She stared at her lap. She'd pulled the first book she'd come to off the shelf and let it fall open. She'd tried reading a few paragraphs, but what was the point of coming in half-way through a story? She'd never been much of a reader. School had put her off Dickens for life. She wondered what a book—the right book—could have told her now.

'I think I'll have a look outside,' she heard herself saying, and got to her feet. She was conscious of Cedric looking at her as she laid down the book and then walked off across the room: watching her not with his usual pride, she guessed, but with the concern she'd been aware of ever since the incident with the dropped tumbler.

She looked over her shoulder and smiled at him. She only

362

wished she might have been able to tell him. But, even if none of the Wednesdays had happened, she wondered if she could ever have ventured an intimacy of that kind with him. Not that she didn't think he was the most trustworthy and honest man she could have had for a husband. But it was occurring to her more and more often that it would have been like telling an uncle rather than a husband. She didn't think she could go on pretending to herself that the difference in their ages didn't matter. Perhaps she'd originally been drawn to him precisely *because* her father was dead, and—unconsciously, if all the psychology books were true—because she had been looking for someone as close to that model as possible? But you don't marry your father—he has lived out the best part of his life already—you look to marry a complementary half and to attempt to form with that man a fulfilling whole.

Too many of Cedric's tastes and hers didn't *quite* match. She guessed that if they were ever to discuss deeper things—moral questions—the attitudes they would each have declared would have belonged to two different generations. They nobly pretended that certain pursuits coincided: his beachcombing and gardening, her tennis and swimming. She'd read in a magazine (in, of all places, the hairdressing salon) that a writer called Vita Something-Or-Other had said, shared interests in a marriage are less important than holding your values in common. From that point on she'd known that, ultimately, the two of them were doomed.

And doomed too for the sake of another person she couldn't have cared less about, Norman Pargiter. All that had mattered to her was that he was the type of person he was: a go-getter with no conscience but with the susceptibility of a mercury barometer where social differentials were concerned.

Outside she stood on the gravel path. Every spring, bulbs came up through the grass where she didn't expect them to be, because she'd forgotten. She knew she would forget again when this season of hyacinths and daffodils and tulips was over. Next year they would reappear in the same spots, and for years after that. How different would Cedric look the spring after this one, she asked herself, how much older? And what about herself, how well would she have survived her year?— presuming that she did.

She stared about her, at the tranquillity of 'The Laurels' ' garden, and thought how much depended on it and how little now supported it, and how fragile was this protective web of calm and peace.

★

Ruth watched the talking heads through the lit windows of the vicarage. She didn't believe she could face them tonight. They gathered once a fortnight, like a coven in a place consecrated to be holy. When he'd originally taken over the duties of the parish, her father had had the idea of a women's discussion group—maybe because he was unused to the sound of female voices in the house?—and, haphazardly, the Sandmouth Ladies' Circle had begun. Ostensibly they discussed the state of the world, and they agreed to read a particular book every couple of weeks, one which the bookshop could order half a dozen copies of: tonight it was Elizabeth Taylor's *A View of the Harbour*. Probably no more than half of them ever read a book through to its end.

Really, Ruth knew, it was gossip which bound the women into their circle: the voices always grew more enthusiastic whenever she and her father left the sitting-room to attend to the tea things in the kitchen. In a way, of course, that *was* discussing the state of the world, but it can't have been how her father intended. After twenty minutes or so Ruth always found the room unbearably stuffy and oppressive, and it had to do with more than the heat of fourteen or fifteen bodies occupying too small a space without adequate ventilation. She could feel the women's eyes like hooks and their words like sharp little needle-stabs, always worse if she turned away, and worst of all when she was stacking the tray in the kitchen with her father: she felt she could hear and see through the walls all the injustices that were being done, the sly defamations muttered out the corners of mouths.

It was Constance who suggested that tonight she need have no part in it.

'You only make them worse,' Constance's voice at her shoulder told her. 'They feel the need to justify themselves.'

'They *can't* justify their lives. All those tiny acts of resentment.'

'Can *you* justify *your* life, Ruth? *Can* you?'

364

'Oh, but I'm an interesting case. They know that too. I'm a vicar's daughter who lives without faith.'

'You're not the first in the history of humankind.'

'It may even be a common condition.'

'It's quite likely.'

'If I was a rake—'

'If I *were* a rake, Ruth, please remember—'

'If I *were* a rake—then I could consume myself with guilt.'

'Would you like that, Ruth?'

'At least it would be something—'

'If you were a rake, you wouldn't have time for *me*, Ruth.'

'No, I wouldn't. I don't expect I should give you a second thought. Men would make violent love to me, day and night. Night preferably.'

'Do you ever find Father attractive in that way?'

'What a question!'

'But you've been waiting for me to ask it.'

'I suppose I have.'

'Well . . .? You can tell *me*, Ruth.'

'I used to think it, sometimes. He's grown a little careworn now. About fourteen or fifteen was the worst time. I used to try to bump my knees against his under the table. I haven't told you *that* before.'

'Well, I knew, of course.'

'Why did you ask me, then?'

'Just to make sure you would tell me.'

'What else do you know, Constance?'

'That you've imagined him—Father—in various states of undress.'

'Defrocked, yes. Doesn't that make me worthless? Not worth knowing as a human being?'

'I should think it makes you *very* human.'

'If you weren't so understanding, Constance—'

'Yes?'

'I don't know. I'd commit some terrible deed, I expect. In frustration.'

'How terrible—'

'A dark deed. I'd murder one of those women in there.'

'How?'

'Tip poison into their cups. Any one. There's poison in the outhouse. For the rats.'

'A peculiarly unchristian habit I always thought that, Ruth.'

'Me too.'

'On the whole, though, he's above reproach. Wouldn't you say?'

'Father?'

'The man in our lives.'

'Apart from what he's never told us about being married.'

'Apart from that.'

'Yes, I suppose he is. He's blinded by his goodness, even. Just as well.'

'Blinded to what?'

'To those women. To me. God bless innocence.'

'Is he? Father? "Innocent"?'

'Terribly. By comparison, I'm a woman of the world.'

'What am *I*, then? It was *I* who showed you the fleshpots of London.'

'That reminds me. Someone told Father a story about a bishop who'd flown out to some African nig-nog land. A journalist at the airport asked him, "Are you going to visit our fleshpot towns too?" The bishop was very pure and innocent, and asked the journalist: "Your fleshpot towns? Where are they?" The headline in the newspaper the next day said, *Where are the fleshpot towns?—Bishop's First Words*.'

'How did Father take it?'

'He smiled pleasantly, how he does.'

'Remember the Anstey girl at school?'

'Grace Anstey?'

'Yes.'

'I didn't *know* her. You—'

'*I* knew everybody. Even when you thought I didn't, Ruth.'

'I sort of remember. What about her?'

'I saw her parents once, they were like Mr and Mrs Bland. Small and cherubic.'

' "*Cherubic*"?'

'Grace used to say they were just like two Babes in the Wood. They couldn't manage anything mechanical at all. They had a refrigerator, and it was as much as they could do to work the handle on the door; Grace said it wasn't even switched into the mains for the first six weeks. She felt awfully worldly by comparison, just because she could open a tin of spam with a key.'

366

'Constance—do you think Father's a Babe in the Wood?'

'Not completely. He tries to think the best of people.'

'Is that a fault?'

'I don't think so. It just—it just leaves him unprepared sometimes, that's all.'

'How do you think I could be so different from him?'

'You could be *more* different, though, couldn't you?'

'Ever-tactful Constance—'

'Well, couldn't you?'

'If I was a rake, you mean?'

'If you *were* a rake, yes. But you're not, are you?'

'No. No, I'm not. But I'm not innocent, either. Where do you think I get it all from?'

'Get all *what* from?'

'My unwillingness to believe. From Mother?'

Every so often the word was dropped between them. *'Mother'*. The conversation would stop at that point. Ruth would fall silent. Constance would drift out of thought-range.

Poring over the few surviving photographs hadn't succeeded in telling Ruth any of the things she wanted to know. In the mirror she searched for a trace of her mother in her features, and couldn't seem to find any at all. Perhaps she spoke like her, a little?—the timbres of their voices were similar? Her father gave nothing away—if he remembered even. Or was forgetting a quality of goodness in the end?

But I can't forget, Ruth knew; my life is a continuation of hers. If she is mine, I am also *her* ghost. And yet I am the living spirit of someone I know nothing about: I am the continuation of a mystery, the core of my 'being' is a life which eludes me.

*

'Oh God!'

The actress stood in the doorway, in her accordion-pleated white crêpe dress (Dior copy, Goldheims of Margaret Street), looking round the Clarence's dining-room. Couples with stiff backs confronted one another across their tables; a few guests sat alone, heads slumped over newspapers or books. One woman held up an Agatha Christie paperback with green covers.

'What fun!' Miss Adaire declaimed in that quiet room. 'If

367

someone really *was* to be murdered. I'm sure everyone here must have dreadful secrets.'

Some heads turned round to look at the group.

'Shut up, Adele!' Pennicote hissed at her.

'For God's sake,' she hissed back in imitation. 'Don't tell me,' she said in a slightly louder voice, 'don't tell me you don't like an audience. *You* of all people. A living, breathing audience—sort of.'

'There's a place for everything.'

'The story of your life, I'm told,' she smiled back. 'Isn't it, old cock?'

'Just button it, Adele,' he said, gripping her shoulder in what might have been a playful gesture. 'And less of the old.'

'Hands off,' she said, removing his hand.

'I shall refrain from making any comment,' Pennicote replied. Adele Adaire smiled across to one of the waitresses.

'Good,' she said brightly. 'If you do, you'll get this handbag where it hurts.'

'Promise?'

'Pervert.'

'A lady to your fingertips.'

'Not that *you* would know, darling.'

'Not like you, Adele, eh?' The actor smiled his publicity smile for the room. 'Or are you pitching your sights a little lower these days?'

'Just forget it, Guy.'

'Of course there's a new generation to whom you are but a legend.'

'Forget it,' she said, more sharply.

'I didn't know if it could be *the* Adele Adaire when they told me I'd be working with you.'

'Why not? You thought I was dead, I suppose?'

The actress hailed the waitress.

'I'm afraid, darling, *your* name meant nothing—'

'Good try, Adele.'

'I've a short memory for boys from the chorus.'

'You've a short memory, full stop, Adele.'

'That,' she said, 'is a bit below the belt.'

'Oh, nothing sacred, darling. You must have learnt *that* by now, surely.'

'For three. A table for three, dear.'

The waitress turned and took a few steps forward.

'Sweet girl,' Pennicote said.

'Got an eye for these things, have you?'

'What things?'

'That young woman's attributes.'

'I was rather hoping *you*'d teach *me*, Adele. Just what I should be looking for.'

'You're not even in the race, sweetheart.'

'You know, you should have had a word with that memory-man in Bognor. On the variety-bill. He could have given you some advice.'

'Oh, I would have had a word all right. Darling,' Miss Adaire swung round, '—let me tell you something. Amateurs like *you* don't give professionals like *me*'—she tapped her chest— 'advice. Understand? God picked *you* out for the chorus-line. *I* was in the West End when you were soiling your nappies. God bloody well knew what He was doing. Once a pretty chorus-boy, *always* a chorus-boy.'

The party moved across the room: Adele Adaire first, Guy Pennicote second, followed by the shambling girl.

'Sit down, dear,' said Adele Adaire, and pushed the chair in so abruptly that the girl's knees went from under her and she had no choice. 'I shall sit here,' the actress said, dropping herself on to the next chair. 'And my friend Mr Pennicote will sit—'—she pointed brusquely—'*there*!'

'Well, this should be an experience for you, Dilly,' Pennicote said as he sat down. 'As it should be for us.'

'Dilly is my friend, Guy, may I remind you.'

'But you said *I* was, Adele—'

The actress summoned the waitress in her best 'carrying' voice and asked her for a menu. 'If you please.'

'Well, being a friend,' Pennicote continued. 'That *does* make you a special person, Dilly. Miss Adaire has many—er, acquaintances. But her friends are a very special, very unique breed.'

'Yes, Guy?' Adele Adaire smiled at the wondering girl placed between them. 'How is that?'

'Well, they're dead for a start.'

'You cheap little bastard.'

369

'I don't remember that line, Adele. Where does that come from? "Mrs Kennedy of Kensington"? "Pimlico Secrets"?'

'You remember my oeuvre, Guy? How loyal of you!'

'My mother used to tell me.'

'Oh. *She* enjoyed them?'

'Not really. Her mother took her. My grandmother, that is.'

'So you *did* have a mother, then?'

'Of course.'

'*Of course.*' Adele Adaire nodded her head. 'Not a father, but a mother. You must have been close to her. To be—as you are. A little too close, maybe. And no woman has ever been quite like your dear old ma, is that it?'

'Except you, Adele. You've always reminded me of my mother.'

'Not your grandmother?'

'Oh no. She was a famous beauty.'

'Your mother wasn't?'

'She had a—"lived-in" face.'

'She'd knocked around rather, I expect. But your father was handsome? Or can't you remember?'

'I was too busy admiring your publicity pix to notice, Adele dear.'

'I imagine you were also at the breast rather a lot, Guy. Weren't you?'

'Oh yes. Just like you, Adele.'

'But something put you off it?'

'Unlike you? Yes, I dare say. By about eight years old I'd had my fill.'

'You don't strike me as the sort of person who could ever have his fill of anything, Guy.'

'Oh yes. Of some things. And some people.'

'Thank you, dear,' Adele Adaire said with great politeness as the waitress put the menu into her hand.

'But are you meaning to suggest, Adele dear, that yours truly is actually handsome? Like his dad?'

'Oh, that's all in the eye of the beholder.' She held up the menu card. 'And I'm not beholding.'

'Maybe Dilly thinks I'm handsome?'

'My friend sees the world a little differently from how *you* do Guy. She doesn't have your ego. Sadly, I dare say. Poor child.'

'Poor child,' Pennicote repeated.

'A great loss for her. Dilly is one of the world's innocents. If the word is familiar to you.'

'She has nice hair. Have you noticed, Adele? But yes, I expect you have.'

'Brown windsor soup. Dear God—'

'A modestly but adequately formed upper torso. Particularly in the area of the mammary appendages.'

'Dilly dear, would you like some meat-loaf? Or ox-tail stew? And soup to start with? It'll *have* to be soup to start with.'

'And how are you *finishing*, Adele?'

'Well, first things first, young man,' the actress said, and tossed him the menu across the table.

'Yes.' Pennicote stretched his legs under the table as he picked up the menu and read. 'It is a man's world, isn't it?'

'How would *you* know a thing like that, Guy?'

'Very vexing for you, Adele. In the—in the portico, as it were. At the top of the stairs, and first in the queue. But they can't allow you into the club.'

'Architectural metaphors. Jesus wept, whatever next? Don't tell me one of your pals has taken you to a gentleman's club? I presume they didn't let you in?'

'Quite right, darling. Hopeless!' Pennicote hung his wrists limply in despair. 'So much on offer and nowhere to, er, powder my nose.'

'Are you fussy where you powder it?'

'Oh yes. Some of us *are*, Adele. Or we'd just look like slags—'

'Not from what I've heard. You'd powder yourself with a poodle's arse—'

Adele Adaire stopped in mid-sentence. She smiled unsurely at the girl.

'We're forgetting you, my dear. I'm sorry. With our chit-chat.'

'Auntie Adele loves her chit-chats, Dilly. With chorus boys. She pretends she doesn't, but she does. Auntie Adele's a bit of a hypocrite, quite frankly. She has no one else to have her precious little chit-chats with, you see.'

'Be quiet, Guy.'

'It's why she's giving us the privilege of her company on this piddling little tour. Because *I* know—'

'What the hell d'you—?'

'Because I know Auntie Adele's friends are really—aren't they, Adele?—rather boring. And working's always better than resting, isn't it? *Some* money's better than none, any time. "What are you doing, Adele?" "Oh, I've a Rattigan play coming off." "Has he written you one?" "Wish he would, darling, ha-ha. No, it's a revival. Limited run." *Very* "limited", Adele old thing, but what the hell—?'

The actress sat with her chin resting on the backs of her hands, listening to him, her eyes staring through him: not seeming to see him, only the words appearing to register.

'Yes,' she replied, quite calmly.

'Yes what, dear heart?'

'It *is* a limited run,' she repeated. 'So—so what the hell?'

It was Pennicote's turn to sit and consider her as she opened her bag and rummaged for a cigarette. She found two loose ones, and threw one of them across the table to him.

'You're a little more perceptive, Guy, than I'd given you credit for. Although I wouldn't have *utterly* wasted my time with someone who wasn't perceptive to a point—'

'Like Dilly here?'

'That's different.' Adele laid her hand on the girl's arm.

'What's the word for me?' Pennicote asked her. 'I'm "amusing", is that it? People in your old plays were always "amusing", weren't they?'

'Endlessly amusing.'

'Friends, Dilly,' said Pennicote, leaning forward confidentially, 'in the theatre "friends" are made very easily.'

The girl was looking pained by the sudden attention. 'In the theatre,' Adele said, 'everyone learns everything about you, Dilly. You can't really hide things. People—take you for what you are. You—you learn to—to accommodate yourself to them. Everyone—everyone shakes down.'

She smiled at the girl, abstractedly.

'Well,' she said, 'it's a way of life, Dilly. Oh, the honesty cuts you. So you cut other people. It's quite bloody, really.'

Adele and Pennicote both blew cigarette smoke across the table, like two experienced performers in a scene carefully synchronising their gestures.

'*You're* very smartly got up, Dilly,' Adele said, leaning forward and brightening. 'Did someone help you to get dressed like that?'

The girl looked down at herself, to where the others had directed their eyes. Her head nodded—possibly.

'How good of you. Isn't she smart, Guy?'

'Yes,' Pennicote said, and blew out more smoke.

'It's a bloody awful place to bring you,' Adele said. 'I'd die if I lived here, I really would. If "living" is the word—'

Pennicote crossed himself. 'Thank God for touring.'

'My landlady said there's someone writing a book about this town. And Dilly sits in her kitchen sometimes. A woman.'

'She sits in her kitchen?'

'Yes. And I expect she listens. And she talks—a little bit.'

Pennicote stared at the girl.

'You have to listen carefully to Dilly, that's all,' Adele said. 'To hear what it is she's telling you.'

'Someone's writing a book about this place?'

'Yes. So I was told.'

'I bet if you scratch at the surface with your fingernails . . .'

'What do you mean?'

Pennicote hesitated for several seconds as he observed the girl.

'Just—just that they're more—more uneasy than they seem to be. Than you like to think.'

'Than I like to think?' Adele asked sceptically.

'Than we all like to think. I imagine it's how things were before the War—'

'I knew we'd get back to that,' Adele said. 'When I was entertaining the troops at Mafeking.'

'Wasn't it Khartoum, darling?'

Two clouds of cigarette smoke passed across the table and met in the middle.

'Places aren't like islands any more,' Pennicote said. 'Or they're not supposed to be. Everywhere *belongs*, I mean. Nowhere's apart, or exempt.'

' "Exempt"?'

'From being in Britain.'

Adele drew meditatively on her cigarette.

'So,' she said, 'it's just like "Maids and Masks". We're doing our bit? Still?'

'We're playing in a play about a touring company who don't know what the country wants to see.'

'What *do* they want to see?'

'Plays like they used to write them, about how things used to be. But also about living in the new age. Isn't that what this is supposed to be? A new age? We're all "New Elizabethans". Only—'

' "Only"? Only *what*, mon chéri?'

'Only nothing's happening. Just these bloody old rep companies, and they're as bloody as the people they're trying to play. Everyone pretending things are different, the actors and the characters and the audience, and everyone knows they're not.'

'Why not, then?'

Pennicote shrugged. 'I'm not sure. We don't go for change like that, the race. Too much is ingrained perhaps. How people see, the different ways they're brought up. The "new" people—whoever *they* are!—trying to be like the old. And the old kind envying them, because they need more money to live how they used to. We're supposed to be getting more class-less and all that, but no one can forget the old days. Or even wants to. The sureties that aren't sureties any more.'

'You should have been a politician, darling. At the hustings, up on your soapbox.'

'It's not too late.'

The waitress took their orders. Her tongue appeared between her lips as she wrote them down on her notepad.

Adele watched her as she walked off. She turned round quickly and caught Pennicote smiling at her concentration.

'Something—*amusing* you, Guy?'

'No more than usual. I was thinking, Dilly will be able to tell everyone she had dinner with a very famous actress. So famous, in fact, she was always being mistaken for Fred Astaire's sister.'

'She'll be able to tell everyone in Sandmouth she shared a table with someone who—so he's always telling *me*—is going to be an actor in the films. And then—when his looks faded—he had a useful second string to his bow, and he became a Minister of State and ate cabinet pudding.'

'I think I'll just stick to the movies, Adele.'

'Do you think *they*'ll take to *you*?'

'Oh, they're bound to.'

'Really?'

'That's the plan.'

'Got your casting-couch settled on then, have you?'

'Well, it won't be the one *you* used. What was your first celluloid epic called?'

' "The Brighton Belle". Did very good business, I'll have you know.'

'So what happened?'

Pennicote laughed. The actress narrowed her eyes at him. She examined the chimney of ash at the end of her cigarette.

'So, *you*'re to be our new Richard Todd,' she said. 'Or David Niven, or whoever. Congratulations!'

'I wouldn't mind.'

'Well, don't let me put you off, darling.'

'But—'

'It's a snakepit like everything else, as you'll discover for yourself. I only hope you're not—crushed alive. Or get the fangs sunk into the back of your neck. Or anywhere else.'

The waitress approached their table, carrying a trio of soup plates on a tray.

'So,' Pennicote said, 'you had the viper treatment, let me guess?'

'More a case of a boa constrictor, I should say. A *very* powerful man. Married to such a nice woman. To use an old-fashioned word. Thank you, dear.'

The waitress departed.

'Bon appétit, Dilly dear.'

'And he crushed you?' Pennicote prompted.

'Crushed me. Had a crush.'

'What was so awful—?'

'Maybe it would suit *you*, Guy, but it wasn't quite *my* style, darling. If you get my drift. Hold your spoon like this, Dilly dear.'

'Couldn't you have—?'

'No, I couldn't. But then that's the difference between us, Guy, isn't it? You're "modern" in that respect, and I'm not. You're a chameleon, let me guess. I'm not.'

They both of them exchanged serious glances, then turned their eyes at the same moment to consider their guest.

'*Good*, Dilly,' Adele said. 'You've got an appetite.' She swallowed more soup from her spoon. 'The knack,' she said, addressing Pennicote, 'is knowing how to control them. Appetites. *Including* them. If you'll permit me one final piece of advice, Guy dear.'

Pennicote confined his response to a nod.

'Although, Guy, I *should* say I'm very good at being wise after the event. If you've any sense in you at all, you'll be wise *before* it.'

Tilly Moscombe looked at them both. She smiled, from one to the other, as if *she* were the hostess of the evening, glad that her two guests had arrived at some amicable, if temporary, status quo.

'That's a nice bracelet,' Pennicote said between mouthfuls of soup.

'Dilly is cared for,' Adele told him.

'Lucky Dilly.'

'Yes. Yes, lucky Dilly,' Adele repeated, the staginess momentarily forgotten and absent from her voice.

★

'How do I look?' Mrs Gutteridge asked her husband.

'Fine. Just fine.'

He stood behind her and fastened the catch on her pearls. She was wearing the peachy-pink ottoman dress she'd bought in Bournemouth. He loved how her taffeta *sounded*, and the rustle of stockings that went with it.

'Come on, Ken, cheer up.'

'I'm sorry, I'm fine.'

'*Everything's* fine, then, is it?'

He couldn't forget the afternoon: the actress coming back, the girl seeing him, his wife blowing in with the wind, the (unspecified) trouble later with Christina when she got home from the Convent.

It was the business with Tilly Moscombe which disturbed him most. He didn't want that particular professional ploy to become public knowledge. Any number of hairdressers watered down the shampoo, of course, they'd always been doing it in the salon in Regent Street where he'd served his apprenticeship: only, they didn't advertise the fact to all and sundry.

'*Not* your blazer, Ken. You wore it last time.'

'Did I?'

'Wear your suit.'

He felt he cut a better dash in his blazer: he looked—somehow—more 'leisured'. But Christina must be right: and the Norrises would recognise it from a previous visit, if anyone would.

'They haven't seen you in your suit.'

'Yes. All right, then.'

He took off the blazer and returned it to its hanger. It had cost a packet—Aquascutum, hessian, twin vents, chrome buttons, the waist taken in a fraction—but you didn't want to give the impression it was all you had. Impressions were important after all: appearances.

As he lifted his tanned legs and stepped into the trousers of the suit, he was thinking of Tilly Moscombe again. He felt a cunning little knife-twist of pain in his stomach.

'So you're all right?'

'Yes. Yes, why?'

Christina laughed. *'You* know why. Your stomach.'

'I'm feeling fine.'

'If you don't take the Eno's, you'll only wish you had.'

'I will.'

She never actually offered him pity for having the stomach he did. He tried not to refer to it. It had come with all the hard work in the early days of the salon, washing and cutting and rolling till seven or eight of an evening and his week-ends taken up with house-calls.

'You were gippy at the Norrises' last time.'

'I won't be this time, love.'

'I hope Christina's all right.'

'Are you sure you don't know what's wrong?'

'Of course I'm sure.'

The words were spoken hurriedly, impatiently, it occurred to Gutteridge. His wife hadn't explained the afternoon's trouble, only mentioned that Christina was very down in the dumps.

'That—that's better,' she said as he slipped his arms into the waistcoat.

'What time did they say?'

'Eight-ish.'

'When will we aim for?'

'Ten-past?'

'Right.'

The Norrises had a daughter at the Convent, in Christina's class, also a younger boy at Minster Court. He had a plumbing business he'd built up for himself. The Gutteridges hadn't pursued the friendship, but the Norrises appeared to like them—or to need them. They had more money than sense, and Gutteridge felt he and Christina enjoyed their visits to the vulgar, over-furnished house more than they pretended to each other. He also had a suspicion that Kevin Norris was interested in *them* for a reason he hadn't admitted to yet. Was he really on the look-out for an investment?

Damn Tilly Moscombe, *damn* her! She had to keep her bloody mouth shut. Should he try to offer her money?—or would that only make a bad situation worse?

'Ready, Ken?'

'Coming, love.'

Christina was looking her best tonight, just a shade edgy maybe. Did that have anything to do with Kevin Norris, he wondered.

He would puzzle about it several times in the course of a day. He concentrated so hard to keep himself in physical shape, to dress youthfully, but he didn't know how much that counted with Christina. To look at, Kevin Norris was nothing to write home about, and yet he seemed to hold some fascination for his wife, and vice versa.

Damn Tilly Moscombe, *damn* her!

'Yes, the suit's better.'

'I just thought—the blazer—it looked more relaxed.'

'But they've *seen* the blazer, Ken.'

'Oh well.'

He heard the taffeta, rich and sexy. He leaned forward and planted a kiss on the back of his wife's neck.

She jumped, a good couple of inches.

'Ken!'

'I'm sorry—'

'Warn me first.'

'I'm sorry—'

She smiled—attempted to smile—rather forcedly. Gutteridge rattled his car keys, wishing he was driving them there in Kevin Norris's fancy two-tone Jensen, not in his staid black Lanchester.

Christina continued to smile. Gutteridge continued to stand rattling the car keys. What on earth was happening to them both?

*

Norah Waites, she was called. Back in that London time.

The cocktail bar had lost half its numbers, and Miss Spink was left with the truth of why she had come to Sandmouth.

Norah Waites. Miss Spink had been twelve years younger than her, but she hadn't been uncomfortable with the age difference. 'I'm ancient,' Norah would tell her. 'You should be eating more green vegetables, Vera, and getting out with people of your own age! All of London's there!'

They'd served on different floors of the shop. Miss Spink had been conscious of the older woman's eyes resting on her every time one of them passed through the other's department. They had been introduced, and were only socially polite to each other for a while. One evening Miss Spink had spotted her getting on to the same train as herself; when she'd got off at the other end she'd looked back and seen the woman's face through the crowd of shoulders on the platform. The same thing happened several times. In the lunch-hour there were occasions when Miss Spink would turn round quickly as she was walking alone a busy street and there a few yards behind was Norah Waites.

She'd never mentioned the sightings to her, nor had the woman volunteered back any information: where she went at lunchtime, why she travelled on a train to Norwood when she lived in Mottingham. In spite of that, they did begin to speak to each other about other matters and, with the passing of weeks, they started to become friends of a kind in the shop. Quite early on Miss Spink learned that Miss Waites lived alone, and had a mother in Dagenham. Miss Spink also had a mother. Sometimes it would trouble her to think how long a mother might be alive for: especially a moody and short-tempered one you didn't see eye to eye with on so many things. Norah Waites was fifty-two and still having to do battle with hers.

The prospect of another ten years of week-end visits on the train out to Leyton and having to humour her and holding in her true opinions to herself deeply depressed her. She felt a mixture of sympathy for Norah Waites, being in the same position—intense sympathy for her—but also (she couldn't help feeling, although it made no sense) irritation with her that she continued in her mother's thrall. After a couple of months she started to imagine Norah Waites might even be an image of herself and for that reason she wanted to protect her and to be closer to her—to be to her as she would have wanted others to be to herself—but also to deny her her friendship, afraid of being pledged to thankless customs and routines even more than she was already, afraid too of admitting her patent similarity to her.

Inevitably they talked of their mothers, but only in passing: they preferred their conversations to be as neutral as possible. They discussed what they read in the newpapers, or had heard on the wireless the previous evening, or how so-and-so was dressed, the quality of the goods the shop was stocking.

Their friendship as it developed only existed within the physical confines of the store. There was nothing so very unusual in that. 'Outside' always tended to be a vague 'Beyond' in people's conversation, and the images built up in the store seldom survived if you saw the person in their home surroundings. Miss Spink was also convinced that there was nothing out of the ordinary in their friendship, except for the age difference: unlike the practice in certain other large shops, those on different floors were encouraged to socialise. She continued to be a little apprehensive, however: not only because of their mothers, like phantoms in any conversation, but because of the new interest her acquaintance was taking both in her own appearance *and* in hers.

The younger woman was unaccountably embarrassed by such attention. *She* had always dressed for the shop, for it alone, not for any one person: her only friendship with a man had been years ago, and she had never had the good fortune or even the time since then to find another such. Suddenly she realised what had been happening over the past weeks since her introduction to Norah Waites, that she too was starting to pay more attention than before to how she looked, because unconsciously perhaps she'd been taking in what her friend from the third floor was saying, and she was plucking her eyebrows and using a lighter shade of lipstick and wearing a more flattering support. It wasn't until someone commented that she'd confused the two of them one day that Miss Spink perceived the extent of the changes in herself. It was exactly the case, she saw: her own appearance had taken on more than a little of Norah Waites's, and—rather queerly—vice versa. One lunchtime she also chanced to catch two women winking to each other as she and Norah both made their way across the canteen with their trays. Quite a different realisation occurred to her at that moment.

Nothing had 'happened'. Once in the Staff Ladies' Room she'd found herself alone at the basins with Norah and she'd been aware of an uncomfortable degree of strain in the room. Norah paid the usual compliments on how she was looking and asked a question—how did she think *she* suited her hair pinned back over her ears (as Miss Spink did)—which might have been a very harmless enquiry, or might possibly not have been. She'd tried not to look at Norah or at her hairstyle as she replied. Norah mentioned nylons next. In the shop they could always find themselves stockings—they didn't have any truck with the painted kind, and pencil lines drawn up the backs of their calves—and Norah would always come down from the third floor and present Miss Spink personally with some of the best quality available and tell her how good she thought she looked in them. At the word 'nylons' Miss Spink stiffened. Norah stood back from the basins and said something fulsome about her legs.

'You don't mind my saying so, Vera? From a friend to a friend?'

'No. Not at all.'

'I just thought I'd tell you.'

'Thank you.'

Until that point Miss Spink had come to feel more confident with her friend's attention, homing in on her across the department or the canteen. Seeing it in the Ladies' Room, at such intimately close quarters, it seemed less—what was the word?—less 'natural'. She was conscious that she wasn't looking straight into Norah's eyes as she usually did.

That was all that 'happened'. Until her friend started tailing her again: never pestering her, never that, but intimidating her all the same, because Miss Spink knew she was there, behind her in the street or on the same train at the end of the day. (Norah had told her dozens of times—scores of times—that she lived in Mottingham, which was on another line, from a different station.) Miss Spink wished she could put the question to her, 'Why do you do it, why do you follow me about?' but whenever Norah was with her, she couldn't believe that there was anything suspect or—a funny word to use of a friend—'sinister' in her nature. Certainly Norah did buy a coat on staff discount which was exactly like hers, and an identical pair of shoes, but those were meant to be flattering gestures—weren't they?

It continued like that, Miss Spink being shadowed by her friend. The regular bombing raids started again, and Miss Spink wished she was spared one of these constant round-the-clock pressures at least. One evening she was hurrying to the station—catching glimpses over her shoulder of Norah in her matching coat and shoes—when she thought she couldn't take any more of it. Recently she'd started, a little treacherously, to concentrate her gaze on the signs of age on Norah's face. She would wonder if that was why she had originally drawn her attention in the first place, because she was young, unlined, without a grey hair: now it was as if Norah was *willing* her to worry, so that the frowns and anxiety lines would surely appear.

That particular evening she played a trick on Norah Waites: as the train was pulling out of the station she jumped off and ran back along the platform. She spotted Norah's face at the window of another compartment: the woman struggled to her feet when she noticed, not attempting to disguise herself, as if she was panicking not to have her friend on the same train.

Miss Spink shivered when she saw. At the same instant, outside the station, sirens were beginning to wail in the streets. She heard a sea of running footsteps on the pavements.

On that same unforgettable evening, eleven minutes out of the station, the train was hit. The middle carriages were blown away. Later, in an underground station in the black-out, Miss Spink heard the news and began to shake uncontrollably.

The next day everyone in the store wore long, long faces.

When Miss Spink walked in Mr Tripp stared at her as if he was laying eyes on a living corpse. He had chanced to be on a train in front that had been delayed: sprinting back to the scene and clambering over the wreckage he'd seen a badly mutilated body dressed as he knew Miss Spink to dress, sprawled under an uprooted wooden sleeper from the track.

Miss Spink stayed in London till the end of the month. She didn't tell her mother of her plans, but simply disappeared, went out of circulation. Four months later she surfaced in Sandmouth and rented a couple of rooms, starkly furnished with austerity furniture. The London store provided Crockers' with references, but her mother didn't pursue her through them: or, if she did, she lost track of her daughter somehow. Miss Spink knew her mother's neighbours were too nosey to leave her to her own devices, she would have survived her defection.

Miss Spink sat in the 'Smugglers' cocktail lounge of the Clarence Hotel and wondered if this was God's revenge for abandoning her mother to her neighbours and the Welfare State. He'd given her ten years in Sandmouth. Ten years of freedom was a good run of luck by anyone's calculation, and it was only as much as you can expect in the course of your life, and especially one lived so anonymously. But He hadn't forgotten and He wasn't going to allow *her* to forget either.

Sometimes of late—when she couldn't sleep—Miss Spink would be stricken by remorse. By the morning it had gone. It might be that her mother was dead. Why should a parent make a claim like that, as Norah Waites had let *hers* do? Then at other times, in the Ladies' Rest Room of Crockers', Miss Spink would look at herself in a mirror and see the features of her mother's face poking up through the stretched skin on her fifty-two year old one.

Now there would be no more Crockers'. And too much time to think about her mother. Too much time to let frowns and anxiety lines and crow's feet and the rest take over her face.

Miss Spink peered at the tea leaves in the bottom of her cup.

Or maybe God really couldn't care less after all, and He was leaving her to sort out her own problems; they were of *her* making, not His.

Maybe yes, maybe no.

Miss Spink wasn't sure of a lot of things. She still didn't know if Norah Waites had been 'one of them' or hadn't been. But perhaps that wasn't the point?

What about *herself*? Could she ever positively *know*, be *certain*, about her own inclinations? What if she didn't really *care* whether she was or not, wasn't that worse in some ways?

Sometimes—on charcoal-sky days when Sandmouth was like a tight metal brace round her head—she had tried to convince herself that the person who died on the train wasn't Norah Waites but a person who might have been Vera Spink: who worked in that shop, who looked not so dissimilar, who was unmarried and had a mother, who was travelling on the regular train service to Norwood she always travelled on.

That didn't lay to rest all the ghosts, though. We try to understand a little of what lies beyond ourselves, Miss Spink told herself: but—never mind Mr Aldred's God, forget Him, *damn* Him—it's ourselves where all the secrets and confusions and unanswerables begin and end.

★

Nanny Filbert sat in the 'The Anchor'. She was still wearing her uniform, or what Mrs Mason—with daft memories of Wrens—thought a nanny's uniform ought to look like: flannel A-line skirt, a blazer with silly polished buttons that wouldn't sit properly on the bust.

What would missus have to say if she was to see her here? Bugger Mrs Mason. Bugger her, if anyone could. Not that husband of hers at any rate, she was quite sure of that, working his arse off eighteen hours a day to afford the house. Working himself into an early grave, to leave his wife a widow and with a daughter in her teens she couldn't control.

Oh, Nanny Filbert saw what it was all about. She also realised that she could make herself indispensable to the stupid bitch. *If* she kept her job. The big 'if'. If that loony splay-footed moonchild didn't go and open her mouth, blow the gaff.

Suddenly in a loud voice Nanny Filbert started discussing with the general company the proprietor of the 'Spirit of Good Hope', one Dave Gribben. And his wife. What a miserable pair they made, she said.

For a while people sat listening to her—then they seemed to lose interest, they stood up or shifted chairs. Bugger the lot of you, she thought.

Before this she'd always had to keep out of pubs. House Rules. Rob probably spent all his time in pubs now. Lucky sod.

She saw someone showing photographs. She joined their table. The man had been killed.

'Your husband, dear?'

The woman nodded.

Life like a candle, not worth the tallow. Poor cow you are, thought Nanny Filbert.

And a photograph of the child. A boy standing near water, staring at the camera. Straight into the lens. He looked hypnotised.

Nanny Filbert went back to her own table, and as she seated herself she found she'd left her glass at the other one. She lurched towards the end of the settle, lost her balance, and fell across the seat. Bugger, *bugger*.

Heads turned to watch, then looked away. Not embarrassed, just uncaring.

Effing place, anyway. What was that tune? Always on the wireless. '*It's a lonesome old town . . .*' Sitting in all those bedrooms: and this one, the pretty-prettiest of the lot. She hated it. '*. . . when you're not around . . .*' Doors closing—footsteps fading, disappearing down the street—eyes hypnotised—eyes closing. '*. . . I wish you'd come back—to—me . . .*'

★

The tea must have been stronger than she'd thought, Mrs Spencer realised.

She was listening to Bax. Lush and sickly sweet, she decided as she tried to concentrate on the music instead of her crime: only confirming what she'd suspected for years, that now the composer's usefulness was over, he wasn't worth listening to any more.

She lifted the needle off the record but lost hold of the arm and dropped it. The needle's point jumped across the record, making chips and scratches which sizzled through the machine's speaker.

Mrs Spencer prised the record off the turntable; standing directly under the lampshade, she held the disc up to the light. The surface was scarred and pitted.

It seemed to her like the end of an age: she had passed out of all that time-that-was and was living now in conditions that were new and hard, harder even than her old life's.

The gloves were draped on the back of the armchair. A pair of white chamois gloves. She was terrified to come too close to them. They were laid on top of each other, two lady's hands, elegant and pale; crossed in a fey party pose, or as if they were in death.

Of how they happened to be here, in her sitting-room, Mrs Spencer was becoming less and less sure. They weren't hers, not *her* white hands, and she wanted to explain to the silly Moscombe girl that they weren't, she'd been confused about what she'd seen, terribly mistaken. The hands had nothing to do with *her*, Captain Spencer's wife, not really.

I shall tell her, Mrs Spencer resolved; I shall find her, *make* her understand that she hasn't seen what she thinks she's seen, that appearances are deceptive and no one can truly know the truth about anyone else from what is made apparent to them: of course we needs must scribble down our impressions in speedwriting, otherwise we might have nothing at all . . .

Mrs Spencer returned Bax to his sleeve, a mere formality since they could have no more use for one another, after the thousands of miles travelled together and the dozens of hours endured in each other's company.

She looked round the room, at what she apologetically referred to as her 'bits and pieces' when anyone visited and she felt compelled to comment. Quite often, as was happening now, the irritation she felt for them was physical. A sickness churned in her stomach; she hated those arrogant claims of the inanimate on a life they had shared: something which had chanced to come into her hands at some place, at some particular time in this or that period. Every time the nausea got the better of her she just wanted to be rid of them all, to sweep them off the stands and shelves: and later she always had the inevitable rush of conscience, that it was betraying Ronnie, and it was making her past seem nothing at all, only incidental, when really it was everything and she only existed because of it.

She would try telling that too to the girl, to help her to understand, that really she was the aggregate of all the things the past wouldn't allow her to exorcise from her mind: and that she was to be pitied, even more than the girl was, because the past will never, will absolutely *never*, forget.

★

Ruth Aldred sat in her mackintosh on the promenade wall. She looked across at the bobbing heads behind the lit windows of the Clarence Hotel. She thought she could hear the sound of laughter, carried across the road.

'Oh well,' said Constance, 'it's all right for some, isn't it?'

'They don't mean anything to me.'

'Why do you sit watching them, then?'

'Because I don't understand them.'

'You enjoy not understanding them, don't you, Ruth?'

'Oh, shut up.'

'Father doesn't approve of that expression.'

'Father doesn't approve of a lot of things.'

'Oh, now we're *getting* somewhere!'

Ruth moved to another point of the sea wall still within sight of the Clarence Hotel but further from the lights of the town, nearer the golf course and the darkness.

'What do you think she heard?'

Ruth shook her head.

'Her life's a sin really,' Constance said. 'Against God.'

'She can't help it.'

'Hark at you.'

'Be quiet, Constance.'

'That's an improvement on "shut up".'

'Just be quiet, will you?'

'Why are you protecting her, Ruth?'

'Who?'

'Tilly Moscombe.'

'I'm not.'

'Shouldn't I have said—?'

'But you *did* say it.'

'And her life *is* a sin, Ruth. *You* know that.'

'So?'

'So, where does that leave us with Father? In this best of all possible worlds.'

'Leave me alone, Constance.'

'But *that* doesn't solve anything, Ruth.'

'We knew, anyway.'

' "Knew"?'

'The problems.'

'With what? With whom?'

'*You*-know-who.'

'Tilly Moscombe?'

'With Father! With *Father*!'

Ruth put her hands over her ears. She wished she could be alone. She wished Constance wouldn't come any more. She wished she would go away, and go away for ever.

At first it had been fine, they'd been friends. Then Constance had started to tell her all sorts of things about the world. She'd taken her to London a couple of times. Now she plagued her with what she didn't want to think or talk about, to have to find words for.

Ruth stood up and buried her hands deep in the pockets of her mackintosh. Now Tilly Moscombe had seen Constance or heard her, and she wasn't her own Constance any more, she was someone else's too. She had to put it out of Tilly Moscombe's mind, somehow, that she had ever heard her. Otherwise Constance wouldn't go away, she would always be here, and Ruth knew she wouldn't be able to live with that.

She'd overheard one of her father's women talking about the girl as she walked up the path to the front door of the vicarage. Tilly Moscombe had been seen going into the Clarence Hotel, what was the explanation of *that*, Mrs Mavor, for goodness' sake?

But what did goodness have to do with anything, Ruth wondered. She hated the conceit of goodness, thinking *it* always knew best.

A figure appeared at the front door of the Clarence Hotel. Ruth took several steps forward, to the edge of the pavement.

It wasn't who she was expecting to see. A woman stood at the top of the steps. She was wearing a fur coat. Ruth had spotted her earlier in the evening. She'd looked restless as if she couldn't decide what to do; or maybe she did know what she had to do but she was afraid to do it.

Afraid to do it . . .

Could Constance have *meant* Tilly Moscombe to see? It

might have been that she was trying to give herself away: different parts of her to different people, so Ruth couldn't own her any more.

Ruth realised now that she couldn't trust Constance. Maybe she would turn out to be a traitor, Constance: she had been a kind of impostor all along? She was ready to tell people about her, Ruth, even to tell someone like Tilly Moscombe; she was distancing herself, taking herself away—from Ruth and the vicarage—and she'd found the perfect emptiness she required, her own body to live in? Tilly Moscombe had nothing to do with Ruth: or so Constance thought. But what made her imagine she could put one over on her sister as easily as that?

Ruth believed there must be a conspiracy afoot. Constance and Tilly Moscombe. The craft of it, the guile! But not quite clever enough . . .

She pitied Constance, pitied her, that she should think *she* wasn't able to see through that poor, thin, threadbare disguise of the witless girl from 'Hallam House'.

★

'May I?'

Miss Spink had been conscious of someone drunkenly steering—or trying to steer—his way round the cocktail lounge. In a mirror like a fish's eye she saw he was making in her direction. She immediately reached down for her handbag under her chair and was about to get to her feet when she looked up and recognised who it was. 'That old buffer' Mavis Clark had called him. The ungrateful trollop.

'May I?' he repeated.

She bowed her head. 'Please do,' she said, in her very best accent, which she kept for occasions when she used the telephone in Crockers'. *Used* to use the telephone . . .

'Bit warmer in here.'

'Oh, yes,' she said, distorting the sound of the word to an ultra-polite 'yaze'.

The Major dropped into the chair, negotiating his dead leg.

'This peg gets a bloody weight by the end of the day.'

Although not quite approving of the expletive, Miss Spink inclined her head, graciously like Miss Mansell, like royalty. As she did so she caught an overwhelming stench of spirits.

'What a shag,' he said.

389

Miss Spink didn't see the connection, but continued to smile, charmingly.

'Yaze,' she said. 'Eh ixpict so.'

'You foreign?' the Major asked, screwing up his nose and eyes suspiciously.

Miss Spink wriggled in her chair with discomfort. She didn't think she would stay on after all.

'Oh no,' she said, as airily as she could. 'Sandmouth bawn and braid.'

'Oh.' He nodded his head. 'Just thought I'd ask.'

'Quate raight. To esk.'

'What's it like, then?'

'Eh'm sawry?'

'Sandmouth.'

'Oh.' She shrugged her shoulders, lifted her hands.

'The world's *my* oyster,' Fitt said. 'Don't know where to call my home. Somewhere with young people, I dare say, that's what *I* want. Young folk around me.'

'Eh'm not sure.'

'Aren't there many?'

'Here? Oh yes. Some.' Miss Spink was losing her refined accent. She was remembering the day just past. 'I'm not so fond of the young people myself,' she found herself saying.

'Aren't you?'

'Not awf'lly.'

She stared down at the blowzy, over-ripe roses on the pattern of the carpet.

'The hill's a shag. Getting my peg up and down that every day.'

Miss Spink nodded.

'What's the weather like?' Fitt asked.

'Oh.' Miss Spink shrugged again. She started to explain, trying to give him an honest explanation of what might be expected in that respect, the bad as well as the moderately good.

During her explanation she glanced across at her companion. She saw he wasn't listening. His eyes were open but his eyelids looked heavy; his head kept dipping to one side and the breath came whistling out of his mouth. His face in repose was different from the public one he'd worn entering: the skin was flabby and pulpy, his mouth sagged, his chin disappeared into his neck.

Then Miss Spink noticed—she couldn't help noticing—that the Major's trousers were open. She hurriedly averted her eyes.

'I must go,' she said, reaching down for her handbag.

The Major started, like a dog dreaming of rabbits. 'What's that?'

'I must be going.'

'Must—must you?'

'Yes. Quite definitely.'

She was aware that he was leaning forward, or trying to lean forward. She pushed her chair back and stood up. She kept her eyes trained on his tie: on the curling collar tips of his shirt. What a disgusting man.

'Keep me company. I'll promise not to mention my old peg again.'

'No thank you. You must—'

'You're fussing like a hen, madam.' The Major gave a half-hearted impersonation of his famous chuckle.

'No, I'm not,' Miss Spink replied in all seriousness. 'I'm just in a hurry.'

'No one to join me?'

What a selfish, self-centred, disgusting man, thought Miss Spink.

'You'll find—you'll find someone,' she said. 'I must go.'

'Like a cat on a hot tin roof.'

Offensive too.

'I've—I've left something in the oven.'

'Not buns I hope! Mustn't stop you, then.'

Miss Spink stepped past him. He smelt quite revolting: of more than drink too. The newspapers said people had no respect any more, no reverence, the heroes were sent up. She used to shake her head with Norah Waites about it. Perhaps there was reason to it after all.

'Good-bye,' she said very briskly indeed, taking care that her eyes shouldn't stray to the man's open crotch and whatever was showing.

'So long as it's not my peg chasing you away—'

She hated that word. She had a horrible instinct that it might refer to more than his leg.

'Good-*bye*,' she repeated with even more briskness.

She walked away from him, across the floral jungle on the floor. Sometimes men quite turned her stomach. They were so

391

much nearer the animal state than women. Pray he didn't come back to Sandmouth.

Sandmouth. She couldn't possibly stay here now, not with everyone knowing her disgrace. Too old-fashioned, too out-of-touch, not modern enough, not the right 'image' for the new-style Crockers'.

She passed through the doorway into the hall. Ahead of her she saw the sign marked 'Ladies' Powder Room', with its finger pointing to the right.

Miss Spink felt she was about to give in to hysterical tears. She turned for the door, and ran towards it.

★

The telephone rang in the 'Old Rectory'.

The sound startled Pargiter as he walked into the drawing-room (so he always tried—*tried*—to remember to call it).

'You answer it, Mum,' he said. Then it occurred to him that it might be Gloria.

'Here, let me,' he said, snatching the receiver out of his mother's hand. 'Yes?'

A high, nervous giggle floated down the line.

'Norrie?'

He breathed a sigh of relief. He noticed his mother scowling at him with disapproval, rubbing at the marks of the flex on her wrist.

'Is that you, Norrie?'

Pargiter covered the mouthpiece with his palm. 'It's personal.'

'Oh well.' Mrs Pargiter shifted her weight from one foot to the other. 'If it's your friend in Bournemouth, she doesn't want to have anything to do with *me*.'

'Don't be like that, Mum, for God's sake. I'm not in the mood—'

'God hears you talking like that, you know. Maybe you think He can't. In Bournemouth, of course, they say what they like and it doesn't matter.'

'I just want to speak to Gloria.'

'What's stopping you? Not me, I assure you.'

Pargiter watched his mother shuffle out of the room and he shook his head.

392

'Norrie?'

'Gloria?'

'Oh, I'm so glad you're in.'

'Nice to—hear from you, Gloria.'

'Are you all right, Norrie?'

'Yes. Yes, of course. Everything's fine.'

'Oh.' A breathy sigh reached him from Branksome. 'I'm glad.'

Pargiter heard faintly the jangling of the charms on the bracelet.

'I just thought I'd phone you up.'

'That's—that's nice. I'm glad.'

'Are you really glad to hear from me, Norrie?'

'Yes. Yes, of course.'

'Good. I—I thought you must be busy. And I was interrupting you—'

'No. No, I'm not busy.'

'Are you *sure* you're not busy?'

'Yes, I'm sure I'm not busy.'

'Oh good.' A little giggle trickled into his ear.

'Can you hear Argos?'

'I'm sorry?'

'Can you hear Argos? I'm trying to feed him.'

Pargiter nodded to himself. 'Are you, darling?'

'Oh, Norrie!'

'What? What is it, dear?'

'You called me that word.'

'What word? "Dear"?'

'No, silly.' Another throaty little laugh.

'What, then?'

'That other word. The one Daddy heard you say. And you told me he looked grumpy.'

'Oh, "darling". Well, he can't hear us now, can he?'

'I don't *think* so. Would it matter?'

'Would what matter?'

'Would it matter if he did hear us?'

'No I don't suppose so. But why should he?'

'*Why?*'

'This is a private conversation.'

'Yes, I suppose it is.'

'Of course it is, Gloria.'

Pargiter made a mental note to check out how many phones and extensions there were the next time he was over. Louis Barlow Senior wasn't above listening in on his pure and treasured daughter.

'Oh, Argos, *no*! You've had two biscuits already. You'll grow so *terribly* fat.'

Pargiter smiled into his cuff.

'Argos is being very naughty. And next Jason will want a biscuit too. You *are* naughty, Argos. I'm very *very* cross with you.'

'What are you doing, Gloria?'

'I think I'm going to biff Argos's nose. If he isn't jolly careful. Did I show you the doggies' biscuits, Norrie? Will I tell you what it says on the box?'

'I—I have to see someone now, Gloria.'

'What?' The voice suddenly sounded despondent. 'Oh, *do* you?'

'In a few moments. I've an appointment to see someone. It's awfully boring of me.'

Pargiter was speaking in his public school voice, which seemed to be how Gloria expected him to speak. Her two brothers always looked rather sceptical, and seemed to be trying to catch him out with their remembered slang from schooldays.

'*Must* you, Norrie?'

'I—I *must*. Darling.'

'Daddy always has to see people too. Oh Norrie.' The confused voice became another little giggle. Sometimes Pargiter wondered if she was stringing him along, she was really just a tease: a cockteaser. Whenever she giggled like that or breathed into the mouthpiece, a hot shiver passed down his neck and back, to his buttocks.

He leaned against the wall, imagining her in her white American woollens and her white pleated cotton skirt. When she spoke into the telephone she had a delightful habit of pulling at the little ringlets that overhung her ear.

'Norrie?'

'Yes?'

She spoke in her simpering, coaxing voice.

394

'Are you coming over? On Sunday?'

'Yes. Of course, Gloria. Don't I always?'

'Yes. Almost always. I only meant, you must come *this* Sunday.'

'I *must* come?' He laughed. 'Why *must* I come?'

'But you *have* to come.'

'Jealous I've got another lady?'

'What was that, Norrie? Argos is jumping up—*No*, Argos! Naughty boy!'

'I'm going to be there on Sunday, Gloria.'

'I've got a surprise for you. You *must* come, Norrie.'

There was so much expectation in her voice he realised he had no choice.

'Of course I'm coming, darling. Just keep me from coming!'

'I'll count the hours.'

It sounded like an expression she'd read in one of the romantic novels she whiled away her time with.

'Now, Gloria, I really *must* go.'

'*Must* go?' Her voice dropped in register. For the first time in the exchange he caught a trace of London. Vaguely Pargiter saw the dangers for the future, that Gloria had the makings of a highly petulant and unpredictable—as well as loving—nature. While she still enjoyed the comforts of her father's house, the negative aspects were minimised. But what about when they had their own green-roofed villa in Branksome?

'I'll see you on Sunday, Gloria.'

'*Promise* me.'

'Promise.'

'Kiss a promise.'

He obliged.

'Oh Norrie.'

When they were engaged he would take it beyond kisses. Preparing her for the wedding night. Petting, feeling her up.

'I'll keep your surprise for you. You'll have to guess.'

'I'll try to guess.'

The conversation continued for another couple of minutes but at last the receiver went down—slowly, lingeringly, with kisses being blown into the mouthpiece in that most congenial and salubrious house on Branksome cliffs.

Pargiter stood for a few moments with the receiver still in

his hand. In the mirror he saw his face fall, his mouth hang slack. He forgot about Gloria and her lucky life and thought about himself and what had taken place this afternoon. It would have been bad enough if only *he* had been implicated: but there was his fellow-conspirator too. His worry wasn't for her moral virtue, but because he knew he couldn't fully control the situation. She'd been predictably well-mannered and discreet on all the past occasions, but this wasn't like any of the past occasions. Did she have the resolve that *he* did?

Suddenly there were lots of imponderables in his life. Gloria's father's reaction when he would ask him for her hand ceased to be the major one. Sunday would be a kind of holiday compared to this: a few hours' reprieve.

His mother shuffled back into the room. Pargiter noticed she was wearing her slippers.

'For God's sake,' he said, 'why d'you wear these? You never used to.'

'Now is now.'

'I bought you shoes. Good shoes.'

'They're *too* good.'

'For God's—'

'Don't take the Lord's name in vain, Norman. He'll give you your deserts—'

'That's superstitious nonsense.'

'He *does* hear.'

'Did Aldred tell you that?'

'*Mr* Aldred.'

'I just wish you'd wear shoes. It's a simple enough request. You look as if you're down-and-out.'

His mother was going to reply—when she decided to, she had an answer for everything—but he'd had enough of it and brusquely walked past her, out of the sitting-room. The sleeve of his blazer caught the door handle and pulled the door shut; it banged behind him, which wasn't what he'd meant to happen.

As usual, it would mean another two or three hours—or a sleep-over—until his mother had thawed enough to speak to him. In some respects, they were far too like each other for comfort.

Pargiter marched into his study: moodily, like one of the dark men out of Gloria's novelettes. Momentarily he felt ready to submit, to be defeated by everything, all the events conspiring against him.

But after a few seconds in his business nest he'd recovered; he honed and primed his brain to think how to deal most effectively with this lowest point in his fortunes, how to give fickle Lady Luck a lesson—a kick in the twat—she would never forget.

★

From the dining-room Adele Adaire caught sight of Miss Spink as she rushed headlong down the front hall. A shop assistant, she had no difficulty in deciding. Lacy handkerchiefs smelling of eau-de-cologne, no-nonsense knickers, a little mother holed up somewhere.

She'd spotted the woman earlier. For a single moment their eyes had met across the cocktail lounge. The woman had looked away first. Funny, how a split second was just long enough to tell you.

★

Miss Spink pushed open the door of the Ladies' cloakroom and blundered past someone standing at a mirror, towards the first of the two open doors. She squeezed herself inside the compartment and pushed the door shut behind her. It slammed, much louder than she'd meant, and she imagined the explosion carrying all over the building.

She found a handkerchief in her bag and stood blowing her nose into it and dabbing at her eyes. It had been her worst day during all her time in Sandmouth, she had no doubt about that. After her years of care and discretion, this was what she was reduced to.

She also felt—why?—exceptionally impressionable, about what was happening to her. Maybe she should have drunk something alcoholic instead of tea? She felt she was remembering too much now. About the man, about the scene in Cheevy's office, and the scene in the department that was the start of the whole rotten business. But the show-down with Mavis Clark wasn't some chance, unforeseeable incident, it had been a year-and-a-half in coming: pressure building up to the point where the load had become too much and one of

397

them had had to give. She'd tried so hard to make sure that it was the girl who would weaken first: but Mavis Clark's insensitivity knew no bounds.

Miss Spink's tears started to dry. She rubbed at her eyes, then blew her nose again. She dropped the handkerchief into her bag and snapped the clasp shut.

She undid the lock on the door and it swung inwards. She caught sight of a shape, the person she'd seen when she'd rushed in. Holding her handbag flat against her stomach, she manoeuvred herself out of the compartment, reluctant to raise her eyes.

When she did, she saw—of all people—that daft girl: the one who went walking through the streets, following patterns on the pavements and speaking mumbo-jumbo to herself.

Miss Spink was conscious that her face was louring. All the time she was behind the door she'd felt the person was still there, half-aware of her distress.

It turned out it was only Tilly Moscombe. Miss Spink stared at her staring back at her. She was supposed to have something to do with Lady de Castellet, of course, but Miss Spink had never believed the story. The girl received the old woman's charity, that was all. It was only in novels that orphans turned out to be blood-relations, novels about cobwebby houses and secret walled gardens. Lucky Tilly Moscombe, though, to stay where she did: but it was the least she deserved, being born how she had been.

Tonight she was in her best clothes. The sight appalled Miss Spink. The girl was like a travesty of womanhood, deportment, fashion. Somehow, though, she got by, against all the odds. She could stand in front of her and smile, as if nothing in the world was wrong: grinning like an organ-grinder's monkey while other people sank to the depths. Tilly Moscombe smiled: and it was the sentient, sensitive dispositions like Miss Spink's which had to take the full measure of other people's neglect and their own suffering, because that was the way they were made and they couldn't smile at the end of the worst day of their lives because there wasn't the courage left to will it.

The tears pricked again behind Miss Spink's eyes. They welled up before she was ready for them and bubbled out of the ducts. She fumbled with the catch on her bag.

'Damn!' she said.

Why in heaven's name did the girl just stand there staring at her?

'Damn!' she repeated, struggling and not able to see properly.

She pulled so hard at the clasp that one of its halves broke and came away in her hand.

'Damnation!'

She held the broken piece in her hand, then clenched it tightly in her fist. She lifted her eyes and looked across at the girl.

Miss Spink glared at her through her tears. The tears wouldn't stop. She felt quite helpless, also angry—*invaded*.

'What are you looking at?' she shouted at her.

The girl shook her head. Some people said she wasn't so daft after all, partly it was an act, to wheedle sympathy out of you. She's not going to get mine, Miss Spink always told herself, I'm on to *you*, my lady.

Now she hadn't a notion what the girl could know or understand. It was sinister how she just stood there: able to bear the brunt of her embarrassment, also looking as if she expected some confidence from her, some admission.

'*What are you staring at?*' Miss Spink hurled at her, aiming the words like bullets.

The girl just stood and gave nothing more away. Miss Spink felt powerless, intimidated, laughed at. She snorted, and then she felt the peppery tears welling up again, stinging in the corners of her eyes.

'W—ell?'

Miss Spink croaked the word out. She fixed the girl, trying to outstare her, to hold her fast—like a rabbit unto the serpent.

'Can't you *speak*?'

Her voice broke on the third word, and hot tears rolled out of her eyes. She felt for the clasp on her bag with her fingers, wanting her handkerchief, then she realised the two halves couldn't open.

A couple of seconds was all the time it took. Miss Spink lifted the bag to shoulder height and—deliberately, calculatingly—she flung it as hard as she could in the direction of the girl.

It caught her on the shoulder. For a few seconds the girl

399

looked stunned. The bag went slithering across the floor.

Miss Spink stood shaking her head at what she'd just done, not able to believe it.

The bag burst open, spilling its contents. A lipstick, emery boards, a comb, coins rattled across the linoleum. It was the final humiliation for Miss Spink.

She sank down on to the solitary dining-chair in front of the wall mirror. She covered her face with her hands and, quite absurdly, she howled. She heard herself, and felt her sobs must be audible to the whole hotel, sending shudders echoing up through the floors above. 'How stupid!' she kept repeating to herself, trying to dam her tears. 'This is stupid! How stupid!'

Slowly she became aware that the girl was still standing behind her, in exactly the same position, with her shoulder turned away. She lifted her face out of her hands and looked for the girl in the mirror.

She turned from the wondering face and looked at her own, and couldn't recognise it as hers. Red eyes—the shiny tracks of tears running down the gutters on either side of her nose—her top teeth biting on her lower lip. She shook her head, as if to tell herself that that woman wasn't really her, not Vera Spink, she couldn't be.

She was looking straight ahead, into the glass, and she didn't see the girl tiptoeing forward. Her hand had touched her own before she realised and she jumped as if she'd made contact with a live wire.

She stared at herself in the mirror. It was only for two or three seconds. Then she realised what was happening: the girl—that girl!—was trying to offer her sympathy.

She dodged down, out of reach of the hand, and twisted herself out of the chair. She hurried over to the bag and its litter of debris on the floor. She crouched down and tossed everything into the open hold.

She only wanted to get away, as fast as she possibly could.

She stood up and reached for the door handle. She grabbed at it and clumsily pulled open the heavy door on its tight spring.

There were some people standing about in the corridor outside. The lights seemed particularly bright when they'd seemed quite the opposite earlier.

Miss Spink tucked her bag under her arm. She lowered her

head, looking down at the floor, and hurried down the corridor and into the front hall, avoiding other people's eyes.

She turned right at the desk. Someone said something, an enquiry, in a superior-sounding voice, but she carried on without stopping. She pulled up her collar. Near the front door people stood looking at an Ordnance Survey map on the wall. She skirted round them, still concentrating on the floor, on the red runner of carpet on the black-and-white tiles.

A man reached forward to open the door for her. She murmured her thanks without lifting her head. Old-fashioned chivalry, when she'd least expected it: the man presuming she was a lady, that she deserved it.

She smelt the sea and felt the chill of a breeze on her face. She'd never been so grateful for Sandmouth: ridiculously grateful for a town she had no affection for.

She'd never been so glad to be alone as she moved out of the shine of the electric lights and down the flight of stairs flanked by the low white walls. Momentarily a memory disturbed her, of what she'd allowed to happen a couple of minutes before, but she put it aside for later, to torment her then.

It was enough to be away. Down on the flat of pavement her legs started running under her; she felt like one of the crabs washed up on every night tide when the hunters prowled with their lanterns, speeding past them for the safe cover of dark, planning in their pink guts on the next tide.

★

'Well, Dilly dear, if you *must* go.'

The actress straightened the collar of the girl's blouse. She'd watched her becoming restless during the latter stages of their meal.

'Although we *don't* want to lose you.'

She'd been an ally—albeit a tacit one—to help counter the cynicism her colleague was so adept at.

'I'm so glad you were free, Dilly. And remembered to come.'

She hated the cynicism, and she also believed she deserved it.

'Do come and see me tomorrow, Dilly. I shall be rising late. And no lunch before an opening. I must do my lines in the afternoon—and my hair, of course. Come *then*, dear, will you?'

The girl nodded at the question mark in the actress's voice. Adele wondered if she was responding too readily for understanding.

'I'm staying at the 'Camelot' Guest House. It's not Claridge's, but I was told it was clean. *Do* come, Dilly.'

The actress leaned forward and planted a friendly kiss on the girl's right cheek.

'Safe home, my dear.'

She stood behind the glass in the sun lounge beside the front doors waving as the girl hurried off. She could go to the Ladies and, with instruction, she could hold a knife and fork—rather more expertly than some of the other guests in the diningroom—so she wasn't a hopeless case. Not at all.

The girl didn't turn round as she passed out of the fall of yellow light from the hotel's windows. Miss Adaire wondered what it was she would remember of the evening; if it would make any special memories for her. Everyone required those. It's why they went to theatres and sat in cinemas, and not just to see 'Odette' and Helen Keller. As Adele Adaire, in white satin and pink georgette, she already lived in people's memories—of happy times, or of happy interludes in not so happy lives—and maybe that was the true nature of her existence: living for others in hundreds and thousands of tiny fragments of experiences she would never know anything about.

*

A full circle of moon hangs over Sandmouth.

On her way to the telephone exchange Alma Stockton walks up Hill Street, past the site roped off by the diggers. What was that silly name again?—'Pythia'. Whatever had the old chap been thinking of to call her that?

The windows of houses were lit. Shadows passed behind curtains.

Passing the entrance to 'The Laurels' Mrs Stockton caught the early summer fragrances from the garden. The Prentices had had the gates removed, leaving only the pillars—a nice egalitarian gesture, if you like, and she wondered how far *those* would be taken in her lifetime. She looked back, down the driveway, but a bank of laurels and rhododendrons hid the house from view.

Mrs Stockton paused a moment, thinking of the beginning of *Rebecca*: the camera leading you down the tangled driveway to the devastated ruin of Manderley: its best days turned to restless and uneasy memories, displaced ghosts with no house to haunt.

★

The telephone rang a second time in the 'Old Rectory'. Pargiter flung down his pen on to the desk top.

His mother put through the call.

'Yes?'

An unknown voice sounded out of the earpiece.

'Speaking.'

'I'm sorry to disturb you, Mr Pargiter. I wanted to speak to you personally. Your secretary—'

'What is it?'

'My name is Lawrence. I—' The man cleared his throat. 'I currently find myself looking for a position of employment.'

'You phone Copplestone's, not me.'

'Oh, it's not that kind of job, sir.'

'What kind, then?'

'A domestic situation, sir.'

'Gardening or something?'

'Oh *no*, sir.'

'I don't think—'

'Previously, sir, I was serving in London. As a valet. What is known as a gentleman's gentleman. I was given *your* name.'

'Mine? Who by?'

There was a pause.

'I'm so sorry, sir. I had to unravel the cord. By a Mr Weston, sir.'

The name didn't mean anything to Pargiter.

'I don't know who—'

'He seemed to have heard of *you*, sir. Through someone else. A gentleman who lives in the Albany, sir.'

'Oh. The Albany?'

'I have attended a friend of his. Also in the Albany, sir.'

'I see.'

'A gentleman's gentleman, as we are called, sir, is a demanding profession. And a very discreet one, of course.'

'Yes, I'm sure.'

'We become a bachelor gentleman's right-hand man. We're presumed to "know" a lot, sir, you see. About what's what.'

' "What's what"?' Pargiter repeated.

'We always keep our masters right. About appearance. The art of presentation—self-presentation—that's very important, sir. Of course we mostly serve in the metropolis. London. As I have done, for quite a number of years now.'

'I see.'

'But perhaps I'm wasting your time, sir? I'm sure a man like yourself is already provided for in that department of life.'

Pargiter was silent and pensive for several seconds.

'No,' he said.

'Or another member of staff attends to your needs?'

'My staff?'

'I was given a description of the "Old Rectory", sir. A house like that—as well as a man in your position, sir—they require certain standards to be maintained. Of course that is the sadness of these times, that so few people understand how important tradition is. Fewer people can afford it, I dare say. If that doesn't strike you as a liberty, sir—'

Pargiter kept mum.

'You will be forming the wrong impression of me, sir. The proper virtue of a gentleman's gentleman is silence. I am being improperly garrulous.'

'What did you say your name was?'

'Lawrence, sir.'

'You could give me *some* kind of reference, I presume?'

'My last employer sadly deceased. In Antibes, where I had accompanied him. But a previous employer could supply you with any reference you might think you require, sir. I immodestly suggest you would find it perfectly in order, sir.'

'Yes. Well, I'm sure I would.'

Pargiter found pleasure in listening to the old-fashioned terminology and turns of phrase.

'Why—why don't you come and see me, Mr Lawrence?' he said, surprising himself that he should be making the request. 'At Copplestone's.'

'With pleasure, sir.'

'Where are you? London?'

'I am currently in Bournemouth, sir. As circumstances

404

would have it. I have been staying with a relative in these parts.'

'You know where we are?'

'I think everyone is acquainted with Copplestone's, sir.'

'When can you come?'

'I can present myself whenever would prove convenient to *you*, sir.'

'Day after tomorrow, then. Ring my secretary, will you?'

'I shall indeed, sir. I am very much obliged to you, Mr Pargiter.'

Pargiter put down the phone. He was conscious of other, much murkier thoughts waiting to crowd out the conversation. But it had made a welcome interlude of relief from the strifeful business of the day. 'A gentleman's gentleman': he even managed to smile at the sound of the expression, at the quality of life three words were able to evoke.

'How did it go?'

The man replaced the receiver.

'I think he might be interested, Mr Barlow.'

'Good for you.'

Good for Waring (or 'Lawrence', as he must be from now on) wasn't the point, they both of them knew. The man stood up. Barlow watched him from his big wing chair behind the desk.

'Let's presume then, for argument's sake, he takes you on. I'll attend to the reference business. You know what you've got to do?'

'Be a gentleman's gentleman, Mr Barlow, and at all times keep my ears and eyes open.'

'Discreetly.'

'Of course, Mr Barlow. It's my middle name.'

'For two incomes it'd better be.'

'Anything at all in particular, sir? That I should be on the look-out for?'

'Anything that catches your eye, or ear. About business. Or—'

'Yes, Mr Barlow?'

'Or if there's anything about any woman you think I should know.'

'Do you think there might be?'

405

'*I* don't know. That's why I'm hiring you. *And* paying you. Why's he not married, for instance. I presume he isn't, but I can't afford to presume.'

'I shall observe, sir.'

'Look in his underpants, if you have to.'

'Very well, sir.'

'And if it's boys, I want to know. But I don't think it is.'

'No, Mr Barlow.'

'Anything you get on the business I want to know as well. I've already got my contacts, but things get done in his house that don't get done at Copplestone's. So I want to know.'

'Yes, Mr Barlow.'

'I was right about the gentleman's gentleman, wasn't I?'

'Hook, line and sinker, Mr Barlow.'

'We'll catch him. If he deserves to be caught. He'll struggle, but it'll be too late then.'

'Yes, Mr Barlow.'

'A certain sort, think they're so clever, they know it all. But if you get yourself the right bait, *exactly* right, it's amazing what a big fish you find you've landed.'

*

And then there are none.

Major Fitt rubs his bleary eyes. The fillies in his dream have bolted, every one of them. Split and run. Vamoosed. Slung their hooks. Naughty, naughty. Spank, spank. Oh, you're quite naughty yourself, sir, quite a handful, has anyone ever told you that?

Less times than you may think, my dear. Men admire me more than women. I'm no threat to them of course. Two legs outrun one and a peg every time. Women try to imagine the complication of straps and trusses and corsets that make my life possible. They stare at my legs, not knowing which of them is the wrong one, the Pretender. Everyone is so careful not to mention it, so terribly careful; except the children, that is, who relish someone's misfortune with all the cruelty they're capable of. It happened before they were born and they're not interested. They're a cocky lot, and forget it was *them* we were doing it for, losing an eye here, an arm there, dropping the odd leg in Flanders. A great pity: I was rather attached to it. As it were.

The Major stared at the empty glasses. Now they're saying Dresden was a mistake. How much else has to be a mistake before you lose a War? You just don't think of things like art galleries and opera houses, they didn't think too much of ours. They had plans to bomb Oxford, all drawn up, the place photographed from the air. War's not like walking into the bar of this hotel—what the hell's its name—you don't hold the door open and step back and say 'After you, sir!'

The Major sits trying to remember the name of the hotel and can't. What the hell difference does it make anyway? What difference does anything make to anything else?—all that matters is getting through the day, and then the evening, and deadening yourself for sleep, so that you don't wake up in the middle of the night. Just reaching morning is what it comes to in the end. Getting past dawn with a white hospital light round the curtains and those bloody birds singing their heads off as if wars have nothing to do with them—it's about that, and launching yourself slowly and gingerly into another day, and surviving another little war that gets played out to no rules at all every twenty-four hours of the sun rising and going down.

★

'Tilly!'

Mrs Stockton shouted the name across Hill Street, but the girl didn't seem to hear.

'Tilly!'

She went careening uphill, as if she had a purpose in mind.

Tilly knew where was where, Mrs Stockton quite understood that. It took many months of perseverance, but in the end you established contact. If she'd asked her to go to this shop or that to collect, and explained which butcher's or bakery she meant, the girl could have managed: that was because they trusted one another. She didn't ask her to do any of these things, it would have been taking advantage of her. People thought she was quite aimless, but they were wrong. There were half a dozen houses where she was welcome, and another six or so where she was used for different purposes: as someone to be spoken to, someone to try to prise knowledge out of, someone to be pitied, someone to eat up the left-overs. She didn't gossip, Mrs Stockton was almost sure of that: at least she didn't *mean* to gossip. It was possible, though, that she might: if she was to see something that struck her as highly unusual, she *would* have been capable of telling, not out of mischief but because she couldn't accommodate the fact all by herself. Maybe that made her a danger to some people: and it was why others grilled her, to find out if Mrs So-and-So was the same person in her own kitchen that she was in someone else's sitting-room.

Mrs Stockton thought it very late for Tilly to be out on her own. She had an inbuilt clock that took her back to 'Hallam House' when it was time to return. Sometimes, though, events could excite her, and the metabolism went to pot: it had happened last year, on the day of the Pageant, when someone had taken her along to see the 'Miss Modern Personality' competition in the Clarence's garden and she'd been ambushed by the Lavezzoli girl, who'd spotted her and given her an ice-cream to eat in their café. A Punch and Judy man had set up his stall—the first time there'd been one in the town—and, after her ice-cream, the sight of Mr Punch hammering Judy with a truncheon had kept her rooted to the spot.

Maybe people didn't realise, and their kindness served to baffle her and bewilder her. That was the irony of the situation, but—as Tilly vanished from sight—Mrs Stockton was quite aware that irony is one of the inevitable and unalterable principles by which humankind conducts its business.

*

'Ruth?'

The Reverend Aldred called the length of the garden, several times.

'Ruth? Ruth, are you there?'

It hadn't ever properly occurred to the vicar that his daughter might in any way be out of the ordinary. The fact was that there was no one in Sandmouth he might have been able to compare Ruth with, no one who was in a similar situation to hers: a motherless daughter with a busy father always in the public eye, who allowed her his attention but gave her less *thought* than he imagined he did. Ruth had always been 'there': the temptation was to take her presence for granted (done quite unconsciously on the vicar's part, of course) and, because the presence was 'fixed' and unchanging, to assume a stability in her character which need not be the case.

It wasn't the case, because the vicar—although he did not know it—really had two daughters. They discussed him at great length, but he never heard or suspected a single word of their exchanges. He would have had difficulty remembering in any degree of detail the stages of Ruth's development (the Bournemouth expedition apart, perhaps): she had always just been 'Ruth', and because he saw the same expressions on her face as he had ten years ago, by no logical process of deduction he concluded that she must be content. He had always spoken to her in the same way, as a child and as a schoolgirl growing up and as an adult: he would discuss with her what was in the newspaper, discreetly (always discreetly) pass on to her any pieces of news about his parishioners he thought it was proper for her to hear, talk about this or that to make their mealtimes pass pleasantly. The result was that, more and more, Ruth would believe she was only being used as a kind of sounding-board, her father made no attempt to account for or include her reactions to anything he said. He always spoke kindly, he never raised his voice or told her off, *but it wasn't a conversation*: which was why Ruth had had to invent her own, and, doing so, she had strayed into a province of her own imagining.

'Ruth?'

No reply.

The vicar told himself, someone must have been taken ill and Ruth had gone to sit with them.

'Ruth, dear?'

Mr Aldred's mind was frequently quite inventive when he applied it to an unexplained situation, but he didn't think beyond what were fundamentally his own concerns and responsibilities. In consequence of which—even though he himself remained quite unaware of the fact—his daughter functioned for him as a satellite consciousness.

There must be a reason for her absence. Nothing untoward had happened to disturb the even tenor of their lives since the Bournemouth incident—which had been the weather's doing anyway—so Mr Aldred felt no particular cause for concern on this particular night. He habitually saw a radius of interests in his own mind—reaching to certain houses and cottages he visited on the perimeter edge of the parish, which was as far as she could have gone—and he always assumed that the possibilities must occur within that span of his own duties.

The vicar of St Andrew and St John's stopped calling for his daughter, and turned back to the house. The over-grown Victorian garden of shady yews and cypresses and Douglas firs and oversized rhododendrons and sprawling Himalayan shrubs returned to its habitual state of silence, as if it had forgotten the name 'Ruth' or had never even known of such a person.

★

And the house like a millstone, 'Hallam House', not having the courage to leave and Aunt Juliana's eyes watching from the wall, even though I turned them to look into the darkest corner, *she* could search me out, *she* knew. I can read your mind like a book, Sybil, I always could, so it's the easy option for you too, isn't that what they call it? *Shirking*, Sybil, and it begins to look to me like ingratitude, although I can't believe that of you. Time would tell, I knew, time would discover if you deserved the house, oh it's a matter of *deserving*, whatever you may think, telling yourself the house was lucky to have you. Luck doesn't come into it, even though the people on the hill think you heaven-blessed to have been born to inherit what you have, it's all right for some, see how the other half lives. If you think you're especially favoured by fortune, then you might think you're not giving anything away by washing your hands of the house, somehow you're paying back or some such nonsense, don't you believe it, Sybil. The test is accepting who you are and what and there being no disadvantages, only responsibilities to serve and the opportunities to prove your caste, and lest you forget (or falter), we watch, ruffed and wigged and crinolined, and these eyes pursue you down the years. There is no virtue in what is past and has amassed itself into the rock weight of history, but no shame either, the centuries are neutral but not indifferent. *You* live—have lived—in the consciousness of time's ebb and flow as those other people on the hill do not, and *we do not wish to be disappointed, to be let down*, there is the pride of ten generations past and others, trust in God, ahead. Your grandmother was christened Sybil, and her mother's names included it, you are the third Sybil, only that, although there might have been

410

another but somehow your courage lost its hold, and it was easier to blame *me*, was it not, for dominating you, enslaving you to inanimate ideas and principles. Not inanimate, Sybil, and now on the threshold of your second past you should understand that as never before, that here we wait for you, as we waited on the riverbank sixty years ago, beside the Cam among those Palaces of Wind (Coleridge was a great favourite of mine in my bygone day), preparing our greetings, not to lavish praise on you since you only did your duty, and rather less than your duty since no one with the true family face sits in filial attendance by your bedside, but to admit you to our number because the initiation is over now, the preparatory rite has been conducted, accomplished, and time-purified, as it were, you enter the presiding company of the spirits.

*

'Tilly dear—'

Miss Meredith Vane, sitting in the lit bay window of 'Convolvulus Cottage', had looked up and seen the girl loping up Windmill Road on her way home to 'Hallam House'. She'd opened the window and called after her.

They had tea and fruit cake in the sitting-room.

'I think I need to leave my characters to themselves for a while, Tilly. Sometimes I do, you know. I like to think they have a will of their own and I am only the transcribing hand, as it were.'

Tilly Moscombe nodded.

'Often I think I should commit my thoughts to paper. My thoughts about the Creative Process.'

Tilly muttered something about the fruit cake.

'Oh good, you like it? I'm so glad, dear. I varied my quantities this time. A little less flour. I felt it was rather heavy last time, didn't you? How nice that you were passing by, Tilly, and I caught you. You rescued me from embroiling myself in the peccadilloes of Mr Trilling. I think he's rather an unpleasant man. Rather crafty with it, you know?—foxy. I can't think what I'm doing in his company. I don't know where all his rashness comes from. That's what I mean, you see, Tilly: I am the transcribing hand. I don't believe it's possible that these characters "live" in me. I can't. I don't believe it's possible *I*

411

could have given them birth. Hence my difficulty getting my thoughts all on to paper. I can disclaim the old theories: but do I have new ones to offer in their place?'

Tilly continued to nod.

'Yes, well I'm sure you're right, dear. I *must* have, mustn't I? Help yourself to another piece of fruit cake. Here, let me—'

Miss Vane wielded the sharp knife so dexterously that Tilly recoiled. Her hostess smiled.

'Don't be silly, dear. Don't be frightened, I'm quite harmless.'

She smiled again at the girl, perhaps less surely. After their years of one another's company, Tilly confused her sometimes with her little frights and anxieties. She couldn't believe that the character she performed for the benefit of Sandmouth— Miss Meredith Vane, published novelist and woman of letters—had any cause to inspire alarm or concern in the young, however ill-blessed by fortune (ie 'fortune' in its original Latin sense, without the monetary application: although Miss Vane believed Fortune might well have a trick up her sleeve for young Miss Elizabeth Moscombe).

'There, dear! Eat as much as you like.'

Miss Vane had a hunch (only a comparatively recent inspiration, and post-dating their friendship) that with Lady de Castellet's imminent demise her young friend might chance to find herself a major beneficiary of the estate. She liked to think that Sandmouth could produce a story-line to rival any of those she read in other people's books or worked into her own.

After their second cup of tea, the french windows opened. Tilly saw first and tugged at Miss Vane's sleeve. Miss Vane turned round. For a couple of seconds her eyes narrowed, then she hazarded a cautious smile of welcome.

'Monica!'

A young woman in her early twenties, dressed quite casually by Sandmouth standards, stepped—indeed sauntered—into the room from the garden. She held out her hands to the flames in the grate.

'Well, Monica, entering through the french doors. This is just like Rattigan, isn't it?'

'Who the fuck's Rattigan?'

'Oh language, Monica dear. I have a friend with me.'

'She's *your* friend?' the woman said incredulously, pointing.

'You heard aright, my dear. We were having tea. Do sit down—'—Miss Vane stood up and went to fetch a third cup and saucer—'—and then you can tell us what has brought you to Sandmouth.'

'A bloody train did, that's what.'

'How droll, Monica!'

'*And* it was late.'

'Oh, I'm sorry. You should have said you were coming. I could have been prepared.'

'What could *you* have done about the train being late?'

'Well, nothing of course. But for my own—' Miss Vane glanced at Tilly. 'For my own peace of mind.'

'Yes, well it was really a piece of *my* mind I was wanting to give *you*. After that letter. You really are a selfish bitch!'

Miss Vane smiled.

'You sound exactly like my Miss Fitzgerald would like to sound.'

'Who the fuck's Miss Fitzgerald?'

'Now, Monica dear, I must remind you we have company.'

'I'm quite aware of that,' the woman said, dropping into an armchair.

'Miss Fitzgerald appears in my new book. My novel. It will be called 'Good Women'.'

'Oh, will it?'

'Indeed.'

'Bloody stupid title. "Good Women" bollocks.'

'You're becoming such a caricature, Monica.'

'Yes, aren't we all, dearie?'

'And why don't you like my title, might I enquire?'

'Suppose *you* know all about "good women", do you?'

'I don't suppose Mr Shakespeare knew about Egypt. Or had met witches. Or had travelled to Denmark. Or had come across a black man even.'

'Let's leave *him* out of it, I'm talking about *you*.'

' "Good Women" arrests the attention.'

'What's it about? Tarts?'

'About all women. And their aspiration to "find their place". Within the morality of their age—'

'Oh my Gawd, give over—'

413

'I thought you'd be interested. If I told you.'

Miss Vane leaned across and, with her little finger delicately crooked, removed a sooty smudge from her unannounced visitor's chin. The woman grimaced.

'I knew you'd get your paws on me soon enough.'

Miss Vane lightly sighed.

'I was rubbing away a mark, Monica dear. From your train journey. *That* part's probably true, anyway.'

'Of course it is.'

'What about the rest of it?'

'What d'you mean?'

'What's your story this time?'

'That's a nice welcome.'

'I'm trying to make it a nice welcome,' said Miss Vane. 'Just as I tried to last time, and the time before, and the time before. So that it'll seem like Woolacombe again.'

'That was bloody years ago.'

'What of that?'

'I was younger then.'

'Young-*er*.'

'I was a minor. Aren't they called?'

'You're *still* young, Monica,' Miss Vane said, as if she hadn't heard.

'I haven't lost my looks, then?'

'I didn't say that. In fact I'd say you'd gained in the looks department. But I dare say you have the sort of appearance that will look rather raddled by forty.'

'Well, forty's a long way behind *you*.'

'I've never pretended to you otherwise. I think I've always been quite honest with you, Monica. Have some more tea?'

'I fancy something stronger.'

'Well, you know where it is. I've never hidden anything from you. Either with a key or with untruths. You've always had the run of this place—'

While the woman was out of the room Miss Vane shifted in her chair as she smiled and considered Tilly.

'Aren't you awfully tired, dear?'

Tilly shook her head.

'I'm sure that you must be.'

The girl shook her head again and mumbled a word like 'No'.

'But you've had such a long day. I need my snoozes to get *me* through the day!'

Miss Vane chuckled. Then she looked up as the door creaked open.

'I was just saying to Tilly—'

' "Tilly" or "Titty"?'

' "Tilly".'

'Hello, Tilly.' The woman slumped down on the sofa. 'Pleased to meet you. I see you get "dear", how I do. Have you earned it the same way? Friendly, isn't she, our Miss Vane?'

There was silence in the room.

'Can't you speak or something?' the woman asked.

'Tilly, like me, inhabits her own world, her realm of fancy.'

'That's an act,' the woman said. 'With *you* it is.'

'Not altogether. Not living like this.' Miss Vane muted her voice. 'It can be very lonely, let me tell you.'

'You don't need to tell *me* that.'

'What do you mean? *You*'ve lots of friends, I'm sure you have.'

'Oh, it's amazing how often you get the cold shoulder. Nice to look at, nice to touch—'

Miss Vane sighed sympathetically.

'Anyway,' the woman said, 'you've brought it on yourself.'

'What do you mean? "I've brought it on myself"?'

' "I have to do my writing this afternoon," you used to say. That means "scarper, you!" Writing your bloody books. For your farty friends.'

'You only give yourself away, Monica. It's very sad—'

'It's *true*!'

'Possibly.'

'Fuck "possibly".'

'It's true. Yes, I see now that it *is* true. But that is my work. It's difficult—'

'I don't see why.'

'You used to turn on the wireless, you played my records.'

'Bloody hell, pardon—'

'I *wanted* you to. You were free to do whatever you wanted to. I told you that, Monica.'

'Well, then?'

'But not at all hours. And so loudly.'

415

'And because *I* was up and *you'd* gone to bed?'

Miss Vane glanced across at Tilly Moscombe.

'If I were you, Tilly dear, I would be getting home now. Don't you think?'

Miss Vane stood up and gently took hold of the girl's elbows. Tilly rose from her chair.

'I'm so worried that we're tiring you. Haven't you had an awfully long day?'

She walked with the girl to the french windows. Miss Vane noticed Monica's reflection in the glass as she stretched herself full out on the sofa. She leaned forward and gave Tilly a parting peck on the cheek. 'Safe home, now,' she said and lightly tapped her bottom.

She turned round as Monica spoke.

'You pick your friends carefully, Merry, don't you?'

'She's a sweet girl.'

'We're all sweet girls.'

'Have you been drinking, Monica?'

'What if I *have* been?'

'Nothing. You're your own mistress, obviously.'

'I found a pub, yes. I needed something. After that bloody train journey.'

'I thought you sounded a little—excitable.'

'I find you entertaining here: of course I should be.'

Miss Vane slowly walked across to the sofa. She perched bird-like on the arm. She picked up some strands of the woman's long brown hair and with the appearance of absent-mindedness threaded it between her fingers.

'I *do* like everyone to be friends,' she said. 'Although you don't believe me, I do.'

'Yes, well there's friends and friends, isn't there?'

'Where on earth have you been?'

'So, what's the interest?'

'I *am* interested. Why shouldn't I be?'

'I don't like people prying.'

'There you are, then. You say I haven't made you welcome. But now you tell me you don't like me asking you questions about yourself. I'm "prying". What am I supposed to do, Monica?'

Miss Vane sighed. 'It always seems to me, Monica—every

416

time we meet—you're ashamed in some way. *You're* the one who can't make the adjustments. It has nothing to do with me, my age. You used to like to make me think it was. I'm still in my fifties. And you can't tell me I'm—I'm—predatory. I'm not that. I always said, you were free to come and go—'

'You're a right con, aren't you? "Miss Meredith Bloody Vane".'

'I don't know what you're talking about, Monica dear.'

'Yes, I'm *sure* you fucking don't know what I'm talking about.'

'Do you learn to say these things from your American friend, Monica?'

'Don't you like it?'

'Oh . . . I can take it. It may surprise you to hear.'

'You don't really surprise me, Merry, ever.'

'That ridiculous name! American too, I expect. No, Monica. My character divides into a hundred selves. For my books, you see.'

'What's it called again, this one?'

' "Good Women".'

'A sexy read, is it?'

'My novel isn't wholly preoccupied with the animal functions, believe it or not.'

'It should be. Everyone thinks about it. And if they don't it's submerged. Repressed. That doesn't mean *they*'re not thinking about it too. "Goodness" is just frustrated sex.'

'A simplistic notion, I fear, Monica. And really rather flippant.'

'So what?'

'*You* think about it a great deal, of course?'

'You've got to if you're not made "normal". What's called "normal". Every time you see a woman, you're wondering. Is she or isn't she? If she's young, what's her cunt like—'

Miss Vane let go the hair.

'You try to humiliate me, Monica,' she said, speaking slowly. '*Humiliate* me. Why do you do it?'

'Jesus Christ!'

'Why, Monica?'

'Why do I humiliate you? Because you *like* it! For fuck's sake!'

417

'What do you—'

'What do I mean? Look at you, look at me. Look at this place. It—it amuses you, I bet—gives you *pleasure*—'

'What? What does?'

'Frigging me.'

'As *she* calls it, no doubt.'

'Not just that. You're ashamed too, more than I am. It *has* to be me, though, doesn't it? It has to be *me*, in this house, on this couch. It's making it not so bad in some ways, coming down to my level?'

'*Your* level?'

'*Social* level, dearie. And I bet it disgusts you to have to, but you like that as well. It's like putting it in a different box of your life, not like the one you're usually in. You wouldn't do this with *real* friends, would you? I bet it's always with younger bints, so *that'll* make it seem like a different box too.'

'You don't know—'

'—what I'm talking about? Yes, I do. What else does "Monica" have to think about anyway? I don't know, there's something in you likes to be unhappy about it. You want it so you don't know when someone's going to walk in these doors and when they're just going to walk out again and not tell you. You'd like someone shitting on you. So long as it wasn't in your living-room—your *sitting*-room.'

Miss Vane knelt down on the Persian rug. She was shaking her head.

'You're wasted, Monica.'

'Forget it.'

'Where *did* you learn it all? From your American friend?'

'She goes to a psychiatrist. She thinks it'll help her to—how does she put it?—it'll help her "adjust", "fit in". All she wants fitted in is this—' Monica held up her hand. 'Up to my wrist, if I can.'

'There *is* a difference between us, Monica. I can't talk like you. See it: visually, I mean.'

'Poor you, then.'

'I'm not pitying myself, Monica. I don't do that.'

'Poor Saint Joan. Think she was one?'

'I've no idea.'

'I just never understand you. I think I do. Then I realise I don't.'

418

'One of my characters—Ainsley Evans—he said something very like that.'

'Have you used *me* yet?'

'Maybe you're in a lot of my characters.'

'Don't you know?'

'I don't know *you*. I couldn't work you out any better on paper.'

'How would you describe me? Cheap and nasty?'

'You don't like yourself much, do you? Or is it—what's the word—a "front"?'

'I'm not so keen on myself, no. Who is?'

'I'm so old, of course—ancient—it doesn't matter. Does it? I don't hate myself, though. Not "hate". I once almost did. I wish—Well, never mind—'

'Everything's wishing.'

It was the cue for Miss Vane to start unbuttoning her guest's cardigan, then her blouse. She slipped her hand into the warm, snug cleavage. Two of her fingers found a nipple and squeezed the teat. Monica writhed and moaned contentedly. Miss Vane's hand weighed the breast and massaged it lightly.

'I always think of Mademoiselle Vinteuil and her friend. At Montjouvain.'

'Who the hell are they?'

'They're French.'

'Where did you meet them?'

'They're in Proust.'

'Where's that?'

'It's a book. Lots of books. They defiled a photograph of Mademoiselle Vinteuil's father. Abused it. But we never discover how.'

'Can't you guess?'

'Oh, there are numerous possibilities.'

'Yes, well the woman who wrote that—'

'A man—'

'Jesus! Well, he can keep his nose out of this one too! Bloody nosey-parker. Here, take my stockings off.'

'Everyone else will be a nosey-parker too if I don't pull the curtains tight shut.'

Miss Vane withdrew her hand and struggled to her feet. Monica smiled up at her.

'Make it slow.'

419

'Don't talk about it please, Monica.'

'That makes it worse, does it?'

'I'm old-fashioned, it's unnecessary.'

'I thought this wasn't old-fashioned, because no one used to believe it happened.'

'I expect it's as old as time, my dear, and has quite a distinguished history if the truth be "out". Probably it kept Cleopatra amused. Good Queen Bess, almost certainly.'

'And millions of women no one's ever heard of.'

'Yes, I should think so. Millions of them. All dust now.'

man lady, trousers, friends Tilly, you me, Tilly tell, fire, friends Tilly, you me, secrets, Mon-ica, not the lady smile, eyes, photo-graph, lady smile, dress, man lady, trousers, friends, you me, friends Tilly, Mon-ica, eyes, not the lady smile, secrets, fire, train, surprise, not the lady smile, friends, you me, friends Tilly, but, late, home, tired, Tilly, now, lady smile, garden, secrets Tilly, home, run, safe, now, garden, window light, Mon-ica, man lady, trousers, hair, car-digan, man, lady smile, hand, finger, buttons, lady thing, pri-vate thing Tilly, Mrs Macey, pri-vate thing Tilly, have to hear, yes, yes, listen, Mrs Macey, lady thing, Mon-ica, man lady, the lady thing, Mon-ica, eyes, eyes open, Jesus, lady thing, hand, man lady, eyes, eyes open, not the lady smile, late, home, run, Tilly, now, run . . .

Miss Vane walked across to the french windows. The curtains had been half-drawn.

'It's her!' Monica cried out behind her.

The older woman looked round.

'It's her, I tell you, what's-her-name.'

'Where?'

'She was looking—'

'Who? Tilly?'

'She had her face against the glass.'

Miss Vane shook her head. 'Oh dear.' She peered out into the garden.

'I can't see her.'

'*I* saw her, she was there.'

'Yes, I dare say she was. Oh dear, how unfortunate.'

'Bloody little sneak.'

'I don't expect she—'

'Fucking little spy.'

'She's—she's not like us.' Miss Vane pulled the curtains fully across the doors. She turned round, with a more concerned expression on her face than the tone of her voice suggested.

'Really not like us at all, my dear.'

'Probably saw my tit,' Monica said.

'I—I don't think so.'

'Cheap thrill for her. I hate that.'

'Hate it? Which do you hate, Monica dear?' Miss Vane asked, balancing on the arm of the sofa. 'Giving her the "thrill"—as you put it—or the "cheapness" of it?'

'Are you or aren't you?'

'What?'

'Going to take my bloody stocking off?'

Miss Vane smiled; the strain eased a little. She preferred to think of these encounters as fitting into a Proustian framework: into the jigsaw of profundities—time, memory, the moment of sensual pleasure and its afterglow.

'Mademoiselle Vinteuil would never have said that,' she told her young friend.

'Well, she probably wasn't desperate for it.'

'And *you* are?'

'Come on, get on with it, will you? I'm not staying.'

'No?'

'Someone's waiting for me.'

It wasn't the most auspicious or most tender or most encouraging of entrées into love-making. But time and experience had equipped these two women to make do with frequently very unpromising preliminaries.

'The last train is at quarter-past-ten, Monica dear,' Miss Vane said. 'We should be finished and done by half-past-nine.'

'I'll be famished by then.'

'I shan't send you away hungry. Whatever you may think of me. There's a veal-and-ham pie. From Sorley's. You can take it with you. Pretend you've stolen it and make me feel properly humiliated.'

'Wouldn't you like that? Wouldn't you *just* like me to do that?'

'In a fond and hateful way, my dear, yes—yes, I rather think I would.'

★

Miss Austen, sitting in the front lounge of the Clarence Hotel, devoured the last pages of her Agatha Christie.

Miss Marple had beaten her again. The sleuth had realised, in the very nick of time, that none other than the refined, mild-mannered and well-spoken housekeeper was the murderer terrorising the quiet village: when her hands were sheathed inside a pair of gloves no one with a claim on her employer's estate could depend on his/her life. *Come with me, my dear, let's go for a walk. We'll take the path over the fields, shall we? Now, would you like to walk on ahead, my dear, by yourself? I shan't be a minute, I just want to—slip on—this pair—of gloves. I shall follow, I shall be—right—RIGHT behind you.*

It always turned out to be the character you least suspected, whom you thought you had accounted for. Maybe in another book, still to be written, the murderer would be exposed as none other than dear, blue-eyed, sweetly beaming Miss Marple herself?

★

Mrs Prentice stepped with scissor strides between the gateposts of 'The Laurels' and out on to Hill Street.

She looked to right and left, then she continued walking, uphill.

Weren't criminals always restless, drawn back in spite of themselves to the scene of the crime?

She wondered what the 'Old Rectory' looked like inside.

She pulled her coat closer about her. Cedric had bought her it—Canadian mink—in Fortnum's, as her wedding present. In the shop she'd looked good in it. She hadn't minded that he should be looking so possessively at her. After all, it was *his* money . . .

Her sister didn't scoff at the trappings. If anything, she guessed, being a farmer's wife had increased Rosalind's respect for them. Possibly she envied her having Cedric . . .

Having Cedric . . .

When she reached the top of Hill Street she couldn't decide

which direction to take. She didn't feel ready to go back yet.

Her legs carried her in the opposite direction from 'The Laurels', on to the road where the telephone exchange was, which became a lane, which became a bridlepath, ribboning round the edge of the golf course.

★

'What are you doing, darling?'

'Writing.'

'Yes, Guy, I can see that. I'm duly amazed. But writing *what*?'

'Oh—'

'If it's letters for auditions, remember you're down for the rest of the run.'

'Yes, well, that won't be for long. By the way, where's Dilly?'

'She's gone home. Do you think she enjoyed herself, Guy?'

'Do you think it matters?'

'I wanted her to have a good time.'

'Jesus, Adele, you'd think you were going for a gong. You're like one of those old bats who put on their ostrich hats and white gloves and go off to every bleeding charity "do" they get wind of. "Dame" wouldn't suit you.'

' "Dame Adele Adaire". It has a certain ring to it—'

'Has it hell!'

'You haven't told me, what are you writing?'

'If you *must* know—it's a diary.'

'Dear God!'

'Everything's going down. For posterity.'

'Oh, so I presume you're not relying on your acting abilities—if such they are—carrying you through the rest of your life?'

'Quite the contrary, my love. This will be sitting in a drawer when I become very famous—as an *actor*—and when the first publisher comes to my Albany apartments I shall be ready to whip it out and let him have a dekko.'

'And the diary too?'

'*And* the diary.'

'I'm sure it'll be fascinating.'

'You'll merit a footnote or two, Adele, I promise you.'

'Oh, I never trust men's promises.'

'Get many, do you?'

'Of course I'll have to make an exception for you. You *are* an exception anyway, aren't you, Guy? Not *quite* matinée idol material, are we?'

'No?'

'I expect you've got more skeletons than you can cram into your cupboard.'

'It's a tight fit, certainly. Not that I ever objected to that—'

'You're very sordid, Guy. Now tell me, what's this precious autobiography going to be called when it's been published?'

'I don't know. What about *Out Of My Depth*?'

'Or—or *In The Shallow End*?'

'Possibly.'

'Or what about—let's see—yes. *Call me Madam*?'

She leaned forward and kissed him on the brow.

'Spoken like the true old bitch and slag you are, Adele.'

'Darling!'

She spoke quietly. 'Only *do* keep your voice down, dear heart. *Entre nous* I suspect the natives are getting *just* a trifle restless.'

★

'Are you sure?'

Mr Arkwright took off his spectacles.

'Quite sure.'

'Damned stupid thing to do.'

'Maybe he thinks he's being discreet about it.'

'Why Prentice's wife?'

'She's a smart-looking woman.'

Mr Arkwright looked across his desk at the man.

'How long have you been at Copplestone's?' he asked.

'Since Mr Copplestone's time. He had his eye on me, I think.'

'And our Mr Pargiter hasn't?'

'I'm sorry?'

'You don't get on?'

'We get on—well, all right.'

'All right? But no better than that?'

'Well, not really, Mr Arkwright. No.'

'I haven't any vacancies here.'

'I know that, sir.'

'I dare say you do. Made it your business to find out, have you?'

'It's a small world, especially in this line. Word gets around.'

'Doubtless you'll want some recompense? Just as *I* shall need proper proof.'

'Of course, Mr Arkwright.'

'Of course what?'

'Of course to both, sir.'

'I don't foresee any vacancies either. Whatever your— whatever your qualifications for a post are. Have to run a tight ship. These days our young friend seems to be sewing most things up roundabout.'

The man nodded.

'What Barlow doesn't get, that is,' Mr Arkwright said. 'But Norman Pargiter's giving him a close run for his money.'

'Yes indeed, Mr Arkwright. Doing *very* well for himself, he is. By hook or by crook.'

Mr Arkwright coughed into his hand.

'Yes, well, it's not a business for saints,' he said. 'But there *are* limits, of course.'

'Yes, sir.'

'Why've you come to *me* exactly?'

'I'm sorry, Mr Arkwright—?'

'I don't believe it's for a job—which doesn't exist anyway. And you'll get money from *him*.'

'I thought—I thought you might be interested in—*using* the information, sir.'

'And if *I* "use" it, it clears *you*, I suppose. Think you'll be out on your ear soon, is that it?'

'I'm—naturally—wary for my future at Copplestone's.'

'Naturally,' Mr Arkwright repeated, with a suggestion of impatience.

'I've taken up your time, sir.'

'I shall have to think about it, Mr Davis.'

'Yes, sir. Of course you will.'

'But I'm sure—I'm sure we can think of something. Come to some agreement. Between us.'

'I'm sure so, Mr Arkwright.'

'No one saw you coming?'

'No, Mr Arkwright.' The man leaned forward in his chair. 'Just one thing, Mr Arkwright—'

'Yes. What is it?'

'I'm—I *am* correct in thinking Mr Pargiter's behaviour—in the past, I mean—'

'No, I haven't forgiven him. Which is what you imagine anyway, isn't it?'

'I didn't think you—'

'I don't like seeing him wooing my customers, no. I'm beginning to be more than a little tired of it, Mr Davis. As you've guessed.'

'As I've guessed.'

'I think it's about time the young man learned a lesson. Relation of mine or not. I don't think I can let *that* stand in my way.'

The interview ended with a handshake. Mr Arkwright stared at the back of the door after the man had gone and he'd heard the front door being closed behind him.

He lifted the telephone receiver and dialled the number of one of his trusted circle.

'Sorry it's so late, Bill. I've had someone in to see me. What do you know about a bloke called Davis? Works at Copplestone's.'

He listened carefully to the reply.

'Can you also enquire around? I want to be quite sure.'

The voice at the other end responded.

'Oh, I don't *trust* him, Bill. He'd sell his grandmother. It's complicated. I'll explain tomorrow. I'll sleep on it. Meanwhile, if you can ask around—keep it very hush-hush—and pick up what you can. Sorry it's late. But it could lead to—well, I don't know what. Good-night, Bill.'

★

Monica Mitchell left 'Convolvulus Cottage' at quarter-to-ten. Miss Meredith Vane waved her off from the french windows. She stood listening till she heard the click of the latch on the gate: the gate in the high privet hedge that had featured in one of her earlier, sunnier books, *Sweet Sings the Lark*.

They'd sat at the kitchen table discussing what Tilly Moscombe could have seen. Miss Vane wished they hadn't ruined the evening thinking about that. But Monica never wanted to do any of the things *she* wanted her to.

For years Miss Vane had hoped she might find herself a proper partner. She'd experimented, but no one had proved suitable. She'd given up imagining that it might be possible. She was no Gertrude Stein: Monica was certainly no devoted Miss Toklas. Virginia and Vita were the patron saints of sensitive sapphic souls, and in a league of their own.

Two women alike in background could always pass as 'companions' and never mind the tongue-wagging, the jabber-jabber. One sighting of Monica leaving the house and she really had no defence. In Sandmouth it paid to have your defences.

Miss Vane appreciated that Tilly was a far from lost cause: they managed to have conversations, of a kind. She also knew the 'trigger' words and her hostess often picked up an interesting tit-bit or two about certain of her fellow townsfolk. She realised that what Tilly had seen tonight must have fed images into her wayward mind, which maybe she would try to find words for. Miss Vane had as much affection for the girl as she did for anyone in Sandmouth, and custom had strengthened it. But what if someone else were now to feed different 'trigger' words: 'Miss Meredith Vane', 'Convolvulus Cottage'?

The authoress wondered how her characters would have coped with the situation. Angrily, or stealthily, or uncaringly—or even violently?

Monica had set off in a frightening mood.

'If that fucking little creep comes round here again, tell her to sling her fucking hook. And quick. If she pretends she doesn't know what you're talking about, just shout it at her. "Up yours, you little twat!" '

For some reason Monica had intensely resented her breast being seen as it was kneaded. (What was it Proust's narrator saw, glancing through the windows of the spine-chilling Chateau Vinteuil on its crag?) Monica had asked her if the girl had a bosom of her own, and she'd replied, most certainly, an unpretentious one but undeniably a bosom.

'She probably goes around sneaking into gardens and peering through windows at night. Tit-hunting.'

'I'm sure she doesn't.'

'How do you know? Maybe she wants it?'

427

Wants *what*? Miss Vane hadn't asked.

Tilly wouldn't come back again, which was a pity. Miss Vane was in the habit of reading untested passages of dialogue aloud to Tilly, and although the girl couldn't respond in words she still acquired from her face a 'feeling' about what worked and what didn't. She could try out her most inept dialogue on Tilly and it didn't really matter.

It must be more than an inconvenience, however, not being able to rely on Tilly's continuing presence. Miss Vane earnestly believed she was marked down for posterity, for a life beyond her own on earth, and Sandmouth was the clue to it: in the annals of the town's collective memory would be recorded, Proustian-fashion, the fortunate years when Meredith Vane was one of them. Pride was less responsible for this vision than that quality of detachment which Miss Vane felt all true artists possessed: the ability to view oneself coldly and (she liked the pun) geometrically, either squarely or in the round. She realised now that, after Monica's unexpected visit and the incident in the garden, there was the danger that her reputation ahead of her—on the other side of death and oblivion—might very well suffer.

Curiously she trusted Monica in the final count, for all the unhappiness and jealousy she knew she was likely to cause her in the interim. It was her worries concerning her own poor, dear Tilly that she wished she might dispose of, however that should best be done.

★

Lady de Castellet rang the bell beside her bed. Promptly footsteps sounded along the corridor. One of the double doors opened and Mrs Macey stepped cautiously into the room.

The fire's flames and the weak gaslight from the wall brackets threw confusing, complicated shadows. Mrs Macey peered ahead of her.

'You rang for something, Lady de Castellet?'

'Mrs Macey . . .' A tired voice carried from the huddle of sheets and blankets and heaped pillows on the bed. 'Elizabeth, has she come home?'

'Not yet, Lady de Castellet.'

'Isn't it very late?'

'It's almost ten o'clock, Lady de Castellet.'

'It's *too* late. Why do you think she's not here?'

'Perhaps—perhaps she's in someone's house.'

'She hasn't come back to eat.'

'Maybe she's *been* fed.'

'Would they not have tried to ring us?'

'Perhaps—'

'Yes, Mrs Macey?'

'Perhaps they don't want to ring and disturb? Knowing—'

'I've given her too much freedom, Mrs Macey. No one has so much freedom. No one.'

'What else could—?'

'If she didn't worry me, Mrs Macey—and if I didn't blame myself—probably I should have passed over long ago.'

Mrs Macey looked more apprehensively in the direction of the voice.

'And everyone would know by now. The worst or the best.'

Mrs Macey muttered some soothing sounds by way of reply.

'As it is . . . I seem to thrive on the uncertainty, do I not? If "thrive" is . . .'

'Soon. Tilly will be back home soon.'

'A poet's touch, Mrs Macey.'

'I'm sorry, Lady de Castellet?'

'Returning home.'

Mrs Macey transmitted the sound of a respectful smile. She couldn't make sense of what was being said.

'The longer this goes on, the more uncertain everyone becomes. That poor Mr Aldred. I think *he* thinks I'm stuck, I'm half-way across. I'm not here, and I'm not there. I embarrass him.'

'Oh no.'

'Oh yes, Mrs Macey. Somehow it should be as clean as a whistle. Quite sudden. I should be raptured away. It's like getting the slow train by mistake.'

Mrs Macey thought—she might have sworn to it—that at that point her Ladyship let out a little laugh. But the situation was too desperate for that.

'Don't fret, Lady de Castellet.'

'It's—it's exactly what I must do, Mrs Macey. Oh you really *don't* understand, do you?'

'I'm not sure I do.'

'Except what I require. And Lizzy too. I'm grateful to you.'

'Please, please don't be—And don't go upsetting yourself.'

'Oh my eyes are quite clear, Mrs Macey. Quite clear and dry. Don't fear on that account. There will be no scenes, as they might be called.'

'No,' said Mrs Macey. 'No.'

'Only I wish the child would come home. She *is* a child, isn't she, Mrs Macey?'

'Oh yes. She *is*, Lady de Castellet.'

'I want to know she's safe. Then I can become *un*stuck . . .'

Mrs Macey bit her lip.

'Please—'

'Yes, Mrs Macey?'

'Is there anything else, Lady de Castellet? To eat or drink?'

'Oh no.'

'I shall make enquiries, Lady de Castellet.'

'Please do, Mrs Macey.'

'Don't go fretting yourself, Lady de Castellet. It's bad for—'

'Dear Mrs Macey, you really don't understand but you *are*—you're perfectly obliging.'

The voice sounded as if it had exhausted itself.

'Lady de Castellet,' Mrs Macey said and started to withdraw.

The high-ceilinged bedroom was like a cave beneath the sea, a mise-en-scène of pale, shifting light and solemn shadows and reflections becalmed in mirrors. The white moon shone through the thin curtains like a curious eye.

Mrs Macey wondered if the bright moon was also to blame for keeping the old lady awake and agitated. The newspapers made the strangest claims for the moon. A doctor said our bodies are half water and the moon pulls on them in a way science fails to comprehend.

There's so much we don't know, Mrs Macey had remarked to her husband, we none of us know: even with bombs exploding in the ocean, life beyond our own control is still a mystery to us. Mrs Macey would repeat to her husband that good sense was a virtue and no harm could come to you just for keeping an open mind.

★

430

Major Fitt woke with some damned fool shaking his arm.

'Are you all right, sir?'

He looked up bleerily, at the stinging light on the ceiling.

'Sir? Are you all right?'

Damned silly question. He'd damned well tell him so if he could get the words out. *If . . .*

'I thought you looked a bit—'

I'd tell you how I feel if I could bloody well find the words. They're here somewhere, muddling around. Like catching an apple in a bran barrel. Used to play that game when it was a bit quietish and everyone was lying low, getting up their strength. Playing it in twos, you and another fellow stuck your hands down deep into a barrel. You groped about in the bran. Sometimes you found you'd grasped the other chap's fingers! Sometimes they put in things to fox you and get a belly laugh: a woman's suspender, a baby's teat, once someone got hold of a rubber John Thomas and, between his fingers, it felt just like the real thing. Great days!

'Please excuse me, sir. I didn't mean to disturb you. Only—'

Who had he been talking to? There'd been someone here. Some plain-jane female, they'd got talking, how on earth . . .?

The centre light in the ceiling was making his eyes ache. Switch the damned bloody thing off!

'The lady you—'

Where had she gone? He looked over the man's shoulders. He saw some faces but couldn't focus on them.

He had a woolly memory of something happening earlier in the day. People cheering, lads, women in hats, a white marquee. Something to do with the peg. Some silly woman's face turning as white as the marquee. Saying she was going to be sick . . .

More memories for the memory box. Put them away for another day.

'Would you like a breather, sir?'

Suddenly he seemed to be up on the perpendicular, floating above the floor, the chair. Strong arms supported him, under his armpits.

'You'll feel better, sir.'

He was sailing through the room, past the other faces. A doorway loomed ahead and more bright lights.

'—just a little pasty.'

Over a strip of red carpet. The front door was open. Into a glassy vestibule.

Now he was sitting in a basket chair, in a draught. He opened his mouth and was able to taste—yes—the salt sea on the back of his tongue.

Street lights twinkled outside. A funny-looking girl toddled past, wearing just a cardigan on top of her dress. His vision started to clear, mysteriously; the wooziness started to lift.

He remembered more of the day. His peg coming off, the woman shrieking at him. The speech—the speech he always gave—still in his pocket. The other woman he'd met, with so little to say for herself, and a lost look. The afternoon in a tea-shop.

When the others had gone—abandoned him—and the vestibule felt too lonely to endure (a fish tank, an aquarium) he got gingerly to his feet. Tried to. Tried again. Did it on the third attempt.

It was turning dark outside. She was nowhere in sight. Given him the slip. If he caught her, he'd playfully trip her up, tell her he was going to give her a damned good hiding, a bloody good spanking she would always remember.

He sank back into the chair. He'd tried with women her age, he'd tried but it never worked. Spanks only made their delicious echoes off young, fresh, firm, taut skin. Buttocks sagged and sank with time and growing older, just like people's spirits.

His own spirit didn't rise in him when he thought of the years' damage, the weathering. The sap *did* rise when he saw a haunch of young, unblemished flesh. Look at it like that and spanking was only celebrating the flesh's resistance, the giggles escaped like little bright bubbles . . .

He pulled at the straps under his trousers and hitched up his peg. He hadn't seen many girls of spankable age in the town. Fillies, he always called them. Ten and sixteen were his choice limits, not that it paid to enquire, they only told you little white ones anyway. Gave you a reason to spank them anyway, if you suspected.

'Spank . . .' He relished the sound of the word, the reverberations. Change the vowel, of course, add an '-up', and you got something very different, what chaps used to brag about in the mess.

The Major frowned. At the back of his mind he really felt he was rather a moral man. It distressed him that young girls had to grow up to learn about things like that. The things chaps talked about—if it was true or not—depressed him sometimes, turned his stomach.

In his own way he was trying to warn the girls—bless them—trying to tell them it was naughty to flaunt themselves, also to let them see that not all men were like those other ones, talking about their John Thomases all the time; he wasn't *hurting* them, the girls, he wasn't really hurting their *feelings* anyway, sometimes you have to be a little hurtful—in the physical sense—you have to cause a very little pain, but just to let your kindness show.

★

This evening, more than any of the others since his marriage, Howard Trevis is restless. He can't settle to his usual routine, lighting his pipe and submerging himself beneath the lines of newsprint, while Maureen sits close to the wireless and knits the arms or shoulders of a jumper for him or turns one of his socks or pens a tactful note to one of their elder relations. His crotch itches, and he can hear the blood pumping behind his ears; his breath feels crammed into his chest. Maureen has already asked him, would he like her to fetch the indigestion salts, and he has been making a particular effort to give the impression that all is quite normal.

He can't get the day out of his head. For once it doesn't have to do with the Bendall boy, who is never far from his thoughts when his mind customarily relaxes a little after supper, before the long preparations for bed begin with their military-like precision. Tonight it's the actor he remembers—every word and gesture they exchanged through the grille—and, several times, he finds himself stranded in mid-sentence on the page of the newspaper, not able to follow the paragraph's drift.

'What's on at the Alhambra?' he asked. 'Do you know?'

He lowered the newspaper. Maureen smiled across at him.

'A play. Terence Rattigan. Would you like to go?'

'Not really.'

'Oh.'

'I just wondered what it was.'

' "Harlequinade".'

433

He forced a smile. 'You're very knowledgeable.'

'I was standing at the counter in Sorley's. There was a notice up. I wasn't really—'

'When does it start?'

' "When does it start?" Eight o'clock, I—'

'No, which day?'

'Oh.' The wooden toadstool was drawn out of the sock's heel. 'Tomorrow, I think.'

Trevis held up the newspaper again.

'How long for?' he asked, meaning to sound quite casual about it.

'Three nights. Till Saturday. There isn't a matinée.'

The conversation stopped at that point. Trevis found himself smiling: a smile he couldn't get to leave his lips.

He'd stood up before he had the words sorted out in his head to speak.

'Is that the time?' his wife asked him, seeming baffled, looking up from her sewing in the pool of lamplight to the clock on the high mantelpiece.

'I've got a bit of a headache.'

'Oh, I'm sorry, Howard. I thought there was something—'

'It's nothing.'

'Let me—'

'No. Just some air.' He strode across the room. 'That's all I need.'

'Maybe the light doesn't help.'

'The light?'

'If we put on the centre-light—'

He hated the room with the centre-light lit. It only ever went on by mistake. When it did he felt all the objects in the room suddenly showed themselves as the enemies they'd been all along. They seemed to fill every shelf and corner; the same memory occurred to him each time, seeing a cartoon film with a kitchen shelf of pots and pans and scrubbing-brushes come alive and dancing to an orchestra, and it wasn't a children's joke any more. In the unsparing glare of the centre-light domesticity crowded every inch of the room; he hadn't understood they had surrounded themselves with so much, and he felt threatened by their *there*-ness; they deprived them of valuable air to breathe.

434

'Maybe we should start putting it on.'

'What's that?'

'The centre-light.'

'No, no.'

'It might be better for our eyes.'

'*I* can see all right.'

'I think it's a nice night outside, Howard.'

'I'll just look out. Might go for a walk.'

Upstairs he took his jacket out of the wardrobe. He hadn't changed out of his trousers after work. A suit was too formal for a stroll, but he looked best in a suit. He combed his hair with the brush. He allowed himself a starched, approving smile in the dressing-table mirror.

'Good-bye,' he called in through the living-room door.

He saw Maureen's head was bent over the wireless speaker. She didn't hear him and didn't look up.

He pulled the oak front door shut behind him. He could always breathe more easily outside. Now the clock and Maureen's glass animals and the bowl of perfumed, sick-room hyacinths with their roots growing obscenely in water and the inherited standard lamp with the fringed shade which was their saviour and Aunt Madge's wedding present chair with the spindly legs they weren't able to sit on, they could all waltz and quick-step together to their hearts' content and Maureen could listen to Ray Ellington or Geraldo or Ted Heath and they would all of them have their escape and freedom for the night.

★

Some of her lines from the play floated into the actress's head as she picked her way along unfamiliar pavements in the speeding darkness.

'*I think I know what was the matter—we all of us suffer from an occasional* crise de nerfs.'

'*Ah, well. There is no purpose to be served, I suppose, in kicking against the pricks.*'

God save her from places like Sandmouth, she'd always told herself: but now here she was, in it, and without even the mean comforts that the people in the houses had. Her own little flat in Bayswater was cramped but cosy, and yet she could convince herself when she was there that it was only somewhere to roost, temporarily. Her 'real' life was spent touring. But when she reached these end-of-the-line places they scared her; even without a city's smoke and fumes and with all their health-giving qualities, they made her breathless for air. They reminded her, 'You don't belong here', and she was always left asking herself, 'But where *do* I belong?'

In the War, and in the seasons just after it finished, there had seemed to be a purpose in travelling the country: they were reviving the public's spirits, they were feeding them the uplifting thoughts of great dramatic minds eternally British. Or so they'd believed. Now the old troupers were starting to sound a little dated in delivery and content, and a little hoarse. Guy blithely talked about going into television, or trying America. Unless she reminded him afresh, he seemed to forget or ignore the fact that she'd had her own career in films, that she'd had her own brief hour of shining glory. Had it been because she didn't know the right people that she'd failed to make it last longer? Two or three times she'd let herself be drawn into tawdry affairs with producers, and they didn't even deserve the honour of the term 'affairs'. The men had found her not very receptive, and she'd hated it, but not for very moral reasons. (Morality was a modern fiction: and the War had damn all to do with it, she knew only too well.) They'd liked to imagine she might be a sort of Garbo or Dietrich, leading them to destruction: but it was a game, for the fag ends of afternoons, the half-hour before their wives sounded the true siren-calls.

If she'd held out, what might have happened? She had received three pay-offs: two cellophaned bouquets of roses, and one (from a man guiltier than the others) of outsized gladioli and orchids. If she'd told them 'no' at the beginning, would that have made the vital difference? Goodness would have guaranteed her her reward? Maybe the good *do* get the best of it, on all counts, and it's worth it just for that?

Coming to the lights of a pub, she debated whether or not to go inside. She glanced in the windows and saw louche types swigging and sawdust strewn on the floor. She looked for the door of the saloon and, as she turned round, she bumped into someone. Her hand brushed against an arm clad in rough wool. She opened her eyes wide and stared at the woman.

She knew from the brown, cow eyes staring back at her, and

there was something about the lines at the corners of her mouth which set the warning bells ringing.

'I'm so sorry,' she said.

'That's all right. I'm not complaining, am I?'

The woman had a common London voice. Adele forced a smile.

'I—I was looking for the saloon bar actually.'

'That's funny, so was I. I'm parched.' The woman's tongue appeared between her teeth and she licked her upper lip. 'Looking for the same thing, are you?'

'What?'

'Something wet?'

' "Wet"?' Adele repeated. A drink. Or more than a drink. 'Yes. Yes, I am.'

For some reason, every time it happened the actress felt she put back her career even more. Stupid to think it when she remembered the three pay-offs. The theatre was the place for it, anyway. But every time it happened it seemed to fill her thoughts—densely, like a gas—for days and nights on end and she hadn't the space left to concentrate on her lines. Her performance suffered, she knew that.

'I'm supposed to be getting a train. Fuck it.'

The woman wasn't at all her usual.

'*I*'m staying in a guest house. I'm an actress, you see. I think my landlady said she had a spare bedroom.'

'No, I'll thumb a lift back. I'm a bit short. Skint, all but.'

'Oh.' Adele wondered if she should offer, mention money.

'When I've had a noggin or two I'll go. I've some business to do, that's why.'

' "Business"?'

The woman laughed. 'Yes. What's yours?'

Adele hesitated.

'I'm an actress—'

'So you said. I meant—well, just as it comes, dear, I'll bet.'

'Yes,' Adele said. 'Yes, I should say so. Pretty much.'

'I'm sure we'll find it if we look up there.'

'The saloon?'

'What you're looking for.'

The woman nodded towards the corner of the building and

the darkness of the lane. ' "Spirit of Good Hope",' she read aloud from the signboard.

'It's a very odd name, isn't it?' the actress said in her Rattigan voice.

'Pretty much,' the woman imitated her.

Adele smiled. She'd stopped caring, that she was made a fool of time and time again.

'Come on, then,' said the woman in the cardigan which felt not at all like Dilly's to the touch, more like wire wool. She went walking on. 'Thought you told me we were both looking to find something?'

★

Mr Symington-Berry had stepped outside for a breath of air before retiring. He looked up at the upstairs windows to check that there were no tracks of torchlight. End-of-term was worst for that, but on the whole he achieved discipline not too badly.

He was always a little apprehensive about what he *might* discover. One unforgettable evening he'd come out and found that Creggan the classics 'filler' had parked his car behind the rhododendrons. He'd walked over and been confronted by a vision of the young man's bare bottom squashed against the front passenger window, writhing dementedly. He'd not had the stomach to explore further, and the situation hadn't recurred, at least not in the school grounds. A new matron in her early thirties had just arrived at the school, and he preferred to think that *she* had been the object of his passion rather than any of the minors in his charge. The woman had left a few months later, rather hastily, giving them only a week's notice in mid-term; he'd been afraid to enquire what the reason might be, and complied with her request only too willingly. Now Creggan had gone too, and he hoped he would never witness such raw and brutal animal lust again: not on school property anyway, so long as he continued to be a headmaster.

The erectors were coming in the morning to dismantle the marquee. It looked ghostly in the moonlight. A length of fallen bunting almost tripped the Headmaster up, and he thought— as he had been thinking all day—of the heroic Major's visit in the morning. Perhaps they had been over-ambitious: even so, they couldn't ever have foreseen such an unfortunate accident happening. Maybe it was a warning of sorts, though? (Mr Symington-Berry was turning to God in his approaching middle-age: or if not to God, to His antecedents, the capricious deities of the ancients.) Maybe they were being instructed, in roundabout and farcical fashion, not to overshoot the limits or to range beyond practicality and moderation? Someone Else knew what was what about the Symington-Berrys—or the Berrys, as they had been—and they shouldn't forget that human powers of invention are finite.

The longer the Headmaster stood in the deserted marquee thinking of the day, the more absurd it seemed to him. He smiled, then he began to snigger with the embarrassment of it; his shoulders started shaking, and a loud laugh came rumbling up from the pit of his stomach. For a while he forgot all about the shame.

The Headmaster's laughter rolled around inside the canvas. He felt genial, lightened: standing in this enclosed space that had been made possible for the day by their own efforts and vision. They would survive the fall of a one-legged, wheezy man turning geriatric before his time. This was a progressive establishment.

In July they would have Commem.: Lavinia was insisting on strawberries as a sop to tradition, but the choice of play would raise a few eyebrows—'Macbeth'.

The laughter became less abandoned, more decorous. At that moment the Headmaster chanced to look over his shoulder. Miss Jones was standing in the entrance, her hand resting on one of the supporting ropes.

The Headmaster's eyes fixed. She'd come to replace the woman who'd replaced the matron Creggan had had his spirited way with. He'd puzzled why such a pretty girl as Miss Hilary Jones should have wanted to be a matron in a school for pre-pubescent boys. In spite of the better paper qualifications of the other interviewees and against his better judgment and even in the face of Lavinia's opinions on the matter, he'd taken her on. 'Welcome to the ship,' he'd told her and gripped her hand in a businesslike grasp.

A month later she was still here. In the course of the four weeks Lavinia had invited her only once into the private wing, for a very hasty and insouciant glass of extra dry sherry which she'd pushed into her hand. 'Well, d'you think you'll last the pace, Miss Jones?' Lavinia had asked her, her mouth shrinking as she heard the girl's unruffled reply in an impeccable accent.

'Hello there,' the Headmaster said.

'I wondered—if everything was all right?'

She never called him 'sir', which was a relief. Looking round the trestle tables, he noticed a bottle of French wine which must have been removed from the boys' notice or which the boys might have removed from the masters' gaze. (The official beverage for pupils and the run-of-the-mill parents had been tea: something a little stronger, on request, for the dignitaries.)

He walked over and retrieved it. It had been uncorked.

'There are teacups in the box behind you, Miss Jones.'

She didn't pretend not to understand. The other young women she replaced had never quite believed their luck at first in serving in a pukka prep school where things were done (more or less) properly, with all the trimmings and no trouble spared.

She held out the cups. The Headmaster averted his eyes from her face, dropping them to her breasts—then to the cups.

'What a day,' he said.

'A nice day, I hope?'

He heard a tone suspiciously like mockery in her voice.

'It's had its moments. Not that it's over.' He tipped the bottle. 'And it's had moments I'd rather forget, I think.'

The Burgundy flowed from the bottle, a generous measure. The Headmaster didn't feel—or sound—his usual self.

'Hold your cup steady, please, Miss Jones.'

She didn't try to tease him with an 'Oh, no, sir'.

'It's not always been like this,' he said, and realised he was being tempted into imprudence.

'No?'

'I mean,' he said, 'the country. Hiding the bottles.'

'No,' she replied, not asking what in hell he was meaning.

'Let's drink to better times.'

She smiled. They chinked china cups.

He looked at her then, into her eyes, as he tilted his head back and swallowed. What the devil kept her here? How and why our paths cross, he thought, it's sometimes better not to enquire: only content thyself that they do.

Mrs Spencer could stand the house no longer. Under the influence of the tea her mind was beginning to imagine the walls were moving in on her. The bits and bobs she'd bought with Ronnie weighed down on every laying surface with a density she thought must crack and shatter the table-tops and shelves. The zebra skin above the fireplace was like a gash, a hole punched in the wall. The brass pots and the shiny brass inlay on the table glinted slily, winked like watching and knowing eyes; she thought she could hear the rich, ringing reverberations of the gong striking from the other side of the room, even though its stick had been lost many years ago in transit.

She pulled on her mackintosh and instinctively reached out for a pair of gloves. *Gloves.* But that was exactly the point, wasn't it?

She picked up her handbag. She remembered—another instinct—to look inside, to check that she had her front door key. She looked in the hold, she rattled the many and varied contents, but no sign of the key. Damn . . .

She didn't think she could bear to be in the house any longer, not a minute longer, and she didn't know where to start searching for the key. So she did what was simpler and unsnibbed the lock on the front door. Abroad, she'd started to keep the doors locked: the natives were invariably hostile, anyone planning a robbery could have just walked in otherwise, the gesture gave her a minimal sense of security, of secrecy at least. When she'd come here to live, to Sandmouth, she was told it was rare for people to lock their doors. She'd been conscious she was most definitely being frowned upon for doing so. But old habits die very hard.

Abroad it hadn't been material loss she was afraid of, but the possibility that others might want to discover more about her. That fear hadn't left her in Sandmouth, where she'd never felt at home. Perhaps it had only perpetuated the unease, and intensified it, but she didn't want to lead the life of an inside-out person, like the ones who'd conducted their lives so transparently in the settlements Ronnie had been posted to.

She pulled the door to behind her, missing the reassuring sound and weight of it locking shut. She didn't care who might go in if they chose to, what they might discover about Mrs Ronald Spencer.

The girl, she must be somewhere. Even in the darkness she must be *some*where. She had to explain to her, she needed a chance to put everything into its proper perspective, all that Sandmouth didn't understand about her, which it never would now.

Mrs Spencer buttoned up her mackintosh. She knew that if she'd been able to sleep it would have been the girl's face that was watching her from the other side, *her* rigmarole of words she was hearing.

She would reply to her as clearly as she could. Clearly, firmly. Not excusing necessarily, not justifying: just asking, requesting, requiring, demanding that she should *understand*, understand and forgive. No more and no less.

Forgiveness, Tilly Moscombe, please. For the life I've led. You must understand me and forgive me, you must. You *must*.

★

Later in the evening Alma Stockton starts her rota duty at the telephone exchange. She opens the detective novel from the library and finds her place.

Leadbetter saw how interested his sister was in determining the exact spot where the body had been found. He explained to her as precisely as he, a stranger in the locality, was capable of doing.

'How curious!' Alice Leadbetter exclaimed. 'You're quite sure?'

'That's what I heard the policemen say. Let me think again. Badger Lane—next to the stile—next to the bridleway up to—up to Hang Wood, is it?'

'Yes, that's right—Hang Wood.' Miss Leadbetter nodded her head vigorously. 'Well, well!'

Her brother sat watching her closely. Although in recent years they had been seeing less of each other than previously, he was well enough versed in all her mannerisms to realise that the information was intriguing and exciting her.

'Fancy that now!'

'Fancy what now?' he asked.

442

'That was one of the points of intersection, you see.'

' "Intersection"?' Leadbetter repeated.

'In Roman days. Where the new straight road to Selby crossed the old pagan track up to the wood.'

Leadbetter sucked on his pipe.

'So?' he said, prompting his sister to continue.

Miss Leadbetter shook her head.

'I don't know,' she announced.

'It's just—a coincidence?'

'A couple of years ago old Miss Thomas was found dead. Supposedly of a heart attack while she was out walking. The body was lying not in Badger Lane but Gimble Lane.' Miss Leadbetter made a cradle of her arms. 'Gimble Lane is a continuation of the Roman road, you see. I discovered that from some medieval maps.'

'So?' Leadbetter bit on the mouthpiece of his pipe.

'To this day no one quite knows how she died. "Heart failure", it was said. Officially, I mean. It was known she had a weak heart. A sudden shock—perhaps someone deliberately did it, who knows?—that would have been enough to cause her to collapse.'

Leadbetter allowed a moment's respectful silence before enquiring.

'But what does this have to do—'

'You see, Basil, where she was found was where the Roman road crossed another of those ancient tracks: between the ford and where the standing stones are, out near Weydon village. Well, well, how very strange!'

'Coincidence again?'

'But that's not how we live our lives here, Basil. Time is always at our shoulders.'

'What's that?' Leadbetter expostulated.

'Time here doesn't just finish. It goes round on a loop. Chasing—But you don't understand me, do you?' Miss Leadbetter asked, seeming concerned.

Her brother scratched his head.

'I don't see what that has to do—with this day and age.'

'Time chases its tail, catching up on unfinished business. In-breeding means different generations are continually in touch: by a kind of thought transference.' Miss Leadbetter *smiled, as if to inform her brother that this was all quite reasonable and not in the least way surprising. 'It's like a web, you see, all the fine silk spokes meeting and connecting. Do something now, and you make echoes just as you catch echoes.'*

At which point, mercifully (the book is turning out to be a slow read, a bit cerebral), a call comes on to the switchboard. It's being made on a public telephone. Alma Stockton connects the number. The voice is a woman's, but no one's she recognises; it sounds thick and croaky and the words are hazarded nervously. Mrs Stockton senses that the voice is being disguised.

'I'm putting you through now, madam.'

The number being requested is the 'Old Rectory' 's. A full minute passes before the receiver is picked up.

Alma Stockton hears another woman's voice, the mother's, and she is intrigued to hear more. The caller asks for Mr Pargiter, please. His mother says he is not at home.

'It's very late.'

'Yes, I know. I was in bed.'

'Oh, I'm so sorry—'

'That's what I'm here in the house *for*.'

The caller's voice wavered, it lost its croakiness and Alma Stockton almost thought she recognised it.

'Can I tell him who's been calling?'

'Oh no. Don't trouble him. I'm troubling *you*.'

'You're not troubling *me*. Who is this calling?'

The woman attempted to lower her voice; she said it didn't really matter, she was making a nuisance of herself.

'Please yourself. Good-night, then.'

The receiver was replaced on the telephone. It was several seconds before the other receiver was put down.

Alma Stockton undid the connection, replaced the plug, then picked up her knitting. She tucked the ends of the needles beneath her arms. Her mouth always worked when her mind was occupied with thoughts she couldn't sort out properly into any order.

She was trying to hear the voice without the thickness and the croak. From habit her mind was making a connection between the voice and the 'Old Rectory', but in another part of her brain she suspected the woman had never called that

444

number before. Even when she felt it didn't, Alma Stockton's mind worked its own night-shift: sifting, distinguishing, discriminating, sorting out. The two, she believed—the women at either end of the line—had never had dealings with one another before; the caller belonged to one compartment on one side of the ironwork social grid Mrs Stockton carried a mental vision of—a contraption which complemented her own switchboard and whose elements required as strict mastery on her part to learn the system of—while the latest occupants of the 'Old Rectory', for all their material possessions, belonged to a compartment squarely set on the other, lesser side.

★

'How old are you, Miss Jones?'

The Headmaster and the young matron were sitting on a felled tree bole in the sylvan grounds of Minster Court. The china cups lay on the turf.

'I thought it was a lady's privilege to keep that a secret.'

'Yes, indeed. But I am your employer, Miss Jones.'

'Ladies don't normally *have* employers, is that it?'

'I didn't say that. But on the whole I suppose not.'

'So I'm not properly a "lady" at all, am I to understand?'

'I think you are. Which makes me curious as to why you should seek to be employed in the first place. And why— methinks—should it be at Minster Court?'

In front of them lay the ghostly white hulk of the marquee. The shining guy ropes might have been silvered twists of barley sugar, so delightful was the prospect to the Headmaster. Beyond that the restrained mock-Gothic façade of Minster Court lay largely in darkness. Only the downstairs bedroom window was lit.

They both sat looking at the view.

'A few deer would make the scene perfect, don't you think, Miss Jones? Nibbling at the grass, striding on their long legs.'

'A scene for Saint George's Day?'

'Next year we should celebrate Mr Shakespeare's birthday instead. You must stay to see it, Miss Jones. What could we call it?'

'Please don't ask *me*. *I'm* just a humble matron, remember.'

'Humble? Why should—' The Headmaster thought, damn

the consequences. 'Why should a pretty young lady like your-self want to be humble?'

Her back straightened, and the Headmaster noticed.

'You were telling me : . .'

'What?'

'About next year,' she said.

'Was I?'

'What you were going to call your Shakespeare extravaganza.'

'Oh yes. What about—let's see—"An Arden Miscellany" perhaps?'

'You have a poetic soul, Headmaster.'

'Are you surprised?'

'I should have thought—to be frank—that having the charge of sixty-two over-active boys heading straight for puberty would have—crushed it out of you.'

'It's a shared charge, Miss Jones.' The Headmaster leaned backwards on the log, preparing himself for a confidence. 'And I don't believe all that sentimental Mr Chips stuff either,' he said. 'I have sixty-two children and they're all boys. Twaddle!'

'Robert Donat made me cry.'

'The film's not why you came?'

'Oh no.'

'I don't let *them* rule my life.'

'Films?'

'*Boys*, Miss Jones. Remember—you are a matron. The matron of Minster Court.'

She smiled, then repeated the words.

'And you don't let *them* rule your life?'

'Certainly not,' the Headmaster replied. He took a deep breath, and again he thought damn the consequences. 'Away from here, Miss Jones, they'll grow up into—well, two kinds, at least. Loud-mouthed, empty-headed men like their fathers, who always land on their feet and will live comfortably for the rest of their mortal days. Or else they'll become the loud-mouthed snobs their fathers want them to be, who'll have just enough common sense in their souls—and the minimum number of scruples, my dear Miss Jones—to know how to run the piffling little businesses that pay the fees here: and be the second generation that makes all the scrimping and saving and sacrificing worthwhile. Which it's not, of course: not worthwhile. Most of them will end up the nonentities they deserve to be, but driving Jaguars and learning every fiddle in the book.'

The matron's reaction to the speech was to smile again. The Headmaster watched her.

'Well,' she said, 'that's refreshingly honest of you.'

'And what do *you* think, Miss Jones? I should like to know. I never have an inkling of what *your* thoughts might be.'

'I didn't know you—you paid me such attention.'

'Indeed I do.'

'I'm not paid to air my thoughts.'

'Do I detect a certain commercial bias in your nature from things you say, Miss Jones?'

'It accounts for the humility, I think.'

'But I should *like* you to air your thoughts, as you put it. After all, you tell them to that Moscombe girl, don't you?'

Miss Jones appeared to freeze, to go rigid.

'Thought I hadn't noticed, didn't you?' the Headmaster asked her in a jocular voice.

There was a pause. The matron's voice when she spoke was attempting to make light of the matter, but struck the Headmaster—even in his partially disordered condition—as somewhat less than convincing.

'Once or twice I may have spoken to her.'

'Oh, more than that, Miss Jones, surely.'

She said nothing.

'I'm sorry. I didn't mean to embarrass you. I've caught sight of you both, that's all. From my window.'

'She just—well, materialises. From nowhere.'

'Lavinia—my wife, rather—she found it rather distressing at first. She thinks she should be in caring hands. I quite agree with her. She must have been about this morning too. My wife didn't want the parents to see her.'

Miss Jones's fingers knotted together.

'Every town has one, I suppose,' the Headmaster said. 'You put up with them.'

'She's not—just another one, though, is she?'

'Isn't she?'

'There are stories about her.'

'About her and Lady de Castellet, you mean? Oh, a lot of nonsense. That's just in books.'

'You can't be sure, though.'

'I don't bother myself thinking about it,' the Headmaster said in his jaunty, jokey voice. 'And neither should you, Miss Jones. I can't think what you two get to talk about. Not—not Minster Court secrets, I hope?'

' "*Secrets*"?'

The Headmaster laughed.

'Just a little joke,' he said.

'You *can't* speak to her anyway. Not really. Although . . .'

'Although what?'

'They say she does know, really, only she can't communicate that back to you. Or she doesn't to *me*, anyway.'

'Oh, there's a failure of communication all right, Miss Jones. The girl's a daftie, and that's the long and the short of it surely.'

The matron appeared less certain on the point.

The Headmaster sat studying her.

'There's something not quite right about *you*, either, Miss Jones,' he said.

She stared back at him. He looked at her eyes: the pupils floated in the whites and seemed intent, suspicious too.

'I mean, you're not like the other matrons we've had.'

'I've no idea if I am or not,' came the reply—a little testily, to the Headmaster's ear.

'Of course you did have your references, Miss Jones.'

'Yes. Of course.'

'I *am* right, aren't I?' the Headmaster asked. 'It *is* "Miss Jones", is it not?'

★

Miss Vane had never felt less like Ginette Spanier, so she put on a reefer jacket over her sailing-trousers and fisherman's jumper. Her fingers fumbled with the wooden toggles. She found a pair of woollen gloves in the pockets and chucked them down among the shiny copper on top of the coffer in her Mrs Tiggywinkle hall. She slammed her felt fedora on top of her head and pulled down the brim purposefully.

She was Tilly's friend, that's what she wanted her to know. She would explain, so reasonably. *I am your friend, Tilly, you must forget what you saw earlier. I am another person as well as that one. That one is not the person you know, she is reserved for someone else. My other friend was joking, you mustn't mind her, although I know you store it up. You mustn't tell anyone, please, Tilly, ever. It's our secret, and we shall just be as we were. Nothing changes. Nothing needs to be any different. I am how people will remember me here—for my fame to come, for posterity. (Because really, Tilly, my talents have yet to be discovered properly and appreciated.) I am not how you may be tempted to say I am, in your own language, if someone only feeds you the words you need, 'Miss Meredith Vane'. I am Miss Vane your friend, Tilly. Look at me: please look at me, Tilly. Hear me, what it is I'm telling you. Only look, Tilly Moscombe.*

★

Behind the high privet hedge of the Reverend Aldred's rectory an object lies gathering dew on the damp grass. A streetlight lends it a *ghostly* hue. The stark yellow light plays over it and seems to turn it, as if it were wood sculpture or some weirdly whorled specimen of shell-life.

But no one has seen; the object goes unnoticed. A few days lends it a spectral hue. The stark yellow light plays over it and inspects the lawn for mole diggings and worm casts.

At first, in the new frame of mind that has taken possession of the whole town, he suspects the worst. Then he sees his mistake, and although it seems out of order to smile at such a juncture, he does so—with relief. Only afterwards does the oddness of the find strike him: what should a plaster hand be doing in his garden, how does it fit into the savage jigsaw of events? Presumably, yes, it has been tossed over the high hedge. Is it intended—could it possibly be—as some kind of reminder, a *memento mori*?

By that time such an episode will have acquired an alarmingly surreal quality.

Now it's as if people have temporarily lost their hold on the logic and system of daily events: either God's methodical workings, or merely the exercise of the pragmatically causal.

★

The Headmaster had moved forward. He stood behind Minster Court's young matron.

449

She looked over her shoulder. She hadn't been sure at first what the Headmaster sought from her; now she guessed. She didn't refuse when he reached out his hand, took hers, and laid it on his arm. She allowed it to stay there.

'To put it quite bluntly, Miss Jones, or whoever you are, you're above all this, aren't you?'

'Well, if that's what you think, think it.'

'You do learn something from this business, you know,' the Headmaster said as he led her forward and they started walking in the direction of the sports pavilion. 'You learn something from educating the little buggers. About who's the genuine article and who's not.'

' "Genuine"?'

'Maybe a foreigner wouldn't understand. But the British understand. We've got all that shorthand at our fingertips. We've a sixth sense for it.'

'For what?'

'Class.'

'Oh, I see.'

'You are—you *are* a foreigner, Miss Jones, are you not? Not completely foreign, I'd guess. Commonwealth, perhaps?'

Her eyes stared at him.

'I gave you references,' she said.

'Yes. Yes, of course you did.'

'I don't understand.'

'References don't go unchecked. Conveniently for me.'

'For *you*?'

'I like to—to protect Minster Court's integrity. For reasons I shall not go into.'

They climbed up the steps on to the verandah of the pavilion, the Headmaster leading. The matron drew back her hand.

'I don't,' she said, 'seek anything other than a professional relationship with your little boys, Mr Symington-Berry. Your little buggers as you prefer to call them.'

The Headmaster nodded his head at the change of tone, the edge, the brahmin demeanour. In those moments he realised he won another little victory as he once again found himself deferring to the indicators of a superior being. Very probably Miss Jones outdid Lavinia in her connections.

450

'Snotty little bastards *I*'d call them,' she said.

The Headmaster smiled.

'I should guess Australian, Miss Jones? It *is* Miss Jones?'

'Let's just leave it as it is.'

'Australian?'

'So—if I am?'

'My wife said I was imagining it.'

'You've discussed me with your wife?' She sounded indignant. She lost what was left of her Jane Eyre manner.

'Now and then.'

'What have you said?'

'Pardon?'

'To your wife.'

'I sang your praises, Miss—'

'*She* doesn't, I suppose? Sing my praises?'

The Headmaster shrugged his shoulders. He dropped his eyes to the swelling outline of the matron's breasts under her tweed coat. He opened his mouth, pitched his voice lower and softer.

'I'm an ardent admirer of yours, Miss—'

She interrupted him. 'Is that what you say to all your matrons, Headmaster?'

'Please. Call me Philip.'

'Is this part of your seduction process? I presume that's the intention? For us to become intimate?'

'Please—'

She shook her head.

'Please don't,' he said.

'Don't what?'

'Say "no" like that.'

'I'm not.' She stood still. 'I'm just—surprised I didn't notice. Notice before.'

'Are you. . .' The Headmaster hesitated.

'Am I what?'

'Are you running away?'

' "Running away"?'

'Isn't that why you're here?'

'No, that's *not* why I'm here.'

The Headmaster passed his eyes over the rest of her.

'It's none of your business,' she said.

'No?'

'If you're not satisfied, put me out.'

'Oh, I'm satisfied, Miss Jones. I'm *very* satisfied.'

'And I presume you've told your wife that?'

The Headmaster smiled, cautiously.

The matron crossed her arms and took a few steps forward, past a canvas chair with an empty wine glass underneath, to a point where she could see across the rolled cricket pitch, to the marquee like a white ship.

'Clever you, Mr Symington-Berry.'

The Headmaster winced. She said his name so disbelievingly.

'You—' He chased a frog out of his throat. Try again.

'Your home was in Australia?'

'Don't sound so flabbergasted.'

'I'm not.'

'If you could call *my* home a "home".'

'No? Oh. I'm sorry. I didn't—'

'You're "sorry" about Australia? Or you didn't "know", you didn't "suspect" about my home life? Why the hell should you? That's the point. We girls, we were meant to be more English than the English. My house in school was called "Cheltenham". We walked about in deportment classes with books on our heads, we wore white gloves, the lot.'

'So—so what are you doing here?'

'At the end of the world?'

'I suppose it is.' The Headmaster nodded. 'More or less. Yes.'

'But it could be worse, you think? Yes, it probably could be worse. Which is the frightening thing.'

'You haven't told me.'

'What I'm doing here? I don't really think you need to concern yourself with that.'

The Headmaster shrugged.

'It's just friendly interest, is it?' she asked, with rather less disdain.

'You—well, you interest me frankly, yes.'

'I do, do I? I see.'

The Headmaster reached out for her hand. She ringed his wrist with hers, and reached for his other hand, and held it. They stayed in the same position for several seconds.

The Headmaster cleared his throat.

'Miss Jones, I'm a fake,' he said. 'I'm a charlatan.'

'Well, that makes us quits,' she replied. 'How a fake?'

'A non-believer.'

'In what?'

'What I do. You'd have to be one, a believer, to want to run a place like this.'

'Just think of what you're giving the country. Sir.'

'I try *not* to think of that.'

'Tomorrow's men. Gin-drinking farmers, your Jaguar-driving businessmen. All top quality turds, I should say.'

The Headmaster blinked.

'Tomorrow's men,' she said. 'With no promise at all.'

The Headmaster blinked again.

'Is my language too antipodean?'

'I was in the Navy.'

'That part's true?'

'Oh yes.'

The Headmaster moved closer to her.

'I've seen you here at night,' he told her. 'With your friend Miss Moscombe.'

'I didn't appreciate I was being watched.'

'My study is my own.'

'Your cell.'

'There are cells and cells,' he said.

'I don't pretend to understand that,' she said.

'Don't bother,' he told her.

Her lips were soft where Lavinia's were cracked and parched after years of lipstick gloss. There was a sweet taste inside her mouth. She touched his tongue with hers and hot shivers shot through him. Their noses fitted comfortably together like jigsaw pieces and then the rest of their persons drew closer and touched, automatically.

On the verandah of the sports pavilion they stood in a conspiracy of moonlight and shadows. His hands caressed her back; hers clamped on his waist. She moaned, and it didn't matter to him if she meant it or not. His groin pressed on the flat of her stomach; she pushed herself close against him and he felt a knot gathering at his fork, urgent and hard.

A gasp from neither of them caused them to hesitate, then to unlock. At the same second they each looked over their

453

shoulder. A face peered up at them over the balustrade, open-mouthed with astonishment. The Headmaster and the matron stared back, transfixed.

The Headmaster started shaking his head, as if to wish the sight away.

'Piss off!' the matron hissed. 'Go on, piss off out of it!'

Tilly Moscombe did nothing. The Headmaster cleared his throat, but the matron had turned for the balustrade before he could open his mouth to speak.

Tilly Moscombe turned on her heels and was suddenly gone. The undergrowth shook as if a startled deer had taken cover.

'She—she saw?' the Headmaster said weakly.

'This is where she comes.'

'But she saw us?'

'You saw she did.'

'Do you think she heard?' he asked huskily.

'I don't *know* what she hears. A hell of a lot, it must be, in the course of a day. People just need someone to talk to—'

'But what *we* were saying just now?' the Headmaster asked, his anxiety unmistakable.

'Oh, I expect so.'

'Does she—does she understand?'

'She can speak sometimes. She writes things down. Messages. Pictures, sort of, and it looks like old baloney. But *she* knows.'

hat lady's man, no hat lady, nurse, lady, tell Tilly, friends, you me, Miss Jones, smiles, talk talk, treefall quiet, Miss Jones, hat lady's man, smiles, talk talk, but, not hat lady, call me, Philip please, treefall quiet, stars, look, Miss Jones, tell Tilly, friends, you me, secrets, Tilly, Philip please, fake, char-lat-an, smiles, non bel-iev-er, smiles, Miss Jones, quits, the rough school, Sir, end of the world, Miss Jones, secrets Tilly, hat lady's man, treefall quiet, fake, char-lat-an, smiles, no hat lady, hands, wrists, waist, kiss, Miss Jones, Tilly tell, treefall quiet, stars, Philip please, kiss, oh, hat lady's man, oh, no hat lady, quiet, moon, fake, end of the world, look, stars, eyes, secrets, piss off out, friends Tilly, no smiles, eyes . . .

For the Headmaster the scene had lost all its vernal charm as they both left the pavilion and walked back—he meanwhile sunk deep in grim perplexity—across the lawn to the house.

'What if . . .?' he ventured.

'What if what?'

'What if Lavinia finds out? My wife.'

'How?'

'The girl—she might blurt it out to someone else. Nothing stays a secret in this bloody place.'

'I don't expect it'll be the only emergency you've faced. You can bluff your way out of it, if you're worth your salt.'

The Headmaster was taken aback.

'That's easy to say—'

'Think of your problems and what might happen,' the matron told him. 'What you've got to stop happening. That concentrates the mind wonderfully.'

The Headmaster looked away.

'Or—'

'Yes?' he said. 'Or what?'

'Or you could get rid of her.'

'What?' He turned and stared at her.

'Get up a petition. Say she should be looked after. She'll be on the loose soon, anyway.'

'How?'

'When Lady de Castellet dies.'

They were both silent as they made their way back. Unfortunately they'd allowed expediency to be overlooked in the course of the evening's dramas and both crossed the threshold of Minster Court's main building at precisely the same second, their steps exactly in time.

The study door was open. Mrs Symington-Berry in her nightgown and slippers was standing at the desk, listening to the earpiece of the telephone receiver and pushing on the buttons. She looked out and saw her husband and the personable young matron arriving in tandem.

She sounded very crisp indeed as she replaced the receiver on the telephone and walked over to the door.

'I'm not dressed for a social encounter,' she announced. 'Even if I felt like it. Which I'm not. Not at this time of night.'

'I met Miss Jones—'

'Yes. I was aware Miss Jones was not in her quarters. A man

called to speak to you, Miss Jones. A Mr Willie McSporran. I can't believe that's his real name. He didn't have a very Scotch voice. He said I was to tell you "Yes", whatever that means. Code, is it? I've passed on his message at any rate, my conscience is clear.'

'Thank you, Mrs Symington-Berry,' the matron said, with becoming modesty and good grace. 'It was news I was expecting.'

'I'm off to bed. I'm so sorry I couldn't join you in your moonlight stroll. You smell of drink, Philip,' she said as she swept off down the corridor. 'That must account for it,' was her parting remark.

The Headmaster smiled painfully at the black and white tiles on the floor.

'I'm off to my quarters,' the matron said as the blue slippers vanished from view, as loudly and distinctly as if she'd been addressing a School Assembly.

'Good night, Miss Jones.'

'Good night, Headmaster.'

Neither moved.

'I hope, Miss Jones, we might continue our conversation another time.'

'I'm sure we will. Sleep well.'

'I doubt that. I doubt it very much.'

'Just think, then. Tomorrow might be even worse.'

'I doubt that too.'

'Oh, I wouldn't be too certain.'

A sound that might have been sniggering carried down from the upstairs gallery in the main house, where the dormitories were. They were standing only a few feet away from the staircase. The Headmaster looked upwards furtively.

'What's that?' he whispered.

The matron didn't lower her voice. 'It sounds to me,' she said, 'very much as if tomorrow's taking shape already.'

And that guffaw, she meant, sounded very much like the contrary music of the gods laughing up their proverbial sleeves.

★

'I think it's his time.'

At the words Mr Messiter raised his eyes from his Margery Allingham.

'What's that, Betty?'

Mrs Messiter instinctively blenched at the name. All her days she'd had to suffer it. 'Elizabeth' had so much more dignity.

'Laddie,' she said.

Mr Messiter looked at his watch.

'So it is.'

The labrador recognised its name; it wagged its tail and clambered up on to its legs, sniffing freedom from the stuffy room.

'We won't be long,' Mr Messiter said.

He always said it, every time he left the house with Laddie. The remark irritated his wife to distraction. So, what if they *were* a long time? Why *shouldn't* they be? — did he think she fretted till she heard them coming back?

Mr Messiter put on his sports jacket and picked up the walking stick that had been his wife's birthday present to him one year. She wished he would learn to use it properly, not just to prod at stones that caught his eye and to lop the heads off dandelions.

'I think my tip's about to fall off.'

'What?'

'The metal bit on my stick.'

'You should be more careful what you do with it. It's not a golf club.'

'No, dear.'

So often what Mr Messiter felt was a harmless and inoffensive observation provoked an unambiguously dismissive response. He tried not to be defeated by them.

'We'll go down by the golf course.'

They always did. Why was he forever telling her, as if she could possibly have forgotten?

'Well, *I*'ll wash up the cups then.'

It was what she said every time, without fail. Mr Messiter shifted uneasily, as was his usual form. Why did Betty make it seem that by taking Laddie out for a walk he was being let off some other much more onerous and bothersome household duty?

'Won't be long, dear.'

He whistled to Laddie. Mrs Messiter wished he wouldn't, for her nerves' sake, and she'd told him about it often enough. The

457

only reservation she had on the point was that she'd read Georgian and Victorian gentlemen often whistled to their pets and hounds, and she couldn't remember if they'd done it indoors as well, in those vast, gaunt mansions of theirs.

When the front door was shut she listened to the whistles rudely ruffling 'The Wyldnesse' 's calm. She didn't know what their neighbours must think. On the whole they were a genteel lot: some of them had traded larger houses for these more easily maintained ones. A number of them spoke in public school accents, and Mrs Messiter took care that she was nicely dressed whenever she hung out a washing or even went to the dustbin, in case anyone should look out and catch sight of her. That wasn't a problem to her, not really: she felt it was a spur not to drop one's standards. She wished Brian wouldn't answer the front door in his slippers or leave the curtains open and the light on in the bathroom when he attended to his business. She was thankful they had a downstairs W.C. now, should anyone call by and require to use it: she forbade Brian to go in, shedding so many curly black hairs into the lavatory bowl that her stomach would turn over on itself. After he'd had a bath upstairs she had to sluice it out again, unblocking the plug of hairs with a wodge of toilet paper. Now she disliked hairy men on principle.

Mr Messiter strode ahead of Laddie. The dog was over-weight. Really he thought of him (just like Tara the tabby) as Betty's, not his. He'd told her it didn't do him any good when she fed him 'Nice' biscuits, but he had the feeling it was almost a nervous gesture with her: easier than sitting still and just talking to *him*. Absurdly she would sometimes try to bring Laddie into the conversation.

'*You* don't think so, Laddie, do you?'

'Laddie wouldn't say that to me, would you, Laddie?'

He was in the mood for a longer walk tonight. The advantage of 'The Wyldnesse' was that it was in easy reach of the golf course and the front. By cutting across the greens you could do a kind of circle, an oval. Tonight there was more than enough moonlight to see by.

Mr Messiter whistled.

'Laddie! Here, boy!'

He would have been just as happy not to have a dog. But if you did have to have one, a black labrador was as good as any: a straightforward, uncomplicated, masculine breed. He was grateful for that much good sense in Betty at least.

'Golf course, Laddie! Hope you feel like a long walk, old chap!'

In a way he felt they were akin: both of them domesticated, a little ponderous maybe, docile. *He* was less overweight, thank God, and had fought off a jowl. On their walks with each other he'd felt an indefinable closeness develop: a kind of contentment he sensed they each of them had for one another's company: they were 'easy' together.

He was glad of it. More grateful, he was conscious, than it should have been necessary for him to be—a reasonably well-adjusted, not unhealthy husband with the leisure of a premature retirement to fill.

*

Miss Jones, of course, is indeed otherwise.

She is one Naomi Spedding. She was born in London, but her first memories are of broad tree-lined streets in another city, under a wide blue antipodean sky—Melbourne, in the state of Victoria, federal dominion of Australia.

Her father was not her mother's husband. She has no recollection of either. Her mother was married to Charles Spedding, proprietor of a fashionable riverside hotel on the Thames. She has seen photographs of 'The Hare and Hounds'. To her Australian eyes they showed a scene quintessentially English: a long and uneven timbered building with leaded windows and swathes of creeper and a high steep hog's-back roof. Guests sauntered on the velvet lawn, beside the smooth-flowing river. White birds perched on top of a dovecote, fluttering their wings. Shiny black cars with running-boards sprawled on the driveway. Someone waved from the open casement of an upstairs window among the—was it?—ivy.

'It must be so old,' she used to say to her mother.

'Not really,' would come the reply she was always hoping she wouldn't hear. 'It was made like that to *look* old.'

'Oh.'

Rich, prosperous, leisured England. The girl was sure that it

459

was from England that the money came to pay the fees at the various schools she had attended before the one with the Houses called 'Cheltenham' and 'Malvern' and 'Clifton' and 'Roedean'. (She wasn't an easy child to educate, and it was only an occasional sharp reminder from her mother of what it was costing that would keep her from running away from them.)

When she was at home she saw the envelopes with the London postmarks being pushed beneath the others, for reading later. It was only in her middle-teens when she was written to herself, without any forewarning, by a Scotsman with no address and the oddest name—Alistair Meiklejohn de Castellet—that she started to make any vague sense of the situation. In reference volumes she found the statutory information about the man referred to in the letter as her natural father and provider: *George Edward Oliver Sturgeon de Castellet, 6th Baron S 1922.* What his connections with 'The Hare and Hounds' could have been, she had no idea. It puzzled her at that most deeply sexual age to think that very probably she was conceived there, one summer's afternoon in an upstairs bedroom among the ivy, with bees knocking against the open casement window and the scent of floribunda roses and honeysuckle wafting up into the room.

On her seventeenth birthday her mother provided her with some of the details she insisted she required and, meshing those with what she'd learned from her correspondent, she began to piece together a history for herself. It started with Lord George de Castellet's visits to the hotel, either for business purposes (?) or to see a little more of her attractive mother, the proprietor's wife. Charles Spedding divorced his wife afterwards, but marriage held no appeal for the rakish de Castellet, and Mrs Spedding elected to leave England for Australia with her baby daughter. In Melbourne the unfortunate woman's relations accommodated the pair in their modest and not very capacious bungalow. The next chapter in the story began when a Sydney lawyer wrote to Mrs Spedding (much later the schoolgirl Naomi found the obscurely worded letter in a drawer); he invited Mrs Spedding to travel to Sydney (expenses to be reimbursed) to discuss certain financial transactions to be implemented by a client of the practice.

In her later teens Naomi had come to imagine George de

Castellet as—elderly, of course—but also rather an avuncular, generous type: with charm enough to have seduced her pretty but very matter-of-fact mother. She didn't feel unkindly disposed to him, not at first. After all, he could have refused to have anything to do with her mother, but he hadn't.

It was only when she'd left school and was touting for a job in Melbourne, then Sydney, that she started to have second thoughts. She would ask herself, what had been the purpose of educating her out of what seemed to be her expected station in life? Then she would remember that her mother *had* lived comfortably and rather grandly at one time, till her seducer had made it impossible for her to continue in that life.

By chance she saw a report of his death in a copy of the London *Times*. He turned out to have been an older man than she'd calculated him to be. There was no mention of a wife in the obituary, no indication that he'd been a widower. At more expense than she could afford she bought copies of *The Times* every day until she saw mention of his estate: amounting to almost half-a-million English pounds.

For three or four months she was obliged to serve in small dress shops and milliners' in Sydney, suffering the pride of customers in each until she would reach breaking point with one of them and lose her temper and she would know as she did it she couldn't return to that shop tomorrow. Her employers were besotted with her accent and manners, but they weren't able to handle the patrician hauteur when it asserted itself. 'You're too good for *us* here, madam,' she was told more than once.

Then another letter—more detailed and containing an address—arrived from the man who called himself a not so distant relation, Alistair Meiklejohn de Castellet. Apparently he'd done much foraging around. He told her about Lady de Castellet's condition. He also described the household and domestic routine of 'Hallam House', and recounted the various theories concerning the mysterious Tilly Moscombe. He also let her know that the Depression had brought his own father down in the world—he'd had a button and hook-and-eye factory and two hundred and thirty workers—and he'd never forgiven the other de Castellets their aloof disinterest.

She'd not known what to do about it until the telephone rang one day at her lodgings in Woollahra and she found herself speaking to the man. He'd been sent out on business by the firm of civil engineers he worked for, and could he see her? She had no objections—she was curious, in fact—and they duly met. She judged him very definitely in the 'mad, bad, and dangerous to know' category they used to discuss avidly in 'Cheltenham' House. They sparred with one another, she gave back as good as she got. She found it easy to steel herself to cope with him, even—at that time—enjoyable. 'If I send you the money out,' he asked her, 'will you come over?'

'What for?'

'We'll pay the old bird a visit.'

'Why?'

'Seems to me there are people with better claims on her loot than certain others. Only she doesn't know that. Or conveniently forgets.'

They'd met up again in London, and had a bit of a fling. Afterwards he'd driven her down to Sandmouth and shown her the place. Back in London he handed her an insertion from *The Lady* advertising for the services of a matron at a private preparatory school in Sandmouth. It would let her be 'on the spot', he told her: she could keep her ears open, and quiz the girl. She'd returned to the town, had her interview, and immediately afterwards phoned Meiklejohn de Castellet from the Clarence Hotel with a report: the Headmaster had taken a shine to her, no doubt about that.

'Why did he advertise in *The Lady*?'

'I think it's his thing,' she told him. 'He's a kind of social masochist.'

'A "masochist", eh? *You* know a lot about the world, don't you?'

'Of course I do. I've lived at its other end.'

'You didn't tell *him* you were an Aussie?'

'No, of course not,' she said. 'But I'm not anyway.'

'Good girl!'

She'd been at Minster Court for longer than she'd thought she would have to be, holed up in her cramped room with the chianti bottle lamp and shade of postage stamps and the inherited cacti pots along the window sill. She still hadn't visited 'Hallam House', although her Scots kinsman had. They heard a story that Tilly Moscombe might not be a blood relation after all, and the checking up on that delayed them: 'MacCastellet' (as she called him) wanted to make absolutely sure before confronting her ladyship. In the meantime the problem remained unsolved: who had the better claim—Naomi Spedding, because she was older, or Tilly Moscombe, because it was rumoured that she might be the brother's child by his much younger half-sister?

Presuming, that was, there were no other bastards cast out into the wilds and waiting to be discovered. 'Bastards': Naomi Spedding hated the word. She also hated having to serve in the school—doing work 'Mac' had made up false references for, over-extravagantly praising her capacities—and she resented having to kowtow to people like the Symington-Berry's. Just to be on the safe side, she'd also checked up on the Headmaster's credentials, and had discovered them to be as untrustworthy as her own. If she did nothing else of note at Minster Court (what a godawful name), she was determined to throw a spanner in the works of that phoney marriage arrangement, and she'd ceased to be fussy about how she was going to accomplish it.

During her month in the 'san' she'd been biding her time. But now she was starting to become impatient. She felt the angry pride she'd inherited from she didn't know where—school, her mother, her father—bubbling away, simmering, ready to froth and boil up and blow its lid.

★

Howard Trevis had the War Memorial Gardens in his sights when he heard footsteps behind him.

The voice was just as he remembered it from the afternoon: low, precise, self-conscious, manly, *thrilling*.

'Hello, there.'

Trevis stopped and swung round.

'Oh. Hello.'

His own voice sounded high and anxious. The actor smiled.

'Just getting to know my way around.'

'It's—it's a nice evening.'

'Yes.' The voice paused. 'A little chilly. Didn't think to put my jacket on.'

'It's—good for the time of year, though.'

463

'Oh yes.'

They walked forward together, in time, the clicks of their heels coinciding.

'I take it you're not about your business?'

Trevis laughed nervously.

'No. No, I'm not.'

'Like it here?'

'Sandmouth? I don't know. Yes and no.'

'Got all the things you want?'

'I—' Trevis hesitated. 'It's where I was brought up, you see.'

'Don't you mind that? Still living here?'

'A bit.'

No one had ever asked him that question before.

'A bit,' he repeated.

'Don't you want to—see life sometimes?'

'Sometimes.'

'I suppose you could? Get away?'

'I'm—' Trevis hesitated again.

The man prompted him. 'You're—?'

'I'm married.'

The actor's face split with a grin. Trevis watched in the fall of the streetlight.

'Oh, I see.'

'It's not easy for me,' he said. 'To move. Maybe one day.'

'Does your wife come from here too?'

'Yes. Quite close by. It was—' Trevis swallowed. 'I don't know, a kind of "arranged" marriage, almost.'

He heard himself with alarm.

The actor's face became more confidential.

'At least you're—honest about it.'

'Only to you.'

'To me?'

'I'm not usually—honest.'

'You in a bank too?'

'Not about—not about that, I mean.'

'But you're honest to me?'

'Well, I—'

'I'm a stranger, aren't I?'

'Yes.' Trevis passed his hand across his eyes. 'Sometimes—'

He felt his arm touched by the actor's hand. Reassuring him.

464

'One advantage of the glamorous life,' the man told him in a stage whisper. 'You never stop long enough to ask yourself questions.'

Trevis shook his head. Their two worlds had nothing in common. He'd heard about actors.

'I suppose it's all pretty much on the surface too,' the man was saying. 'Take it or leave it.'

'*On the surface*'. In that instant Trevis recognised a different interpretation of the words: he saw the possibility it allowed for honesty, to waste no time, to nail your colours to the mast.

He turned round and looked into the actor's face. The man gave off a charge, it crackled between them. He'd never met anyone like him. He was aware he was smiling: grateful for just one occasion in his life to say what he believed to be true.

They'd reached the War Memorial Gardens. Trevis felt his legs carrying him unbidden: the way he performed every function in his life. Except the one on which their marriage depended, the love-act which wasn't.

'Think I need a leak,' the man said. He nodded towards the public lavatories.

'Good idea,' Trevis replied. He'd spoken the words without giving himself a chance to consider them. He suddenly felt breath massing in his chest like a stone.

Their feet turned in time towards the steps up to the gardens. Only one streetlamp lit the walled rectangle of rose-beds and rustic pergolas. It seemed further away and more other-worldly than anywhere he travelled to in his dreams, with his stevedore friends. The pole's top-half disappeared into the branches of the fir-tree and the light from the glass was green and pale. Thick shadows striped the path. Trevis had never been here at night, and only two or three times by daylight. He smelt the lavatory stalls before they reached the doorway.

Inside, one light-bulb shone fitfully in the middle of the ceiling. Trevis smiled, remembering his last words with Maureen: he smiled to himself with sweet satisfaction, already knowing what was about to happen. The reality was going to be gentler, easier, more unthinking than in any of his dreams.

He caught the man noticing his smile. It didn't make him want to be serious. He kept the smile in place as he stood at the stall and unbuttoned himself.

He forgot later which of the two turned his eyes first, who was quicker to respond to the other's attention. He wanted it to be himself who went down on his knees but the man was too quick, too knowing, for him.

It might have been a dream. But if it *had* been, how could his imagination have devised sensations he'd never experienced before.

Afterwards . . .

Afterwards they walked to the doorway. There were no cars passing on the esplanade, no footsteps approaching along the pavement.

'It's such a fucking dead end,' the man said, quietly.

Trevis sighed. 'Yes. Yes, it is.'

'How d'you stand it?'

Trevis shook his head. He felt tears welling in his eyes: for simple gratitude's sake.

'You should get out.'

'There's . . . Well, there's Maureen.'

He hadn't meant to say her name: a stupid superstition, that maybe it could be used against him.

The streetlamp concealed among the waving fir branches patterned a moving grid of shadows on the little geometric-angled lawns and flower beds. Something in that moment gave Trevis an instantaneous vision of joy: he'd waited eighteen months, and much longer than that—all his schoolboy and adult life—to discover it. It was a secret none of the women who had ruled his life could have the remotest access to, with all their neat system and goodness: they would never have the sickening thrill of achievement, debasement, joy like strangulation. He pitied them for never knowing the ecstasy of sex with a stranger who doesn't have a name: only a man could have shown him the potential for euphoria and delirious satisfaction his own body allowed him.

Then the swell of unadulterated happiness started to pass from him and, trying to salvage something, he wrapped his arm round the man's waist. The women who'd brought him up had educated him to believe that it was a man's natural right to initiate, to command, but they had continued to dominate him so that the theory had never been tested. For the first time he was close enough, literally, to be able to feel that power of command, the surging of strength in the man's arms, in the muscles of his back, it was there in the firmness of his lean hips.

The arm fell away with fright as they walked forward, out into the gloomy green gardens, no longer the gardens of a night dream.

Trevis laid his hand on the man's arm. He wanted to ask, when can I meet you again, but he didn't know how to. The night air was disorientating him even more than the sex, a sickness and chill churned in his stomach.

Thank God the words had been said, Sandmouth was a fucking dead end. At least there was the cover of ignorance and respectability.

It was as he was withdrawing his hand that Trevis, so decently presentable in his charcoal flannel suit for the bank, chanced to notice a movement on the pavement side of one of the shrubs. He looked ahead, down the drop of shallow steps on to the promenade. His eyes gazed in horror.

The girl hadn't even the sense to wait and keep hidden but was staggering backwards with her mismatching feet, her hands paddling the air. She looked up at them both, her face fish-white and confused.

Trevis motioned the man to stay where he was but he didn't notice. Trevis held back. The man smiled over his shoulder.

' 'Night-'night. And thanks.'

Trevis watched him walk down the steps and pause when he noticed the girl. They both stared at each other for a few seconds. The man turned and looked back. He was still smiling.

He walked off, whistling a tune, past the girl who was floundering and didn't seem to know which direction to take. *Who cares to define what chemistry this is, Who cares with your lips on mine how ignorant bliss is . . .*

Trevis shook his head. He buttoned his office jacket, then rammed his hands into the pockets, as if to conceal evidence.

He stood summoning up all the courage expected of a man before taking the steps at a run. He hurried across the road, to the opposite pavement, without daring to look at the girl.

Once, fifty yards or so further on, he permitted himself to

look back. She was standing more or less where he'd spotted her; she'd turned round and was watching him watching her.

They passed each other in the street most days but did she know who he was? Would she be able to put two and two together and realise?

He took his right hand out of his pocket and held it in front of his eyes, as if to wish away the sight of her. He could feel the sickness travelling up from his stomach into his chest. He remembered the constable, officiously and conscientiously plodding the length of George Street; reporting back to smiling Sergeant Wavell, standing tall in the same all-weather boots with the reinforced steel toe-caps.

On the way back, outside 'The Anchor', he encountered the pert girl from the ground floor in Crockers'. She was calling good-bye to one of her drinking pals and fastening the toggles on her duffle coat. He saw her observing him from the doorway of the pub with a brazen, come-hither expression. A brisk, worldly, daylight-bright smile flashed across her face.

Could women think of him that way? It had never occurred to him that they could. What was it the women in the audience saw when the actor went through his paces?—where did they train their eyes in the dark?

A few yards beyond the pub, he looked back. The Crockers' girl had turned her head and was looking the other way, towards the promenade; she was studying the distance.

Was the Moscombe girl still where he'd left her? He pressed his right hand against his brow.

He felt a raw, complicated pain drilling through his bowels. He became aware of the night chill, and shivered, and sensed it was more than that to blame. In the next few moments, as the cold settled on him, he knew what it really was: the onset of despair. First, joy like no other—then this, the certain fall.

'ONLY you can hear and see, behind the eyes of the sleepers, the movements and countries and mazes and colours and dismays and rainbows and tunes and wishes and flight and fall and despairs and big seas of their dreams.'

DYLAN THOMAS, *Under Milk Wood*

EPILOGUE

'The moon is afloat over our town like a watching eye.'

It is the best sentence in Miss Vane's book, but it leads her nowhere. The disc's purpose escapes her.

Perhaps life in Sandmouth doesn't equip one to understand and the truest thing that might be said is this, that none of us has the wisdom to escape the moon and its purposes.

The eye watches, and we can only watch back. It shines out of multifarious eyes: cats' eyes as they stalk tidy domestic gardens which to them are degrees of wilderness; the matching green eyes of the Tierneys, mother and son, who are laying the garden with nets to catch the feline invaders they despise beyond words; in the liquid eyes of teenage romantic Delia Hutton watching the edge of the shore she can catch sight of, just, from her bedroom window above the corner shop, and listening for the hooves of white stallions and Rex Harrison's voice; in the Gutteridges' eyes as the couple walk on the beach, talking privately in the accent of their childhood, about their plans for themselves; in the ever alert eyes of PC Ingilby, who is grateful to have such a quiet beat after his last; in the waking eyes of everyone who is kept awake beyond the mean time of retiring to bed in Sandmouth, because they are too troubled to sleep; in the tired and innocent eyes of Miss Meredith Vane, who sits at the bureau in her sitting-room with a cup of Ovaltine and a virgin sheet of paper and cannot think of a thing to write—of anything *deserving* to be written. So the English Novel continues to wait . . .

The moon shines on them dispassionately: they are all life. To show no favour, it also shines on what can only return the compliment glassily: the impossibly blue painted eyes of the dummies in the windows of Crockers' department store; the weathered eyes of no colour at all belonging to 'The Old King', George III, who sways tipsily on his creaking signboard; the carved downcast eyes of Christ on the Convent crucifixes; the wide almond coquettish eyes of the beauty pinned to the wall of the Gutteridges' salon; Valerie Hobson's eyes caught in a photographer's flashlight, looking out of a magazine which lies open on the coverlet in front of the Lavezzoli's slumbering daughter as she dreams of other places, different lives.

Another pair of eyes between the two states—human but without life—reflects two white orbs. The moon fills the irises, which stare up through damp undergrowth and the budding branches of trees. The eyes seem to be fixed steadily on it: but as the moon continues its climb in the sky, the shine glazes the irises and whites, and there can be no doubt that the eyes see nothing at all of the moon's lonely beauty swimming in the night sky.

The moon pales the surrounding face and the long fair hair fanned out like a drowning woman's. The head is lying in grass; the grass is damp and, where it has collected a drop of dew, each blade holds its own reflection of the moon. The grass sparkles, and the leaves gleam on the trees under which the body lies, front down, head corkscrewed round. The moon's sheen steals across the splayed, abandoned limbs, it alights on details of the girl's dress: the mother-of-pearl bead buttons on the grey cardigan, the tiny sprigs of flowers patterned on the fabric of the skirt, the buckle fastenings on the child's sandals, which are turned soles upward. The cardigan and the skirt are starting to take the dampness and they cling to the outlines of arms and legs. One hand clutches at something, an object, evidence, which will transpire to be a chrome button when the fingers are uncurled; the other hand seems to claw at a tussock of the wet grass, but it holds nothing at all—it is the pose of anguished desperation which will strike people who witness it as particularly affecting. The rumpled dress has risen up and exposes the backs of the girl's thighs; naturally people's first assumption will be that the girl's virtue has been tampered with, but expert examination will dispel that fear.

In the headlights of the police cars and the ambulance the girl's eyes will continue to stare up at the moon, fixed above Sandmouth like a lantern to light the dark, but its reflection in each iris will have been overlaid by those of the night's commotion. A blanket is produced to cover the body from head to foot and only then do the eyes cease to hold all the images of lunar and human activity. Beneath the blanket they— presumably—see nothing.

The moon's passage isn't over yet, however, and while policemen from Bournemouth walk the grass and arrangements are made to tape off the dank, dewy copse and to seal the roads circling the golf course, it shines wherever it can: on rooftops, on rainpipes, on windows, it seeps through curtains and where they haven't been drawn it floods into east- and south-facing bedrooms and washes into their corners like a searchlight, picking out objects with particular clarity and seeming to deny any element of mystery in human affairs.

But what of those in west- and north-facing bedrooms, sleeping or attempting to sleep? What secrets are they allowed to escape with?—unless perhaps the secrets have a will of their own, and trawl like pike just beneath the surface of sleep?

★

Alma Stockton looks up from her knitting.

She stares up at the skylight, at the stars stirred into the black.

For a moment she sees the blackness as the inside of a hat. A gent's topper.

The hat lies on a table-top. There are holes pricked in the lining, and the stars occur where bright light shines through from the room containing the table with the hat laid on top of it. Mrs Stockton imagines a lot of light: she imagines party voices, and a room full of laughter.

But that is a fancy. She shakes her head. She has a 'here and now' to have to cope with, without needing to invent others for herself. She may think a little bit backwards and forwards, but only a little.

Often to Mrs Stockton Sandmouth seems to have more than its share of the 'here and now'. What's outside them touches

471

them so little, it can be digested at the breakfast table. Other people make decisions. Once after the War the Queen—waving a grey-gloved hand—drove through in a long black car, a Daimler, down Hill Street, a right turn at the bottom, along Britannia Terrace, and out of the town again. And once Kay Kendall was supposed to have spent a couple of nights incognito at the Clarence Hotel.

Sandmouth is Sandmouth. It minds its own business, more or less. It has no sights beyond itself, nor any expectations. Presumably the world will still be turning tomorrow: in another twenty-four hours everything will be just as it is now, more or less. In this year of God's grace, with a new and becoming young Queen on the throne, England lies like a lazy, slumbering cat on a window-sill, catching what sun it can.

If the sun were shining, that is: but it may tomorrow, as it did during the day that's now almost done. Saint George's Day, Mrs Stockton reminds herself as she clicks her needles. A pleasant, breezy day, when England was England. Nothing too much has happened, not that you would notice. Once upon a time a man in armour slew a dragon but she forgets just how and why, if indeed she has ever known the explanation, the key.

★

Tilly continues walking along the promenade.

The moonstruck sea is like crinkled silver paper. The beach is bleached white. The chalky cliffs gleam.

The surface of the road has a pale greasy sheen to it. Tilly walks along it, past where the pavement ends, drawn by the unusual sparkle the tar is carrying. White is the significant colour tonight.

On Tilly's left, on the other side of the road, is the beach. The sea grinds up on to the ramp of sand and pulls back again, and might be sighing. On the girl's right is the golf course.

Further on she comes to a car-track—two ruts marked by tyre prints, with a high grassy ridge in the middle—which cuts across the greens. The moon shines down between the high banks of wild rhododendrons; it silvers the leaves and sets the flints and pebbles glittering. Tilly's eyes notice and her legs follow the track's curve. Behind her the main road continues in a straight line, towards the cliffs. Unheard by her a car slowly cruises by, its engine whispering behind the bright chrome grille and its tyres slily silent on the smoothness of tarmacadam.

★

Christina Gutteridge lies in bed watching the shadows growing on the wall. They take different shapes, all fantastic but equally believable: nuns, ravens, dolls, nuns, ravens, dolls.

Her parents haven't come back yet. The Norrises are their most modern friends.

Given the chance, they like to stay out late. It makes her feel neglected, even with Granny Leek snoring downstairs.

Tomorrow her class are coming down into Sandmouth to watch the archaeologists' dig. Sister Teresa has told them that 'history is alive', but it's hard for Christina to take the pronouncement seriously when she knows that all the people in history are dead. (Why else are there ghosts?)

For a few moments one of the shadows becomes, not Sister Teresa, but the fabled golden head that lies such a long way down in the black, slurpy mud. What, Tina is pondering, if it turns out to be not as they imagined, but chipped and noseless and with the gold flaking away? Why should people have gone on presuming when really all they can do is guess?

★

The actress stretched out an arm from inside the folds of her cape and grasped one of the ropes that marks off the site of the dig.

She was dreading going back to the 'Camelot' Guest House and facing her smalls in the linen bag. She was too muddled after two port-and-lemons to think straight. The girl had grabbed the five pound note in her purse and she'd left and told her she'd pay her back. *She* knew better, that she would never see either of them again.

All her life she'd been used—right, left, and centre. She'd tried—tit for tat—to use all that came her way, for what she could get from it, but somehow 'it' always seemed to get away before she could lay her hands on it.

Now 'it' lived behind the curtained windows of proper hotels with 'AA' stars and travelled first class on trains and paid every bill on receipt.

She hated 'it'.

'*Hate*'. She dropped the word into the black pit beneath the ropes. It hissed and slithered about for a while, then it sank out of hearing.

How had she learned about the golden head? From the girl, it must have been: the other one—squinty, bevelled Dilly Mushroom, all over on one side like a holed ship.

Leave the thing alone. There was something tricksy, shifty, about the past, and she knew too well that it wasn't to be trusted: even when you thought you could see it again, how it was, it turned out to be not quite the same. Sometimes nothing like.

She hadn't *believed* in herself, she hadn't been selfish enough. She'd read somewhere that Garbo was always thinking of how other people were seeing her, that was her life's energy—her *vanity*, like Dietrich's, like all the stars'. She'd never been able to believe that she *deserved* better than she got. Maybe in her opportunities she'd been lucky: but why hadn't she capitalised on them? At heart she'd never considered that she was any good—or good *enough*—at what she did. Except surviving, and how come—if she could do that—she was stuck in a dump, a rat-hole, like this?

'Bitch!'

The word fell into the pit, but she didn't know who it was she meant it for—the bint who'd robbed her, or that head of gold, beautiful and wily as fortune, or herself, for being her own worst enemy.

★

Major Fitt removed his soiled gaberdine mac, undid the buttons of his suit jacket, and stretched out on the chaise. He unhitched his leg.

Through the glass doors he looked out at the white flank of the big house. A car had caught him in its headlights as he stumbled into the driveway. Nothing had been said—oddly enough—but you let fate decide that for you. No use bothering yourself.

He closed his eyes. Who'd have bet ten bob it would be *him* who'd prove his mettle under the Jerries' fire? Not that he'd done it for England's glory. His sister had gone on a cycling trip through Europe once and she'd had her bicycle stolen in Heidelberg: it was that he was thinking of the first few times, his sister's pristine black Argyll. In the citation ceremony they quoted 'A Shropshire Lad' and there was a lot about 'the grandeur of our fate'.

> 'Spirit of England, ardent-eyed,
> Enkindle this dear earth that bore us,
> In the hour of peril purified.'

He'd had to sit listening to it with his dead leg: all about dwelling in Arcady, 'boys with windy hair and wine-wet lips dancing on the sun-splashed grass'. A load of bollocks.

That was for the nancy poets. But for him in a different way, he knew, the trenches *had* been his golden moment: he'd known it then, that nothing would ever be so good again, and it wouldn't be so bad to die like this, not thinking of anything at all—hardly. Mind-less.

The Major heard the breath grow thick in his throat. Why not sleep? It had been a shag of a day. Not one of the better sort: but it could have been worse, possibly. The sun would wake him, time enough for an early departure before the town was awake.

No fond farewells. He knew he wouldn't be back in these parts again. Except in his sleep, maybe: but if you drank enough you forgot enough and no one and nothing could haul you all that long way back.

★

Mr Messiter whistled for Laddie. He'd seen him making for the brake behind the thirteenth green. He whistled again, then shouted. 'Laddie! Here, boy!'

He walked on slowly, waiting for the dog to reappear. He tapped the leash against the side of his leg.

Every evening without fail he waited for Laddie to emerge sniffing and snuffling from the bushes, perhaps half-heartedly growling at a bird as it soared, squeaky-winged, above him.

Now there was no sign of him. The brake was quite still.

Mr Messiter whistled. He listened for the usual lethargic, panting response, the familiar rattle of the neck chain, but he heard nothing.

He started walking towards the bushes.

★

When it's discovered, the murder will become a *cause célèbre*, uniting the nation in its interest in the activities and personalities of a small seaside town most of the population didn't know existed.

But that is still to come. Tilly Moscombe's body is undiscovered as yet. It lies face-down in wet grass. The marks of the strangler are on her throat. Her fingers claw the rich red damp clay.

For the moment it is only a body without any scheme of reference except the most general. The body lies beside a road, and the road leads out of and into Sandmouth, and Sandmouth in the first years of this second half of the twentieth century is a faint dot on the map of Britain, and Britain is a red smudge on an atlas map of the northern hemisphere, and all the red countries of a diminishing empire amount to just a blur on a whirring globe on a table-top, and the globe of the world as it spins at one thousand miles an hour in an unending void (at a velocity of sixty-six thousand miles an hour in its orbit about the sun) is only a clouded silver round of cooling gas, stranded in one galaxy out of many, among countless other stars of more and less life.

RONALD FRAME

A LONG WEEKEND WITH MARCEL PROUST

Seven stories and a novel

Winner of the Scottish Arts Council Book Award, 1987

'Ronald Frame's new collection of seven short stories and a novella enhances his reputation as one of our most gifted younger writers'

John Nicholson, The Times

'His style is achieved and elegant . . . On this form, he is one of the most interesting writers around, capable of narrative radiance, and of articulating the virtually unspeakable depths of his characters'

Douglas Dunn, Glasgow Herald

'Frame is interested in the way apparently minor events in the past continue to rule people's lives and their conceptions of themselves . . . This is an ambitious project, the successes of which are more than adequate'

The Literary Review

'Varied and talented . . . All exhibit a superb technique backed by clever twists in their plots'

Martin Goff, Daily Telegraph

ALLAN MASSIE

AUGUSTUS

AUGUSTUS reconstructs the lost memoirs of Augustus, true founder of the Roman Empire, son of Julius Caesar, friend and later foe of Mark Antony, patron of Horace and Virgil. Massie has breathed conviction and realism into one of the greatest periods of the past, creating an unforgettable array of characters and incidents.

'Far more entertaining than I, CLAUDIUS . . . proves that Massie is the best living Scottish novelist'
The Times

'Allan Massie's best novel to date – it revivifies a great historical figure with mischievous wit and a serious respect'
Paul Bailey, author of GABRIEL'S LAMENT

'A fine historical novel'
Peter Ackroyd, author of HAWKSMOOR

'A great achievement by any standards'
The Scotsman

sceptre

STEPHEN GREGORY

THE CORMORANT

From the moment of its arrival at the cottage in the Welsh mountains one drizzling October afternoon, the cormorant's malignant presence creates turmoil and spreads fear. As blizzards shroud the mountains in snow, the cormorant's evil power takes shape, hunting and haunting the family into fear and frenzy . . .

'A considerable delight . . . assured and restrained . . . The quality of prose is particularly impressive, as too is his economy of expression'

Time Out

'Promising and bizarre with some excellent set pieces'

The Times

'I liked it. Intelligent and well-written with a natural feel for the avian vandal of the title which brings to mind the poetry of Ted Hughes'

Iain Banks, author of THE WASP FACTORY

JEREMY COOPER

RUTH

A searingly evocative portrait of a young artist living and working in rural Somerset, and of her struggle to overcome a debilitating mental illness. RUTH is as compassionate as it is memorable.

'Flavoured with a richness of incidental detail rare amid the growing aridity of modern English fiction . . . Cooper's professionalism is absolute'

The Observer

'In his first novel, RUTH, Jeremy Cooper dwells with sense and sensitivity on creativity and mental illness'

The Listener

'Written in a calm and clear style, with excellent detail . . . reading it is to be reminded what a noble activity the craft of novel writing still is'

The London Standard